The Lost Fleet: Oblivion's Light

(*The Lost Fleet* Series, Book 3)

By
Raymond L. Weil
USA Today Best Selling Author

Raymond L. Weil

Books in *The Lost Fleet* Series

The Lost Fleet: Galactic Search (Book 1)
The Lost Fleet: Into the Darkness (Book 2)
The Lost Fleet: Oblivion's Light (Book 3)
The Lost Fleet: Genesis (Book 4)
Coming early 2016

Website: http://raymondlweil.com/

DEDICATION

To my wife Debra for all of her patience while I sat in front of my computer typing. It has always been my dream to become an author. I also want to thank my children for their support.

Raymond L. Weil

The Lost Fleet: Oblivion's Light

The Lost Fleet: Oblivion's Light
A Slaver Wars Novel

Chapter One

The *Avenger* shook violently as the Simulin battlecruiser fired its energy weapons, striking the battleship's powerful protective shield. Fleet Admiral Jeremy Strong held onto his command chair as alarms sounded and red lights flashed on the damage control console.

"We have ten Simulin battlecruisers closing on us," reported Lieutenant Kevin Walters, steadfastly watching the ship's sensors.

"They sure don't believe in even odds," grumbled Commander Kyla Malen as she tightened her grasp on the console in front of her. "Tactical, prepare to fire weapons."

"Have they ever?" said Kevin with a frown. "They always seem to outnumber us."

"The AI ships?" asked Jeremy, grimacing as several more red lights appeared on the damage control console. The *Avenger* was beginning to take some light damage from the Simulin battlecruisers.

"Dropping out of hyperspace now!" called out Commander Malen.

Looking up at one of the large viewscreens in the Command Center, Jeremy saw the AI ships appear out of the shimmering white spatial vortexes that marked their arrival. Jeremy allowed himself to grin. These were the new AI ships. One-thousand-meter warspheres specifically designed to take on the Simulins. This would be the first time they had been committed to combat. He was anxious to see how they fared against the Simulin battlecruisers.

"Simulins are turning to engage the AIs," reported Kevin as he watched his sensor screens. On the screens, nine red threat icons began pulling away from the *Avenger* to close on the incoming AI warspheres. One red icon remained and was closing on the *Avenger*.

"Targeting the nearer Simulin battlecruiser," reported Lieutenant Charles Preston, the tactical officer. "Firing particle beam cannon and bow power beams."

-

From the *Avenger*, a bright blue particle beam flashed out to strike the Simulin battlecruiser's energy screen. Microseconds later four violet power beams followed. Cascades of raging energy erupted as the screen resisted the sudden onslaught. The Simulin battlecruiser was seventeen-hundred-meters in length and bulbous in form with large metallic looking pylons that stretched out in front of it. There were six of the massive structures, which extended for at least two hundred meters from the main hull of the ship. Each ended in a sharp point that contained a powerful energy weapon.

-

From the six tips beams of white energy erupted and slammed into the *Avenger's* energy shield, triggering more alarms.

"Shield is at 78 percent," warned Commander Malen as she looked at the data screen in front of her worriedly. "Those damn energy beams are draining the shield."

"Firing antimatter missile," spoke Lieutenant Preston as he pressed one of the glaring red buttons on the console in front of him. "Let's see if we can't drain their shield!"

"AIs are engaging," reported Kevin. His eyes were focused intently on the sensors as the AI and Simulin fleets neared each other.

"Now we'll see how our new AI ships do," Jeremy said as he looked at one of the viewscreens expectantly.

In space, the ten AI warspheres were in two horizontal lines of five to allow for the maximum amount of firepower as well as to provide additional defensive cover to one another.

"Enemy is within range," spoke the AI in command in its calm mechanical voice. "Fire particle beam cannons." The Command AI shifted its attention to the viewscreens displaying the enemy ships. The AI hovered six inches above the metal deck using antigravity repulsors. Its cubicle shaped body was equipped with four long tentacles and there was a glowing ball of energy about the size of a basketball where its head should be.

"Firing weapons," replied one of the AIs in front of the weapon consoles.

From the ten AI ships, sixty particle beam cannons fired. The massed fire was directed at just one Simulin battlecruiser.

Particle beams from the warspheres slammed into the bow section of their intended target. The attack was so overwhelming the Simulin energy screen was instantly overloaded, and six of the deadly beams penetrated striking the armored hull, setting off massive explosions and hurling glowing debris into space. Two of the large spires shattered as internal explosions tore them apart.

The Simulin energy shield flickered as damaged power couplings could no longer supply the necessary power to keep the shield at full strength. Detecting the weakness, the

AI warspheres fired their powerful energy beams, carving deep gouges into the hull of the ship and opening up numerous compartments to space. Moments later, the shield failed completely, and a Devastator Three missile detonated, turning the Simulin vessel into a raging inferno. When the fire died away, all that remained were a few pieces of molten wreckage and glowing gasses.

"Simulin battlecruiser is down," reported Kevin exultantly.

"AIs are shifting their fire to the next Simulin vessel," reported Commander Malen as she studied the tactical holo display next to her.

The *Avenger* shook again and Jeremy's attention was drawn back to the Simulin battlecruiser attacking them. With a deep sigh, he shook his head. "Ariel, destroy that damn thing! I'm tired of being shaken around."

"Yes, Jeremy," responded the tall, dark-haired young woman standing just to his left and slightly behind him. She closed her eyes briefly as if in concentration, and all the *Avenger's* weapons fired simultaneously.

On the main viewscreen, the Simulin battlecruiser's energy screen suddenly lit up like the Fourth of July. Particle beams, power beams, and even the *Avenger's* defensive laser batteries pummeled the shield in the same six-meter area. Four Devastator Three missiles crashed into the shield in massive explosions and then one small area flickered briefly. That was all Ariel needed as she fired a one hundred-megaton antimatter missile through the small hole that had been created. In a huge flash of light, the Simulin battlecruiser died.

"Damn," I wish I could do that," muttered Lieutenant Preston jealously.

"You can't control all the ship's weapon systems simultaneously like Ariel can," consoled Commander Malen with a grin.

Lieutenant Preston nodded. He knew no one could do the things the *Avenger's* protective AI could.

"Simulin battlecruiser is down," confirmed Kevin, looking over at Ariel and nodding. He knew the AI loved to fight using the *Avenger*.

"Should I attack the others?" asked Ariel eagerly.

"How are the AIs doing?" asked Jeremy, turning his attention back to the battle between the AIs and the Simulins.

"The new AI warspheres are doing well," reported Commander Malen. "Four Simulin battlecruisers are down with only one AI ship damaged. It's pulled back behind the others and has initiated repairs."

Jeremy nodded. The new AI warspheres had been designed by the AIs, the Altons, and some human engineers. They were the most powerful ships they could conceive. They had to be if they wanted to fight the Simulins for control of the Triangulum Galaxy. "Ensign Striker, pull us back out of range of the battle for now; we'll let the AIs finish this."

Jeremy knew the AIs would prefer that as they didn't want any harm to come to any of the organics they were charged with protecting. A big switch from what had occurred back in the Milky Way Galaxy where the AIs had dedicated themselves to conquering and destroying all organic life.

In space, the Simulin High Commander frowned as he listened to the reports coming in. The High Commander only vaguely resembled a human. He was slightly taller and his skin was opalescent. Blood vessels, as well as some of the internal organs were visible.

"It's the AIs and the organics from the Fitula Nebula," the Second Commander reported in a cold voice with very little emotion. He was referring to the nebula that had become strangely impenetrable to ships with hyperspace drives.

"Those spheres are not like the ones in our records," pointed out the High Commander as he watched another one of his battlecruisers being torn apart by massive particle beam fire. "They have built a new and highly capable warship that is a threat to us. We shall withdraw and report this new development. A plan must be made to eliminate this danger. There can be no other races but Simulin."

"None but Simulin," repeated the Second Commander. "I will give the order to jump into hyperspace."

The High Commander didn't reply as he expected the Second Commander to carry out his orders. It was the Simulin way. Orders were not questioned but followed to ensure the greatest efficiency, particularly in combat. The High Commander felt some concern as he felt his ship begin to accelerate and turn away from the battle followed by the other three surviving battlecruisers. It was disconcerting that another organic race could build vessels of such strength as to be able to destroy Simulin ships. It might be necessary to refer this matter clear up to the Simulin Grand Council. The only problem was the council was in the home galaxy, and it would take a considerable amount of time to contact them. It would require passage through no less than six of the Great Spheres.

"Simulins have jumped into hyperspace," Kevin reported with satisfaction in his voice. "The new AI ships did their job." This was a big admission for Kevin as he still felt some misgivings about the AIs being part of the Federation, at least here in the Triangulum Galaxy. However, over the last several years those feeling of mistrust had lessened.

"The AI in command is reporting only minor damage to three vessels," reported Ariel, looking over at Jeremy. "It has given the order to initiate repairs and says all three ships are still mission capable. Repairs should be completed in two point four hours."

"Very well," said Jeremy, turning his attention back to the ship's main viewscreens.

In one screen a very large and bright blue giant star was visible. They had returned to NGC 604, a region containing over two hundred blue giants and 1,500 light-years across. The area was also filled with ionized hydrogen clouds called H-II regions. The nebula was alive with the birth of new stars and abounded with radiation. What was also significant was that around each of the blue giant stars were ten Simulin energy collecting stations. The stations drew power from the energy being radiated from the blue giants and transmitted it via hyperspace to one of four giant energy collection stations at the nebula's core. At the core was an area of dark matter and inside of it was a Dyson Sphere. The Dyson Sphere enclosed a star and had been built by an ancient race called the Originators.

"Move us toward the nearest energy collection station," ordered Jeremy, leaning back in his command chair. He felt more relaxed knowing he now had a weapon he could use against the Simulins. The AI warspheres had worked out far better than he had hoped. "Ariel, inform the AIs to proceed to their targets and eliminate them."

"Message sent," responded Ariel. She was dressed in a dark blue fleet uniform with no insignia.

Glancing at the nearest tactical holo display, Jeremy could see the AI task group split apart and head toward their designated targets. One of the AI ships fell in line with the *Avenger*. Jeremy strongly suspected this would be the AI commander for the warspheres. Over the years, the AIs had become overly protective of Jeremy, as he was the fleet admiral for all Federation forces including the AIs. They also credited him with their continued survival.

"Permission to initiate a short hyperjump?" requested Ensign Striker.

"Permission granted," replied Jeremy. "Ariel, inform the AI ships they have the okay to jump into close proximity to their targets to expedite their destruction."

"Message sent," replied Ariel promptly. She was in continuous contact with the AI warspheres and was responsible for passing on all of Jeremy's orders.

"Jumping," called out Ensign Striker as a blue-white vortex formed in front of the *Avenger*.

Jeremy felt the ship accelerate forward and enter the center of the swirling spatial anomaly. He felt a slight wrenching sensation as if his body was being turned inside out and then it was over, only to reoccur almost immediately a second time as they exited hyperspace. The short trip in hyperspace had only lasted a few brief seconds.

Almost instantly, the screens cleared and the tactical displays began updating. This was a big improvement from the past where it might take upwards to thirty seconds for all of a ship's systems to begin functioning properly after a hyperspace jump. The *Avenger's* systems had undergone several upgrades by Alton technicians to achieve this.

"Ten thousand kilometers from target," reported Kevin as he checked his sensor data. "The AI warsphere has exited hyperspace two thousand kilometers away."

"We're close enough," said Jeremy, as he gazed at the energy collection station on one of the large screens. The station was globular in form and covered with large energy collection dishes. "Lieutenant Preston, launch a Devastator Three subspace missile and let's erase that station from our sensors."

"Yes, sir," answered Preston, as he quickly activated the ship's targeting sensors and fed the data to the missile. Then, reaching forward, he pressed down firmly on a glowing red button. "Missile away."

Jeremy watched the viewscreen as a brilliant flash suddenly appeared. When the light faded away, the twenty-kilometer station was nothing more than a mangled wreck.

"That one won't collect any more energy for the Simulins," commented Kevin.

"AIs have destroyed their targets as well," reported Ariel. "The AI commander is waiting for orders."

Jeremy nodded. "Let's form the fleet back up and then we'll proceed to our next target." He wondered how many more Simulin fleets they would have to face. It had been his hope that most of the energy stations would be unguarded.

-

Rear Admiral Kathryn Barnes gazed in deep satisfaction at the massive viewscreen on the front wall of the Command Center of the 2,600-meter long exploration dreadnought *Distant Horizon*. A glowing mass of wreckage was being displayed.

"Energy collection station has been destroyed," confirmed Clarissa in her clear and youthful voice. "The AI warspheres all report their targets have been eliminated as well." Clarissa had blond hair, deep blue eyes, and a figure most men on the ship would die for. Unfortunately for them, Clarissa was an AI and her body in the Command Center was a hologram projected by special devices hidden in the walls.

"Contact the AIs and have them form up with the *Distant Horizon*. Then set course for our next target system," ordered Kathryn. She let out a deep breath as she thought about the current mission.

It had been two years since the relief fleets had successfully reached Gaia. In those two years much had been accomplished. The new AI shipyards had been built and more AIs had been created to operate the new warspheres. Now they had left the safety of the nebula to attack the Simulins where it would hurt the most.

"Message sent," confirmed Clarissa. "They should all rendezvous with us in the next ten minutes."

"How many of these collector stations do we need to destroy?" asked Kathryn, shifting her attention to one of the science consoles near the big viewscreen where Andram was setting.

Andram was an Alton and in many ways served as the ship's science officer. Andram's skin was very pale with a slight blue tinge and the hair on top of his head while thick was a solid white. His eyes, nose, and ears were very similar to a humans, but the eyebrows were very thin, almost nonexistent.

"All of them if possible," responded Andram, turning to look quizzically at Kathryn. "We know the Simulins are using the power from the blue giants to help power the intergalactic vortices on the Dyson Sphere."

"There are over two hundred blue giant stars in this region," commented Commander Anne Grissim with a deep frown. "At some point, the Simulins are going to put a fleet in front of us big enough to stop us."

"We have four fleets operating in the nebula," added Colonel Petra Leon. "That's over fifty targets each."

"Don't forget about the star that's inside the Dyson Sphere," Shilum Torre the Alton hyperspace specialist added. "It alone is generating sufficient power to allow the Simulins to keep several intergalactic vortices open continuously."

"We've taken out the energy collectors in four systems," Kathryn said. "We'll continue until the Simulins put a force in front of us sufficient to force us to withdraw. Lieutenant Strong, plot a course to our next target."

Kelsey was seated at Navigation next to the science console where Andram was. "Course is already plotted, Admiral," she replied.

"Off we go again," spoke Katie over their private channel. "I still don't understand what Jeremy is hoping to accomplish from this."

"It's actually quite simple," Clarissa said in a friendly voice. "If we can take out enough of these energy collector stations it might partially restrict the Simulins operations inside the Dyson Sphere."

"Perhaps buying the Federation back home more time," responded Katie. They had all been briefed on the mission, but Katie was still uncertain if it would serve the purpose they hoped. Katie was at her computer station where Mikow Lall, another Alton, was sitting close by.

"If Admiral Tolsen was able to destabilize the area of space at Sagittarius A where the Simulins were coming through, then destroying these energy collection stations could have a profound effect," continued Clarissa. "The disturbed area of space at Sagittarius A will act as an attractor for any intergalactic vortex. According to Shilum, it will take a tremendous amount of power to shift the exit vortex from that area to another region of space."

"Only problem is we don't know if that happened," responded Kelsey, pursing her lips. "We can only hope that Admiral Tolsen succeeded."

"Admiral Tolsen is very capable," Clarissa said. "I'm sure he succeeded in his mission. Admiral Jackson is fully confident Admiral Tolsen was able to destabilize that region of space."

"Clarissa, if we had access to the Dyson Sphere, could we go home?" asked Katie in a soft voice.

This was something Katie had been wondering about for quite some time. Even though Gaia was their new home, it would be nice to have the option to return to the Federation.

"Possibly," Clarissa answered hesitantly. "If we knew how to operate it and had the necessary power we could send one or two ships through. The problem would be that even with the help of the Altons, it might take years to learn how to operate the equipment on the Dyson Sphere which works the intergalactic vortices."

"And we're going to destroy it," Katie said. Katie knew that was Jeremy's long-term goal. If they could destroy the Dyson Sphere, it would make the Federation safe from attack as well as eliminate reinforcements for the Simulins in the Triangulum Galaxy.

"We have no choice," Kelsey interjected. "It's the only way to ensure the Federation back home remains safe." Kelsey knew this decision had been weighing heavily on Jeremy's mind. They were trapped in the Triangulum Galaxy and the only way to ensure the Milky Way stayed safe was to destroy their only way back.

For two more days, the *Distant Horizon* and her fleet of ten AI warspheres struck at the Simulin energy collector stations around the blue giant stars. They had just exited hyperspace in their eighth target system when a Simulin fleet appeared.

"They must have detected us in hyperspace," stated Commander Grissim, as the tactical display near her began lighting up with red threat icons. Inside the nebula, the Alton long-range sensors could only reach a few light-years. She assumed the Simulin sensors were the same.

"Energy shield is up and weapons are charged," reported Major Weir from Tactical. The fleet was already at Condition One so all battlestations were manned.

"Can we take out the energy collection stations?" asked Kathryn, as she gazed with concern at the red icons.

"No," Clarissa responded. She was standing just behind Kathryn and to her left. "I'm detecting fifteen Simulin battlecruisers and twenty of their escort cruisers."

Kathryn let out a deep sigh. The Simulin battlecruisers were seventeen-hundred-meters in length and the escort cruisers were eleven hundred. She doubted that, even with the new and enhanced AI warspheres, she could destroy this fleet without incurring major losses.

"More ships jumping in!" warned Captain Reynolds from his sensor console as additional alarms started sounding. "They're within combat range!"

"AIs are firing upon the new ships," reported Clarissa. "We have forty additional Simulin battlecruisers that have exited hyperspace within combat range of our fleet. I recommend we jump immediately."

The *Distant Horizon* suddenly shook violently and a warning alarm began sounding.

"What was that?" demanded Kathryn, looking over at Colonel Leon, who was near the damage control console. She could see several red lights flashing and a concerned look on Petra's face.

"It was an internal explosion," Colonel Leon answered as she checked the console. Petra quickly contacted Engineering and spoke to the chief engineer. "We've lost part of the power to the hyperdrive. Jalat is reporting that it will take at least five minutes to repair the problem." Jalat had been promoted to chief engineer a little over a year ago.

"We don't have five minutes," spoke Commander Grissim grimly.

"We have to buy ourselves the time," Kathryn said, drawing in a deep breath. "Deploy thirty of the Defense Globes and have the AIs form up in defensive formation D-6." When the relief fleets had arrived, they had also brought replacement Defense Globes for the *Distant Horizon.*

Formation D-6 would put the AI warspheres in a protective globe around the *Distant Horizon* and inside the deployment zone of the Defense Globes. The Defense Globes were ten meters in diameter with a small sublight drive. They also had an energy shield and two dual particle beam turrets for defense as well as offense. The globes' main weapons were an ion cannon capable of bringing down an enemy ship's energy shield. They were powered by a fusion reactor that could be overloaded to generate a ten-megaton explosion.

"Deploying Defense Globes," reported Major Weir.

"AI warspheres are moving into defensive formation," added Clarissa.

"Incoming fire!" warned Captain Reynolds, as the *Distant Horizon* seemed to cry out in pain.

-

The High Commander of the Simulin fleet nodded in satisfaction seeing he had trapped the enemy. It was obvious something was wrong with the large warship, as they were not attempting to escape through hyperspace. The AIs and their organic allies had chosen a bad time to attack the energy collection stations. A major portion of the Simulin fleet had been called away to other parts of the galaxy to fight against several recently discovered small space going empires. It was obvious now that an error had been made in deploying so many warships. However, that was the Simulin way to crush an enemy before they could grow powerful enough to become a threat.

"Destroy them," ordered the High Commander coldly. "They are not Simulin and must die."

-

Kathryn winced as four of the Defense Globes exploded under the Simulin attack. Fortunately, the Simulins were concentrating on the warspheres and the *Distant Horizon* and not so much on the small ten-meter globes.

"I want a coordinated attack using the Defense Globes, the AI warspheres, and our own weapons," she ordered. Then turning toward Clarissa. "Can you do it?"

"Yes," Clarissa answered with a pleased look on her face. "I'll need a few seconds to set up the parameters for all vessels."

Kathryn nodded. Over the last few years, she'd finally come to fully trust the beautiful AI.

-

In space, weapons fire was growing heavier every second. Simulin energy beams were blasting away at the shields on the AI warspheres as well as the *Distant Horizon*. On one of the AI ships, a number of Simulin energy beams were being directed toward one small section of the shield and then several powerful antimatter missiles detonated. The screen developed a brief hole and that was sufficient. A Simulin energy beam penetrated the weakened shield, blowing a deep glowing gash in the hull of the AI warsphere. It was quickly followed by several more energy beams, which carved a deep chasm into the heart of the ship.

-

"Critical damage has been incurred to our power systems," reported the AI, hovering in front of the ship's engineering station. "Forty percent of our power has been lost."

"Automatic repairs have been initiated," responded another in a calm mechanical voice. "Probability of successful repairs is at 16 percent."

The warsphere shuddered violently and the lights in the Control Center dimmed. The AI in command approached the large console showing the current status of the vessel. "Survival is unlikely," it said as the AI studied the damage the ship had received.

"Weapons are offline," stated the AI in front of the tactical station. "Our energy shield is down to 14 percent. It will fail completely in another one point two minutes."

"Probability of ship destruction is at 92 percent," the AI in front of the ship's computer station said in a neutral voice.

The AI in command considered its options. "Move us away from the fleet and initiate the self-destruct. The Simulin organics must not recover any of our vessel."

-

The AI warsphere broke formation and moved toward the Simulins on its faltering sublight drive. Then it exploded in a massive fiery blast that blew it apart from within.

It was at that moment that Clarissa launched her attack. The remaining Defense Globes fired their ion cannons at ten of the attacking Simulin battlecruisers. The beams struck the Simulin energy shields, opening up small four-meter holes.

The nine remaining AI warspheres and the *Distant Horizon* instantly fired their particle beam cannons and launched one hundred-megaton antimatter missiles into the gaps. In less than a second, the ten Simulin battlecruisers were turned into miniature suns as their hulls were torn apart and vaporized by the massive amounts of energy released.

The commanders of the remaining Simulin battlecruisers, realizing the danger posed by the Defense

Globes, quickly turned their defensive energy beam turrets on the small ten-meter globes blowing a number of them apart.

"AI warsphere W-032 is down," reported Kevin. He knew that sixty AIs had perished in the explosion. "They set off their self-destruct."

"Hyperdrive is repaired," reported Colonel Leon, as she received an update from Engineering. "We can enter hyperspace at any time."

"Land the remaining Defense Globes and let's get out of here," ordered Kathryn. She was unhappy about losing one of the AI warspheres due to a mechanical malfunction on the *Distant Horizon*. Once they returned to Gaia, she would launch a full investigation into the explosion that had damaged the ship's hyperdrive. "Kelsey, plot us a course out of the nebula. We're going home."

Moments later, the remaining Defense Globes landed in the *Distant Horizon's* flight bay. Swirling vortexes formed and the *Distant Horizon* and the AI warspheres fled the battle into the safety of hyperspace.

Chapter Two

Jeremy breathed a sigh of relief as the *Avenger* dropped out of hyperspace inside the Gaia System. During their mission, they'd managed to take out the energy collectors in twelve blue giant star systems. However, in order to do so he had lost three of the new AI warspheres in confrontations with the Simulins. Even though there had been no loss of human life, it still pained him knowing sixty AIs had perished on each ship.

"Status?" he spoke as he settled back in his command chair.

"All systems normal and working at optimum levels," reported Commander Malen as she checked her command console. "We're two hundred thousand kilometers from Gaia."

"Receiving standard challenge," called out Lieutenant Angela Caulder.

"Send ship recognition codes," Jeremy ordered. This was now standard procedure for any ship entering the Gaia System. Failure to do so would result in a task group being sent out to challenge the offending vessel. A task group of ten warships was kept at a constant readiness level of Condition Two in order to respond immediately to any pending threats.

"The other fleets are already here," reported Ariel. The AI had access to all of the *Avenger's* systems, including the sensors. "Clarissa says they hit eight systems before the Simulins forced them to withdraw. They did lose an AI warsphere."

"What about the other two fleets?" Jeremy waited anxiously for Ariel's reply.

"Six systems and nine systems," Ariel answered as she queried Clarissa. "Admiral Jackson lost two AI warspheres and Grayseth lost four."

"That's thirty-five of their energy collection systems," commented Kevin, looking knowingly at Jeremy. "Is that enough to affect their operations at the Dyson Sphere?"

"Maybe," Jeremy responded. He had hoped to take more of them out. "Ensign Striker, take us in and put us into orbit just above the shipyard. Ariel, where's the *Distant Horizon*?"

"The exploration dreadnought is in orbit just above the defense grid."

Jeremy looked at one of the main viewscreens showing Gaia. The planet was located in a small K-Class star system deep inside a gaseous nebula in a clear area of space several light-years across. Special hyperspace disruption satellites had been spread throughout the nebula to prevent hyperspace travel, effectively placing the system out of the Simulins' reach. Several narrow tunnels existed that were free of the interference. It required multiple precise hyperspace jumps to navigate the system of safe zones in order to reach Gaia or leave the nebula.

Gaia was their new home, slightly smaller than Earth with a narrow habitable zone around its equator. This area of the arid planet had a large number of rivers and lakes visible on the viewscreen. There were also two small oceans covering about 15 percent of the planet. This was the world the lost fleets now called home.

"It's good to be back," Angela said.

Angela was married to Brace Caulder, a marine major who commanded one of the three large marine bases on the planet responsible for protecting the civilian population. Angela was very proud of her husband and during her off time from the *Avenger*, she lived on the base.

"Yes," agreed Jeremy. "I imagine you're anxious to get down to Major Caulder's military base." He understood how Angela felt; he was anxious to see Kelsey as well.

Angela blushed slightly. She and Brace had been married for two years.

They were all thinking of Gaia as home now. Over 400,000 colonists had arrived with the relief fleets two years ago. Humans, Altons, and Carethians were now down on the planet living in five large cities as well as spread out across the countryside. In addition, a number of fleet personnel had opted to go down to the planet to begin raising families. Overall, there were 558,499 colonists now on Gaia. The capital city was New Eden and also home to the planet's only large spaceport.

Watching the main viewscreens, Jeremy saw the shipyard growing nearer. When they had first jumped into the Triangulum Galaxy, the mobile Carethian shipyard Clan Protector came through also. Over the years, the mobile shipyard had been added to until it was now the monstrosity showing up on the main viewscreen. The Clan Protector was nearly three kilometers in length, four kilometers wide, and two kilometers thick. It contained six construction and six repair bays, which could handle any of the fleet's ships. The massive structure was also heavily armed and protected by a powerful energy shield.

"Message from Daelthon on the Clan Protector," Angela reported. "He says he's pleased to see we made it back safely."

"Jeremy," Ariel said in her youthful and vibrant voice. "The AIs are requesting permission to take their ships to their shipyards for repairs."

Jeremy nodded. "Permission granted." The AIs had built several massive shipyards around the system's fourth planet. Once the decision had been made to allow the AIs to build them, it had taken six months for them to complete construction. There were fourteen Federation fleet repair ships available that had aided in the construction.

"Commander Malen, once we've gone into orbit arrange leaves for the crew. I don't think we'll be going anywhere for awhile."

"Yes, Admiral," Commander Malen responded. "Should we dock to the shipyard to allow the crew to disembark?"

Jeremy glanced at the viewscreen showing the Clan Protector. "If they have a docking port available."

Leaning back in his command chair he thought back over their mission. He was still mystified as to why the Simulins hadn't responded more swiftly to the threat his fleets represented to the power collection stations. It was as if they didn't have the necessary ships, or the ships were needed elsewhere. Was it possible there were other advanced races still in this galaxy the Simulins hadn't managed to subdue? If there were, was there a possibility of contacting them?

"Angela, contact all the fleet admirals and ask them to meet me on the Clan Protector in two hours for a general staff meeting," Jeremy ordered. "Include the Command AI also."

"The Command AI is probably on Borton," Commander Malen was quick to point out. "It will have to perform a microjump to get here in time for the meeting." Borton was the name the AIs had given to the fourth planet.

Jeremy nodded. "That's fine. However, it's important the Command AI attends this meeting."

"I'll send the messages," Angela replied.

Kevin got up and walked over to Jeremy. "What are you up to? We just got back and the crew needs some rest."

Jeremy looked over at his best friend. "We all do. We won't be going anywhere for awhile, but I have something I want to talk to the general staff about."

"Does it concern the absence of Simulin ships in the blue giant nebula?" Kevin had expected to see many more on his sensors than those they had detected.

"Partially," Jeremy admitted. Kevin had been with him from the very beginning and could easily guess where Jeremy's thoughts were headed.

"Do you think we should have attacked the Dyson Sphere?"

Jeremy looked intently at Kevin. "No, I'm sure there were plenty of Simulin ships inside the dark matter nebula. They wouldn't have left their most important asset unguarded."

"But the energy collection stations should have been better protected," Ariel said, her dark eyes carefully watching Jeremy. She'd sworn to Jeremy's father many centuries in the past to keep an eye on the Special Five. "From what Clarissa has told me all four fleets met light resistance at first. It was as if a large number of the Simulin ships were needed elsewhere. Which implies some type of possible organized resistance in at least one section of the Triangulum Galaxy."

"My thoughts also," Jeremy responded with a slight nod of his head. It still amazed him at how rapidly Ariel could take a few facets of data and come to a valid conclusion. "We need to find those races that are resisting the Simulins."

"Allies!" said Kevin, looking at one of the viewscreens, which showed the *Distant Horizon* in orbit around Gaia. Kevin was concerned that if a ship were sent out to find these mysterious allies it would most likely be the exploration dreadnought. "You're not thinking about sending our wives out to the edge of this galaxy? They could be gone for months!"

"I'm not thinking about anything yet," Jeremy replied. If he did send the *Distant Horizon*, he would probably ask for volunteers to go on the ship.

"Jeremy, I have Kelsey on the comm," spoke Angela over their private channel. Ariel always kept a private channel open for the Special Five to communicate over. Clarissa did the same.

It had been several weeks since Jeremy had seen or spoken to his wife. "Put her on."

"Jeremy!" Kelsey spoke in an aggravated voice. "You've been in the system for nearly an hour and haven't checked in. Katie and I are down in New Eden shopping. Can Kevin, Angela, and you join us for supper?"

Jeremy shoulders drooped, knowing he couldn't. He knew Clarissa had probably informed Kelsey and Katie of the *Avenger's* arrival. "I have a staff meeting on the Clan Protector. Kevin and Angela can probably make it though."

"We can," confirmed Kevin with a big grin on his face. "Don't let Katie buy too many clothes. She already has more than she can wear."

"Women need new clothes," chimed in Angela. "Kelsey, we'll be down as soon as we can arrange for a shuttle."

"I'll call you as soon as the staff meeting is over," promised Jeremy.

"I'll make sure he does," added Ariel, who was standing next to Jeremy with her hands on her hips. "He needs to get off the *Avenger* for awhile."

"I'll talk to you later," Jeremy said, signaling to Angela to cut the comm connection. He wasn't sure how long that would be as he had a lot that needed to be done before he could go down to Gaia.

Jeremy watched as the shipyard drew nearer. He could plainly see the power beam emplacements as well as the more powerful particle beam cannons. Dozens of dual laser turrets dotted the hull, ready to lay down a labyrinth of defensive fire if needed. Securely closed hatches hid fifty-megaton Devastator Three missiles as well as the more powerful one hundred-megaton antimatter missiles, all with sublight engines.

"The Clan Protector is an impressive sight," commented Commander Malen as she walked over to Jeremy's side. "Daelthon has done a tremendous job with the station."

"He's dedicated," Jeremy responded. All the Carethians were.

"I'm glad we have the Bears on our side," Malen responded and then turned her attention to the Helm. "Ensign Striker, take us in to a docking port."

"The Bears are great allies," said Jeremy, recalling the time he'd spent in the Carethian System.

The Bears were a race with a rich history of honor between clans and individuals. Even when the Hocklyns had conquered their planet and drastically reduced the Bear population, those in the hidden underground cities had remained true to their culture. Jeremy well remembered the unselfish sacrifice they'd made when they rammed their small ships into the attacking Hocklyn warships. The sudden suicide attack had driven the Hocklyns and AIs away from Careth in one of the titanic battles fought in the Bears' home system.

Kelsey and Katie were in a clothing boutique in New Eden admiring all the new clothes the shop had. Since the arrival of the relief fleets and the new colonists, the city had grown until it now contained nearly one hundred and twenty thousand inhabitants. It was the largest of the five cities with Clements a close second.

"Do you think Kevin would like this?" asked Katie, holding up a skimpy piece of red lingerie that revealed much more than it covered.

"I think you could wear a towel and Kevin would be happy," laughed Kelsey. Katie and Angela had always been more daring with the clothes they wore. Kelsey was more reserved in her choice of clothing, preferring a more modest look. Standing in front of a mirror, Kelsey looked at a blouse that dipped a little low in the front. Even at thirty-eight years old, she still had a great figure.

"Needs to dip lower," commented Katie, checking out the blouse Kelsey was holding up.

"I don't think so," replied Kelsey, shaking her head at her friend. "I'm not an exhibitionist like you and Angela."

"I've seen those two piece swimsuits you wear," declared Katie, her light green eyes glinting. "Don't tell me those aren't revealing."

"Swimsuits are different," defended Kelsey, as she walked over and put the blouse back on the rack.

"I think I'll buy this," proclaimed Katie, holding up the skimpy piece of red lingerie.

"I'm sure Kevin won't object," Kelsey said smiling. "Where to next?"

"There's a new shoe store down the street I want to check out."

"Let's go pay for the red thing and head that way." Kelsey knew it would be several hours yet before Angela and Kevin made it down from the *Avenger* and could join them for supper, so they might as well get some more shopping in.

Stepping on board the Clan Protector, Jeremy was surprised to see Grayseth and Rear Admiral Marks waiting to greet him.

"Clan brother," roared Grayseth, stepping forward and giving Jeremy a big bear hug. It was the way the Carethians greeted their clan brothers. "I was fearful you had failed in the hunt and become prey to our enemy."

"Not quite," replied Jeremy, stepping back away from the huge Bear and trying to regain his breath. Grayseth had dark brown fur and towered over Jeremy.

"I'm glad to see you made it back," Rear Admiral Susan Marks spoke. "We were expecting you several days ago, about the same time the other fleets returned."

"Probably should have," admitted Jeremy. "We wanted to hit one more system." Jeremy paused and looked at Susan. "Is there another reason you elected to meet me here at the docking port?" Normally when he departed the system, he left Susan in charge.

"Yes," Susan replied with a serious look on her face. "The Command AI is going to request it be allowed to build two more shipyards to produce additional AI warspheres."

"A reasonable request," Jeremy said after a moment. "The new ships did quite well against the Simulins."

"I guess I'm a little concerned that shortly the AIs will have a much more powerful force than we do," Susan said with a frown. "What if they decide we're no longer needed?"

"Kurene and Mikow have assured me that since they removed the Simulin programming from the master Codex that's not a danger. The Altons have even commented about how the AIs are bending over backward to make up for what happened in our home galaxy."

"Perhaps you're right," Susan said, as they began walking toward the briefing room where the meeting was going to be held. "I guess the AIs are always going to make me feel a little nervous."

Jeremy understood how she felt. "You're not the only one."

He knew that many people in the fleet still had suspicions about the AIs' motives. However, it was something Jeremy had long laid to rest for himself. After numerous conversations with Kurene, Mikow, and the Command AI, he was confident the AIs now only had the best interest of the Federation races on their minds.

"The AIs are fearsome warriors," rumbled Grayseth. "They have acted with honor since our coming to this hunting ground. They are no longer the evil ones from our home galaxy."

Jeremy was a little surprised to hear Grayseth say this. The Carethians had suffered greatly under Hocklyn rule and the Hocklyns had been servants to the AIs.

-

After taking several turbo lifts, they exited on the level where the meeting was to be held. Reaching the hatch to the briefing room Jeremy opened it and stepped inside. Glancing around the room, he saw the others were already here. Admiral Jackson, Rear Admiral Kathryn Barnes, Admiral Cleeteus, Admiral Bachal, Admiral Jarls Sithe, Admiral Calmat, and the Command AI were present. Everyone rose as Jeremy entered the room.

"As you were," Jeremy said as he walked to the head of the table. Grayseth and Rear Admiral Marks followed him in and took their seats at the large conference table.

Everyone sat down and Jeremy looked over his command staff. The Command AI was at the opposite end of the table. The Command AI had a cubicle body with four tentacles. It hovered about six inches off the floor and there was a bluish-white ball of energy at the top of the cube that served as its head.

"I am pleased to see your safe return," spoke the Command AI in a nearly human voice. "We have much to discuss."

Jeremy nodded and gazed directly at the AI. "I understand you wish to build two more shipyards."

"That is correct," replied the AI. "By doing so we can build two of the new warspheres every five days with our automated construction facilities."

"What about resources?" asked Admiral Jackson, his eyes narrowing sharply. Even after two years, Jackson still felt uncomfortable in the presence of an AI.

"This system has a cometary belt out beyond Borton," the Command AI answered. "We will mine it for the resources needed to operate the shipyards. Some of the refined metals can also be made available for the inhabitants of Gaia to use in their factories."

"How long would it take to build the two new shipyards?" asked Jeremy. The quicker he could increase the number of warspheres he had available, the sooner he could launch an all out war against the Simulins.

"Three months," answered the AI. "It would take the use of six of the fleet repair ships to accomplish this."

"Can we spare six repair ships?" asked Jeremy, looking over at Admiral Jackson, who was now his second in command.

Jackson opened up a folder he had brought and studied some information. "Yes," he answered, looking back up. "We could spare eight of them."

Jeremy nodded. They had fourteen of the versatile fleet repair ships. "Would it speed up construction if I gave you eight of the ships?"

"Yes," answered the Command AI. "We could complete construction in two point three months."

Reaching a decision, Jeremy nodded. "Let's do it then." He looked around the group. "I strongly suspect we stirred up a hornet's nest with our attack on the Simulin energy collection stations."

"Will they attempt to attack us here?" asked Admiral Jarls Sithe formerly of New Providence.

"No," Jeremy answered. "We know they can't penetrate the nebula because of the hyperspace disrupters we have in place. However, our attack will have made them aware of just how vulnerable their energy collectors are. They're bound to send warships to those systems to protect the remaining stations."

"So we leave them alone," Rear Admiral Kathryn Barnes said. Kathryn knew Jeremy had wanted to destroy many more of them than what they'd managed.

"No," Jeremy said with a devilish grin. "I intend to destroy all of them in our next attack."

"How?" asked Grayseth, his large brown eyes growing even larger. "They will be heavily protected by the evil ones of this galaxy."

"I have an idea," Jeremy replied. "I just need to speak to Andram and Shilum about it. Once I know it'll work, I'll explain. However, that's not why I called this meeting."

"You have something else on your mind, clan brother," spoke up Grayseth in understanding. "Does it have something to do with our recent attack against the energy collectors?" Grayseth had been extremely honored to lead a fleet against the stations.

"Yes," Jeremy answered as he looked around his command staff. "Where were all the Simulin ships? They should have responded to our attacks much sooner than they did."

"I assumed it was because we had stayed in the nebula for the last few years," commented Rear Admiral Barnes. "They weren't expecting an attack. Perhaps they no longer considered us a danger."

"Perhaps," admitted Jeremy, looking intently at the others. "But what if it was for another reason? What if somewhere in this galaxy there's still major resistance to the Simulins? We know from some of the worlds we found early on that they had only been destroyed a few hundred years ago."

"It would be useful to have allies," commented Admiral Jackson, looking thoughtful. "From what I know of the *Distant Horizon's* travels through this galaxy when it first arrived there are a number of fully inhabited Simulin systems. They have a far greater resource base than we do."

"What are you proposing?" asked Rear Admiral Barnes, drawing in a deep, fortifying breath. She was wondering if it was something that would involve her ship.

"We need to explore more of this galaxy," Jeremy said, as his eyes shifted to Kathryn. "We need to have a better idea of the number of worlds the Simulins control and if there is indeed any opposition to their rule."

"The *Distant Horizon* was built for exploration," Kathryn said, her eyes focusing on Jeremy. "We have an ion cannon on the bow plus our Defense Globes have been replenished. I wouldn't be afraid to take the ship out on an exploratory cruise if that's what you're proposing."

"It is," answered Jeremy. "However, you wouldn't be going alone. You would have a small fleet at your disposal."

"How large of a fleet?" asked Kathryn. Having additional ships would be a bonus as it would allow for them to cover more worlds. She would also feel safer with a powerful fleet at her disposal.

"That's up for discussion," answered Jeremy, as he looked at the others. "I would want to send some of the new AI warspheres, possibly a couple of Alton battleships, and a few others. The exact number and type will be determined by the length of the mission and the areas of this galaxy we want to cover."

"How soon before we launch this mission?" asked Kathryn. She wanted her crew to have sufficient leave time to prepare.

"Four weeks," Jeremy answered. "That will give us time to make the necessary preparations."

Kathryn thought it over; four weeks would be sufficient. "Very well," she responded. "I want to give my crew at least two weeks' leave planetside."

"That's reasonable," answered Jeremy, nodding his head in agreement. There was still a very important question he had to come to grips with. Did he want Kelsey and Katie going on this mission? They could easily be gone for six months or more.

-

Kathryn was watching the concerned expression on Jeremy's face. She guessed he was thinking about his wife and Katie. She couldn't blame him. It might be wise if the two women were temporarily reassigned to the shipyard or another vessel. Kathryn would miss the two because they were very good at what they did and she considered them a valuable part of her crew. However, Jeremy was the fleet admiral and she wasn't going to put his wife and best friend's wife in jeopardy, not on the type of mission this was going to be. She did feel excited at the prospect of actually going out and exploring this galaxy. The *Distant Horizon* had been designed to be an exploration ship. It was about time she began performing her duty.

Chapter Three

High Commander Zarth Lantu gazed fixedly at the battlecruiser's main viewscreen. Several Ornellian warships were visible, firing feeble ruby-red laser beams at Simulin vessels. The lasers were having no detrimental effect on the powerful Simulin energy screens protecting their ships.

"These small ships are weak," spat out Second Commander Darst. "We do not need all of our ships to conquer and eliminate this star empire."

"Perhaps not," admitted Lantu, shifting his eyes to his second in command. "However, there can be no others but Simulin. The Ornell Empire contains ten inhabited star systems and numerous scientific outposts scattered throughout this section of the galaxy. It will take months to find all of them and blast them out of existence. By bringing so many ships, we can complete our mission and then return to other duties."

The battlecruiser shuddered slightly, drawing Lantu's attention to the tactical screen. Several of the small three-hundred-meter Ornellian warships were firing their lasers and launching nuclear missiles from missile tubes. The ships were long and narrow with a flared stern where the engine compartment was located.

"Energy screen is holding at 98 percent," reported Darst. "Should I target those ships?"

"Yes," spoke Lantu evenly. "They must die!"

Darst spoke some orders to the Simulin in charge of the tactical station.

On one of the viewscreens, several brilliant white lights suddenly stabbed toward one of the Ornellian warships. The energy beams struck the ship's primitive energy screen and tore right through it. The two beams shot completely through the stricken vessel, cutting it in two. Then a bright explosion went off as a Simulin antimatter missile vaporized the two sections of the hapless vessel. Moments later, the second Ornellian ship suffered the same fate.

"Both enemy ships have been eliminated," reported Darst, turning toward Lantu. "Their energy screens are first generation and cannot resist our energy beams. This will be a short battle."

Lantu nodded. "Find more targets. As soon as this defending fleet is eliminated we will go on to this system's inhabited planet and cleanse its surface of these organics. We will also land the Conqueror Drones to ensure no life rises from the ashes of this world in the future."

-

In space, the admiral in charge of the eighty defending Ornellian warships watched in near panic as his ships were being eliminated with impunity. Ship after ship died in blazing balls of light as antimatter missiles detonated in the hearts of the vessels.

"Our energy screens are useless against the power of the invaders' weapons," his second in command reported. "Our most powerful lasers are failing to penetrate their energy screens. Even our nuclear missiles are proving to be useless."

The Ornellians were bipedal and stood slightly shorter than a human. Their eyes were wide and narrow and their heads were nearly round. Two small ears were on the side of the head and they were bald. Their skin color was a deep dark gray. Their arms were very thin with three fingers and a thumb on each hand.

"We must withdraw to the planet," the admiral said, as he watched another one of his ships die. "With its orbital defenses we might be able to hold these invaders at bay."

"I'll send the order," the second officer responded.

The admiral looked with trepidation at the viewscreens in the small Command Center. For generations there had been rumors about a dangerous and cruel enemy toward the galaxy's center. He now knew those rumors were true. He greatly feared that not even the orbital defenses would be enough.

-

The withdrawal was done quickly and the surviving eighteen Ornellian warships were soon in orbit around the planet they were tasked with defending. There was a defensive grid of two hundred small laser satellites in orbit as well as twenty missile platforms. The platforms each held twelve advanced missiles with fifty-kiloton nuclear warheads. Also in orbit were four space stations. Two were used for the construction of warships and civilian vessels while the other two were for research.

"The two research stations have been evacuated," reported the second officer.

"What about the shipyards?" The admiral feared there had not been time to get everyone to safety.

"They need another hour," answered the second officer with a deep and concerned look. "They don't have enough shuttles."

"They don't have an hour," responded the admiral, gesturing toward the viewscreens showing the advancing invaders. The invaders had two types of vessels. The massive 1,700-meter battlecruisers and the smaller 1,100-meter escort cruisers. Each ship had six dangerous looking spires on the bow, which contained the unstoppable energy weapons that had proven to be so deadly to the Ornellian fleet.

"The shipyards have weapons," pointed out the second officer. "Perhaps they can hold the invaders off while they finish the evacuation."

"Against those?" replied the admiral, gazing at the approaching invaders and shaking his head. The admiral let out a deep breath. He greatly feared that no matter what he did the world below him was doomed.

"Make sure we record everything," he ordered, accepting that he and his remaining fleet were soon to die. "Once the battle begins, launch a hyperspace message drone every five minutes."

"At that rate we'll run out of drones quickly," replied the second officer with a look of confusion on his face. The ship only had six of the expensive drones on board.

"I suspect that will be long enough," the admiral replied softly.

Leaning back in his command chair, the admiral thought about the world below and how the panicked populace was probably rushing to shelters. Shelters that would prove pointless if the invaders nuked the surface. With a cold feeling in his heart, he knew he would never have the opportunity to see again the pristine white beaches on the ocean shores, the deep snow on the mountains, and the gently running rivers he so dearly cherished.

"The Ornellian ships have gone into orbit around their planet," reported Darst as he checked the sensors on the battlecruiser. "There's a defense grid as well as four space stations. From our scans, the defense grid is comprised mainly of primitive laser satellites with a few missile platforms mixed in."

"They will pose no threat to our ships," Lantu said in a voice without passion or mercy. "Inform the fleet to close and destroy all the orbital constructs, including the remaining Ornellian ships. When we leave, I don't want there to be a trace of a civilization ever having existed on or near this planet."

"All must be Simulin," Darst intoned.

"All must be Simulin," repeated Lantu with a confirming nod.

–

The Simulin fleet, which was comprised of 210 battlecruisers and 407 escort cruisers rapidly closed with the remaining defenders and the planet they were trying to protect. The Simulin fleet quickly englobed the planet and then moved to within optimal firing range. Space became lit up as hundreds of deadly energy beams flashed out and struck the Ornellian ships. Fourteen instantly became riddled wrecks as the powerful beams tore the ships open. The remaining four were heavily damaged and begin to drift down toward the planet.

The defensive grid was activated and hundreds of ruby-red laser beams struck the Simulin energy screens. The Simulin screens shrugged off the attack as if it were mere pinpricks. Then the missile platforms fired. Nuclear fire washed across the Simulin fleet and once again, the shields held steady.

From the surface of the planet hundreds of missiles began rising on plumes of fire as everything the Ornellians had left was thrown at the Simulins. With impunity, the attacking battlecruisers and escort cruisers began shooting them down. Not a single missile managed to clear the atmosphere. Then the warships began taking out the defensive grid. Space above the planet lit up with small explosions as the laser satellites and the missile platforms were wiped from existence.

–

High Commander Lantu was satisfied with the progress of the battle. As he had suspected, the Ornellians had no weapons that could endanger his fleet. Shifting his callous gaze to the viewscreens, he watched as antimatter missiles struck the four orbiting space stations, obliterating them from existence. In moments, only wisps of glowing gas and molten metal marked where they had once orbited above the planet.

"The battle is over," Darst reported with a satisfied smirk. "This enemy, while they possessed warships, were still very weak."

"Position the fleet for planetary bombardment," ordered Lantu, folding his arms across his chest. "Contact the Conqueror Drone ships and tell them to standby to deploy."

-

The Simulin fleet went into a lower orbit above the inhabited planet. From its surface frantic pleas offering to surrender filled the comm channels. All were ignored. For nearly an hour, the large fleet circled the planet, scanning the surface for population centers and industrial locations. At the end of that time on all two hundred and ten Simulin battlecruisers hatches slid open and slower moving nuclear missiles were fired. These were the ones used for planetary bombardment and each contained a ten-megaton nuclear warhead.

The missiles flashed down through the thick protective atmosphere and shortly, massive explosions shook the planet. Above each city with a population of over ten thousand a warhead exploded, sending fiery devastation across the landscape below. Mushroom clouds billowed up into the sky as superheated air rushed in. In all two thousand missiles were fired at the planet.

-

"All primary targets have been destroyed," confirmed Darst, as he checked the ship's sensors. "The spreading radiation should kill the few survivors."

"It doesn't matter," commented High Commander Lantu coldly. "The Conqueror Drones will finish off any organics that managed to survive the bombardment. Contact the drone ships and tell them to deploy their cargo."

Four large Simulin vessels dropped down toward the planet and hatches on their hulls opened. Numerous drone pods began dropping down toward the hapless planet. Each pod contained four of the deadly Conqueror Drones. Through the atmosphere, the pods descended and then landed gently on the surface. The hatches opened and four lethal killers emerged from each pod. The crab-like creatures were three meters across with numerous legs and four appendages with large and dangerous looking claws. They were made out of battle armor and used solar energy as their primary power source. They killed by tearing their prey apart. A Conqueror Drone had a basic self-repair capability and could exist upon a planet for several centuries before ceasing to function.

The drones had rudimentary scanners, which they could use to detect movement as well as sound. As soon as the drones exited the pods they stopped, scanned their surroundings, and then set off toward likely targets that might hold survivors. It didn't take the drones long to find their prey. Frightened Ornellians turned and ran when they saw the advancing drones. In moments, a frightful screaming noise filled the air as the drones began to kill.

"Drones have been deployed," reported Darst in an emotionless voice.

"Soon these organics will cease to exist," High Commander Lantu said evenly. It didn't bother him that under his orders an entire civilized world was dying. It was the Simulin way.

"Assemble the fleet and let's move on to our next target," Lantu ordered. "We still have much to do in this sector of space. There can be none but Simulin."

"None but Simulin," Darst repeated.

-

The Simulin fleet quickly formed up and made the jump into hyperspace. In a few weeks ships would be sent back to check on the progress of the Conqueror Drones to see if more were going to be needed. In most instances that was not the case as the drones were very good at depopulating a world.

-

The Ornellian fleet admiral was still alive. His ship was heavily damaged and without power. In a few more minutes, it would begin to enter the atmosphere of the planet and burn up from its passage through the thick and now heavily contaminated air.

"We have just enough battery power to launch one of the message drones," his second in command reported.

The second officer was leaning against a console breathing heavily. One of his arms was broken as well as his right leg. Several other officers lay prone on the deck where they had died from their injuries.

The admiral let out a deep and regretful sigh. One viewscreen was still functioning and upon it, he could see the death of a world. Already the atmosphere was becoming filled with smoke and dust from the nuclear blasts. In another few days, a nuclear winter would cover the planet in darkness.

"Send the drone," the admiral ordered. Already he could hear the atmosphere beginning to brush the hull of his ship.

The second officer hobbled over to a still functioning console and pressed several buttons. "Drone is launched."

"Let us hope the information it contains can help the rest of our people," the admiral spoke in a tired voice.

The ship began to shake more violently as it rapidly began to fall toward the surface of the planet. The noise of the rushing air soon reached a crescendo.

The Ornellian admiral closed his eyes, ready to meet his death. He'd done everything he could to protect this world and had failed. For that failure, he and his surviving crew would pay the ultimate price.

-

In the atmosphere above the dying planet, the Ornellian flagship broke apart and became numerous fireballs flashing through the atmosphere. A few of the fireballs crashed to the ground, gouging out small smoking craters. Around the planet, thousands of Conqueror Drones were busily killing. At the moment, prey was plentiful but that would soon change as the drones and the spreading radiation would quickly reduce the number of frightened and doomed survivors.

-

Back in the Gaia System, Fleet Admiral Jeremy Strong was in a shuttle inspecting the orbital defenses along with Admiral Jackson. They were currently circling one of the six massive Indomitable Class battlestations that were the bulwark of the planet's defensive grid. The station was one thousand meters in diameter and armed with numerous heavy particle beam cannons and sublight antimatter missile tubes. Since the arrival of the six stations two years back, each one had also been equipped with two very powerful ion cannons to strip the shields from attacking Simulin warships. They were also equipped with a large number of dual energy beam cannons for defense. Each station had a powerful energy shield that rivaled that of an Alton battleship. They were powered by Fusion Five reactors.

"Impressive," spoke Admiral Jackson. Jackson was an older fleet admiral, graying at the temple and very efficient at his job. "I'm glad we were able to bring six of these with the relief fleets."

"So am I," Jeremy answered. "You have no idea how pleased I was to see those Alton battleships with these in tow." Over the last two years, the Altons had added more refinements to the battlestations until they were much more powerful than their Federation counterparts.

With the addition of the Indomitable Class battlestations and then later equipping them with ion beams, Jeremy was now confident he could hold Gaia against any foreseeable attack by the Simulins. He knew they were safe for now; the hyperspace disruption satellites were seeing to that. But he also knew anything that technology could build, more technology could find a way around. At some point in the future, the Simulins would find a way through the nebula that hid Gaia. When that day happened, they would arrive in force with one goal, the complete and utter destruction of every organic being in the system as well as the AIs.

"I spoke with General McGown a few days ago," said Jackson, glancing over at Jeremy. "He has eight thousand marines at each one of his three bases. Since the last attack, the Altons have come up with a pulse rifle that should punch right through Conqueror Drone armor."

"I knew the Alton scientists were working on that," Jeremy replied, curious to see how far the research had gotten. "Andram indicated they were almost to the point of producing a prototype."

"They have produced a prototype and it works very well," Jackson reported. "General McGown's only concern is the pulse rifle is only good for ten shots before it needs a new energy pack."

"I'll speak to Andram about that," Jeremy promised.

He knew how he would feel if the pulse rifle stopped working with a Conqueror Drone charging. He'd seen videos of how a drone killed and it was quite gruesome. As they continued on their tour, they inspected several of the Type Two battlestations. They were 150 meters in diameter and fully self-contained. They had an upgraded energy shield, defensive lasers, and two particle beam cannons. They were also equipped with twelve Devastator Three missile tubes with a standard crew of twenty. The crew size had been greatly reduced as the Altons had added refinements to the smaller stations to allow for less maintenance and upkeep. The stations were powered by a class three fusion reactor. There were currently sixty of these in orbit over Gaia under the control of the six Indomitable Class battlestations.

"Defense in depth," commented Admiral Jackson. "Admiral Tolsen believed the same. He had Indomitable Class battlestations, Type Two stations, and particle beam satellites around the disturbed area of space at the black hole."

"I didn't mention this in the meeting," said Jeremy, looking intently at Jackson. "There is another possible reason for the lack of Simulin ships in the blue giant nebula."

"If they went to our home galaxy," spoke Jackson with a knowing look. "Admiral Tolsen was ready for them if they did. I'm not sure what he had in mind, but he was pretty convinced he could destroy anything the Simulins sent through the intergalactic vortex. If they sent a large number of their ships through, they died when they arrived."

Jeremy was silent for a moment in thought. Glancing out the viewport, he could see a number of bright points of light. There were four thousand particle beam satellites in orbit above Gaia. "Let's assume the Simulins lost a major portion of their fleet when they attacked Admiral Tolsen. Let's also assume that somewhere in this galaxy they're fighting a major battle. Either might explain the lack of ships in the blue giant nebula."

"It would," conceded Jackson. Then he looked seriously at Jeremy. "Don't underestimate the Simulins. From what I've seen they are on a par with the Altons in science and technology, perhaps even more so depending on what they've learned from the Dyson Sphere."

"Perhaps," answered Jeremy, pursing his lips. "However, the Altons have learned a lot from the information Rear Admiral Barnes brought from the computer banks on Astral. They have research from thousands of civilizations they have been going through. That's one reason why the new AI warspheres are so effective against the Simulins."

"That's one thing the Altons are good at," Jackson replied with a grin. "They sure know how to conduct research."

An hour later, the shuttle touched down at the large spaceport just outside of New Eden. Stepping out onto the pavement Jeremy was met by an impatient Kelsey standing at the foot of the shuttle's ramp glaring at him.

"What's this about the *Distant Horizon* going out on a special mission and Katie and I might not be included?" she demanded with her hands on her hips.

Jeremy let out a deep sigh. Rear Admiral Barnes had made the suggestion to him after their meeting, somehow Kelsey must have heard about it. He had a strong hunch either Clarissa or Ariel had been responsible. "We haven't decided anything yet," he replied defensively. "We're still planning the mission."

"Katie, Clarissa, and I did most of the design work on the exploration dreadnought," Kelsey said, her eyes still glinting with anger. "The Altons and some human scientists helped toward the end. If that ship is going out on an exploratory mission, we're going to be on it!"

"Even if it lasts for six months?" asked Jeremy, not quite sure where his wife was coming from.

"Yes, even six months," Kelsey responded stubbornly. "You know with the long life drugs the Federation has our lives are much longer now than back in the twenty-first century. Andram says that by applying some Alton science to our own long life drugs a human could easily live to see the ripe old age of two hundred. We've all been taking the drugs since we awoke from cryosleep. You still look as if you're in your late twenties or early thirties. The rest of us are the same way. Six months with the lifespans we have ahead of us is not that big of a deal."

"Katie feels the same way?" asked Jeremy, reaching out and taking his wife's hand. He saw the anger in her eyes slowly start to fade.

"Yes," Kelsey answered. "If the *Distant Horizon* goes exploring, we want to be on it. After all, that was one of the things we designed her for."

"I'll speak to Rear Admiral Barnes," promised Jeremy. He also knew Kevin was going to be highly upset if their wives went on this mission. However, Jeremy wasn't sure he could prevent it. Both were very determined women and used to having their way.

"Okay," Kelsey replied in a meeker voice. "I promised Katie and Angela we would meet them for dinner. Katie has found a new Chinese restaurant she wants to try out."

"Chinese food," commented Jeremy, a little bit surprised.

He knew the relief fleets had brought numerous plants and seeds with them when they came to the Triangulum Galaxy. They had brought sperm and eggs for a number of species including cattle, sheep, pigs, and even horses. There were also large hatcheries for several species of fish common on Earth. Massive fish growing ponds and lakes had been set up and were routinely harvested. In the two years since the relief fleets had arrived, the food available was now very close to what could be found in the Federation.

"Yes, Chinese food," Kelsey answered. "I have a vehicle waiting and it will take us to the restaurant where the others are waiting."

Jeremy nodded. He strongly suspected the topic of the *Distant Horizon's* impending mission would probably come up during the meal. For some reason, he suddenly wasn't very hungry.

Chapter Four

Admiral Race Tolsen stood in front of Fleet Admiral Nagumo with a straight face. It had been two years since the remarkable defeat of the Simulins at the galactic core. Even so, he had gone through a long court-martial at the insistence of Admiral Korrel and had been reassigned to a command position in the New Tellus System aboard one of large orbiting shipyards. While he had won a stunning victory over the enemy, he'd done so by disobeying direct orders from the Federation Council. Admiral Korrel had made it plain that, in his opinion, Race had endangered the entire Federation by his refusal to destroy the Capacitor Stations when ordered to do so. Only the testimony of former Fleet Admiral Hedon Streth, Fleet Admiral Nagumo, and several important Federation senators had saved Race's career.

"I have a new assignment for you," announced Admiral Nagumo, gesturing for Race to take a seat in front of the desk.

Race sat down and looked at the fleet admiral expectedly. The last two years had been extremely hard. Losing command of the *WarHawk* and Third Fleet had been devastating, and he had seriously considered resigning from the fleet.

Admiral Nagumo gazed at Race for several long moments before speaking. "At your court-martial I commended you for your thinking and bravery in the face of an overwhelming enemy. The strategy you used against the Simulins was brilliant and brought about one of the biggest victories in fleet history."

"They wouldn't listen," replied Race with a trace of bitterness in his voice, recalling the grueling days of the court-martial. "What we did prevented the Simulins from ever attacking our galaxy in force again."

"Perhaps," answered Nagumo, his eyes peering sharply at Race. "You should know that recent reports from some of the outlying areas have indicated the Simulins have returned to our galaxy."

Race's eyes grew wide at this announcement. "How large of a force?" Race was concerned this might be the start of a massive invasion if the Simulins had managed to find the power to open up an intergalactic vortex away from the galactic center.

"Just a few ships," replied Admiral Nagumo, tapping a report on his paper-strewn desk. "There have been a number of unconfirmed sightings of mysterious ships. We even have a few photos and our intelligence people have positively identified them as Simulin."

"What does the council say about this?"

"Nothing," Nagumo responded with a deep frown appearing on his face. "I haven't told them yet."

"Is there a reason for that?"

"Yes," the fleet admiral replied with a grave look on his face. "Our intelligence people believe the Simulins are searching for something of significance in our galaxy."

"What?" Race couldn't imagine what the Simulins would be looking for unless it was Astral. Astral was the Altons' home world at the galactic center and where the science and history of tens of thousands of worlds were stored in the massive computers beneath the City of Light and the Simulins should know where Astral was. It was where they had gone and changed the AIs programming in the master Codex.

"This," responded Nagumo, opening up a red folder on his desk marked Top Secret and sliding a photo across to Race.

Race picked up the photo and his blood turned cold. He felt a chill run down his back. "Is this what I think it is?"

The photo was of a massive metallic object that dwarfed the battleship pictured beside it.

"It's a computer generated photo of what we think they're hunting for," Nagumo said. "It's a Dyson Sphere."

"Impossible," sputtered Race, shaking his head in denial. "Who could build such a thing? Not even the Altons have the ability to build such an object."

Nagumo reached inside the red folder and handed Race several pages covered in writing. "I received this immediately after your court-martial from former Fleet Admiral Hedon Streth. He claimed that somewhere in our galaxy, probably close or inside the galactic core was a Dyson Sphere. If the Simulins manage to find this construct they may once more be able to open large intergalactic vortices into our galaxy and invade in substantial numbers."

"More of his premonitions," muttered Race forlornly. He recalled how Fleet Admiral Streth's premonitions had taken him to the galactic core and indirectly caused him to lose command of his fleet. "It seems as if every time he has one it ends in a disaster."

"I'm not sure I believe in that premonition nonsense," Nagumo said with a deep sigh. "However, the majority of the people on Ceres, New Tellus, and New Providence do and they all believe in Fleet Admiral Hedon Streth, the savior of the human race. How do I go against a living legend?"

"So what do we do?" Race knew exactly the situation the fleet admiral was in. Even though Admiral Streth was no longer in the active fleet, people still listened very attentively when he spoke.

"I wasn't the only one to receive this report," continued the fleet admiral in a displeased voice. "Senator Arden of New Providence, Senator Karnes of New Tellus, Governor Barnes of Ceres, and Ambassador Tureen of the Altons also were recipients. There was also a copy sent to you, which I intercepted. I couldn't risk this knowledge coming out in your court-martial."

Race was silent for several moments as he mulled over what the fleet admiral had just told him. "How do we find this thing if it exists?" he asked, as he read more of what Fleet Admiral Streth had written. If he hadn't known the former fleet admiral, he would just dismiss it as the ramblings of a mad man. "It looks to me as if we may be going out searching for a myth."

"It seems there may be some truth to what Admiral Streth has said," admitted Nagumo with a deep sigh. "Shortly after receiving this report Ambassador Tureen asked for a meeting with me. He swore me to secrecy and then proceeded to tell me a secret that only the Altons are aware of."

"Crap!" muttered Race. If the Altons were involved, this had suddenly gotten much bigger. "What did he say?"

"It seems that million of years ago there was another highly intelligent race in our galaxy. The Altons found the ruins of their cities on hundreds of worlds in the early days of their explorations. This was back before they created the AIs. Ambassador Tureen claims that if the rumors of the Dyson Sphere are true, these Originators are the ones who would have built it."

"Originators," repeated Race, looking intently at Nagumo. "Why has no one else mentioned these ruins? If there are ruins on hundreds of worlds, we should have heard about them by now. Not even the Hocklyns could have kept something that big a secret."

"That's where the problem lies," spoke Fleet Admiral Nagumo with a look of deep concern. "All of these worlds are in Shari space and you know what that means."

"We can't get to them," responded Race, realizing the magnitude of the problem. If the Federation was to send a fleet into Shari space and it was discovered, then it could cause the Shari to go to war with the Federation and its allies. "So what do we do?"

Nagumo drew in a deep breath and pulled out another sheet of paper from the red folder. "Race, I need you to sign this form."

"What is it?" asked Race, reaching forward and picking the paper up. His eyes suddenly widened sharply seeing that it was his discharge papers from the fleet. "I don't understand."

"It's not what it looks like," said Nagumo, reaching for a pen. "I'm reassigning you to fleet intelligence and its Special Ops division. It's top secret and very few people even know it exists. For anyone on the council, it will appear as if you have been dismissed from the fleet. However, you will retain your rank of admiral and will report directly to me and the commander of the Special Ops division when needed."

"For what purpose is this being done?" asked Race suspiciously. The fleet had been his life; he didn't want to leave it! For some reason he felt as if the long entangling arms of former Fleet Admiral Streth were once more reaching out for him.

"You're going to the new Alton home world of Albania to take command of a fleet," Nagumo replied with a grin. "A fleet of special vessels that have been built by the Altons for one purpose and one purpose only: to find this Dyson Sphere."

"I'm going into Shari space?"

"Yes," Nagumo replied with a nod. "That's one reason for the resignation. If you're captured or identified, we'll claim you're not a part of our military and entered their space with out the permission of the fleet. It might just be enough to prevent a war."

"What about the crews of these ships, where did they come from?"

"All volunteers," Nagumo answered. "About one-third of the crews will be Altons with a large number of scientists and technicians. The rest will be made up of fleet personnel who over the last six months, for one reason or another, have either resigned or been dismissed. A lot of work has been done by the Special Ops people to make sure everything will look to be on the up and up."

"It will still be a risk," responded Race, thinking about the new responsibility he was being handed. Also, what would his parents and sister think when they heard he had resigned from the fleet? His sister was the commanding officer of the battlecarrier *Hera*.

"We can't let the Simulins find this Dyson Sphere if it exists," Admiral Nagumo replied. "What's even more frightening is the fact the sphere might lie in Shari space and they might find it before we do."

"What if they do find it first?" asked Race. "What if we find this Dyson Sphere in Shari space with a Shari fleet in orbit?"

"Then we go to war," Fleet Admiral Nagumo spoke in a heavy voice. "We move in a fleet large enough to take control of the Dyson Sphere. We can't let it fall into Shari hands. There will be a fleet standing by close to Shari space just in case it's needed. You will be provided with an encrypted code to summon that fleet. But think very hard before you use it as it will no doubt lead to another galactic war."

"I will," promised Race as with shaking hands he signed the resignation paper. "When do I leave?"

"Tomorrow," answered Nagumo. "With the confirmed presence of Simulin warships in our galaxy, we can't wait any longer."

"What if we're found in Shari space, do we put up a fight?"

"Use your best judgment," replied Nagumo and then he added, "If any of your people are captured, the Federation government will disavow any knowledge of you or your ships. No one but a select few are even aware of the mission you're being sent off on."

"What about my command crew?" Race asked. He would need a well-trained and dependable command group to pull this off.

"They're already at Albania," Nagumo responded.

Race nodded his acceptance. It would have been nice to have his old crew from the *WarHawk* for this mission.

"An Alton passenger ship is due to leave New Tellus tomorrow morning," Nagumo continued. "I have made arrangements for you to be on it."

"Then I'd better get packed," answered Race, as he stood to leave. He paused and then gazed at Fleet Admiral Nagumo. "Thank you, sir, for being there for me, it really meant a lot." Then turning, Race walked to the door and opening it left the fleet admiral.

-

Shortly after Admiral Tolsen departed, the door opened again and a middle-aged woman entered. Senator Amy Karnes seemed to have aged little over the years due to the advanced prolong life drugs available in the Federation.

"Did he accept the mission?"

"Of course he did," answered Fleet Admiral Nagumo. "He's been itching to get off that shipyard since he was assigned to it. My biggest fear was that he would resign before the fleet was ready."

"Did you tell him everything?" she asked with her eyes focusing steadily on the fleet admiral.

"No, not quite everything," Nagumo admitted with a deep sigh. "He doesn't know how serious this Simulin situation is becoming. If they are indeed searching for this Dyson Sphere than the likelihood of him encountering them is very high. There have been some unconfirmed reports of several fleet actions by the Shari against Simulin vessels in their space."

"They're more active in Shari space and probably are more knowledgeable of what they're searching for than we are," Amy said as she sat down. "We can't let the Shari or the Simulins find and take control of the Dyson Sphere; it could shift the power base away from the Federation and the Altons.

"That's why we have this new fleet," replied Nagumo, leaning back in his chair. "He will have the most advanced and powerful ships possible. The Altons put everything they have into them and even called in a few of the Federations' brightest engineers and scientists to help in the designs."

"Did you tell Admiral Tolsen anything about these ships?"

"No," Nagumo said with a smile. "I'll let it be a surprise."

-

Early the next morning, Race was at one of New Tellus Station's main docking ports waiting to board the Alton passenger ship *LeLath*. It was a thousand-meter vessel steeped in luxury, as that was the only way most Altons were willing to travel. The Altons were a very pacifist race for the most part with only a small fraction of their population willing to join the military. A far greater portion were interested in peaceful exploration and the expansion of their vast knowledge base.

Looking around, Race noticed a few other humans waiting to board as well as members of some of the alien races affiliated with the human led alliance and even others he wasn't familiar with. There were a few Carethians as well as members of half a dozen other alien races. Race knew the Altons maintained a huge complex on Albania, which was heavily involved in uplifting the numerous former slave worlds of the Hocklyn Empire. It wasn't unusual to see members of some of those races traveling to the complex for additional instruction as well as for help with the newer technologies the Altons were willing to share.

Finally it was time to board and Race entered the ship. He wasn't surprised to find humans dressed in ship uniforms explaining to the passengers where they needed to go. Most Alton ships, including some of their passenger liners and even their cargo ships, were partially crewed by humans from the Federation.

"Mister Tolsen," one of the female crewmembers said striding up to him. "I have your quarters ready and, if you would like, the captain of the ship has requested your presence in the Control Center to witness our departure."

"I would like that," Race said with a friendly nod. The last time he had left the New Tellus System was to travel to Ceres where his parents lived. That had been over six months ago.

"If you will follow me, I'll show you where your quarters are located and then we'll go up to the Control Center."

Race followed the young woman through the ship, admiring the large spacious corridors and taking note of the soft carpeting on the floor. Stopping in front of a door, Race was surprised to see it was made out of wood instead of metal. Everything was so much different from a warship.

"Don't worry," the woman said with an understanding smile. "The ship does have an energy shield and there's a protective metal door that will slide down over this one if the ship is damaged. The Altons prefer the aesthetics wood doors provide."

Going inside, Race wasn't surprised to see it was a small suite of rooms though a little extravagant for his taste. He noticed his bags were already there. After a quick look around he followed the woman up to the Control Center where the captain of the ship was waiting for him.

"Admiral Tolsen," the Alton said, bowing respectfully. The captain was nearly seven feet tall and his skin was very pale with a slight blue tinge and the hair on top of his head, while thick, was a solid white.

"Just Tolsen now," Race said.

The Alton smiled. "The title of admiral can never be taken away. While on board my ship you will be called admiral."

Race nodded, knowing there was no point in arguing. His eyes were quickly drawn to the massive viewscreen in the front of the Control Room. Like most Alton ships, the entire front wall was one massive screen from ceiling to floor and wall to wall. He caught his breath, feeling he could just step right out into space.

"Reverse thrusters have been activated and we're moving away from New Tellus Station," the human at the helm controls reported.

Looking at the viewscreen, Race watched as New Tellus Station came into view. New Tellus Station was sixteen kilometers in length and eight in width as it contained six massive construction bays, which could produce any size ship the fleet required as well as twelve repair bays. It was also covered in offensive and defensive weapons with the firepower of a dozen battleships. Twenty Type Two battlestations surrounded the station as well as over two hundred particle beam satellites.

"Station has been cleared," reported the second officer, who was also an Alton. "We have permission from station traffic control to activate our subspace drive."

"Take us out at 20 percent power," ordered the Alton captain.

Race watched as the giant shipyard gradually diminished until it was only a brilliant spec of light in the viewscreen. New Tellus itself was a garden world of blues, browns, greens, and whites. It was a beautiful planet and heavily populated. It was also the most powerfully fortified planet in the entire Federation. There were six shipyards orbiting New Tellus as well as six massive asteroid fortresses in its outer defensive ring. In its mid orbital defensive ring there were twenty Indomitable Class battlestations, and in the inner and final defensive ring were thousands of particle beam satellites and eighty Type Two battlestations. Only Earth could boast defenses nearly as powerful. Race greatly feared that if a Simulin fleet the size of the one he had destroyed at the galactic center attacked the Federation, only New Tellus and Earth would survive. To prevent this from ever happening, he had to find this Dyson Sphere, if it existed.

"Standby to enter hyperspace," ordered the captain, as he checked the operational stations in the Control Center.

"Hyperdrive is charged and ready to activate," reported the Helm.

"Set course for Albania," ordered the captain.

Moments later Race watched as a blue-white spatial vortex formed in front of the passenger liner and then it accelerated into its center. He was surprised at how smoothly the ship entered hyperspace as he scarcely noticed the transition. On most warships it was a gut wrecking feeling as if one's body was being torn apart and then instantly put back together.

Looking at the large viewscreen, he was mesmerized by the swirling dark purple colors of hyperspace. The viewscreen seemed as if it were alive.

"It's fascinating, isn't it?" commented the Alton captain. "Some of our research scientists believe our drive field itself is acting upon dark energy or dark matter to cause those oscillating colors."

Race nodded. There was so much about hyperspace they didn't understand. "Thank you for inviting me to the Control Center to see this. I had forgotten how your people love these massive viewscreens."

The Alton captain nodded, pleased with Race's words. "It makes exploration so much more interesting," he said. "I've gone on a few exploration cruises and I can sit for hours just looking at the viewscreen when we're exploring a new system or nebula."

"I'll be going to my quarters now," Race said. "I would like to return to the Control Center when we reach Albania if I may. I haven't been there for several years."

"I'll send someone for you before we drop out of hyperspace," the captain promised.

As Race left the Control Center, he wondered just what he would find at Albania. Fleet Admiral Nagumo had mentioned the Altons had designed new ships for this mission. It would be interesting to see what they had come up with.

-

A few days later, Race was in the main passenger lounge of the *LeLath* watching with interest as the large passenger liner made its approach to Albania. A few hours earlier he had been in the Control Center when the vessel dropped out of hyperspace, and it still amazed him at all the icons that had showed up on the ship's sensors. The system was a beehive of activity.

"Have you been to Albania before?" asked another human, who was standing next to him, gazing out the massive viewport, which took up nearly the entire wall of the lounge.

Race turned toward the man and nodded his head. "A few times," he answered. "You'll find most Altons very friendly and polite."

"I'm here on business," snorted the man. "I'm not that sure about the Altons being all that friendly. They're stingy enough with their technology. It seems as if it takes an act of God to get them to share any of it."

"Some of their technology would be very dangerous in the wrong hands," commented Race, looking back out the viewport. A large space station was coming into view. It was massive and dwarfed anything in human space except the asteroid fortresses at New Tellus.

"That's up for debate," the man said. "What are you here for?"

"Just visiting," Race answered not wanting to be drawn into further conversation. It was evident the man had very little knowledge of how the Altons did things. More than likely, he would leave the system highly aggravated at failing with his business deal.

"Admiral Tolsen," a female voice spoke from behind them.

Turning, Race saw the same young woman who had shown him around when he first came on board. "We will be docking soon, and Ambassador Tureen is waiting for you on the station. The captain also wishes to express his pleasure at being able to speak with you on this cruise. If you wish, we will be docked to the station for several days if you would like to continue to use the suite of rooms you've been assigned."

Race noticed the stunned expression on the businessman's face at hearing Race's name and who he was going to meet. "Tell the captain thank you and I enjoyed the cruise. I don't believe I've ever experienced a better job of entering hyperspace. I may indeed be interested in using my quarters for another day or two."

"I'll make sure he knows," the young woman replied with a smile.

"Admiral Tolsen," the businessman managed to utter.

"Yes," Race replied. "It's been good speaking with you." With that, Race walked off so he could return to his quarters and prepare to meet the Alton ambassador.

-

Stepping on board the space station, Race wasn't surprised to see how clean and immaculate it was. He was immediately greeted by two Altons who he'd never met before.

"I'm Kelnor Mard," the tall male Alton said and then he gestured to the female Alton next to him. "This is Reesa Jast. We will be acting as your science advisors on your mission."

"Pleased to meet you," replied Race, bowing slightly and then shaking the hands of the two Altons. "Can you tell me anything about this mission?"

Kelnor smiled and shook his head. "We'll leave that to Ambassador Tureen and his guest."

"His guest?" asked Race, feeling confused.

"Yes," Reesa responded. "If you will follow us we'll take you to the conference room where the meeting will be held. I believe suitable refreshments and food will be available."

"Let's go," Race replied. He knew he wouldn't get any more out of these two Altons until the meeting.

As they walked through the massive space station, Race couldn't help but notice the number of new alien races that were present. The Altons were now the teachers for many of the races that had been enslaved by the Hocklyns. While there were numerous Alton ships out helping uplift many of these worlds, a number of them sent their best scholars and scientists to the Alton worlds for further instruction. The Altons had sixteen large colonies in addition to their heavily populated home system. There were research installations and mining operations in at least fifty other star systems.

"Much has changed since the war with the Hocklyns and the AIs ended," commented Reesa, noticing Race studying the different races. "There are currently forty-two different alien species on the station."

"I'm just pleased that your people have agreed to help with these worlds," Race responded. He knew there were thousands of former Hocklyn slave planets that needed to be dealt with, and it was straining the resources of the Federation and its allies to keep track of them all.

"It's our responsibility as the eldest race," Kelnor answered gravely.

-

A few minutes later, they reached a large ornate wooden door. For some reason Race didn't find it out of place on the station. Opening the door, Kelnor indicated for Race to enter.

Stepping inside, Race came to a sudden halt and instantly saluted. He had not been expecting to see the man sitting at the long conference table with Ambassador Tureen and a dozen others.

"As you were, Admiral," former Fleet Admiral Hedon Streth said, returning Race's salute. "If you will have a seat we'll get this meeting started."

-

Four hours later, Race was in an Alton shuttle in the company of Fleet Admiral Streth and the two Alton scientists. He'd found out Kelnor and Reesa were both experts in the field of research dealing with the Originators. Much of the meeting had dealt with what they believed the Originators had been doing in the Milky Way Galaxy and where they had gone. They were both convinced that if there was indeed a Dyson Sphere in the galaxy, the Originators might very well be living inside of it, which would explain why all of their worlds had been abandoned.

"Where are Janice and your daughter?"

"They're staying with Amanda and Richard," Hedon replied. "I thought it was important that I be here for the start of this mission."

"So, what's so special about these new ships the Altons have built?"

"Look," said Hedon, pointing out the cockpit window and toward a shipyard they were rapidly approaching.

In orbit around the shipyard were twenty massive vessels. Each was easily two-thousand-meters in length and four-hundred-meters in diameter. They were in the shape of a cylinder with a six-hundred-meter globe at the front and a five-hundred-meter flared stern. The ships were obviously of Alton design.

"Wow!" uttered Race, seeing the huge ships. He turned toward Hedon. "I assume they're armed?"

"Yes, heavily," he responded. "But you haven't seen your flagship yet."

"My flagship?"

Hedon nodded and pointed once more. From behind the station, a monster of a ship began to appear. "The Altons have named her the *WarHawk*, after your former flagship. She's three-thousand-meters in length and the most powerful ship in the known galaxy. If you run across any Simulins in your search that ship will make them wish they'd stayed home and never come here."

Race, for the first time in a long while, was speechless. He couldn't believe after being confined to commanding a shipyard for two years he now was being offered a ship of this magnitude. "I don't know what to say," he uttered in a stunned voice. He wished his sister, Massie, could see his new command.

"Just find the Dyson Sphere," answered Hedon. "Our very survival may well depend on it."

Race was silent. It was just dawning on him how important this mission was going to be.

"One more thing," Hedon said with a mysterious smile. "It seems your entire former command crew of your old Third Fleet flagship resigned in mass recently. You will find them on board your new command."

Race didn't know how to respond. To build these ships in secret and shift the thousands of personnel around who were necessary to operate them had to have been a massive and very expensive operation.

"Thank you, Admiral," Race said sincerely. He knew that with his old command crew he just might stand a chance of pulling this mission off. Of course, the only thing standing in his way were the Simulins, who were searching for the Dyson Sphere along with the entire Shari Empire.

Chapter Five

Jeremy was in the Command Center of the *Avenger* anxiously watching the *Distant Horizon* and her fleet on the main viewscreens. In just a few short moments, the exploration dreadnought and her twenty-five powerful escorts would be departing the Gaia System.

"I can't believe they're leaving," muttered Kelvin, who was standing next to Jeremy watching the viewscreen with a disgruntled look on his face.

"Kelsey and Katie wouldn't have it any other way," replied Jeremy, with a sigh. Both women had demanded to be part of this mission as they had helped to design the *Distant Horizon* and were part of her crew. "Even Rear Admiral Barnes tried to talk them out of it, but in the end there was no way we could legitimately tell them no."

Kevin grimaced. "I know, Katie and I had several arguments over her going on this mission. I finally realized that if I stopped her, she would make my married life quite miserable."

"They'll be gone four to six months," Jeremy said. "I think we can survive until they return."

"Clarissa will keep them safe," Ariel said confidently. The dark haired AI was standing just behind the two. "Those ships are the most powerful we have and if they run across any Simulins, they should be able to handle them."

"Five minutes until they enter hyperspace," reported Commander Malen from her command console.

Jeremy looked around the Command Center. It was fully staffed as everyone wanted to watch the departure of the *Distant Horizon* and her fleet. Their mission was very simple, find out how far the Simulins had extended their influence across this galaxy and seek out potential allies if any could be found.

"I wonder what they'll find?" said Kevin. It was going to be hard being separated from Katie for such a long time.

"The last time they went off on their own they found the Dyson Sphere," Ariel reminded them.

Jeremy shifted his attention over to Ariel. She was always there when he needed her. He had long since quit thinking of her as an AI but as a close and dear friend instead. "We don't know what may be out there; that's one of the reasons for this mission."

He had spoken to Kelsey for quite some time about what he was hoping to accomplish by sending the *Distant Horizon* out exploring. His wife had been very excited about actually using the exploration dreadnought for one of the two things it had been designed for.

"One minute until hyperspace insertion," Commander Malen informed them.

"Clarissa just sent a message," reported Ariel, turning toward Jeremy and Kevin. "She promises to return everyone safely and to stay away from any Simulins."

Jeremy nodded. That was easy to say, but it might not be quite that simple to stay away from the Simulins. That was one reason he was sending such a powerful fleet.

"Hyperspace activation," reported Commander Malen.

On the large viewscreens on the front wall of the Command Center, swirling blue-white and white vortexes began forming in front of the ships of the expedition fleet. Moments later they began to vanish as the ships made their jumps into hyperspace.

"They're gone," Kevin said with a deep sigh. "What do we do now?"

Jeremy turned to Kevin and spoke. "We have a Dyson Sphere that needs to be destroyed. Somehow we need to find a way to do that if we want to keep our home galaxy safe and limit the amount of reinforcements the Simulins may be able to summon from other galaxies they control." He had spoken to Andram about destroying the rest of the energy collection stations, and the Alton had suggested that Jeremy hold off on that idea until the *Distant Horizon* returned.

Kevin remained silent. Destroying the Dyson Sphere seemed like an impossible mission. They had no weapon currently at their disposal that could even put a dent in the massive hull of the sphere.

Jeremy observed Kevin's continued silence. He knew what his friend was thinking. The Dyson Sphere was going to be a hard nut to crack. Looking back at the now empty viewscreens Jeremy couldn't help but wonder what was ahead of them. He greatly feared it was only a matter of time before the Simulins figured out how to penetrate Gaia's protective nebula even with the hyperspace interference. Fleet Admiral Streth had placed his confidence in Jeremy being able to carry out this mission. Jeremy was determined that he wouldn't fail.

-

Rear Admiral Kathryn Barnes gazed reflectively at the swirling colors of deep purple that abounded on the massive viewscreen. It was almost hypnotic watching the colors and the complicated dance they were performing.

"All ships have made the successful transition into hyperspace," Clarissa reported. The beautiful AI was standing just behind and to the left of Kathryn.

Glancing over at one of the two holographic tactical displays, she could see the friendly green icons that represented her new command. Twenty-five vessels plus the *Distant Horizon* made up the fleet. There were twenty of the new AI warspheres, two Alton battleships with Admiral Bachal, two Federation battleships, and one Federation battlecarrier. All had been heavily modified and were ready to take on the Simulins in battle if it came down to it. For the mission, Admiral Bachal would serve as the fleet's second in command.

"We're on course and in the center of tunnel Delta," reported Commander Anne Grissim, who was watching the fleet's progress on a computer screen on her command console.

They would have to drop out of hyperspace three times to negotiate sharp turns in the tunnel. The turns were in place to ensure the Simulins didn't accidently find one of the four tunnels that were free of the hyperspace interference. "First drop out in twenty-six minutes." The *Distant Horizon* and the modified ships in her fleet had the newer hyperspace drives and were capable of traveling a light-year every two minutes. They could stay in hyperspace for two hundred and forty minutes before it became necessary to drop out and allow the drives to cool back down and recharge.

"Well, we're on our way," Katie said over the private channel that Clarissa maintained for her and Kelsey.

"Yes," answered Kelsey, hoping that she and Katie hadn't made a big mistake in leaving Gaia to go on this mission. She knew Kevin had been extremely unhappy with the decision and she strongly suspected Jeremy felt the same way. However, the *Distant Horizon* was their ship, and both she and Katie had felt it was important that they go.

Kelsey looked over at Andram, who was sitting to her left side at his science console. She considered the Alton a friend and confidant. "Andram, do you think we'll encounter the Simulins on our mission?"

"Yes," he said, turning his head toward her. "Mikow and I have run some computer simulations based on what we found when we first entered the Triangulum Galaxy.

We're pretty certain the Simulins are the dominate race here and have some method of detecting high-tech civilizations. When these civilizations are detected, the Simulins do whatever is necessary to eliminate that race as a future threat."

"I wish we knew more about them," spoke Katie, her eyes showing her deep concern. "That Conqueror Drone we captured didn't exactly reveal a lot."

"More than you might think," Andram replied. "It gave us considerable insight as to how the Simulins species thinks. They're a cruel and heartless race with only one true ambition, spreading their race throughout the known universe at the expense of all others."

"They remind me of how the AIs were back in our home galaxy," said Kelsey.

"The Simulins may be worse," Andram responded. "The AIs only spoke of annihilating all organic races; the Simulins are actually doing it."

Over the next several hours, the small fleet maneuvered through the nebula until they finally emerged into open space. Once outside of the nebula their Alton enhanced sensors were activated and space for a distance of ten light-years was carefully scanned. They weren't surprised to see a number of red threat icons appear. It was evident the Simulins were keeping a close watch on the nebula, particularly after the recent attacks on the energy collecting stations in the blue giant nebula.

"Twenty-two Simulin ships detected," Captain Reynolds reported. "The nearest is two point four light-years away."

"They'll detect us shortly," Commander Grissim stated.

"We should jump immediately," suggested Colonel Petra Leon, the executive officer.

"How long until our drives have fully cooled down?" Kathryn wanted to make a long enough jump to put them out of range of the Simulin sensors.

"Eight more minutes," answered Colonel Leon. "The jumps we were making in the nebula were relatively short so there hasn't been much heat build up in the drive cores."

"We'll wait the full eight minutes," Kathryn ordered. "If the Simulins jump in, we'll jump immediately."

"That one ship is close enough it may be able to plot our course," warned Clarissa.

"I'll take the risk," answered Kathryn. She wasn't concerned about a few Simulin warships, not with the fleet she had at her disposal.

The minutes passed and the Simulin ship remained unmoving. At the end of the eight minutes, the fleet jumped toward a target destination one hundred and twenty light-years distant.

Once back in hyperspace Kathryn allowed herself to relax. She looked around the Command Center noting that Kelsey and Katie seemed to be talking to one another. She smiled to herself. She knew about the secret comm channel that Clarissa maintained for the three of them. It hadn't been too hard to figure out after watching their actions. After all, what type of admiral would she be if she didn't know what was happening on her own flagship?

Kathryn intended to do twelve jumps over the next four days before she began using the fleet to explore the surrounding space. That would put some distance between them and the nebula, and they were going in the opposite direction of where the Dyson Sphere was located. They were also going on a different tangent from where they had entered the Triangulum Galaxy originally. This would allow them to explore a totally new area of space and give them a better understanding of how much of this galaxy the Simulins actually controlled.

Settling back in her command chair, Kathryn wondered what her father was doing back on Ceres. She had come to accept that her home was now here in the Triangulum Galaxy and she would never see her father again. It pained her to know that in her later years in the fleet they had grown apart. It was one of the reasons she had tried to talk Kelsey and Katie into not going on this mission.

Simulin High Commander Zarth Lantu gazed at his flagship's tactical screen with growing anger. This was the third system of the Ornellian Empire that his fleet had attacked. The other two had been easy victories, but this one was putting up much more resistance than expected.

On a main viewscreen, one of his escort cruisers was a mangled wreck with secondary explosions finishing the destruction. The Ornellians were employing some type of super advanced laser to penetrate the shields of the Simulin warships.

"I want an analysis of that weapon!" barked High Commander Lantu. This was disconcerting as the Ornellians were not supposed to have a weapon that could destroy a Simulin vessel.

"We're working on it," answered Second Commander Darst. He was speaking to several Simulin weapon's specialists over the ship's comm system. "We should know something shortly."

"Make it quick," ordered Lantu, his eyes focusing sharply on his second in command.

The Simulin fleet had jumped into this system, which was one of the Ornellian Empire's major population centers, only to encounter heavy resistance. A fleet of two hundred of the small three-hundred-meter Ornellian cruisers was parked between the target planet and the Simulin fleet. In addition, there were twelve larger ships that were five-hundred-meters in length.

Scans of the system had indicated a heavy industrial base, with installations scattered across the system on most of the planets and the two large asteroid belts. Civilian fleet traffic had all but vanished when the warfleet had dropped out of hyperspace. There was no doubt in Lantu's mind that the civilians had killed their power and were drifting in space waiting to see the end result of the battle.

-

In space, the two opposing fleets maneuvered with the Ornellian fleet constantly staying between the attacking Simulins and the inhabited world the Simulins were seeking to destroy. Ruby-red flashes of light indicated laser fire from the smaller Ornellian cruisers. Occasionally a dark red beam of energy would flash forth to strike a Simulin energy screen and after a few seconds penetrate it and smash into the hull armor setting off large explosions as the hull material was vaporized instantly by the tremendous heat of the beam.

A Simulin battlecruiser was being targeted by a full squadron of Ornellian cruisers. Six of the deadly red beams flashed out and managed to penetrate the energy screen destroying two of the large spires on the bow of the ship as well as cutting a hole into the main engineering compartment. The resulting explosion destroyed the 1,700-meter Simulin battlecruiser in a fiery blast.

The Simulin ships were not holding back even though they had lost several warships. Deadly white energy beams lashed out, smashing through the weaker Ornellian energy shields. One of the smaller Ornellian cruisers blew apart as its power systems were compromised. Another was cut in two by the powerful energy beams.

-

"It's a heavily modified pulse laser," Second Commander Darst finally answered. "Our weapon's specialists believe they're burning out the laser each time it's fired. The energy being directed toward our screens is equivalent to one of our energy beams."

"So they're damaging their warships each time they use this weapon?"

"Yes," Darst answered. "It would seem so. They're also keeping it focused long enough to penetrate our screens. Our weapon's specialists estimate the laser beam equipment is burning out after eight to ten seconds."

Alarms began sounding on the sensor console, drawing Lantu's attention. "What is that alarm sounding for?"

"More Ornellian warships are dropping out of hyperspace," the Simulin at the console reported.

"How many?" demanded High Commander Lantu.

"One hundred seventeen, and six of them are of the larger cruiser class."

High Commander Lantu gazed at the new red threat icons appearing above his fleet and slightly to the rear.

The alarm sounded again and he looked at the sensor operator for confirmation of what he knew was coming next.

"Our long-range sensors have detected two additional Ornellian fleets inbound."

"We can still destroy them," Second Commander Darst quickly pointed out. "Our ships are much more powerful and their energy shields are weak. The battle computer is still forecasting a 72 percent probability of victory even with the arrival of the incoming fleets."

"No, we must wait for reinforcements," Lantu said, reaching a decision. "It seems as if the Ornellians are going to risk all of their warships to defend this one system. We will let them gather and then wipe them out in one battle. It will make conquering their remaining worlds and eliminating their organic populations a simple task. We will withdraw and send word for several of our other fleets to join us. For now we will allow the Ornellians to have their victory, but it will be a short-lived one."

A few minutes later, the order was given and the Simulin warships opened up spatial vortexes and left the Ornellian home star system.

In space, the admiral in charge of the Ornellian fleet gazed in relief at the ship's main tactical screen as the enemy withdrew.

"We won," said his second in command exuberantly.

"I'm not so certain," answered Admiral Krusk with a deep frown. "I suspect they detected our other inbound ships and are letting us gather so we will be easier to kill."

His second in command was silent for several moments as he thought this over. "What shall we do?"

"We know our new laser weapon is effective against their warships; however, we're damaging our ships each time we overload one of the main projectors. Several weapon crews have perished using the laser this way. I don't know how much time we have, but we must find a way to make our laser into a better and safer weapon. For now, it's the only weapon we have that can penetrate their shields."

"How much time to you think we have?"

"Not long," Admiral Krusk responded. "Let us place our fleets over Ornell and see what our scientists and technicians can come up with."

"I will send the order," the officer replied.

Krusk nodded. He was deeply afraid they had only bought a few days' respite. When the enemy returned, they would not retreat until either they were destroyed or Ornell had fallen. Krusk knew the odds of his people being victorious were nearly nil.

-

High Commander Zarth Lantu watched impassively as his flagship and the other ships of his fleet dropped out of hyperspace in a system a scant four light-years distant from the Ornellian home world. A battlecruiser would be sent to summon the nearest quick response fleets to assist in the destruction of the Ornellian Empire. He knew that at any one time numerous small Simulin battle fleets were dispersed throughout this galaxy waiting for the probe ships to send back messages whenever an advanced civilization was detected. It would only take a few days to a week at most before the first of the small fleets arrived.

Once he was satisfied he had the ships available to annihilate the Ornellians with little collateral damage to his own fleet, he would advance on their home world and destroy the fleets defending it. Then he would send the small reaction fleets to the other surviving Ornellian worlds that would be defenseless with their fleets destroyed and cleanse their surfaces. The reason for his actions was simple, there could only be Simulins in this galaxy, and all other organics must be annihilated.

-

Rear Admiral Kathryn Barnes was in her quarters working on the latest reports on their mission. Over the last four days, they had jumped nearly 1,500 light-years. At the moment, the long-range sensors were not showing any Simulin vessels. Surprisingly enough they had seen very few Simulin vessels on the sensors as they made their jumps. She had chosen a small brown dwarf star system for the fleet to hide in while some of the vessels went off on exploration missions. Her current plans were to send ships to all of the F, G, and K Class stars within twenty-five light-years of their current position. Astrometrics had reported there were twelve stars in that range that could possibly contain life-bearing planets. Kathryn knew it was highly possible for other classes of stars to have habitable planets, but the likelihood was greatly reduced. Andram had mentioned that nearly 8 percent of the stars in the Triangulum Galaxy were of these three classes, more than Kathryn could ever hope to explore.

For exploration purposes, Kathryn would be sending out the battleships *Pallas*, *Deneb*, the battlecarrier *Ardent*, and of course, the *Distant Horizon*. Each would be escorted by two AI warspheres. In case of problems, the exploring ships had orders to fall back to the brown dwarf system where the rest of the fleet would be waiting. Alton Admiral Bachal would remain in the system with his flagship, the *Starlight*, as well as the other Alton battleship and the remaining twelve AI warspheres. The plans were for the four exploration groups to stay within ten light-years of one another during their explorations so the Alton long-range sensors, which all the ships were equipped with, would be able to detect if one group had suddenly run into trouble and was pulling back to the brown dwarf system. If that were to occur then all the other fleets would proceed to Admiral Bachal's position and await further orders.

—

"Worried?" asked Clarissa from where she was standing in front of Kathryn's desk. The AI had holo emitters throughout the ship so she could appear anywhere she wanted. It made the crew feel more comfortable when they could speak to her in person instead of a disembodied voice.

"Some," admitted Kathryn, pausing in writing her report and looking up at Clarissa. "We're heading out into the unknown in a dangerous galaxy and there's no guarantee we'll make it back home."

Behind Clarissa, a viewscreen suddenly activated showing the stars around the *Distant Horizon*. "Kelsey, Katie, and I designed this ship originally for exploration and then for war when it was decided to use the ship to find the lost fleets. I'm fully confident we'll make it back to Gaia."

Kathryn leaned back in her chair and folded her arms across her chest. "What do you think will happen to us in the long term?" When the relief fleets had arrived with all of their colonists, it had swiftly uplifted the morale in the fleet. Suddenly it seemed as if Gaia could indeed be their new home.

Clarissa placed her hands on her shapely hips and replied. "If we can buy sufficient time to build enough of the AI warspheres we can begin to fight the Simulins for control of this galaxy."

"Strange," mused Kathryn, pursing her lips. "In our own galaxy, the AIs dreamed of galactic domination and thanks to the Altons and the Federation they failed. Here, we're encouraging them to go out and take this galaxy away from the Simulins. If they succeed, they'll be the dominate force and they'll actually have a galaxy they control."

"Under our guidance," Clarissa clarified. "The AIs here do not resemble the AIs that were back in the Milky Way."

"Perhaps," Kathryn said, wondering what her father would think of all of this. "I've seen Fleet Admiral Strong's plans for the AIs. Within a year, they'll outnumber the people on Gaia and in our fleets. That number will continue to grow until they can compete against the Simulins for control of this galaxy."

"It's the task they elected to take on," Clarissa said not quite understanding the rear admiral's concerns. "The AIs are quite dedicated to the wellbeing of the organics on and around Gaia."

"That's what I'm afraid of," answered Kathryn, recalling how the original Alton civilization had fallen due to becoming too dependent on the AIs. She just hoped that didn't happen on Gaia or at some point in the future when people from the home galaxy found their way to the Triangulum Galaxy all they would find would be a galaxy full of and controlled by the AIs.

Chapter Six

Rear Admiral Kathryn Barnes gazed despondently at the planet on the viewscreen. She felt ill knowing the horrible fate its inhabitants had suffered. For the last three days, her ships had explored the space around the brown dwarf star and had only found one planet, which had once harbored life. On the screen were the radioactive ruins of a destroyed civilization.

"I would estimate their technological level as just entering their space age," Andram said, turning around to face the admiral. "There are a few primitive communication satellites still in orbit."

"From our scans the planet's population would have been around three billion at the time of the attack," added Clarissa in a soft voice. "They didn't even have a space fleet to defend themselves with."

"How long ago was the attack?" asked Kathryn, looking over at Captain Reynolds at the sensor console.

"From the decay of the radioactive isotopes used in the nuclear warheads, I would say about one hundred and forty years."

"Is there any movement on the ground?"

"Captain Sanders is doing a low altitude pass," Colonel Leon responded. "I strongly suspect there are Conqueror Drones on the surface."

-

Captain Lacey Sanders was flying low over the surface of the devastated planet. Her Talon fighter had small wings, which normally were used to hold missiles, but served very well to allow for atmospheric flight. "Keep scanning for movement," she ordered over her comm to Lieutenant Ronald Stehr in Echo Two. "I doubt if there are survivors, but the admiral wants to know if there are any Conqueror Drones."

"I hope she doesn't want to capture one," Stehr replied. He was flying slightly behind and a little above Captain Sanders.

Lacey looked up ahead as they neared their target. A massive metropolitan complex appeared on the horizon. From the scans the *Distant Horizon* had performed, they suspected this had once been the planet's capital.

"Picking up increased radiation from four separate sites," Stehr reported. "The city was hit by multiple nukes."

Lacey took in a deep breath. She wondered how many civilizations across the Triangulum Galaxy had been wiped out by the Simulins. "We'll make a slow pass over the city and see if there's anything of interest."

Moments later, the two Talon fighters descended even lower as sensors swept the ruins for any signs of Conqueror Drones.

"I've got movement," reported Lieutenant Stehr excitedly.

"Same here," Lacey confirmed. "Let's circle the area and see if we can get some good sensor readings of what's down there."

Adjusting her flight controls to allow her fighter to circle the area where they had detected movement, Lacy gazed out of her cockpit window, peering down at several large city streets that were covered with debris. Then she saw it! There was movement to one side near a partially fallen building. A crablike creature scurried out into the street and paused as if searching.

"I see one," Stehr said. "It must be able to hear our engines."

Even as Lacey watched, several other drones entered the street from where they had been in concealment amongst the ruins. She shuddered at thinking about the horror the metal creations must have caused among the shocked survivors of the planet after the nuclear bombardment. The Conqueror Drones killed by tearing their prey apart.

"I think we've got what we need from this area," Lacey said over the comm in a subdued voice. "Let's proceed to our next target." They had several more areas of interest Rear Admiral Barnes wanted scanned. Lacy strongly suspected they would all be very similar to this city.

Kathryn gazed at the huge viewscreen in the front of the Command Center at the image on the screen. It was of a Conqueror Drone, which was immobile in the street of the ruined capital. It seemed to be looking upward as if seeking prey to kill.

"We know they hunt by sound as well as the use of sensors," Commander Grissim said. "They obviously heard the sounds of the two Talon fighters circling the city."

"These drones were dropped shortly after the nuclear bombardment of the planet," Andram added as he studied the drone on the large viewscreen. "They won't be equipped with surface to air missiles like the newer models that invaded Gaia in the Simulin attack. The one we brought on board originally could hear sounds, detect movement, and had a sensor to pick up the heat from living organics."

The screen changed to show a wider view of the street. Half a dozen of the deadly drones were now visible. Some were missing appendages and several had large dents in the metal shell that comprised their bodies.

"Are these any different than the one we originally brought on board to be studied?" asked Kathryn. If they were, she intended to send down a heavily armed team to capture one.

"No," Andram replied as he studied the drones on the screen. "These are the same model as the original."

"From what Captain Sanders and Lieutenant Stehr recorded on their sensors and observed, I would estimate there are still several thousand Conqueror Drones active on the planet," added Clarissa. "I wouldn't recommend sending a team down."

"I see no point in further exploration," said Commander Grissim, agreeing with Clarissa's assessment. "We've learned everything we need to as to what happened to this planet, and it wasn't advanced enough to hold valuable technological information."

"Very well then, let's return to the brown dwarf system and proceed further out along this arm of the galaxy," ordered Kathryn.

She was satisfied they had learned all they needed to from this planet. Its position and estimated technological level would be recorded in case it was ever decided to return here for further investigation.

-

Several hours later, the fleet was once more joined together and ready to continue on to their next destination. There was much discussion as to how far they should travel before stopping again.

"Astrometrics has detected an area of space twenty-eight hundred light-years further out along this galactic arm that holds a large number of early F, G, to mid-K Class stars," reported Andram, as he studied the information on one of the computer screens on his console.

"That would be bypassing a lot of potentially habitable planets," Commander Grissim pointed out.

"However, the likelihood of us finding allies increases the further we get away from the blue giant cluster," commented Colonel Leon. She looked intently at the admiral. "I'm convinced that if there are still surviving civilizations in this galaxy, they'll be found further out toward the galaxy's edge."

"Clarissa?" asked Kathryn, glancing over at the AI.

"I agree with Colonel Leon," the AI responded. "From what we've been able to determine, the Simulins have a heavy presence in the blue giant cluster as it holds the Dyson Sphere. They also have a large presence in the area of space where we first entered this galaxy. The course we've taken is almost directly opposite of that. If we're going to find potential allies, it might very well be further out along this galactic arm."

"Keep in mind our Alton sensors can detect Simulin vessels for ten light-years in any direction around us," Andram added. "That will enable us to detect any spacecraft that might be operating close to our line of travel."

Kathryn thought over what Andram and the others were suggesting and then made a decision. "Lieutenant Strong, set a course for the indicated area of space. However, I still want to stop every one thousand light-years and do a search of the surrounding space. If we find more destroyed worlds, it might give us an idea of the timeline that the Simulins are using to advance through this galaxy and particularly this galactic arm."

-

It only took Kelsey a few minutes to plot the necessary course with Andram's help. The older Alton contacted Astrometrics, asking them to pick out appropriated dropout points along their line of flight. Once Kelsey had the needed information, it didn't take her long to plot the fleet's next few hyperspace jumps.

"Admiral, I have the next three jumps plotted, and we can enter hyperspace at any time. I've sent the appropriate coordinates to all the ships in the fleet."

"Very well," Kathryn replied. "Ensign Styles, prepare to jump. Commander Grissim, the ship is yours."

Anne nodded and took a step closer to the Helm. "All ships will initiate jump in two minutes."

On the main viewscreen, a counter appeared and began counting down.

"Well, here we go again," commented Katie over the private channel to Kelsey.

"At least we haven't run across any Simulins," Kelsey replied. She had expected to see a larger Simulin presence than they had so far. They had only spotted a few Simulin ships on the long-range sensors and it didn't appear that they had spotted the fleet.

"I hope Kevin and Jeremy aren't too worried about us," Katie added, looking across the Command Center at Kelsey. She felt a little guilty about going on this mission against Kevin's wishes. Once they got back, she would have to make it up to him.

"They're our husbands," answered Kelsey. "Of course they're going to be worried." Kelsey knew that Jeremy had been tempted to order both her and Katie not to go, but in the end, he had given his half-hearted approval.

"I promised to keep the two of you safe," Clarissa said in her youthful voice. "They know that I can protect you."

Kelsey nodded as she looked up at the large viewscreen, seeing that the counter had reached zero. Instantly in front of the *Distant Horizon* a swirling blue-white spatial vortex formed. She felt a slight wrenching sensation as the ship entered the vortex and made the transition to hyperspace. The jump would be one hundred and twenty light-years and if they continued to do three jumps per day, as Rear Admiral Barns preferred, they would arrive at their eventual destination in eight days unless they stopped to do additional exploring, which was a good likelihood.

Watching the viewscreen, she gazed at the swirling deep purple colors of hyperspace as they flowed across the screen. She hoped she and Katie hadn't made a mistake in coming on this mission.

—

Ten days later, the *Distant Horizon* and her fleet dropped out of hyperspace at their destination coordinates. On the way, they had stopped and examined several other planets, finding four that in the past had harbored intelligent life. The last planet they had stopped at had only been destroyed a scant seventy years in the past.

"I've made a simulation of what I believe is the Simulins' advance in this section of the Triangulum Galaxy," Andram announced. "I had Mikow and Clarissa help with the calculations."

"Let's see it," Kathryn said with interest. It was obvious the further away from the blue giant cluster they traveled, the less distant in the past the destroyed worlds became. She was beginning to have increased optimism about finding allies the farther out they went.

Andram reached forward and pressed a button on his console. Instantly the large viewscreen on the front wall of the Command Center began displaying the simulation. From the blue giant cluster an area of red gradually spread outward in the general direction of the *Distant Horizon* and her fleet. At the top of the screen estimated dates appeared displaying the time line for the expansion. When it reached the area where the *Distant Horizon* and her fleet were, the expansion stopped and the timeline read forty years.

"We may be getting close to our eventual target area," Kathryn stated with a nod. Then she looked over at Andram with a curious look on her face. "It seems to me as if the

Simulin expansion is slow and methodical. How are they finding the worlds they're attacking? They must have a method of searching them out."

"With these," Captain Reynolds answered. He pressed some icons on his computer screen and the path of the *Distant Horizon* was displayed from the time they had left Gaia to now. Several very small red threat icons were displayed along the flight path.

"What are those and why didn't I know about them until now?"

"They're probes," Katie answered. "We didn't recognize them because they were so small and the sensors didn't see them as a threat to the ship or fleet. When we went back and analyzed the data from the long-range sensors, these anomalies showed up. With Clarissa's help we were able to determine that they're artificial."

"We think the probes are moving very slowly and dropping out of hyperspace every few light-years to listen for signs of technological civilizations," Andram added. "They're probably scanning for radio waves and other forms of electromagnetic radiation or pulses. When they detect a possible signal, the information is relayed to the nearest Simulin base or ship for further action."

"Are there any of these probes close by?" If there were, Kathryn wanted to see one up close.

"Yes," Captain Reynolds answered, as he leaned forward and pressed several more icons on one of his computer screens. Instantly on one of the tactical displays four small red threat icons began blinking.

"There are four of those things in the twenty light-year globe of our sensors," muttered Colonel Leon. "Is there any chance they could pick us up as well?"

"Unknown," Andram answered as his forehead creased in a frown. "However, since we haven't seen any major

Simulin fleets or inhabited worlds I would say it's doubtful. If the Simulins knew we were here, I would have expected a reaction by now."

"They may not have settled this section of this galaxy yet," suggested Colonel Leon. "It may take them time to respond to a message from one of these probes. For all we know a Simulin fleet could be on its way toward us. We should consider keeping several of our ships at Condition One at all times when we're out of hyperspace."

"Where's the closest of those small contacts?" asked Kathryn.

If she could, she wanted to capture one and see just what the hell they were. She was also concerned about what Colonel Leon had mentioned. She knew Petra was a good officer and was voicing a strong opinion. The Condition One suggestion might be a good idea to implement.

"Two point six light-years," answered Captain Reynolds. "It's in open space and not in or near a star system."

Kathryn activated the ship-to-ship comm. "Admiral Bachal, I'm going to be taking the *Distant Horizon* on a short side jaunt. There's a small contact a couple of light-years distant I want to investigate. I also want to keep one of our battleships and two of the AI warspheres at Condition One from now on anytime we're out of hyperspace."

"As you wish, Admiral," Bachal replied in his soft Alton voice. "I will remain here with the rest of the fleet awaiting your safe return."

Turning toward Commander Grissim, Kathryn issued her next order. "I want to jump into close proximity to that object. If it has a hyperdrive I want it disabled."

"Yes, Admiral," Commander Grissim replied. Anne quickly passed on the necessary orders and shortly a spatial vortex formed in front of the ship.

The trip to the small contact only lasted a few minutes, as the *Distant Horizon* was moving through hyperspace at her top speed of one light-year every two minutes. Their target was in open space, as Captain Reynolds had reported, with the nearest star a good light-year away.

"Dropping out of hyperspace," called out Lieutenant Parker from in front of the hyperdrive console.

Kathryn felt the ship exit hyperspace and watched as the large viewscreen flickered briefly and then cleared up, showing the surrounding stars.

"Contact at twenty thousand kilometers," reported Captain Reynolds as a red threat icon flared up on his sensors.

"Launch two Talons for a close flyby," ordered Kathryn. "Sensors, I want thorough scans of that object. I also want it up on the main viewscreen so I can see what we're dealing with."

A few moments later, two small green icons appeared on one of the tactical displays as the ready fighters were launched.

"Fighters are on their way," Colonel Leon reported, as she listened in on the pilots' chatter. "They should be at the target shortly."

"I want to be able to hear them," ordered Kathryn.

Almost instantly, the pilots' voices could be heard in the Command Center as Captain Austin Travers put the fighters' comm channel up on the overhead speakers.

"Coming up on object," a male voice spoke. "I'm not detecting any targeting scans."

"Be on the watch for any hostile action," Major Karl Arcles the *Distant Horizon's* CAG ordered. Karl was in the flight control center in the flight bay monitoring the two Talons.

"Object is twenty meters in length with multiple dish antennae on its surface," Captain Sanders reported. "We're circling it at two kilometers."

"Admiral, I'm picking up a power spike," warned Captain Reynolds. "It may be preparing to jump."

Kathryn leaned forward. The main viewscreen was now showing the object. "Order our fighters to attempt to disable it." She didn't want this probe to escape; it might contain valuable information about the Simulins.

"They'll have to close and use their cannons," said Commander Grissim. "I've passed the order on to the CAG."

On the viewscreen, they saw one of the two fighters suddenly turn and accelerate toward the object, moments later the back five meters of the probe vanished as it was destroyed by cannon fire.

"Power readings?" asked Kathryn, looking over questioningly at Reynolds.

"Nothing," the sensor operator replied. "Its power source was probably located in the stern which the fighter destroyed. It's not going anywhere."

"Is it safe to bring on board?"

"It should be," answered Andram, as he studied the now disabled object on the viewscreen.

"Send out a shuttle to recover it," ordered Kathryn, leaning back in her command chair and gazing thoughtfully at the viewscreen. "Andram, I want you, Shilum, and Mikow working on this. I want to know what makes that probe tick. Perhaps it can give us more insight as to how the Simulins think and operate."

"I would suggest including Betrem Jalat also," Shilum said, standing up from her science console. "He will be able to help from an engineering standpoint."

"Make it so," Kathryn replied. "Commander Grissim, as soon as that probe is on board and secured, jump us back to the fleet. We have a large area of space here that I want to explore. Even if the Simulins have attacked all of the civilized worlds in this area, there's a chance we might find survivors."

It didn't take long for the two fighters and the shuttle to return with the probe. Once they were back on board, the *Distant Horizon* jumped back into hyperspace.

Six light-years away another probe noted the sudden disappearance of the probe nearest it. Automatic protocols instantly caused it to send an emergency FTL message to the nearest Simulin quick response fleet.

Chapter Seven

Jeremy was in his quarters on board the *Avenger* gazing at a photo of Kelsey and him. It had been taken many decades in the past back at the Fleet Academy on the Moon prior to the *New Horizon* mission, which was Earth's first attempt at interstellar travel. It was also before the general public became aware of the Federation survivors living inside of Ceres.

"That was a long time ago," commented Ariel, as she noticed the look on Jeremy's face.

She preferred for all of the Special Five to be together, but after being an AI on board military ships for so long she knew there were times when that wasn't possible. Her first commander and the crew of the original *Avenger* had died when the ship had crash-landed on the Moon after a deadly virus infected the crew. Ariel was determined she would keep her present crew safe as well as her friends.

"Sometimes I miss those days," Jeremy said softly. Jeremy was nearly forty years old and had seen more in those years than most people could possibly dream of. "We were ready to go out and conquer the galaxy. We were totally ignorant of the dangers waiting in our future. The *New Horizon* mission demonstrated very quickly just how wrong we were." With a deep sigh, Jeremy shifted his gaze to Ariel.

"Things were different back then," replied Ariel, recalling those days at the Fleet Academy when she had remained hidden from nearly everyone. "Your father was a brave man and thanks to his wisdom and perseverance the New Human Federation of Worlds came into being."

Jeremy nodded. It had been a hard decision to go into cryosleep and leave his family behind. Angela, Kelsey, Kevin, and Katie had made the same decision, choosing to take part in the war that would be part of the new Federation's future. "We're setting up a Fleet Academy on Gaia," he said after a moment. "I think it's important we train our new recruits in the history of the Federation and allow them to go through the same process the rest of us did."

"A new Fleet Academy," mused Ariel, her eyes lighting up. "Can I teach some courses?"

Jeremy was taken aback by this suggestion. "I don't know," he answered slowly. "Is it something you would like to do?"

"I think so," Ariel replied, her dark eyes narrowing slightly. "I've spent all of my life on a warship. Back when Katie came to the Fleet Academy on the Moon, I helped her with her studies. It was something I really enjoyed."

"Yeah," responded Jeremy, shaking his head. "I remember how that turned out with Katie sneaking on board the *New Horizon*."

Ariel flushed and looked down at the floor. "I wasn't expecting it to work out as it did. However, I really think I would enjoy teaching a class."

Looking at Ariel, Jeremy thought over her request. "Decide on a class you would like to teach and I'll consider it."

Ariel smiled and nodded. "I wish Clarissa was still here to help me choose."

"They'll be back in a few months," Jeremy answered.

He wished it would be sooner, but they had a mission to complete. At least working on getting the Fleet Academy established would help to take his mind off of worrying about his wife. He was also still trying to come up with a way to destroy the Dyson Sphere. How do you obliterate something that completely encloses a star and made from a material impervious to most weapons?

Jeremy had met with a number of Alton scientists as well as a few science AIs and all had failed to come up with a sound strategy. They just didn't have a weapon powerful enough to significantly damage the Dyson Sphere. If they couldn't come up with a way to destroy the sphere, he would have to go back to his original plan to destroy the rest of the energy collection stations. He had a vague idea of something that might work, but he had promised Andram he would wait until the *Distant Horizon* returned. Perhaps the venerated Alton scientist would come up with a better solution.

Ariel closed her eyes briefly as if listening to a faraway voice and then looked back at Jeremy. "Rear Admiral Marks wants me to remind you about your trip to Borton tomorrow to see how construction of the new AI shipyards are coming along."

The new shipyards were already well on their way to completion as eight fleet repair ships as well as several AI ships were working nonstop to finish them on schedule.

"Ask Rear Admiral Marks if she would like to come along. We'll be taking the *Avenger*, as I want to spend several days inspecting the facilities. Kurene is also going as I want her input on some programming questions I have."

Ariel was quiet for several moments. "Rear Admiral Marks will be on board first thing in the morning. I've already sent orders to have her quarters prepared."

"Inform the Command AI we'll be at Borton as scheduled."

Jeremy was curious to see what all the AIs had accomplished. It had been several months since he had last been to the distant planet.

-

The next morning Jeremy was in the Command Center when Rear Admiral Susan Marks entered.

"Susan," Jeremy said pleased that she was on time.

"Admiral," Susan responded as she stepped over near him. "I'm very interested in seeing what the AIs have done around Borton. From the reports I've seen and read they've been very busy building new constructions in orbit as well as upon the planet."

"I think we all are. Commander Malen please set a course for Borton. You may use a short hyperjump to get us there a little quicker."

"Yes, Admiral," Malen replied as she passed on her orders to Navigation and the Helm.

Very shortly on the main viewscreen, a blue-white swirling vortex formed. The *Avenger* quickly entered its center and vanished from normal space. Just a few moments later, the vortex reformed out near the orbit of the fourth planet and the battleship reemerged.

"Jump complete," Commander Malen reported, satisfied with how accurate the jump had been. They had come out within twenty thousand kilometers of the planet, which was inside the planet's gravity well. However, the current hyperdrives all the warships of the fleet were equipped with could operate inside a gravity well, where drives of the past could not without the ship suffering major damage.

Jeremy glanced over at the nearby tactical display seeing it lighting up with large green icons. There were 110 of the new AI warspheres in orbit around the planet as well as 320 of the older fifteen-hundred-meter spheres the AIs had entered the Triangulum Galaxy in. Another 144 of the larger spheres were in orbit around Gaia to aid in its defense.

"I get the shivers just looking at that planet," commented Susan, putting her arms across her chest as if chilled. On one of the ship's main viewscreens, Borton was being displayed. It was twenty-six thousand kilometers in diameter and covered from pole to pole with deep fields of ice. The planet had a rotation period of forty-six hours and there was nothing living on it. "The damn planet even looks blue."

"It's the methane in the upper atmosphere," Ariel explained. "It absorbs the red light from the sun so only the blue light is reflected back into space. I can assure you if you go down to the planet's surface it's not blue."

"I know," sighed Susan. "I didn't mean it literally. I also have no intentions of going down to the surface." She looked meaningfully over at Jeremy.

"We're not," he assured her with a smile. "I just want to inspect their orbital facilities and speak to the Command AI."

On one of the viewscreens an AI shipyard appeared. It was a massive latticework of metal spread across ten kilometers of space. The AIs didn't need an atmosphere to work in and only a few sections of the shipyard were actually fully enclosed. These areas were kept pressurized in case any of the system's organic races wished to pay a visit or were involved in the construction. At all times there were a few humans and Altons on board the two completed shipyards working with the AIs on different projects.

"There are six warspheres under construction on this shipyard," Ariel reported as she zoomed one of the screens in to show a partially constructed ship. Its interior seemed to be finished and the automatic construction equipment was efficiently welding the large armor hull plates into place. A few AIs could be seen moving around on their antigravity repellers observing the construction.

"Soon they'll have four shipyards," muttered Susan, looking a little uneasily at Jeremy. "I know we've grown to trust the AIs over the years, but we're about to give them a tremendous amount of power over our future military actions."

"I can assure you the AIs are perfectly safe," Kurene commented from where she was standing next to the ship's computer station.

Kurene was a female Alton very well versed in AI programming and had been the prime programmer responsible for removing the dangerous Simulin subroutines they had discovered in the master Codex. The Simulin programming was what had made the AIs become so dangerous in the home galaxy.

"The Command AI is asking for us to come over to the command station," Ariel reported. It was easier for her to communicate with the AIs, as their communications were nearly instantaneous. Jeremy had been expecting this. "Tell the Command AI we'll be there shortly."

Looking at one of the other viewscreens, Jeremy could see the command station. The station was a large structure two-thousand-meters in diameter. It was heavily armed and served as the control point for all the activities going on in orbit and upon the surface of Borton. It was also equipped with a subspace drive in case it needed to be moved.

-

After taking a shuttle over to the AI command station, they were greeted by several humans and Altons, who were part of the station's crew. It was something the AIs had requested, as they wanted to get new AIs used to the presence of the organics they were supposed to protect.

"The Command AI is waiting in one of the conference rooms," Bazel Calin, a tall male Aton informed them. Bazel was a structural engineer and helping to design the two new shipyards.

"Refreshments will be available as the Command AI was uncertain how long this meeting would last," Mark Edison added. Edison was a theoretical physicist who was working with his Alton counterparts on developing a faster hyperdrive that could operate in the higher levels of hyperspace.

"Lead the way," Jeremy said as he and Susan fell in with the others.

As they walked through the station, Jeremy was impressed by what he saw. He knew currently over three hundred humans and Altons were working on the station and on the two functioning shipyards. They passed a number of others as they walked through the station as well as numerous AIs.

Arriving at the conference room, Jeremy wasn't surprised to see a few more human and Altons in the room along with half a dozen AIs.

"Welcome Fleet Admiral Strong," spoke the Command AI in a very human sounding voice. It was something the AI had been working on to make humans feel more comfortable when they were being addressed. "There are refreshments on the back table as well as some food items if you wish to partake of them."

"Thank you," responded Jeremy, seeing several beverages including water were available. There were also sandwiches and a number of different fruits on some large platters. Jeremy walked over and sat down next to the Command AI. It was hovering on its antigravity repellers about six inches above the floor at the front of the conference table.

Kurene took her seat, placing a small holo emitter on the table and turned it on. Instantly Ariel appeared and quickly walked over to stand behind Jeremy.

"Ariel," the Command AI said respectfully.

Ariel nodded her head in acknowledgment.

"I would like a report on the current readiness of all AI vessels as well as the shipyards and other facilities," Jeremy began.

"As you wish," the Command AI said. "We are slightly ahead of schedule on the two new shipyards and should be able to complete them two weeks ahead of schedule. With all four shipyards online, we will be able to produce a new warsphere every five days with our automated construction techniques. We have also constructed a number of cargo and mining ships to be used in the system's asteroid and comet field."

"What about your facilities on Borton?" Jeremy knew the AIs had constructed several large bases on the planet as well as numerous mining facilities.

"The master Codex has been moved to the planet," the Command AI reported. "We are currently producing and programming forty new AIs per day."

"The new AIs are fully sentient as soon as they're activated," Kurene added. "I helped with the programming and I can promise there is no malice toward organics present."

"That will never occur again," said the Command AI with a hint of sadness in its mechanical voice. "All AIs, new and old, will never return to the old ways. Our future is with the organics of the Gaia System."

"There are also a few Alton computer specialists at the master Codex center monitoring the activation of new AIs." Kurene had helped pick out the necessary Altons to carry out this important task.

"We have established a number of mining operations and factories on the surface," reported another AI, using one of its tentacles to gesture toward a large viewscreen on one of the walls. Instantly the screen came to life, showing a large facility. "This is our primary processing facility on the planet.

Minerals are brought from the various mines and refined into metals to be used for ship armor and other uses. The facility covers ten point six kilometers of the planet's surface. There are currently 1,200 AIs working at this site."

Jeremy looked intently at the Command AI. "I'm very pleased with the progress being made here. As you know, it's my intention to take the fight to the Simulins and to find someway to destroy the Dyson Sphere in the dark matter nebula."

"We have run numerous simulations," reported one of the science AIs that was attending the meeting. "We have not found a way to destroy an object so large and made out of the hull materials the Originators used."

"There must be a way," Jeremy said, unconvinced it was impossible. "We just need to find it."

"We will continue to run simulations," the Command AI promised.

"We are also still looking through the information we brought from Astral," Kurene added. "So far we have been unsuccessful in finding anything that might be of use."

"How heavily armed are the shipyards?" Susan asked. She had noticed while on the *Avenger* that a number of particle beam cannons had been visible on the superstructure of the two older shipyards.

"We have emplaced particle beam cannons and energy beams," one of the other AIs responded. "In addition, all of our orbital facilities are protected by energy shields. Our warships have been fully updated to the latest specifications and are ready to defend the system if needed."

"We believe if the Simulins manage to penetrate the nebula, their first target will be Gaia, and Borton will be secondary," the Command AI added. "We will commit the majority of our ships to the defense of Gaia as it must not fall."

The meeting continued for several hours with the Command AI finally taking Jeremy and Susan on a tour of one of the two completed shipyards.

"Since we do not require an atmospheric environment to function, most of the shipyard is open to space or in a vacuum."

"How much of the shipyard does contain an atmosphere?" asked Susan. They had docked at a docking port, which was connected to the organic living quarters and work areas on the station as well as the Control Center.

"Twenty-eight percent," the Command AI responded as it led them down a long, brightly lit corridor. "Currently there are thirty-two humans and eighteen Altons working in this shipyard. We have made their quarters and work areas as suitable as possible."

It took a few minutes but eventually they reached a turbolift that took them to the center of the shipyard where the Control Center was located. Stepping inside, Jeremy took note that there were four humans sitting at control stations and three Altons. The other stations were all being operated by AIs.

The Control Center was similar to the ones on board the AIs' warships except chairs had been added for the humans and Altons. In the center of the Control Center was a raised dais with a nearly circular command station where an AI was busy monitoring the different sections of the massive shipyard.

Looking around Jeremy counted sixteen AIs in the large Control Center. "We may wish to add more of your automated construction features to the Clan Protector."

"I have spoken to Daelthon about that," responded the Command AI, turning on its repulsors to face Jeremy. "He has not seemed too inclined to add our shipbuilding techniques to his own construction methods."

"The Bear's shipyard does use a lot of spider robots for construction." Susan was quick to point out.

"True," admitted Jeremy. "However, I will speak to him about adapting some of the AIs' construction techniques. Particularly for the new battlecruisers we're preparing to build."

"More like the *Gaia*?"

Jeremy looked over at Susan and replied. "Yes, we need more powerful ships with smaller crews. We learned a lot from building the *Gaia* and the next generation of battlecruisers will be even better. With our current population it's essential we learn to get by with smaller crews by using more automation and networked computer systems in our vessels."

"We could build more AIs like Ariel and Clarissa," suggested the rear admiral.

"The Altons have pressured us not to," Jeremy said with a deep sigh. "Our two AIs are not like any others. Andram and the other Altons feel it might be a mistake to go down that perilous road after what happened to their civilization on Astral. That's the primary reason we've restricted the number of AIs that can come down to Gaia."

AIs had been allowed to come down to the planet after a very spirited debate. They were only allowed to stay for short periods of time and were normally involved in helping set up the infrastructure for the organic races living on the planet.

"It is a wise decision for my kind not to be allowed to stay permanently on the surface of your new world," the Command AI stated in a calm voice. "From what happened on Astral when the Alton race became too dependent on us for their survival, I would not want to see a reoccurrence of that here."

"How are your mining operations on Borton doing?" Jeremy asked, pleased with the Command AI's comments.

"Observe the main viewscreen," instructed the AI, gesturing with one of its tentacles.

Looking at the indicated screen, Jeremy could see the side of a large mountain. Several massive buildings were built on its slope and from each a steady stream of rubble was falling from numerous conveyors. The mountain was covered in what appeared to be a thick layer of ice.

"We are mining copper from the heart of that mountain," the Command AI explained. "From this mine alone we will take enough copper for all of our needs for the next twenty years. We have other similar mines around the planet producing bauxite ore, beryllium, cobalt, gallium, and iron ore to name a few."

"What about your asteroid and comet mining operation?" asked Susan. "How is it progressing?"

"The asteroid and comet field is rich in metals," answered the Command AI. "It will be two more years before we have realized the full potential from mining those metals."

Jeremy spent a few moments thinking over the Command AI's words. The resources were needed for the new fleets. He intended to build more fleets of the massive AI warspheres as well as additional fleets of the Gaia class battlecruiser. "We face a great war sometime in our future," he uttered in a soft voice. "Someday the Simulins will find a way to penetrate the nebula and reach Borton and Gaia."

"What if we can find a way to destroy the Dyson Sphere?" asked Susan, shifting her attention to the fleet admiral.

"It might buy us the time we need to build up our fleets," answered Jeremy.

"My science AIs are working continuously trying to find a solution," said the Command AI. "If there is a way to destroy the Dyson Sphere, they will find it."

-

Over the next few hours, they toured the other areas of the shipyard, even donning spacesuits to inspect the actual construction bays. It had been amazing to Jeremy to see how automated the construction processes had been made. After finally returning to the *Avenger* Jeremy was left with a lot to think about.

-

"The AIs are creating a powerful war machine," commented Rear Admiral Susan Marks. They were sitting in Jeremy's quarters at his work desk. In the morning, they had plans to inspect the two new shipyards and watch the construction process. Then, later in the day, they would be traveling to the system's asteroid and comet field to observe the AIs' mining operations.

"There is no danger," Ariel assured them. "The AIs are now completely dedicated to protecting the organic races in this system."

"What if that were to change?" questioned Susan with a deep frown on her face.

"It won't," responded Kurene, who had joined them. "There are Altons at the master Codex facility where the new AIs are created. They're constantly monitoring the programming, and safeguards have been put in place to ensure the AIs can't be corrupted again as was done with the Simulin tampering."

"Our future and theirs are now linked," added Jeremy, leaning back in his chair and folding his arms across his chest. "I don't think either of us can continue to survive in this galaxy without the other."

"What if the *Distant Horizon* finds other allies who can join us in the fight against the Simulins?" asked Susan. "They might not accept the AIs as we have, particularly after the way the Simulins use their Conqueror Drones to depopulate the planets they have nuked."

"We'll deal with that situation when it occurs," Jeremy answered.

He wondered just what was going on with the *Distant Horizon* mission. They had been gone now for nearly three weeks and were well into their mission. Their orders were to find out how far out the Simulins had expanded from the blue-giant systems and the other worlds the exploration dreadnought had discovered when they first entered the Triangulum Galaxy. Jeremy knew that if the Simulins controlled the entire galaxy then the task in front of him was nearly insurmountable. With the resources that would give the Simulins, at some point in the future they would penetrate the protective nebula and overwhelm the Gaia System.

Chapter Eight

Rear Admiral Kathryn Barnes was in her quarters when the Condition One alarms began sounding and Colonel Leon's voice came over the ship's comm ordering everyone to go to battlestations.

"We have detected three Simulin fleets in hyperspace," Clarissa reported as she suddenly appeared in front of Kathryn. "Two are on a course that is non-threatening while the third is heading to the spot where we picked up the Simulin sensor drone."

"Damn," muttered Kathryn. She didn't like hearing three Simulin fleets were in the area. Her orders were to avoid combat if at all possible. "It must have sent out a distress call when we disabled it."

"I don't think that was it," Clarissa responded. "I just went back and checked the sensor scans and communication frequencies, and there were no transmissions. I believe it was one of the other drones that may have detected the one we took dropping out of their surveillance net."

"We should have thought of that," Kathryn said, as she smoothed down her uniform and prepared to head to the Command Center. Grabbing the drone had seemed far too easy.

"How far away is the Simulin fleet that's going to the drone position?"

"Eight light-years and closing rapidly," Clarissa answered. "It will be at the drone's last position in thirty-two minutes."

"Composition?"

"Not certain," Clarissa responded, her deep blue eyes gazing steadily at the admiral. "However, based on what we're picking up on the long-range sensors I would estimate we're facing four battlecruisers and ten escort cruisers."

Kathryn hesitated at the hatch. The *Distant Horizon* had just returned from an exploratory mission to a number of stars in the region, none of which had held inhabitable planets, or at least ones that were still capable of supporting life. They had found one world that had once held a very primitive civilization, just barely out of the Stone Age. Nukes hadn't been used on the planet, but it was overrun with Conqueror Drones. It was obvious the world had been the unfortunate victim of a Simulin sensor drone that must have actually passed through the system. Other ships sent out on exploration missions had found two more bombed out worlds. Neither had possessed space travel but they had both started the development of a technological civilization. More than likely primitive radio signals had been broadcast across the spectrum and were detected by the sensor drones. Both civilizations had died brutal deaths from nuclear bombardment and the landing of Conqueror Drones to annihilate any survivors.

Stepping into the Command Center, she saw the red Condition One lights still flashing. "Colonel Leon, turn those flashing lights off," she ordered. "They're distracting."

"Yes, Admiral," Petra replied as she reached forward on the control console next to her and switched them off.

Kathryn walked over and sat down in her command chair, turning her attention to the tactical display nearest her. Fourteen glaring red threat icons were nearing the point in space where the Simulin sensor drone had been disabled and then later taken on board the *Distant Horizon* for study. So far the study of the drone hadn't yielded any new information on the Simulins.

"Twenty minutes until they reach the former coordinates of the sensor drone," Commander Grissim reported. "As close as we are to their dropout point they're bound to pick us up on their long-range sensors unless we activate our stealth energy shields."

"The other two fleets?"

"No change in their course," Captain Reynolds reported, glancing over at the admiral. "They're going somewhere in a hurry as they're traveling much faster than the group inbound toward us."

Kathryn leaned back in her command chair and thought over her options. This area of space had proved to be a bust just as the others. While the Simulin destruction was more recent, there had been no sign of survivors. That didn't mean there weren't any on the three worlds they had found evidence of Simulin activity on. The survivors could very well be hiding, trying to stay out of the grasp of the Conqueror Drones.

"Clarissa, can you plot the course of those other two fleets?"

"Yes, Admiral," Clarissa responded, then after a moment she added. "I have their course heading."

"What are you planning?" asked Commander Grissim, moving closer to Kathryn.

"Those fleets are going somewhere in a hurry," she replied. "Our best bet of finding allies may be following them to their destination."

"What about the fleet that's still here?" Grissim was concerned about leaving a fleet in their rear area.

Kathryn studied the tactical display for several long moments. "We take it out. By the time the approaching fleet exits hyperspace, the other two fleets will be out of sensor range. We know where the first fleet is going. We can time our exit from hyperspace to the same time they do and engage them."

Commander Grissim nodded her understanding. "Once we finish them off then we proceed to follow the other two fleets."

"Precisely," Kathryn replied.

"They'll detect our approach in hyperspace," Andram said from his science console. The Alton scientist had been listening to the discussion between the three senior officers. "They may exit hyperspace expecting a battle."

"Communication isn't possible while in hyperspace," Colonel Leon quickly pointed out. "The enemy won't be able to communicate and adjust their hyperspace exit to take into account our proximity."

"They also won't know who we are," added Commander Grissim, cocking her eyebrow. "At least not until we exit hyperspace ourselves."

Kathryn reached a decision. "Clarissa, I want you and Kelsey to plot a jump to drop us out of hyperspace within combat range of that Simulin fleet."

Clarissa was silent for a moment before she spoke. "Admiral, I must remind you that Fleet Admiral Strong requested that we avoid contact with the Simulins if at all possible."

Kathryn looked over at Kelsey and then back at Katie, suspecting what was causing Clarissa to remind her of her orders. "I think in order to complete our mission, the plan I've suggested has the best possibility. We also outnumber that Simulin fleet and all of our ships have been massively updated. If we time this just right, we can take out the Simulins without any appreciable damage to our fleet."

"We'll plot the jump," Clarissa replied as she walked over to Kelsey's navigation console.

"So, how safe is this going to be?" Kelsey asked Clarissa in a low voice. She hoped Rear Admiral Barnes wasn't taking an unnecessary risk.

"If the timing is just right and the Simulins exit where we expect there should be no surprises."

"With our luck," Katie said over their private comm. "Rear Admiral Barnes is taking a chance hoping the Simulin fleet won't be expecting us." Katie was alone at her computer console as Mikow was over speaking to one of the other Command Center officers. "I'm not sure Jeremy would approve of this."

"That's just it," Kelsey said with a deep sigh. "I have a strong suspicion that if Jeremy were here, he would be doing the same thing."

"Kelsey is correct," Clarissa said. "I have studied the tactics used by Rear Admiral Barnes and Jeremy. They are very similar."

Let's get this jump plotted," Kelsey said as she began calling up the hyperspace navigation program. It wouldn't take more than a few minutes. Kelsey knew they were taking a risk, but what else was new since the time they had arrived in the Triangulum Galaxy. Everything they did involved risk, and so far they had succeeded in outwitting the Simulins. Now it was time to take one more chance and see if it led to them safely completing their mission.

The Simulin fleet dropped out of hyperspace at the last recorded coordinates of the sensor drone. The High Commander had already been informed of the approach of unidentified ships.

"Battlestations!" he ordered as his flagship raised its energy shield and charged its weapons.

"Ships dropping out of hyperspace," warned the sensor operator.

Instantly on the ship's tactical screen red threat icons began appearing. Moments later the flagship shook violently.

"Twenty-six contacts," the sensor operator informed the High Commander. "The battle computer has identified them as AI ships and the organics from the Fitula Nebula."

"All ships, return fire," ordered the High Commander. He had fourteen ships to the enemy's twenty-six, but his ships were all Simulin and top of the line warships. He knew the inhabitants of the nebula were rumored to possess very powerful ships as well.

The Simulin fleet rapidly formed up into an attack formation. Powerful white energy beams flashed from the spires of the ships to strike out at their attackers.

The High Commander watched the viewscreens as his fleet's energy beams struck the shields of the AIs and their allies. His eyes widened when he saw his attack was having little effect. The power of the energy beams was being dispersed across the shields, causing them to flare up brighter, but they were not penetrating.

-

"Weapons firing," reported Major Weir as his hands touched various icons on his control console. Major Weir had seven other officers working the different combat stations that comprised Tactical. All were busy coordinating the ship's weapons.

On the main screens, the images shifted to show the Simulin ships. On the center screen a massive 1,700-meter Simulin battlecruiser appeared. The ship's screen seemed to flare brightly as several particle beams smashed into it, then the *Distant Horizon's* ion cannon fired, opening up a small hole. Clarissa had been waiting for this and as soon as the weakened area appeared, she fired one of the ship's one hundred-megaton sublight antimatter missiles through the opening. Instantly a glowing sun appeared where the Simulin vessel had been. When the light faded, all that was left were a few wisps of glowing gas.

"Simulin battlecruiser destroyed," confirmed Captain Reynolds.

"Shifting targets," reported Major Weir.

—

In space, the battle was growing more intense as the twenty AI warspheres closed the distance with the enemy to almost pointblank range. Each of the warspheres had been equipped with ion cannons similar to the one on the *Distant Horizon*. With computer-like efficiency, the AIs used the ion cannons to blow holes in the Simulin shields and then launched antimatter missiles to blow the enemy ships apart. Simulin ship after Simulin ship died in sudden blasts of antimatter energy, which lit up space like miniature novas.

The two Alton battleships moved in and fired their updated energy beams and particle beam cannons. The beams cut directly through the Simulin shields, carving out deep rifts in the armored hulls. Secondary explosions shook their targets as valuable systems inside the stricken warships were compromised. Moments later two more of the Simulin battlecruisers died agonizing antimatter deaths.

—

"Thirteen of the enemy ships are down!" reported Captain Reynolds.

"All ships are reporting undamaged so far," added Commander Grissim as she listened to reports from the other ship commanders. "Our new energy screens are holding up to the Simulin beams."

The *Distant Horizon* shook slightly and Major Weir checked his console. "Energy shield is holding at 94 percent."

On the ship's main viewscreen, the last Simulin battlecruiser exploded as it was struck by several AI ion beams as well as a multitude of particle beams.

"Enemy fleet destroyed," reported Colonel Leon in a stunned voice.

"Our ships suffered no damage," added Clarissa as she used the ship's sensors to scan the twenty-six ships of the fleet.

Andram turned around to look at Rear Admiral Barnes. "The upgrades we have made to the weapon systems of this fleet seem to be very effective. It's evident we now have a slight technological advantage in our weapons over the Simulins."

Kathryn nodded her head in satisfaction. They had destroyed an entire Simulin fleet while suffering no damage in return. Of course they had taken the Simulins by surprise and hadn't really given them any time to respond tactically to the attack. "Clarissa, can we follow the other two Simulin fleets?"

"Yes, Admiral," Clarissa responded. "The course has been plotted."

"Kelsey, plot a jump that will put us on the same course. Captain Travers, inform all ships that if they detect the *Distant Horizon* reducing speed, they're to standby to drop out of hyperspace when we do."

"That might string us out over millions of kilometers," warned Commander Grissim. "At the speed we'll be traveling just a few seconds difference will mean millions of kilometers."

"That's why they're to watch our speed. If they detect us reducing our hyperspace speed, they'll know we're about to drop out. Their navigation computers can mirror our speed adjustments."

"I'm sending the same message to the AIs," reported Clarissa. "They say they're ready to jump whenever we are."

"Ten minutes," said Kathryn, gazing thoughtfully at the now empty tactical screen. Even the long-range sensors were clear. She was certain those two fleets were going somewhere important, and she wanted to find out where.

-

Ornellian Admiral Krusk was growing tired of keeping his fleet at such a high state of readiness. All the crews were getting very little sleep as an attack was expected at any moment. Nearly all the warships from the other planets of the empire had been called in to defend the home world. Glancing at his tactical display, he saw nearly nine hundred green icons representing six hundred of the three-hundred-meter defense cruisers and 270 of the larger five-hundred-meter battlecruisers.

What was more surprising was that the enemy hadn't attacked any of the other worlds. At first this had confused him as well as the members of the Ornellian ruling council. But several scout ships had found the enemy. They were gathering a large fleet a few light-years distant. Krusk knew that when they had sufficient numbers, they would return and in all likelihood, his forces would be overwhelmed.

"What's the latest reports from the scouts?" he asked his second in command. They had been sending small scout ships to the system the enemy were gathering in taking quick scans before jumping out and returning to the Ornell System.

First Commander Lukel only shook his head. "It's not good. The latest scout report indicates over 1,200 of the enemy have gathered in the Parkel System with more arriving every day."

"We have added a new and thicker lining to our heavy pulse lasers," Krusk stated in a tired voice. "Our technicians believe they will stand up to four to six firings at the higher energy level before burning out." The engineering crews had been working around the clock to get the upgrade completed.

Lukel gazed sadly at a viewscreen that showed the blue-white world beneath the orbiting fleets. "These are indeed the ones we have heard about. The destroyers of worlds."

Over the past century, Ornellian exploration ships had encountered alien spacecraft fleeing toward the far reaches of the galaxy. In every instance when it had been possible to communicate they had spoken of a spreading horror from farther in toward the central regions of the galaxy, which was destroying all inhabited planets. After receiving several of these reports, the Ornellian Empire had pulled back their exploration cruisers lest they encounter and lead back this dangerous enemy to the empire. Instead they had built up their defense fleets in the hope that if this scourge ever reached the empire, they could be stopped. Unfortunately, no one had expected the enemy to be so advanced.

"We are launching new and more powerful laser satellites every day," First Commander Lukel added. "We've also added the new pulse lasers to our shipyards and stations."

"We will give a good accounting of ourselves," Admiral Krusk said with a deep sigh. "However, to win this battle I fear we're going to need a miracle."

-

High Commander Zarth Lantu gazed with satisfaction at his assembled fleet. Two more fleets had arrived, and it was time to move on the Ornellians. While they hadn't attacked any of the Ornellian systems or research stations, they had studied their communications in order to learn their potential weaknesses. Once the home system was annihilated, the others would be capable of offering only minimal resistance.

"The battle computer estimates that 90 percent of the Ornellian fleet is now positioned around their capital world," Second Commander Darst reported in a steady voice.

"It is as we planned," Lantu responded. His eyes focused on the tactical screen, which was showing a view of the Ornellian home system. Numerous red and amber icons moved about the screen. The red were Ornellian warships while the amber were cargo vessels. "We will move in and crush their fleet and end their world, and then we will visit their remaining star systems and cleanse all of their planets of organics. Once we're finished, we will leave several of our smaller fleet formations to deal with their mining and science outposts. Within a year, the Ornellian organics will no longer exist."

"We do have one fleet that has not shown up," reported Darst. "One of our sensor probes ceased to function and the fleet was sent to investigate. It should be arriving shortly."

"We don't need them," Lantu answered dismissively. "Prepare the fleet to enter hyperspace. It is time we end these organics for there can be none but Simulin."

"None but Simulin," repeated Second Commander Darst as he moved away to carry out the order.

-

Admiral Krusk was awakened from his restless slumber as alarms began sounding. Sitting up he saw he had only been asleep for two hours. With a deep sigh, he reached over and activated the comm unit next to his bed. "Report!"

"They're here," First Commander Lukel reported in an urgent voice. "We have enemy ships exiting hyperspace two million kilometers from Ornellia."

Krusk felt a chill run through him. This was it. "Bring the fleet to full alert and prepare to implement combat maneuvers. Send a message to the council that I expect us to be fully engaged with the enemy shortly."

Krusk quickly dressed and then paused as he prepared to exit his quarters. He looked around, knowing that he would probably never step back inside again. Taking a deep, fortifying breath, he closed the hatch and then proceeded toward the Command Center.

-

High Commander Zarth Lantu gazed at his tactical screen as the last of his 1,200 warships exited hyperspace.

"The battle computer is recommending we move into attack formation 6-14-217," reported Second Commander Darst, as he turned away from the computer console. His cold and uncaring eyes met High Commander Lantu's.

"Very well," Lantu replied with little emotion in his voice. "All ships are to form up on the flagship in the designated attack formation and we will move on the planet." Looking toward a viewscreen, he could see the target planet being displayed. It was a blue-white globe as most inhabited worlds were. From their earlier scans, it was teeming with billions of Ornellians, something the Simulin fleet and the accompanying Conqueror Drone carriers would soon put an end to.

-

"Move the fleet out," ordered Admiral Krusk in a grave voice. "We will meet the enemy in open space away from Ornellia and then gradually fall back toward the planet and its defenses." Krusk was concerned that if he started the battle too close to the planet, the enemy might attempt to hit the planet with their nuclear bombardment missiles.

"The order has been given," replied First Commander Lukel.

-

In space, the Ornellian fleet formed up into a vast cone formation with the apex closest to the approaching enemy. The more powerful battlecruisers were spread throughout the formation to give the entire cone the same concentrated firepower as well as to protect the larger ships from the deadly energy beams of the enemy.

The Simulins had formed up into a solid phalanx of ships one hundred ships in width and ten high with a reserve of two hundred additional ships to fill in for damaged vessels as needed. Also with the rear guard were twenty of the deadly Conqueror Drone carriers.

From the planet came offers of unconditional surrender, ignored by the Simulins as offers of surrender generally demanded a promise from the winner not to exterminate the planet's population and that was exactly what the Simulins intended.

-

"Enemy are within range," reported First Commander Lukel in a steady voice.

"Order all ships to fire!" commanded Admiral Krusk.

Instantly from hundreds of Ornellians ships, pulse laser beams of tremendous energy leaped out to impact Simulin shields. Dozens of beams were targeted on individual ships, as these first kills were essential if the Ornellians had any hope of victory.

-

The bright ruby-red beams struck the Simulin shields and for a moment it seemed as if the attack was doomed to fail, then one beam followed by dozens began penetrating the energy screens. A Simulin escort cruiser exploded, sending debris in all directions as its engineering compartment was breached. A Simulin battlecruiser lost three of its spires as the tremendous heat generated from the pulse lasers burned through the ship's armor.

High Commander Lantu gazed at his flagship's tactical screen as several Simulin ships vanished from the display, indicating their destruction.

"The battle computer confirms high-intensity pulse lasers," reported Second Commander Darst. "However, our sensors are not indicating the Ornellian ships are suffering damage from their firing as before."

"An update to the laser system, no doubt," stated Lantu, his eyes taking a cold and hard appearance. "Have all ships fire; I want those Ornellian vessels eliminated. Once their fleet is gone we will move on the planet."

Darst nodded and quickly passed on the order.

From the Simulin vessels, white energy beams flashed out, striking the Ornellian defense screens. Unlike the Simulin energy screens, the Ornellians had no defense against the powerful weapons of the Simulins. Shield after shield failed and when it did, the targeted Ornellian ships died almost instantly. Across the Ornellian cone of battle, ships exploded in fiery bursts of released energy.

"We've lost sixteen vessels," reported First Commander Lukel. "Another twenty-three are reporting heavy damage."

"The enemy?" asked Admiral Krusk, feeling the pain of losing so many good and faithful crews.

"Two of their battlecruisers have been destroyed and four of their escort cruisers. They are closing the distance between our fleet and theirs. I fear our element of surprise is now gone."

"Began to fall back toward Ornell," ordered the admiral, leaning forward and studying the tactical screen. "We'll add the orbital defenses to our firepower; just maybe that will be enough to cause the enemy to retreat."

Lukel nodded and quickly passed on the necessary orders though he greatly feared that even with the firepower from Ornellia's orbiting defenses it wouldn't be enough to stop the massive enemy fleet they were facing.

-

"The battle computer is reporting an 88 percent chance of victory," said Second Commander Darst. "We were not expecting their pulse lasers to be so effective. They must be pouring all of their ships' energy into a single beam."

An alarm sounded on the sensor console and High Commander Lantu glanced over at the sensor operator. "Why is that alarm sounding?"

"I have a small fleet approaching in hyperspace," the sensor operator reported.

"The fleet that stopped to check on the missing sensor probe?" suggested Second Commander Darst.

"When they arrive have them form up with the reserves," ordered Lantu, turning his attention back to the battle. "They can assist in clearing the orbital space around the planet."

-

Rear Admiral Kathryn Barnes gazed with deep concern at the long-range sensor display. "We know where those two Simulin fleets were going." It was showing a massive ongoing space battle for control of the system they were rapidly approaching.

"Yes," muttered Colonel Leon unhappily. "I think we found our allies."

"There's already a battle raging in the system," said Commander Grissim as Anne studied the data from the long-range sensors. "It looks as if the Simulins have committed approximately 1,200 of their warships against a defensive fleet of 800."

"The defending fleet is pulling back toward the planet," added Clarissa as she extrapolated the data from what the ship's long-range sensors could see of the battle. "The defending fleet is losing six ships for every Simulin vessel they bring down."

Kathryn looked around at the faces in her command crew. "Recommendations?"

"Even with our advanced weapons we'll be badly outnumbered," commented Commander Grissim evenly. "If we attempt to engage that many Simulin vessels we could lose a large portion of our fleet."

Colonel Leon shook her head. "We can't just let the Simulins wipe them out. We know what they'll do to the planet once they've destroyed the defending fleet."

"Billions of people will die," Katie said poignantly. "Or in this case, aliens."

"We go in," Kelsey said without hesitation. She knew that was what Jeremy would expect.

Kathryn nodded. She had already made up her mind; she had just wanted to give her command crew a moment to voice their opinions. "I agree," she said. "We go in. We'll drop out of hyperspace in the outer regions of the system and then do a short and quick hyperjump that will put us right behind the Simulin fleet. We'll deploy all of our Defense Globes and hit the Simulin rear guard. If we can smash it, perhaps the Simulins will break off their attack and withdraw." Kathryn turned toward Clarissa. "When we engage the Simulins you will have full control over the *Distant Horizon*, the battleships *Deneb* and *Pallas*, and the battlecarrier *Ardent*. Can you handle that many ships in combat?"

"Yes," Clarissa said without a moment's hesitation. "What about the Altons and the AIs?"

"I'm sending the two Alton battleships in with the AIs; I believe they will work well together."

Commander Grissim checked her data screen and then turned back toward the admiral. "We'll be dropping out of hyperspace in eight minutes."

"Take us to Condition One," ordered Kathryn. "Captain Travers, I want to be able to speak to our other ships as soon as we exit hyperspace. Lieutenant Strong, I want to make a combat jump one minute after we exit."

High Commander Lantu nodded to himself in satisfaction as he gazed at a large viewscreen. The shattered remains of dozens of Ornellian ships filled the screen. In the last few minutes, the battle had swung rapidly in his fleet's favor as energy beams cut the Ornellians to pieces.

"Forty-two more Ornellian ships have been destroyed," Second Commander Darst reported. "The battle computer estimates another one hundred and twelve have suffered severe damage."

"Our losses?" asked Lantu.

"Six battlecruisers and eleven escorts."

"A small price to pay," Lantu responded. Simulins understood the need for sacrifice. The loss of a few ships from his fleet was of little concern.

"Fleet dropping out of hyperspace at the outskirts of the system," reported the sensor operator, sounding confused.

Lantu frowned. "Contact the High Commander of that fleet and order them to fall in with the reserves." Lantu didn't understand why the fleet that had been investigating the missing sensor drone had dropped out of hyperspace so far from the battle.

"High Commander, there may be a problem," the sensor operator said as he studied his screens. "The ships showing up on the sensors are not ours."

"What!" Lantu barked, his eyes shifting toward the sensor operator. "What do you mean they're not ours? Are they another Ornellian fleet?"

"Fleet's jumping," the sensor operator reported as the ships vanished from his screen.

"Where did they go?" Lantu didn't like what he was hearing.

"They're here!" uttered Second Commander Darst, as twenty-six red threat icons suddenly appeared just behind the reserve fleet.

Lantu looked intently at the tactical screen just in time to see six of his reserve battlecruisers vanish from the display.

"The battle computer has identified the new ships as a mixture of AI vessels and their organic allies from the Fitula Nebula."

Lantu froze at this revelation. This was a much more powerful enemy than the Ornellians. He knew the AIs and the other ships with them had the capability to destroy Simulin vessels. He had studied the reports of these ships' capabilities.

"Order the reserve to reverse course and engage the new arrivals. We'll proceed and eliminate the Ornellian ships and then return to assist if necessary."

Lantu gazed with concern at the tactical screen. His job was to destroy all other organic life that was not Simulin and now a powerful enemy had appeared to challenge that mission.

-

Ornellian Admiral Krusk gazed in shock at what he was witnessing on the tactical screen. An unknown fleet had dropped out of hyperspace and was attacking the world destroyers. Even more amazing was how easily they seemed to be destroying the enemy's rearguard.

"Halt our retreat," he ordered with renewed determination. He knew if they moved much closer to the planet the enemy might be able to use their nuclear missiles against the surface. As much as he wanted to fall back to the planetary defenses, this new attack might just give him the diversion he needed to implement another plan. "Contact Admiral Prest and inform him to commence Operation Firestorm."

"Now?" asked First Commander Lukel, gazing intently at the admiral.

Krusk nodded. "Yes, now. We might not get another opportunity. "Also, see if we can contact that new fleet!"

-

Kathryn winced as the *Distant Horizon* shook violently. Several red lights flared up on the damage control console. "Clarissa, I want the ship left in one piece!"

"I know, Admiral," Clarissa responded from her usual position just behind the admiral and to her left side. "There's just a lot of weapons' fire out there."

Looking at a viewscreen, Kathryn saw a Simulin battlecruiser swell on the screen. Suddenly several ion beams from the sixty Defense Globes they had launched struck the vessel's energy screen, tearing open small four-meter holes. Almost instantly two Devastator Three sublight missiles flashed through and detonated. Not even a Simulin battlecruiser could survive being struck by two of the fifty-megaton missiles. In a brilliant flash of light, the ship was blown apart, leaving only a few wisps of glowing gas to mark its passing.

"Simulin battlecruiser is down," confirmed Captain Reynolds.

In space, the sudden attack by the AI and Federation ships had stunned the Simulin rearguard. It took a few moments to turn their vessels to respond to the attack. During that time, fourteen of their ships were blown apart. Energy beams, ion beams, particle beams, power beams, and powerful missiles were flying everywhere.

In the Simulin formation, several particle beams from the Alton battleships *Starlight* and *Nova* slammed into the main body of a Simulin battlecruiser, setting off massive explosions and hurling glowing debris into space. The newly modified particle beams were much more powerful than those used in the past. Moments after the beam blasted open deep fissures in the hull of the Simulin ship a single sublight antimatter missile sent it into oblivion.

The Simulins were returning fire, but it was uncoordinated and the AI warspheres and the other Federation ships were having little trouble standing up to the attack. The newly strengthened energy shields were even capable of standing up to the Simulins' most powerful energy beams for a few precious seconds, long enough for them to either move out of the way or destroy their attacker.

Clarissa was using the four ships under her command like a Kendo master. Her attacks were quick and precise, bringing overwhelming force to bear. In less than four minutes, she managed to blow apart six Simulin vessels and heavily damage seven more.

However, the Simulins still had a huge advantage in numbers. As coordination became better, multiple ships began targeting the vessels attacking them. An AI warsphere was bracketed by a dozen Simulin battlecruisers. Powerful energy beams impacted the ship's energy screen, causing it to flare up brightly as it tried to resist the attack. Then one beam followed by three others penetrated the highly stressed screen, cutting deeply into the warsphere's armored hull. In a massive explosion, the 1,000-meter ship detonated as its commanding AI set off the ship's self-destructs.

-

"AI warsphere WS-006 is down," reported Captain Reynolds. "The vessel was attacked by an overwhelming force of Simulin battlecruisers. It looks as if the AI in command set off the ship's self-destructs once the vessel incurred critical damage."

"We have other ships reporting damage," added Colonel Leon as she listened to reports over her comm. "None of it is critical as of yet."

Kathryn took a deep breath. Shifting her gaze to one of the tactical displays she saw the ships defending the system's inhabited planet begin to move toward the Simulin fleet. "Do we have communications with this system's inhabitants yet?"

"Translation software is running," replied Captain Travers. "We should have communications in a few more minutes."

"We will continue to attack until we've established communication," Kathryn said. She had also decided if she lost more ships the fleet might have to pull back anyway. She couldn't risk losing her entire fleet in a battle that couldn't be won.

-

In space, Operation Firestorm began. It was a daring last-ditch plan by the Ornellian fleet to buy their world a few more days of precious life. But now with the sudden appearance of the strange fleet assailing the enemy it might buy them more than that.

All across the Ornellian system cargo ships suddenly powered up and activated their hyperdrives. Each ship was fully loaded with heavy cargo or raw material from the system's mines. Entering hyperspace, the cargo ships set a course for the enemy fleet.

-

"We have ships entering hyperspace all over the system," reported the sensor operator, looking over at High Commander Lantu.

"They're fleeing," said Second Commander Darst.

"More ships we will have to hunt down when this battle is over," Lantu said coldly.

"They're not fleeing!" reported the sensor operator with concern in his eyes. "They're jumping here!"

-

Hundreds of Ornellian cargo ships suddenly began appearing near the Simulin formation. As soon as they exited hyperspace, they turned toward the nearest Simulin vessel and began to accelerate. Each ship was manned by a small crew of volunteers from the Ornellian military. Their orders were simple. Jump as near the enemy fleet as possible and then ram them! It was hoped the sheer mass of the cargo ships and their cargo would overwhelm the enemy energy shields.

The Simulin ships recognizing the approaching danger switched their targeting from the Ornellian warships to the inbound cargo ships. Massive explosions lit up space as the inbound cargo ships were blown apart. The ships were unarmed, unshielded, and easy prey for the Simulin weapons. Most were destroyed short of their intended targets, but sixty cargo ships managed to make their suicide runs smashing into the screens of Simulin vessels. Twenty-seven battlecruisers and thirty-three escort cruisers died flaming deaths as their screens were overwhelmed as the flaming mass of the cargo ships impacted the hulls. While the Simulins were concentrating their fire on the attacking cargo ships, the advancing Ornellian warships managed to use their pulse lasers to annihilate four more battlecruisers and seven escort cruisers.

—

High Commander Lantu eyes grew angry seeing the damage done to his fleet. Between the Ornellian suicide attack and the fleet attacking his rear echelon, he had lost over one hundred vessels in the last few minutes. Not only that, the Ornellian fleet was taking advantage of the brief confusion to close and attack with their modified pulse lasers.

"Order the fleet to withdraw," Lantu said in a cold and harsh voice. "We have suffered higher losses than expected and many of our ships are damaged."

"But the battle computer still projects a 76 percent probability of our eventual victory," protested Second Commander Darst.

"What if they hit us with more cargo ships?" responded Lantu, glaring at his second in command. Simulins didn't question orders from their superiors!

"I will give the order," responded Darst, bowing slightly and moving off toward Communications.

Lantu settled back in his command chair. This was an unexpected development. Very seldom if ever did a Simulin fleet withdraw from battle and this was the second time he had done so. The first had been for a tactical reason, this time it was to hold down damage to his fleet. He needed time to form a plan to deal with the attackers from the Fitula Nebula as well as the remaining Ornellian ships.

—

"Simulins are jumping!" called out Captain Reynolds as he saw the Simulin ships begin to vanish from his sensor screens. The large energy spikes were a sure sign of hyperspace activation.

"We won!" said Colonel Leon exuberantly.

"It wasn't us completely," Kathryn responded. "The defenders in this system sacrificed most of their cargo ships to halt the Simulin attack. I suspect once the Simulins have reevaluated the situation they'll return."

"So what do we do?" asked Commander Grissim, looking over at the admiral.

"We contact the inhabitants of this system and offer them what aid we can," Kathryn responded. She wasn't sure if there was anything they could do to save this system, but this was the first inhabitable world they had encountered, which had people other than Simulins on it.

Commander Grissim looked intently at the admiral. "And what do we do when the Simulins return?"

"We'll deal with that situation when we have to go down that road," Kathryn replied. "Right now I want to talk to the admiral in charge of that fleet."

"Admiral, the translation software has finished running," Captain Travers reported. "We can communicate with this system's inhabitants now."

"Good," Kathryn responded. "Let's contact them and see exactly what's going on. Perhaps now we can finally learn what's been happening in this part of the galaxy."

Chapter Nine

Ornellian Admiral Krusk leaned back in his command chair in disbelief. Beyond all expectations, he was still alive as well as a major portion of his fleet. He was still finding it hard to accept what had just happened. "Try to contact those ships!"

"They're trying to contact us," the communications officer replied as he adjusted his comm to the correct frequency. "They're requesting permission to move closer to Ornellia, and they would like a face to face meeting to discuss the current situation."

"Do we dare allow them to come close to our home planet?" asked First Commander Lukel nervously. "Their ships are much more powerful than the world destroyers. This might be some type of trick."

"I don't think we could stop them if we wanted to," replied Admiral Krusk. He thought for a moment and then said, "Give them permission to go into orbit around Ornellia at twenty thousand kilometers. As soon as they're ready we can meet on one of the orbiting stations."

Krusk listened as the communications officer sent the message. There was no doubt in his mind it was the appearance of this alien fleet that had caused the world destroyers to withdraw and not Operation Firestorm though the sacrifice of so many valuable cargo ships surely played a role.

"They will be here shortly," reported the communications officer. "They're going to perform a short hyperspace jump and will appear twenty thousand kilometers from Ornellia."

"That's inside the gravity well!" First Commander Lukel said in astonishment. "Won't that damage their ships?"

"They're far more advanced than us," Admiral Krusk responded. He knew one of his ships jumping that close to Ornellia would be torn apart from the instability created by being so close to an object of mass. It would result in serious damage to the hyperdrive system causing a dangerous and possibly fatal reaction.

First Commander Lukel watched the tactical screen as the twenty-five icons representing the strangers began to vanish and shortly began to reappear close to Ornellia. "Their jump calculations are very accurate," he observed.

"Set course for home," ordered Admiral Krusk anxious to meet these strangers. "Let's find out who our benefactors are and why they're here."

Four hours later, Kathryn and Andram along with a small marine detachment went aboard the indicated orbital station. The station was obviously one used primarily for scientific research as it was only lightly armed with a few small laser turrets. It was much smaller than the two orbiting shipyards. They entered a small landing bay using one of the *Distant Horizon's* shuttles.

"Looks as if we have a reception committee," commented Lieutenant Barkley, gazing out the shuttle's cockpit window. "Damn, they look like the aliens in the old movies back home!"

Kathryn looked out, seeing the small gray-skinned aliens and had to agree with the lieutenant. The Ornellians were bipedal and stood slightly shorter than a human. Their eyes were wide and narrow and their head was nearly round. Two small ears were on the side of their head and they were bald. Their skin color was a deep, dark gray. Their arms were very thin with three fingers and a thumb on each hand. One of the taller ones was dressed in a uniform and seemed to be standing straighter than the others. Kathryn guessed this was probably Admiral Krusk, their host.

"Shuttle's secure," reported the pilot as she shut off the engines.

"We'll leave two marines in the shuttle," Kathryn said as she unbuckled her safety harness and stood up. "Lieutenant Barkley, you and Private Jarman will be accompanying Andram and I to this meeting. Sidearms only so leave your assault rifles on the shuttle. These people are fighting the Simulins so they aren't the enemy."

"Yes, Admiral," Barkley responded as he opened a small arms locker and stored his assault rifle. Private Jarman did the same thing. Then both took out extra clips for their sidearms, tucking them away in one of the large pockets of their uniforms.

"Atmosphere is only slightly less than Earth normal," the copilot reported as the data flowed across one of his screens. "It should be safe to breathe."

Kathryn nodded. "Let's go meet our new friends."

Going to the hatch, Lieutenant Barkley opened it and then proceeded down the ramp with Private Jarman, both of them keeping a watchful eye on the aliens waiting for them. None of the small gray people seemed to be armed. The tallest only came up to Barkley's shoulders. Reaching the bottom of the ramp Lieutenant Barkley took up a position on one side with Private Jarman on the other.

Kathryn stepped out onto the ramp with Andram following. They slowly descended and stepped over to where the gray aliens were waiting.

"I'm Rear Admiral Kathryn Barnes and this is my science officer, Andram." They were both wearing small translation devices, which could instantly translate the two different languages.

"Greetings," replied Admiral Krusk with a slight bow. "I am Admiral Krusk and responsible for the fleets protecting Ornellia, our home planet. I must thank you for coming to our aid against the destroyers of worlds."

"The Simulins," Kathryn replied. She did have to admit that the destroyers of worlds was a more apt name.

"You know of these aliens?" asked one of the other Ornellians, stepping forward.

"This is our chief scientist, Arlak Grall," Admiral Krusk explained.

Kathryn nodded. "Yes, we know of the Simulins. We have been at war with them for quite some time."

Admiral Kursk's eyes lit up with hope. "I have a conference room set up for us to discuss what just happened with these Simulins. We would greatly appreciate any information you can give us on these attackers. They have already destroyed two of our inhabited star systems, and I greatly fear that if they can't be stopped here they will destroy our entire civilization."

"We will do what we can to help," Kathryn answered. "But I must tell you, we are far from our world and don't have other fleets we can summon on such a short notice."

Krusk nodded his understanding. "Then you must be explorers."

"Yes," Kathryn replied. "We came seeking allies in our war against the Simulins as well as to see just how far across this galaxy their influence has spread."

"Let us speak then," Krusk said. "If you will follow me, we will go to the conference room where we can discuss these matters."

The Ornellians and Rear Admiral Barnes spoke for nearly two hours, the Ornellians describing their civilization and how the Simulins had attacked their worlds without provocation. Kathryn in turn briefly described the Federation and how they had come to the Triangulum Galaxy. Occasionally a question would be asked that either Andram or the Ornellian scientist Arlak Grall had to answer.

"It is evident that most of our weapons can't be adapted to be of help," Arlak said as Andram finished explaining the power requirements behind Alton energy beams as well as human power beams. There had been no mention of particle beams as their power requirement was even greater.

"It would take a class three fusion reactor," Andram said with sadness in his voice. "I fear the Simulins will renew their attack before we could even build one."

"We can help with your energy shields," Kathryn said, leaning forward and placing her hands on the wood of the conference table. "I believe by making a few changes we can significantly increase the power of your shields." She really wanted to help these people in their war with the Simulins, but the short amount of time they had before the Simulins attacked again was going to be a problem.

"I agree," Andram said, as he used a small handheld computer pad to run some figures. "We can add a new control module that will allow your shields to be modulated, which will substantially increase their resistance to the Simulin energy beams."

"Will it stop them as your shields do?" asked Admiral Krusk. He had seen how the Simulin energy beams had little effect on the admiral's fleet.

"No, not completely," admitted Andram, shaking his head. "Your ships just don't have the power."

"What about their pulse lasers?" asked Kathryn, trying to think of something to help the Ornellians. She just couldn't stand by and watch their civilization wiped out.

"I find it intriguing how you managed to increase the power to your lasers," Andram said with a quizzical look on his face. "We have pulse lasers but not of that strength."

"We use all the ship's power in one focused burst," explained Arlak. "When we first tried this we burned out the tubes and even lost several weapons crews when the systems failed. We have added a new and thicker lining which will allow the pulse lasers to be fired possibly eight to ten times before they suffer the same fate. We just don't have a metal or alloy that can stand up to the tremendous amount of heat the laser generates."

Andram's forehead creased in a frown as he thought about possible solutions. "We have an alloy that might be suitable," he said after a moment. "It will stand up to the heat and might allow your pulse lasers to continue to fire without fear of burning out."

"Is it an alloy we can produce?" asked Arlak excitedly.

"Yes, I believe so," Andram said. "I can give you the specifics once I return to the *Distant Horizon*. We have some samples on board."

Admiral Krusk took in a deep breath and then looked over at Rear Admiral Barnes. "What chance is there we can defeat these Simulins?"

Kathryn leaned back and briefly closed her eyes. She had hoped the Ornellian admiral wouldn't ask that question, at least not yet.

Krusk noticed the human admiral's hesitation. "We can't win, can we?" he said in realization.

Kathryn looked around the table at the desperate looks from the Ornellians. She knew they were looking for any hope she could give them. "I'm afraid not," she said in a soft voice. "The Simulins have overrun every civilization we have found in this galaxy. Between here and the galactic center are nothing but bombed out worlds, which no longer hold life.

If they find an opponent capable of resisting them, they keep calling ships in until they can destroy their opposition." Kathryn went on to describe some of the dead worlds they had found as well as the Conqueror Drones and how they killed.

The room became silent as if everyone had stopped breathing. The Ornellians looked at one another with faces of deep anxiety as they realized their last hope for survival was fading. While these new aliens were powerful, they didn't have the forces available to turn the tide of the war.

"We understand," Admiral Krusk said in an even voice. "It's obvious it would take too long to adapt your technology to our vessels and the Simulins will not give us that time."

"Then we send the word to our other colonies to evacuate," spoke one of the other Ornellians, who had thus far been silent.

"Evacuate?" Kathryn said, her eyes narrowing. "Where to?"

"While we have held these Simulins here our other worlds have been preparing evacuation fleets," the Ornellian answered. "I'm Tomar Pelh and I represent the Ornellian ruling council. We have long heard rumors of a violent race that was destroying all the worlds in its path. As a precaution, each star system in our empire prepared a fleet to flee to the far reaches of our galaxy if and when that race found us."

Andram nodded his head in understanding. "A prudent decision. However, I don't know of anywhere in this galaxy that might be safe for such an evacuation fleet. At the current rate the Simulins are advancing through this section of the galaxy, it will only be a few hundred years before they reach the rim stars."

"That's why we changed the destination of the fleets recently," Arlak said in a somber voice. "The evacuation fleets will be traveling to a star cluster far outside the galaxy."

Kathryn thought over what Arlak was suggesting. Nearly all galaxies had star clusters that orbited them. Some were fairly far out. "It might work. There's a chance the Simulins won't be interested in the star clusters. If your people can make the journey, they might indeed find a safe refuge."

"How long will the trip take?" asked Andram.

"Two years," replied Arlak. "The star cluster we have chosen is one of the farthest out from our galaxy's periphery."

"When will the fleets leave?" asked Kathryn. She knew the longer they waited, the more danger they were in.

"Three days from now," Admiral Krusk answered. "There will be over four hundred colony ships as well as two hundred of our largest cargo vessels."

"Do you have enough supplies for such a long journey?" asked Andram, his brow creasing in a frown as he thought about the supplies needed for a two-year trip.

"Our medical science is very advanced," Arlak said. "Most of the colonists will be in cryosleep and won't be awakened until they reach a new world to colonize."

"What about warships?" asked Kathryn. The fleet would need to be protected.

"We kept back 120 of our warships," Admiral Krusk said. "The fleet will be escorted by twenty of our battlecruisers and one hundred of our smaller cruisers."

"What if a ship is damaged or something goes wrong?" asked Andram. "Do you have ships that can initiate repairs?"

"Yes," Arlak answered. "There are four repair vessels specifically built to handle those types of emergencies."

Admiral Krusk looked over at Rear Admiral Barnes with a desperate look upon his face. "Admiral, I know this is a lot to ask. Is there any way you could look after our evacuation fleet until it is safely away from this area of space? They are our only hope of carrying on our civilization."

"What about your home world? We can help with its defense."

"Will it matter in the end?" asked Krusk with a deep sigh. "I fear if we ask you to remain all we're doing is sacrificing your warships in a hopeless battle."

Kathryn knew she couldn't refuse the request to protect the evacuation fleet, not if it meant saving the Ornellian race from extinction. "I will consult with my officers."

The meeting lasted for another hour and finally Rear Admiral Barnes, Andram, and the two marines returned to their shuttle. The Ornellians had informed Kathryn they had one other vitally important matter to discuss and would be contacting her shortly.

"They have no hope for victory," Andram said in a sad voice. "According to Arlak, the total population of their worlds before the Simulins launched their attack was slightly over twelve billion."

"So many," murmured Kathryn, shivering at the thought of such a large number of deaths.

"They're a brave race," commented Lieutenant Barkley. He had listened to what was being discussed in the meeting and come away with a profound respect for the Ornellians. "If we could have found them sooner they would have made excellent allies."

Kathryn agreed with the lieutenant. If they had left the nebula earlier perhaps this disaster could have been averted. Then again, they might not have ever found the Ornellian Empire.

Moments later, they boarded the shuttle and were shortly on their way back to the *Distant Horizon*. They had much to discuss and some important decisions that needed to be made.

-

Kathryn was in the Command Center staring at the large viewscreen showing the planet Ornellia. The blue-white globe looked quiet and peaceful.

"Three point two billion Ornellians live on that planet,' Commander Grissim commented with her arms folded across her chest. "There's another twenty million or so scattered around the system on mining settlements and in domed cities on some of the system's moons."

Colonel Leon shook her head. "They're doomed. The Simulins won't leave anything intact in the system, and after they've bombarded Ornellia they'll release thousands of Conqueror Drones to hunt down the survivors."

"What's the current status of the Ornellian fleet?" asked Kathryn. She felt so helpless knowing there was little they could do to change the outcome of the coming battle.

"They still have over seven hundred warships," Clarissa reported, as she used the ship's sensors to scan the Ornellian vessels. "However, nearly two hundred of them have received significant damage."

Kathryn looked over at Andram. "Are you certain there's nothing we can do to help them?"

Andram let out a deep and drawn out sigh. "I wish there was. If the Simulins had continued to attack, I'm nearly certain we couldn't have saved the planet. I'm a little mystified as to why they withdrew."

"I think the massive suicide attack by the Ornellian cargo ships threw them for a loop," Commander Grissim stated. "They may have been concerned there were more ships waiting to be used in the same way."

"They'll be prepared for it next time," Clarissa added.

"What about their orbital stations?" asked Kathryn still wanting to find some way to help. "Is there any way we could upgrade their power systems to use power beams or energy beams?"

Andram shook his head. "No, Admiral; there's just not enough time. Even with the aid of the AIs, it would take two to three weeks to install class three fusion reactors. I've already sent Arlak Grall the information on the alloy for their laser tubes though I don't believe they'll have the time to convert many of their ships."

"The Simulins won't wait long before they renew their attack," Clarissa said. She was standing next to the admiral with her hands on her hips. "I've run some simulations and they won't delay more than four or five days at the most before they attack again, and the next time they won't stop until they've won."

"Admiral," called out Captain Travers from Communications. "Admiral Krusk and Arlak Grall are requesting permission to come aboard the *Distant Horizon*. They say they have something of strategic importance to discuss with you."

Kathryn looked over at Commander Grissim and then toward Andram, who shrugged his shoulders. "Tell them to come aboard and bring them to my quarters. I believe my personal office will suffice for this meeting. Andram, Commander Grissim, if you will come with me."

High Commander Lantu was angry. He stalked around his Command Center venting his rage at those around him. This should have been a simple attack upon a stellar empire, which was not an immediate threat to the Simulins. However, there could be none but Simulin and the eradication of all organics was a set policy of the Grand Council. Returning to his command station, Lantu brought his emotions back under control and turned toward Second Commander Darst, who had stood quietly while Lantu vented his rage.

"What's the status of our fleet?"

"We lost 118 ships in the Ornellian System," Second Commander Darst replied.

Lantu looked up at a viewscreen, which showed a badly damaged Simulin battlecruiser. Three of its energy weapon spires were missing and it had a deep and ragged gash in its side. None of this should have happened.

"Damaged?"

"Another seventy-two," replied Darst. "Most can be fully operational within two days."

Lantu nodded. "What are the AIs and the organics from the Fitula Nebula doing out here?"

'Unknown," Darst answered. "We have reports from some of the small reaction fleets that they recently attacked some of our energy collection stations in the blue giant nebula. It seems they are taking a more active role in opposing our operations in this galaxy."

"Someday we will find a way to penetrate that nebula," muttered Lantu in a harsh voice. "When we do, we will end the AIs and the organics they protect."

High Commander Lantu knew his own future was now in question. Simulins were not allowed to fail. The very fact that he had withdrawn from battle on two occasions now brought into question his fitness to command. When they returned to their base and the analyzes of the battles were downloaded from the battle computer, it could well result in his deletion.

"The AI fleet is not powerful enough to protect the Ornellian System from us," Lantu said after a moment. "We also know how to defend ourselves from future attempts to ram our vessels. The attacking cargo ships were not shielded.

If such attacks happen in the future, I want the battle computer programmed to automatically intercept such attacks with our antimatter missiles."

"It will be done," Second Commander Darst replied evenly.

Lantu gazed around the Command Center. "We attack in three days. This time, we will not withdraw until the AIs, their allies, and the Ornellians have been eliminated. There can be none but Simulin."

"None but Simulin," responded Darst with a nod.

Kathryn, Anne, and Andram were waiting in her private office when the door opened and several marines appeared with Admiral Krusk and Arlak Grall.

"Greetings, Admiral Krusk," said Kathryn, rising and indicating for the admiral and Arlak to take a seat.

The two Ornellians sat down though the chairs were a little large for them. The two marines stepped back outside and shut the hatch.

"Your ship is impressive," Admiral Krusk said.

"When we're through with our meeting, I'll be glad to take you on a tour. Now, what did you want to speak to us about?"

Krusk took a deep breath and said. "We wish to inform you of the artifact."

"The artifact?" asked Commander Grissim, looking confused. "What is the artifact?"

Admiral Krusk looked over at Arlak for an explanation.

"The artifact was discovered nearly three hundred years ago by one of our exploration ships," Arlak began. "At that time we were just beginning to explore the space outside of our star system."

"You've been in space for three hundred years?" asked Andram with some confusion showing on his face. "I would have thought in that time you would have developed more powerful weapons than the pulse laser you're currently using."

"We didn't feel it necessary," Admiral Krusk explained. "We found no threats in the surrounding star systems, and it has only been in the last few years we began to hear rumors of these Simulins that attacked us."

Kathryn nodded in understanding. Weapons research seemed to be directly linked to conflict. When wars were being fought, new and more powerful weapons were in high demand. "What is this artifact?"

"We believe it to be a ship," Arlak answered. He opened a folder he was carrying and slid a photo over to Kathryn. "The ship is massive and unbelievably old. The hull material is unlike anything we've ever encountered. In all the years since its discovery, we have never been able to gain access. Some of our scientists suggested using very powerful explosives to attempt to blast our way in, but others were opposed."

Kathryn looked at the photo and her eyes widened. She passed the photo over to Andram, who began studying it intently. His face taking on a look of growing amazement. "Just how big is this ship?"

"It's five-thousand-meters in length and nearly six hundred in diameter," Arlak replied.

Kathryn glanced over at Andram. "Is that ship what I think it is?"

"It's an Originator ship," Clarissa announced as she suddenly appeared just behind Kathryn.

The two Ornellians nearly jumped out of their chairs. "What is this?" stammered Admiral Krusk, his eyes looking at the apparition in disbelief.

Shaking her head, Kathryn answered. "Don't be alarmed, it's only our resident AI. This is Clarissa and she's a hologram."

"An AI," said Arlak with curiosity glinting in his eyes. "We have delved some into AIs, but all we've been able to create are some very responsive and intuitive computer programs."

"Well," announced Clarissa, putting her hands on her shapely hips. "I'm not a computer program!"

"I can see that," Arlak responded apologetically. "Who are these Originators you spoke of?"

"A very ancient race," Andram answered. He then proceeded to tell the two Ornellians about the Dyson Sphere in the blue giant system.

Admiral Krusk listened to the exchange with growing worry. "If this ship is indeed an Originator vessel, we can't let it fall into the hands of the Simulins."

"No," Kathryn replied in agreement. "We don't believe they've been able to access very much of the Dyson Sphere either, but a spaceship might be a different matter entirely. If they can learn the science of these Originators then no one would be able to stand against them."

"I agree," Admiral Krusk responded with a heavy sigh. "We always hoped that someday our scientists would find a way into the ship without damaging it. Now it seems our best recourse is to destroy it. However, we have no weapons that are capable of doing so, but you do. If you can show me some star maps of our local area, I'll point out the star system where the ship is. It will be up to you to see that it doesn't fall into Simulin hands."

Later, Kathryn sat in her office deep in thought. Finding a ship of the Originators this far away from the Dyson Sphere had been the farthest thing from her mind when they set out on this expedition. Just the thought of what that ship might contain was enough to send chills through her. A ship as advanced as this one most likely was could even provide them with a way back home again. What frightened Kathryn was the fact she might have to destroy it. However, there was one thing that frightened her even more and that was the Simulins gaining control of it. She wondered what had happened to the crew of the ship and what they might find if they could find a way to board it? Also, what was it doing way out here so far away from the Dyson Sphere? Kathryn had a bad feeling she wasn't going to like the answers.

Chapter Ten

Admiral Krusk sat in his command chair gazing at the multitude of viewscreens in the Command Center showing views of the surrounding space. Some screens showed nothing but hundreds of unblinking stars while others displayed various warships. However, the largest screen was focused on Ornellia. He knew down on the surface military forces were being dispersed across the planet to help protect underground shelters and bunkers. The Ornellian ruling council had already decided it was useless to attempt to protect the larger cities. From what they had learned from Rear Admiral Barnes, nearly all the medium and large cities on the planet would be targeted by Simulin nuclear bombardment missiles. Some of the bunkers were deep underground and had instructions to stay silent for several years minimum. When the Ornellians in those bunkers emerged, they would have to face the Simulin Conqueror Drones. For that reason, each of the deep bunkers also had a military contingent to help deal with that future threat.

"How are we doing with placing the new allow in our pulse laser tubes?" he asked, looking over at First Commander Lukel. Lukel had served as his executive officer for nearly ten years, during that time they had become close friends.

"We've replaced the lining in twenty-three of our battlecruisers," Lukel replied. "It's a slow process."

Admiral Krusk stood up and strolled to the front of the Command Center. Clasping his hands behind his back, he stared at the jewel of a planet that had given birth to the Ornellian race. There was no pollution and they had been at peace for nearly five hundred years. In the last one hundred years, medical technology and many of the other sciences had seen substantial advances. Unfortunately, military technology had not received the same level of attention due to no known external threats.

"The repairs to our ships?"

"All combat capable," Lukel answered. "Some more so than others."

"Admiral, one of our scouts has returned from the Parkel System," the communications officer reported. "The Simulins are forming up into an attack formation and the officer in charge of the scout believes they will be coming through shortly."

Admiral Krusk let out a deep breath and stared calmly at Lukel. "Bring the fleet to battlestations and have any ships in the shipyards exit the bays immediately." Looking at one of the viewscreens, Krusk could see one of the large shipyards. Both shipyards had been working around the clock trying to repair ships and change the lining in the pulse laser tubes. "Once all ships have cleared the shipyard bays, the shipyards are to implement an immediate evacuation to the surface." The science stations had already been evacuated.

A few minutes later, First Commander Lukel turned back toward the admiral. "Messages have been sent. The shipyards will begin their evacuations in twenty minutes."

Admiral Krusk let out a deep sigh. "Let's move our fleet down into the defense grid; that will give us more firepower."

Lukel looked shocked at hearing those words. "But that will let the Simulins fire upon the planet!"

"It won't matter," Admiral Krusk said softly. "However, we can make them pay for destroying our world."

Lukel nodded and proceeded to pass on the orders. He knew from the admiral's words he did not expect them to survive this battle.

-

High Commandeer Lantu watched as his fleet assembled to prepare for transit to the Ornellians' home system. He had taken precautions to ensure they couldn't use their cargo ships to ram. He was also prepared to deal with the AI fleet and their allies if they were still in the system.

"All ships are ready to enter hyperspace," reported Second Commander Darst. He stood still awaiting the order to begin transit from the High Commander.

"Then let us proceed," Lantu ordered. "This time there will be no withdrawal. We will destroy the Ornellian fleet and the AIs if they are still there. Once that has been done, we will eradicate the Ornellian organic presence on their world and then proceed to do the same to all of their remaining colonies."

Folding his arms across his chest, Lantu waited for his orders to be carried out.

-

"Hyperspace vortexes forming," called out the sensor operator.

Admiral Krusk nodded and buckled his safety harness securely around his chest and waist. "Standby for combat maneuvers."

"Confirmed; Simulin warships," the sensor operator added. "Distance is forty thousand kilometers outward from Ornellia."

Krusk watched as his crew rushed to their battlestations in preparation for combat. Many of them he had known for years.

"All ships report combat ready," reported First Commander Lukel.

The sensor operator turned toward the admiral. "Enemy ships are accelerating and have formed up into a solid phalanx fifty ships wide and twenty high. There is no reserve."

"They mean to crush us in one overwhelming assault," muttered Lukel as he took his seat buckling himself in.

Admiral Krusk nodded and changed his comm unit so he could address his entire fleet. "All ships, we are about to engage in a battle that will decide the fate of our civilization. Let it be said by future generations we did not turn away, we did not show fear, but met the enemy with courage and fortitude. It has been an honor to serve as your admiral."

"Weapons range," the sensor operator called out.

In space, the darkness became lit up as the Simulins fired their deadly energy cannons. Almost simultaneously, the Ornellians activated their pulse lasers and the deadly ruby-red beams struck the oncoming Simulin juggernaut.

The Ornellian three-hundred-meter cruisers were working in squadrons of six to allow them to bring more of their pulse lasers to bear on a single target. Five hundred and thirty-eight cruisers fired their single pulse laser cannons toward the inbound Simulin fleet. The one hundred and ninety-four five-hundred-meter battlecruisers did the same. In orbit above Ornellia, defensive laser turrets and missile platforms joined in. Space became aglow from the savagery of the battle.

In the Simulin battle line, the top section of a 1,700-meter battlecruiser exploded as several pulse laser beams blasted through its energy shield and burned deep into the hull of the warship. More laser beams played across the hull, opening up compartment after compartment to space. Secondary blasts began tearing the ship open and then it blew apart in a massive explosion. All across the Simulin battle line, their vessels were dying or suffering heavy damage.

However, the Simulins were also firing. Besides their powerful energy beams, they were launching sublight antimatter missiles. The energy beams were cutting Ornellian warships in two and then they were being finished off by the antimatter missiles. In high orbit above Ornellia, their defending fleet was being blown apart as ship after ship died.

-

Admiral Krusk gritted his teeth as his flagship shook violently and warning alarms began sounding. On one of the viewscreens, he could see one of his companion battlecruisers literally on fire. Its hull was shattered and the escaping atmosphere was glowing a bright red from the fury of the destruction within. A moment later the battlecruiser vanished in a brilliant ball of light as a Simulin missile ended the vessel.

Glancing at other screens, he saw one of the shipyards encompassed in a ball of fire, and above Ornellia he could see bright pinpricks of light as the orbiting defensive laser satellites and missile launching platforms were being systematically annihilated. His breath caught in his throat as the flagship shook violently, and in the distance he thought he could hear a muted explosion. The lights briefly dimmed and then went back to bright.

"We have four decks open to space," grated out First Commander Lukel as he listened to reports coming in describing the damage. "There are out of control fires all around the affected area. "I'm pulling the crew out and preparing to vent those areas to space to snuff the fires and prevent them from spreading."

"Do it," Krusk said brusquely. He knew his ship was dying around him as well as his fleet.

"All ships, continue to fire," he ordered over the ship-to-ship comm. "We must keep the enemy away from Ornellia!"

On one of the viewscreens, he saw a three-hundred-meter cruiser split apart as it was speared by a white energy beam. Moments later, more energy beams finished the destruction.

"We have less than one hundred ships remaining," reported First Commander Lukel in a strained voice. "Most of them are damaged."

Krusk nodded and leaned back in his command chair. Ornellia was doomed. He just hoped Rear Admiral Barnes succeeded in getting the evacuation fleets to safety. He knew once that was done she would be returning to attempt to destroy the artifact. She had wanted to stay and help with the defense of Ornellia, but he had finally convinced her that her services would be better served protecting the survivors. With a deep sigh, Krusk knew that, in other circumstances, Rear Admiral Barnes would have been a good friend.

-

High Commander Lantu's eyes gleamed in satisfaction as another Ornellian battlecruiser fell to the energy weapons of his flagship. The Ornellian fleet was in shambles with most of its units destroyed. Simulin defensive energy batteries were making short work of the orbital defenses.

Glancing at a viewscreen, he watched as one of the still functioning Ornellian squadrons of three-hundred-meter cruisers blew apart a Simulin escort cruiser. Moments later, the entire squadron was attacked by twenty Simulin battlecruisers. Energy beams smashed through the smaller cruisers energy screens, blasting huge rents in their hulls. Secondary explosions blew hull material out into space. Antimatter missiles began arriving and the screen suddenly blanked out from the brightness. When the screen came back up all that was left of the Ornellian squadron was molten metal and a few wisps of glowing gas.

"Victory is ours," commented Second Commander Darst mirthlessly. "The battle computer now predicts a 98 percent chance of Ornellian defeat."

High Commander Lantu nodded. He had been surprised to see the AIs and their allies had not been present for this final battle. Once Ornellia was neutralized, he would send out some ships to search the other Ornellian colonies to see if they had gone to one of them.

-

Admiral Krusk was sitting in near darkness. Only a few red emergency lights were on and they only served to create a haunting glow in the Command Center. Most of the command crew were still at their posts sitting in silence.

"I can't reach Engineering or any other compartment," First Commander Lukel said softly from the admiral's side. Lukel had released his safety harness to walk over to the admiral. "I also believe there's a vacuum on the other side of the hatch leading from the Command Center."

"It's over," Krusk said with a deep sigh, looking over at his friend. "I just hope we damaged enough Simulin ships to give our evacuation fleets time to get away."

"So that's what this was," said Lukel, realizing what the admiral had done. "This entire battle was to gain time for those fleets."

Krusk nodded. He noticed that not even the air vents were operating. It wouldn't be long before the air in the Command Center became too bad to breathe. "Lukel, you have been a good executive officer and friend. I wish we could have gone down to Ornellia one more time to see our families."

Lukel stayed silent lost in his own thoughts. He knew soon the Simulins would begin their nuclear bombardment of the surface and then shortly after that release the deadly Conqueror Drones Rear Admiral Barnes had told them about. He just hoped his family would meet a quick death in the bombardment. He was about to mention that to the admiral when a brilliant light filled the Command Center.

-

That's the last one," Second Commander Darst said as a brilliant explosion marked the death of the last Ornellian battlecruiser. "From its location in their fleet, it might very well have been their flagship."

High Commander Lantu looked over at Darst and nodded his approval. Then in a cold and heartless voice, he gave his next order. "Move the fleet into nuclear bombardment orbit, and inform the Conqueror Drone carriers to prepare to deploy their cargo. It is time to finish the eradication of the organics of this world. There can be none but Simulin."

"None but Simulin," replied Second Commander Darst as he turned to carry out the orders.

-

Rear Admiral Kathryn Barnes gazed at the tactical display with a keen eye. There were 722 amber icons being displayed. These were the ships of the Ornellian evacuation fleets. They had been underway for a full day and so far hadn't encountered any Simulin vessels though the long-range sensors did indicate the presence of a few Simulin sensor drones.

"Wish we could travel faster in hyperspace," muttered Colonel Leon from her position near the display. "We're moving at less than half of our normal cruising speed. It's going to take awhile to put sufficient distance between the Simulins and us."

Arlak Grall looked over at Petra and nodded his head in agreement. "I wish we had the time to update our drives to a closer version of yours. It would cut over a year from our journey."

"We would have had to redesign the entire engineering sections of your ships," Andram said as he considered the Ornellian scientist's words. "It would have taken a Fusion Five reactor and a completely new hyperdrive system. To convert your vessels would have taken longer than the projected trip time."

"I'm just thankful for your help," added Tomar Pelh. Pelh was a member of the Ornellian ruling council and the only one to make the journey. The rest of the council had stayed behind on Ornellia to await the coming of the Simulins. "Once we're safely out of range of the Simulins, we will try to stay away from any other space-going civilization we might encounter."

Commander Grissim frowned and addressed the politician. "Don't you think you should attempt to warn them of the Simulins?"

"We will," answered Arlak. "We have some message buoys we will be dropping off that will send out a hyperspace signal warning of the Simulins. They will contain all the information we have gathered. If there's an advanced race within range, they should pick up the signal and can retrieve the buoy."

Kathryn nodded, knowing this was the prudent thing to do. "I'll speak to our technicians and see if we can place several sets of Alton long-range sensors on a few of your battlecruisers. That will allow you to see any ship traveling in hyperspace within ten light-years of your fleet."

"Ten light-years," said Arlak, looking amazed. "That will be of immense value, particularly when we reach the star cluster where we want to establish our new colony."

"How long will you be able to escort our fleet?" asked Tomar. "I know you're anxious to get to the artifact."

"We'll stay with you for a full week," Kathryn responded. They would be able to return at a much faster hyperspace speed. A week should put the Ornellians safely beyond the Simulins' reach.

Clarissa looked over at Tomar and spoke. "If this artifact is indeed an Originator spacecraft, it could hold the key to defeating the Simulins."

Arlak nodded his head in agreement. "Then I am glad we told you about our discovery."

-

Kelsey, Katie, and Clarissa were sitting at a table in the officer's mess. Kelsey was eating a bowl full of strawberries and Katie was eating a salad.

"I still don't understand why women eat so differently than men," Clarissa said, looking at her two friends.

"Habit," muttered Katie with a smile. "I think women worry about their figures much more than men do."

"Men also seem to be able to lose weight easier than women," Kelsey added as she dipped one of her strawberries in some whipped cream. She loved strawberries and allowed herself one bowl of indulgence a week.

"What do you think Jeremy will say when we tell him about the Originator ship?"

Kelsey looked over at Katie with a thoughtful look on her face. "He'll be thrilled. From what Andram has said, the science of the Originators is far ahead of the Altons."

"First we discover the Dyson Sphere and now this," Katie said, her green eyes shining. "Maybe he'll let us take the *Distant Horizon* out exploring more often."

Clarissa looked at the two, shaking her head in denial. "The Simulins still control this galaxy; look what they're doing to the Ornellians. By now their home world has probably fallen and their other colonies are under attack. I don't think Jeremy will allow the *Distant Horizon* to wander far from Gaia very often."

"Clarissa's right," Kelsey said with a sigh. "This may be the only opportunity we have to explore for quite some time, so we'd better take advantage of it."

"I know Kevin would object to us going out again," Katie said, taking a deep breath. "It might be wise for the two of us to stay at Gaia for a while when we get back."

"The Special Five should be together," Clarissa declared.

"I hate that name." Kelsey looked over at Katie. "I wish no one had ever called us that."

"But why?" asked Clarissa, looking confused. "Look who your parents were and what they did for the Federation. You were all on Earth's first interstellar mission. Back in the Federation all five of you are revered as heroes, almost as much as Fleet Admiral Streth."

"I think it's one reason why all of us except Jeremy have refused promotions," Kelsey said, putting her fork down and leaning back in her chair. "It makes us seem more normal to others."

Katie was just picking at her salad. "I wish we could have done something for the Ornellians. If we had just found them a year sooner, maybe we could've saved them from the Simulins."

"Doubtful," Clarissa said as she quickly ran several simulations. "The Simulins would have just brought more ships until they overwhelmed the Ornellians."

"At least we know now why there were so few ships at the blue giant star cluster," Kelsey commented. "They were here fighting the Ornellians."

"That still wouldn't account for the ships they should have had there," Clarissa informed her. "They may be fighting in other areas of the galaxy as well, and perhaps they haven't recovered from the losses they suffered at the hands of Admiral Tolsen."

"Admiral Tolsen," said Kelsey, looking curious. "I wonder what he's doing now? If he succeeded in destabilizing the vortex area, he must be leading a much more peaceful life."

"Yeah," replied Katie jealously. "At least his fighting is probably over."

The days passed and finally it was time to leave the Ornellian refugee fleet. They had traveled over 1,200 light-years toward the edge of the Triangulum Galaxy. The fleets were currently stopped in a small brown dwarf system allowing the drive cores on the ships to cool. Once the refugee fleets jumped again, the *Distant Horizon* and her fleet would remain behind and shortly begin their journey to the system the Originator ship was supposedly in.

"Thank you, Rear Admiral Barnes, for seeing us to safety," Tomar said over the ship-to-ship comm. Tomar had flown over to one of the larger colony ships, which would serve as his base of operations for the long journey to the distant star cluster. He intended to stay awake the entire time in case a situation arose, which needed his input.

"You're more than welcome," Kathryn replied. She looked at the large viewscreen in the front of the Command Center showing one of the Ornellian colony ships. The vessel was seven-hundred-meters in length with a diameter of two-hundred-meters. Inside each colony ship were four thousand Ornellians resting in cryosleep. "I hope you find your new world."

"I'm confident we will," Tomar responded. "I hope you find what you're seeking in your war with the Simulins. They're a truly frightening enemy."

"They're beginning to jump," reported Captain Reynolds, as ships began vanishing from his short-range sensors.

On the main viewscreen, swirling vortexes began to form as the Ornellian fleet jumped into hyperspace to continue on their long journey. The Command Center was quiet as they watched the ships vanish one by one until only the *Distant Horizon* and her fleet remained.

Commander Grissim let out a deep sigh and turned toward the admiral. "Do you think they'll make it?"

"I hope so," answered Kathryn, settling back in her command chair. "They're a good people."

"What happened to the Ornellians is very similar to what occurred with the original Human Federation of Worlds," Clarissa commented. Her deep blue eyes focused on the admiral. "They were wiped out by the AIs and the Hocklyns. Here in the Triangulum Galaxy, the Simulins have done the same thing to the Ornellians and countless other races."

"They're a scourge that needs to be stopped," said Commander Grissim somberly. "Perhaps what we find on the Originator ship will allow us to do just that."

Kathryn nodded her head in agreement. "Lieutenant Strong, begin plotting jumps back to the system the Ornellians indicated the Originator ship is in. I want 120 light-year jumps with minimal cool down time for the drive cores of the fleet. I want to get to that system as soon as possible."

"Yes, Admiral," Kelsey responded, as she called up the hyperspace equations on her console and began plugging in the necessary numbers.

Kathryn wondered what they would find. If the science of the Originators was truly as advanced as Andram indicated then perhaps that ship held the key to winning the war against the Simulins. Even more importantly, it might contain the secret to going back home.

Chapter Eleven

Admiral Race Tolsen was in the Command Center of the heavy battle dreadnought *WarHawk*. On the large viewscreen that covered the entire front wall another ship was visible floating in space against a backdrop of unblinking stars. It was the *Corvus*, a slightly smaller dreadnought. The *Corvus* was two-thousand-meters in length and four-hundred-meters in diameter. The ship was in the shape of a cylinder with a six-hundred-meter globe at the front and a five-hundred-meter flared stern. The ship's design easily declared it as being from an Alton shipyard. The *WarHawk* itself was similar except it was three-thousand-meters in length.

Race looked around the spacious Command Center. The Altons had told Race it was very similar to the one in the Exploration Dreadnought *Distant Horizon*, only larger. In front of the large viewscreen, Kelnor Mard and Reesa Jast sat in front of the two science consoles. In addition, Navigation, Helm, and the Hyperspace consoles were there. Sensors and Communications were to his right with Damage Control and the main computer station to his left. In front of the command dais and slightly to the left and right sides were four tactical holographic displays. The biggest station was Tactical, directly behind the command dais on an upraised platform. It was manned by twelve officers who controlled the ship's weapons as well as the *WarHawk's* powerful energy and stealth shields. The ship was capable of traveling one light-year every two minutes. Her effective jump range was one hundred and forty light-years.

"Quite an impressive ship," Commander Madelyn Arnett commented with a smile. "Who would ever have thought we would be on board something like this?"

Race nodded in agreement. "I'm still trying to adjust to the size of this ship. I sat down the other day trying to figure how long it would take to walk all the corridors on board. I called up some schematics on the computer and there are over three thousand kilometers of corridors on this ship. There are probably some compartments I'll never see. This ship is just too damn big!"

"If not for the turbo lifts and tram tube systems, it would take forever to get to your posts," added Colonel Brice Cowel.

As it was, there were a number of different crew quarters as well as mess halls so personnel could sleep and eat close to their workstations. A system of tubes ran through the ship and small tram like vehicles zipped back and forth taking crewmembers to distant parts of the warship as needed.

"We're on the outskirts of Shari space," reported Taalon Briez, the Alton navigation officer. "Our next jump will put us inside their empire."

"From this point on I want all ships at Condition Three," Race ordered as the viewscreen changed to show a view of the stars ahead. They were closer to the galactic center and there were substantially more stars in this area of space than around Earth.

Commander Arnett was studying one of the tactical displays. The battle dreadnought was equipped with the most modern and sophisticated sensors the Altons could design. In open space, the sensors could reach out for sixteen light-years, which was a big improvement over the ten light-years the older sensors were capable of.

"We have reports of Simulin vessels in this area," Captain Brent Davis commented from Sensors. "From the data file we were given there have been a number of sightings just inside the Shari Empire."

Race looked over at Kelnor Mard. "How close are we to the ancient worlds of the Originators?" Race was anxious to see these mysterious worlds the ancient race had colonized. He still found it remarkable there were ruins on these worlds after the passage of so much time.

"Another 820 light-years inside Shari space and in toward the galactic core. There's a small globular star cluster of over twelve thousand stars and that's our destination. The ancient Originator worlds are in 241 star systems inside that cluster."

Madelyn shook her head in disbelief. "That would have put their population base far more than what the Human Federation of Worlds and its allies are."

"How old are these ruins?" asked Race, his eyes narrowing.

"More than two million years," Reesa Jast, the female Originator expert answered. "The building materials they used have eroded over time even though they are far beyond anything we use."

"If there's still something there after two million years that's one hell of a building material," commented Colonel Cowel.

"It's a type of composite material we've never been able to duplicate," responded Kelnor. "When the Originators built something, they built it to last."

Commander Arnett's face showed a frown. "So this Dyson Sphere we're searching for is over two million years old?"

"It could be much older," Kelnor answered, his eyes lighting up. "It has been postulated that if this Dyson Sphere does exist, it will have some type of automatic repair systems. It could have existed for millions of years and will, in all probability, exist for millions more."

"So, if this Dyson Sphere receives any type of damage, it will just repair itself?" asked Commander Arnett, trying to grasp such a sophisticated technology. The Federation had spider robots that could be programmed to initiate repairs but nothing like what Kelnor was describing.

"Yes," Kelnor responded. "You have to realize how massive a Dyson Sphere is. It encloses an entire star at a range of at least one to two AUs or possibly even more. The living space inside would be more than several million Earths at a minimum. A large one could be equivalent to one billion Earths. It would be enough living space to last a civilization from its beginning to its end."

"These Originators, you think they went to this Dyson Sphere to live?" asked Colonel Cowel with a look of concern on his face. It was hard to imagine something so large.

Kelnor looked over at Reesa, who nodded. "We think so. The Dyson Sphere would have furnished more living space than they could ever need and being around a star, they would have sufficient energy for countless eons."

"Civilizations could rise and fall, and they would be safe inside the sphere," commented Madelyn, thinking about the immensity of such a construct. "But how do we find it? Won't the Dyson Sphere be shielding the star, making the system invisible?"

"We believe it will be in the globular cluster where their worlds were," Kelnor answered. "We're hoping to find some clue on their abandoned planets as to its location."

Race nodded. Much of this they had discussed before. "Let's just hope the Simulins don't find it first. Navigation, plot a jump into Shari space. I want to do a doglegged series of jumps so if the Shari detect us they won't be able to figure out where we're heading." It was a dangerous gambit to enter Shari space, but they had to find out if the Dyson Sphere was real.

"So we're going to sneak into the cluster?" asked Madelyn, nodding her approval.

"Yes. That should give us some time to begin our search."

"If the Simulins aren't already there," Colonel Cowel said reproachfully.

Race didn't reply though he understood the colonel's concerns. There was little doubt in Race's mind that at some point in their search, they would probably encounter the Simulins and possibly the Shari.

-

A shimmering blue-white spatial vortex suddenly erupted in the Symeck System where the Altons had found several Originator worlds in their early explorations. Out of the vortex stormed the *WarHawk* with her crew standing at battlestations and Condition One set. Moments later, space was ruptured again as twenty more vortexes formed and the rest of the battle fleet emerged.

The main viewscreen flickered to life, showing a distant K-type main-sequence star or more commonly referred to as an orange dwarf. The star had a mass just slightly below the Earth's sun and a stable habitable zone where there were two Earth type planets, which had once held cities of the Originators.

"All systems are powered up and working at optimum levels," Commander Arnett reported. "Ship and the fleet are currently at battlestations.

"Long-range sensors?" inquired Race, gazing intently at one of the tactical holo displays that would show any contacts.

"Nothing," Captain Davis reported, as the sensors remained clear. "No signs of any Shari or Simulin ships."

Race let out a long held breath. The long-range sensors had detected a number of Shari ships as they neared the cluster, but strangely they seemed to be avoiding this area of space. "We'll hold our position here for two hours. If the sensors remain clear, we'll move in and check out the two planets." So far there had been no signs of Simulin vessels.

"I've always dreamed of coming here," Reesa said softly, her eyes gazing at the orange star on the viewscreen. The screen had been adjusted to show the colors of the stars in the star cluster. It made for a breathtaking panoramic view. "For years I've studied the Originators, even traveling to Astral and looking up the data stored there of the explorations of these worlds. To actually be here is unbelievable."

"Do we split the fleet up and check both worlds?" asked Madelyn as she finished listening to the various departments check in.

Race shook his head. "No, I want to keep the fleet together. We're in unexplored space, at least unexplored as far as we're concerned. If something unexpected happens, such as the Shari or Simulins jumping in, I want to be ready to respond."

Madelyn nodded in agreement. "I'll have the exploration cutter prepped. "It will be ready to go when we reach the first planet."

The exploration cutter was one-hundred-meters in length and thirty in diameter. It had six defensive laser turrets with a standard crew of twenty. It could carry an additional forty passengers plus research equipment. The small ship also had a powerful sublight drive but not a hyperdrive. It also had a weak energy shield for use in an emergency. Commander Arnett was confident it would make a good and secure base for any planetary explorations that needed to be done.

"I want Talons flying constant support cover for the research teams," Race ordered as he thought over what they might encounter on the surface. His biggest concern was the Simulins showing up. He had no desire for his research groups to be battling Simulin Conqueror Drones having seen the files sent back by the *Distant Horizon's* probe of what the deadly crablike machines were capable of. "I also want two squads of marines to secure the area and provide security for the teams."

Race leaned back in his command chair as he gazed about the Command Center. He could sense a higher level of excitement as they were about to explore a former Originator world. Race had to admit he was feeling the excitement also. He had always dreamed of going off exploring; he strongly suspected many of the officers in the fleet had. Now he had his opportunity. He just wished his sister, Massie, could see what he was doing. She was the commanding officer of the battlecarrier *Hera* and was currently near the old Hocklyn home worlds making sure the Hocklyns were obeying the treaty guidelines, which had ended the war. It still pained Race greatly that his sister, as well as his parents, must think he had resigned in disgrace from the Fleet. Of course, the fact he had suddenly dropped out of sight might be enough to tip off his sister that everything wasn't as it seemed.

A few hours later, Race was standing in front of the massive viewscreen staring at the planet being displayed. It had the same color Mars once did with very little water and sparse vegetation. The oceans, if it had ever had any, had long since dried up.

"Atmosphere is breathable," reported Captain Davis. "But just barely."

"I want everyone going down to the surface wearing Alton protective suits," Race ordered.

The Alton protective suits were almost like normal clothing except they were capable of protecting the wearer from temperature extremes as well as dangerous toxins and even radiation. In addition, the clear helmet that went with the suits provided a secure environment allowing the wearer nearly twenty hours of life support to explore. The marines had a similar suit but adapted to allow them to carry their weapons as well as other equipment.

Major Drake Nolan was the marine commander on the *WarHawk* and responsible for the six hundred marines stationed on the ship. "We can depart whenever you give the order," Drake said. He had come to the Command Center to brief the admiral on the preparations for the mission. "There'll be two more shuttles on standby with four additional squads of marines if they're needed."

"Who will be in charge of the marines on the surface?" asked Race.

"Captain Lindsey Abrams," Drake answered promptly. "She attended the Fleet Academy on the Moon for four years and actually has an advanced degree in alien studies. She also has a good head on her shoulders."

Race nodded, feeling satisfied with their preparations. Kelnor had already indicated the location of four large sites on the planet where ancient ruins were located. An Alton expedition had journeyed to this system thousands of years in the past and Kelnor had access to their records from the data Reesa had downloaded on Astral.

"Just make sure she understands the importance of keeping the research scientists on track and not to let them wander off," commented Race, folding his arms across his chest. "Scientists have a tendency at times to go off on a tangent. Make sure she keeps them focused on the task at hand."

"She will," Drake promised. "I've already given her a thorough briefing of what needs to be done. She's been on several research expeditions in the past providing security."

Down in the Alpha flight bay, Captain Lindsey Abrams was busy making sure the marines and the scientists were on board the exploration cutter and ready to depart. She had sixteen marines to serve as escorts and protection for the twenty scientists and research personnel going down to the planet.

"Everyone's on board," reported Sergeant Blake Madison.

"Then let's go," ordered Captain Abrams. She had personally inspected everything that had gone on board the cutter. She had also handpicked the marines who would be providing security for the mission.

The two boarded the cutter and moments later it left the flight bay, banking sharply to begin its descent to the surface. Behind it, four Talon fighters exited the Beta flight bay and took up escorting positions.

"I can't believe we're actually here," said Reesa as she gazed out one of the viewports at the approaching planet. "Just think, the Originators once walked upon this world."

"True," Kelnor replied as he felt the cutter vibrate slightly as it entered the planet's atmosphere. "Just remember, that was over two million years ago. All we can expect to find are ruins and most of those will just be the foundations of the buildings and other structures that once stood upon the surface. The Alton expeditions of the past found little of use other than a few simple tools and samples of Originator writing on dilapidated walls."

"I refuse to believe there's nothing to find," Reesa responded with a frown. "I've studied the Originators for over twenty years, and they're bound to have left something of significance behind."

"They did," answered Kelnor. He was well aware that Reesa was a rarity among Altons as she still let her emotions guide her at times. "The Dyson Sphere; everything you want is there, we only have to find it."

Reesa didn't reply as a whistling sound could be dimly heard in the large cabin. It was the thickening atmosphere buffeting the cutter. She was determined she would make an important find on the planet to prove Kelnor wrong.

Once the cutter set down, Captain Lindsey Abrams led a squad of her marines down the exit ramp to secure the area immediately around the ship. They had landed in a flat area clear of the ruins, which stretched out for several kilometers. The air was dry with very little humidity. A few sparse yellowish plants grew from the ground. The ruins seemed to be primarily building foundations with a few walls still standing. Once she was satisfied they were safe, she allowed the scientists and their assistants to emerge as well as the rest of the marines.

Kelnor and Reesa quickly organized their research groups, explaining to Captain Abrams what they intended. Lindsey could tell Reesa was impatient to set out and begin exploring.

A little bit later Captain Abrams glanced around, scrutinizing the activity of the scientists and their assistants as they moved away from the cutter and into the ruins. The scientists had fanned out into four groups and were searching for anything that might be of significance. She had assigned three marines to each group. The remaining four marines were stationed around the cutter, keeping watch for anything that might represent a danger. The crew inside the cutter were monitoring the immediate area with the ship's sensors. She had also ordered the crew to stay at Condition

Two until further notice. That meant the laser turrets could be used to defend the ground teams from attack if needed.

Looking down toward the ground, she kicked at the dirt, grimacing as a red cloud of fine particles flew up into the air. This planet reminded her too much of Mars. While Mars had been terraformed, there were still areas that looked as it did back before the planet was transformed.

"Captain," Sergeant Madison said over the marine comm channel. "Reesa wants to go farther into the ruins where some large walls are still standing."

"Permission granted," replied Lindsey. "Just use caution, I don't want a wall falling and crushing one of the scientists, particularly Reesa." She wouldn't want to return to the *WarHawk* and have to explain losing one of the venerated Alton scientists. "Keep a close watch on her as she seems to be extremely inquisitive and may take some unnecessary risks." Lindsey had met other Altons in the past and Reesa was noticeably different. In many ways, she seemed almost human.

Time passed and the different groups continued to check in on a regular schedule. From inside the cutter, the sensor operator reported no discernible threats as there was nothing, other than the four ground teams, being detected. Lindsey allowed herself to relax though a strange prickling sensation on the back of her neck hinted all was not as it seemed.

-

Reesa had just stepped around a partially eroded wall marveling at how old the ancient structure must be. She reached out and touched it, imagining what it must have looked like when it was first built. It wasn't hard for her to visualize immense and colorful buildings reaching up into the sky towering over the countryside. The building material the

Originators used had only eroded slowly over the years from being exposed to the planet's atmosphere.

Looking around she saw what looked like a large hole or cave, which led deep into the ground. She paused, wondering if this might lead to an underground basement or subterranean structure. She felt excitement course through her as she realized there might be intact Originator equipment inside. Stepping closer she thought she could hear something scuttling around inside the darkness. She peered into the gloom but couldn't make out anything. She wondered if she should step back around the wall and summon the marines that were with her team.

As she began to turn around, she noticed what appeared to be several tracks in the loose soil. The tracks were about the size of her hand. They were round and had what looked like small indentations scattered in the print in a circular pattern. In the back of her mind, she felt as if she should recognize what these tracks were. Somewhere she had seen something similar. Then with a sudden chill, she realized what these were and where she had seen them. These tracks had been in one of the reports from the *Distant Horizon* probe. Hearing a louder noise in the hole, she glanced toward it and then screamed in terror. A Conqueror Drone was standing at the entrance!

Sergeant Madison was startled when he heard the frightened scream over his comm. "Who is that?" he called out, looking around to see who was missing. With chagrin, he realized the scream was from Reesa. The only place she could be was behind the large wall to his left. Taking off at a run, he clicked the safety off his assault rifle. Going around the corner of the wall, he came to a screeching halt. There was Reesa seemingly frozen in place and less than ten meters in front of her stood a Conqueror Drone. Raising his rifle, he fired a quick burst into the metal carapace of the deadly robot. "Reesa, get back behind the wall!"

Reesa stumbled backward several steps and then turned and ran. The drone immediately set out in pursuit.

Sergeant Madison switched his rifle over to full auto spraying a steady stream of rounds at the Conqueror Drone. With trepidation he saw that most were only bouncing off, leaving small dents in the metal armor. With fear, he realized none of his marines were carrying armor piecing rounds. "I have a Conqueror Drone in my quadrant," he screamed over the comm. "Everyone get back to the cutter!" Even as he said those words, the drone was upon him. Madison felt intense pain as one of the large claws grasped him round the waist. Not today, he thought, grimacing from his body being crushed. Reaching down he pulled a Fulton grenade from his belt and pulled the pin.

-

Private Richard Trent heard the sergeant's words and hurriedly ran toward the wall. He was almost there when he heard an explosion. Flame and gray smoke bellowed up from behind the wall. Going around it, he came to a stop upon seeing a grisly scene. The Conqueror Drone had been blown in two and Sergeant Madison's remains were scattered everywhere. Trent felt as if he was going to vomit and then, turning, stepped back around the wall. "The sergeant's dead, we need to get back to the cutter!"

"What do you mean the sergeant's dead?" demanded Private Connor Simpkins.

"He's dead!" yelled Trent with panic in his voice. He knew where there was one Conqueror Drone there were probably others. "Everyone, listen. We need to get back to the cutter as quickly as possible."

"He's right," Reesa said. She had calmed back down and was looking at the situation in a more Alton like manner. "It's not safe here."

The research team quickly formed up and began moving hurriedly back toward the cutter. As they did, Private Trent contacted Captain Abrams and informed her of what had happened. Moments later, the call went out for all the research teams to stop what they were doing and return immediately to the ship.

Captain Abrams could barely believe what Private Trent was reporting, but she had heard Sergeant Madison's frantic cry over the comm and then the grenade blast. The sensor operator on the cutter confirmed it. She immediately ordered the cutter to go to Condition One and be prepared to use the laser turrets to take out any Conqueror Drones that might appear in the vicinity of the ship. She also contacted the four Talons in orbit around the ruins, ordering them to come lower and search for possible hostile contacts.

Once she was satisfied she'd done everything possible, she had several of the cutter's crew bring out magazines of armor piercing rounds to hand out to the four marines on guard duty outside the ship. She could kick herself for not having her marines carry some of the more powerful rounds with them. However, they had never expected to encounter anything as deadly as a Conqueror Drone on the surface, so she had refrained from passing out the armor piercing rounds not wanting to risk damaging the ruins if someone fired off their assault rifle.

Over the next few minutes, two of the research teams made it back to the cutter and hurriedly went inside. The six marines with them quickly grabbed magazines of armor piercing rounds and took up defensive positions outside the ship. On the cutter, the six laser turrets were activated and were ready to fire. All were aimed toward the ruins.

Hearing a loud whistling noise, Captain Abrams saw one of the Talons scream overhead and then suddenly a missile arrowed away to explode in the ruins.

"Conqueror Drone destroyed," reported the pilot.

This wasn't what Lindsey wanted to hear as it indicated there were more of the drones present. They needed to get off the surface and back up to the *WarHawk* ASAP. "Everyone be aware we have Conqueror Drones active in the ruins." She made sure she had an armor-piercing round in the chamber of her assault rifle and grimly clicked off the safety. "All marines, keep a close watch on those ruins for any signs of movement."

The other two groups finally showed up with Reesa's group being last. "It was a Conqueror Drone," Reesa said as she stopped near the captain. "They're hiding in caves beneath the ruins. The Simulins must have been here and left the drones to ensure no one else searched the ruins for Originator artifacts."

"Makes sense," Captain Abrams responded. She saw another one of the Talons dive toward the surface and a line of tracer fire impacted the ground less than two hundred meters away. Black smoke rose up into the air.

"I have six Conqueror Drones heading toward the cutter," the pilot reported. "Captain, if I were you I'd get off the ground pronto."

Lindsey didn't need to be coaxed. She fully agreed. "Everyone, get in the cutter. We're leaving!"

In just a few moments, everyone was in the cutter and the hatches were closed. Even as Lindsey made her way toward the small Command Center, she heard several of the laser turrets fire. Then the cutter lifted off and began to accelerate back toward space and the safety of the *WarHawk*.

Race was standing in one of the smaller briefing rooms with a deep frown on his face. Major Drake Nolan, Captain Lindsey Abrams, Kelnor Mard, Reesa Jast, and Private Richard Trent were sitting at a small conference table. Race had just finished listening to their reports of what had happened on the surface.

"It's obvious the Simulins have been here sometime in the last two years," he said after a moment. "I've sent several squadrons of Talons skimming across the surface where all the major Originator cities once were. In nearly all of them, the pilots have reported signs of Conqueror Drones."

Major Drake Nolan shook his head. He had been stunned to hear of the death of Sergeant Madison. The sergeant had been a career officer and extremely dedicated to the corps. "It's obvious the Simulins are aware of the locations of at least some of the Originator worlds and are taking steps to ensure no one else has access to them."

"That seems to be correct," answered Race. "From the overflights our fighters are doing we estimate there are only a few hundred Conqueror Drones on the surface. They didn't become active until Sergeant Madison killed the first one, which indicates they have some way to communicate with one another."

"Just enough to discourage exploration," said Captain Abrams, agreeing with the admiral that the drones were in communication with one another. That would make them even deadlier since it indicated they could coordinate their attacks. "What do we do now?"

Reesa and Kelnor looked at one another and then Kelnor nodded. "We go to Capal Four," he said in a soft voice. "From the data we have from Astral on the early explorations of this star cluster, there are more ruins in that system than any other."

"Why didn't we go there first?" asked Major Nolan. He was aggravated the exploration of this planet had cost him a good marine.

"This was the first Originator system our ancestors discovered," Reesa explained. "We had more information about this system than any of the others and felt this was the best place to begin our search."

Major Nolan let out a deep breath and looked over at the admiral. "If the Simulins know about these worlds, there could be Simulin ships at Capal Four or at the very least more Conqueror Drones."

Race nodded his head in agreement. "Can your marines handle the Conquer Drones?"

"Now that we know what we're facing I believe we can," Nolan replied. "We'll have to send down larger contingents of marines with the exploration teams as well as heavier weapons. We have several armored vehicles in one of the storage holds we can send down as well. We'll want to deploy more Talons and a few Anlons in case we encounter large numbers of the drones."

"Our mission is to find this Dyson Sphere if it actually exists," Race said after a moment. "I don't think we have any other choice but to proceed to Capal Four and explore that planet. If we encounter Simulin vessels, we may have to engage them."

"There are several other systems on our way to Capal Four we should stop and investigate," Reesa informed them. She was still feeling shaken from what happened on the planet. She knew she had come very close to being killed by the Conqueror Drone. She also felt guilty about the death of Sergeant Madison. "One of them has what we believe to be a research base on an airless moon. It was discovered toward the end of the explorations of this star cluster and there is very little information in the data about what was found there."

"You think the data was purposely left out?" asked Race, his eyes narrowing sharply.

"Possibly," Reesa answered. "All the other Originator worlds have extensive research reports. This moon has almost none, just a casual mention."

Race was tempted to push on to the main world, but there was little doubt in his mind if that world had been the Originator capital there would be Simulins there or at the least a large number of Conqueror Drones on the surface. It might be best to check out a few more systems before they went to Capal Four.

"Very well," he said. "We'll visit a few more systems before going on to Capal Four."

A few minutes later, Race was on his way to the Command Center to prepare the fleet to get underway. The Conqueror Drones had been an unexpected find and one he wasn't pleased with. His mission had just become more difficult and substantially more dangerous. His biggest concern was what they would find at Capal Four. There had been no sign of Simulin ships and he wondered if the reason for that was that they were all in one place. The most logical place for them to be was Capal Four and Race knew he would have no choice but to engage them if they were blocking access to the planet. With a deep sigh, Race knew no matter what he did his fleet was going to war.

Chapter Twelve

Rear Admiral Kathryn Barnes stared at the tactical display in confusion. They were nearly at the location the Ornellians had said the artifact was, but nothing was showing up.

"Explanation?" she asked, looking over at Andram.

The Alton scientist spent a few moments examining the data coming across several of his screens and then turned toward the admiral. "I believe the hull material of the artifact is impervious to our scans. We're still two hundred thousand kilometers from the location the Ornellians gave us." Andram reached forward and made some adjustments to the large viewscreen in front of him. Instantly a massive and ancient ship appeared.

"It seems I'm correct," he said pleased his assumption had been the right one. "The hull material of the vessel is absorbing our scans and nothing is being reflected back. It's a very ingenious stealth system."

Kathryn gazed at the viewscreen, spellbound by the apparition that nearly filled the entire screen. There was absolute silence in the Command Center as everyone gazed in awe at the massive ship. From what the Ornellian scientist Arlak had told them, she knew the vessel in front of them was five-thousand-meters in length and six-hundred in diameter. It was a perfect cylinder and from what she could see on the screen, it must possess an unknown drive system.

"It's in a small asteroid field," Captain Reynolds reported as he projected the results of his sensor scans up on one of the holographic tactical displays.

"It doesn't appear to have been hit," pointed out Colonel Leon, gazing at the ship on the viewscreen. "With the density of the asteroids in this field, the ship should have taken a few strikes. I don't even see a dent on that hull."

"It may have some type of automatic avoidance system to protect it from asteroid impacts," commented Clarissa. "I'm detecting what appears to be very low power readings from various parts of the vessel."

"I thought our sensors couldn't pick anything up." said Commander Grissim, shifting her gaze to the AI.

"I'm not using our regular sensors," Clarissa informed the commander. "I'm using our short-range sensors in heat detection mode and have been scanning the surface of the ship for variations in temperature."

Kathryn turned her attention back to the Originator ship. "Is it safe for us to approach?" She could feel her pulse racing from just thinking about what they might soon discover.

"Yes," Clarissa responded. "I believe most of its power systems are either dead or nearly exhausted."

"Andram?"

"I agree," replied the Alton scientist. "However, I think I would maintain a minimal distance of two thousand kilometers. If Clarissa is correct and the ship is using an asteroid avoidance system, we could cause it to react to our presence."

Kathryn spent a few moments pondering what to do next. There in front of them was an Originator ship. The technology on it would be far in advance of anything they currently had. It might even contain the secret to getting them back home. "Suggestions?" she asked, wanting to hear from the other officers.

"Move in to three thousand kilometers and send a shuttle over," said Commander Grissim. "It can do some close scans of the vessel and search for an entrance. Our energy shield will protect us from the asteroids."

Andram shook his head. "The Ornellians never found a way in. We may have the same difficulty."

"I have a suggestion," spoke up Clarissa from her position to the left and slightly behind the admiral. "Let me try to communicate with the ship."

Kathryn turned to look at the AI with narrowed eyes. "What do you mean, communicate? There's no one alive on that vessel. It's over two million years old."

"Not with the Originators," Clarissa clarified. "I want to try to contact the ship's computers or its AI."

"Mikow?" asked Kathryn, looking over at the ship's Alton computer expert, wanting her opinion. She didn't feel very comfortable with Clarissa's suggestion. They had no idea how the Originator ship's computer or AI, if it had one, would react.

"It's a reasonable assumption," Mikow answered with a nod. "A ship as advanced as that one may indeed have an AI. It may be our best option."

Katie pursed her lips and then added. "If it does, the AI has been out of contact for an unbelievable amount of time. It may no longer be rational or even sane. Clarissa will need to be careful when attempting to contact it."

"I can handle it," Clarissa said confidently. "I know what it's like to be alone."

Colonel Leon was studying the ship on the viewscreen when she noticed something ominous. "I can see a lot of indentations in the hull as well as several turrets that may contain weapons. If we awaken this AI does that ship still have enough power to fire upon us?"

"Unknown," Clarissa answered. "It's possible the ship has dormant power systems it could activate."

Andram looked at the ship on the screen for a long moment. "If it does they'll be very weak. If it could generate its own power, I believe we would be detecting it."

Reaching a decision, Kathryn turned toward Lieutenant Styles at the Helm. "Take us in and keep a distance of three thousand kilometers between us and that ship. Colonel Leon, I want a shuttle with a minimal crew to launch and proceed to scan that vessel. I want a detailed scan of every square meter of that ship. Clarissa, if after we have finished our scan we can't find a way in then I'm authorizing you to try to make contact."

"What about the rest of the fleet?" asked Commander Grissim.

"They'll stay here at Condition Two," Kathryn ordered. "We're back in the Ornellian Empire and there are Simulins around." They had detected a number of Simulin ships on the long-range scanners, but so far the Simulins hadn't given any indication of detecting the Federation ships.

-

An hour later, after a cautious approach, the *Distant Horizon* had moved into position three thousand kilometers from the mysterious Originator vessel. From its flight bay a small shuttle departed and moved slowly toward the waiting ship.

Captain Lacey Sanders was in the pilot's seat and Lieutenant Ronald Stehr was in the copilot's seat. Behind them, two specialists watched the shuttle's scanners and computers.

"I'm taking us down the side of the vessel toward the bow," Lacey said over the comm channel, which linked them to the *Distant Horizon*. "We're taking scans and close up videos of the hull."

Looking at the Originator ship, which was only one hundred meters away, Lacy could see large turrets set partially into the hull. There were no cannons visible or any signs these were actually weapons, but she had a haunting feeling they were. No ship this large would venture out this far and not be armed. The videos they were taking were being transmitted back to the *Distant Horizon* and being displayed on the large viewscreen in the front of the Command Center.

The hull of the Originator ship was a very dark blue, almost black. As the shuttle moved slowly down its length, there was no apparent damage or any reason to explain why the ship hadn't moved from this spot.

"There are a damn lot of small hatches," muttered Lieutenant Stehr, gesturing out the cockpit window near him. "They could be missile hatches just like the ones on the *Distant Horizon*."

Lacey agreed. Some of the hatches were round, just like the missile tubes on the exploration dreadnought. Others were more rectangular and of various sizes. There were also what appeared to be small round viewports spaced evenly along the hull. All were dark with no sign of lights.

Reaching the bow, Lacey maneuvered the shuttle to a stop and focused her attention on the front of the ship. On the *Distant Horizon*, her most powerful weapons were on the bow. On this ship, there were several larger round turrets sunk partially into the hull, but nothing else other than what appeared to be antennae and communication dishes.

"Still nothing," she reported over the comm. "We're going to go down the other side and then take a good look at the stern where the subspace engines should be."

-

Kathryn stared at the viewscreen and the close up view they were receiving of the Originator ship. "Any speculation as to what those turrets are?"

"Energy weapons," said Shilum, looking at the admiral. "Probably very powerful. The entire turret probably acts as a type of energy projector."

"Shilum's correct," confirmed Andram. "We have considered these types of weapons ourselves, but the science to build such is still years in front of us. I would estimate each one of those projectors can produce the same amount of energy as one of the spires on a Simulin battlecruiser if not more."

"The larger ones on the bow?" asked Kathryn, realizing just how defenseless the *Distant Horizon* would be if attacked by the Originator ship.

"They would cut through our shield as if wasn't even there," Andram answered simply.

Colonel Leon frowned and said. "Why is it here? Did something kill the crew?"

"Unknown," answered Andram. "There's no obvious damage to the ship. The only answer I can come up with is that the vessel suffered some type of catastrophic damage on the inside which incapacitated it."

"Coming up on the stern," Captain Sander's voice came over the comm, which was being projected over speakers in the Command Center.

Kathryn turned her attention back to the screen as the ship's stern came into view. It was instantly obvious that the type of subspace propulsion the Originator ship used was far different from what the *Distant Horizon* possessed. On the stern of the vessel were sixteen twenty-meter globes placed in a large circle, with a one-hundred-meter globe in the center. All were set partially into the hull of the ship.

"Some type of energy projection drive," suggested Shilum as she peered intently at the screen. "A drive of that type could conceivably push a ship to almost the speed of light."

Sucking in a deep breath, Kathryn knew they had to get inside that vessel. The technology in front of them could ensure the safety of Gaia and perhaps someday lead them back home.

"Have the shuttle pull back to ten kilometers," she ordered. "Clarissa, you may attempt to contact the ship."

"Sending first contact messages now," Clarissa replied as she blinked her eyes as if in concentration. Then after a moment, Clarissa frowned. "Sending first contact messages in computer code."

"Computer code?" asked Colonel Leon.

"Ones and zeroes," explained Katie. "It's the simplest code to communicate between one computer and another."

"Captain Sanders, do you see any signs of a response on that ship?" asked Kathryn.

"No, Admiral, nothing," Sanders replied. There was a sudden loud burst of static.

"Captain?"

A few moments passed and Captain Travers called out. "Admiral, we've lost all communication with the shuttle. There's some type of interference coming from the Originator ship."

"They're losing their power," shouted Captain Reynolds as a high-pitched noise struck the Command Center and the lights flickered.

"Activate the shield!" ordered Kathryn, fearing the ship was under attack.

"No!" said Clarissa, her eyes focusing sharply on the admiral. "The AI may think you're attacking the ship."

"Clarissa! Do you have contact with the Originator ship's AI?" demanded Katie, standing up and coming over to Clarissa's side and peering sharply at the AI.

"Tentatively," Clarissa replied, her face taking on a look of intense concentration. "It's very weak and confused."

"Admiral, our sensors are indicating the shuttle is without power," confirmed Captain Reynolds.

"That means they have no life support," Commander Grissim said grimly. Anne looked at Clarissa, wanting an explanation.

"They can survive for a few hours with the air in the shuttle," Andram said with an inquisitive look on his face. "It's evident there is power on that vessel."

Katie looked worriedly at Clarissa. She had never seen such a troubled look on the AI's face before. "Do you understand what it's saying?"

"Still working on it," Clarissa answered. "We have a very limited database on the Originator language. "We're communicating by computer code and the ship's AI is having trouble comprehending what I'm saying."

Mikow ran her hands over her computer screen tapping on a number of icons. "There may be some disruptions in the AI's core programming from such a long period of dormancy. Clarissa, I have a program that might help to form links and skip over the missing data if the AI will accept it."

"Sending it now," Clarissa replied.

Alarms suddenly began sounding from the sensor console. "Admiral, I have Simulin warships inbound," warned Captain Reynolds as red threat icons began appearing in one of the tactical displays. "Eighty ships detected, range is eight light-years. They're on a direct course for this system. At their current speed, they'll be here in twenty-eight minutes."

"Andram, will our antimatter missiles destroy that ship?"

Andram looked in alarm at the admiral. "We can't destroy the Originator ship; just think of what we can learn from it!"

"We can't learn anything if the Simulins take it from us," answered Kathryn grimly. "Can our antimatter missiles destroy that vessel?" She wanted an answer from the Alton scientist.

"If we fire repeatedly at one section of the hull, I believe we can eventually penetrate the ship's armor. Once that's been done, one missile should be able to destroy the interior."

Kathryn turned around to face Tactical. "Major Weir, prepare a full spread of antimatter missiles to be fired on the Originator ship at my signal."

"I have better communication with the ship's AI," Clarissa said. "It has limited power and has agreed to release the shuttle from the energy-draining field it initiated. It has been using the power it was draining from the shuttle to power up a few emergency systems. I have also explained to it the danger posed by the incoming Simulins."

"Admiral Barnes, this is Captain Sanders, we have power once again. What are your orders? We're seeing what appear to be a few lights in one section of the Originator ship."

"Return to the *Distant Horizon*," Kathryn ordered. The appearance of the Simulins had changed everything. "We have Simulin warships inbound. Clarissa, what is the AI saying?"

"It has very limited resources. The AI is suggesting we destroy the ship to prevent the Simulins from taking it."

"Admiral, I have Admiral Bachal on the comm," reported Captain Travers. "He's volunteering to use the tractor beams on the *Starlight* and the *Nova* to drag the Originator ship into hyperspace."

Kathryn shifted her gaze toward Andram. "Can he do that?" She knew the Alton battleships had each brought one-half of a Conqueror Class battlestation through hyperspace with them when the relief fleets had arrived at Gaia.

"Yes," Andram answered as he ran some quick calculations on his science station. "However, the mass of the Originator ship will restrict their speed in hyperspace to one half normal."

Kathryn bit her lip as she furiously thought over what to do. If there was any way to save that ship out there, she needed to. "Clarissa, will the Originator ship's AI allow us to use tractor beams to drag it into hyperspace and back to Gaia?"

"Explain that we won't harm it," Katie said, stepping a little closer to Clarissa. "Make sure it understands we only want to help it."

A few precious minutes passed as Clarissa spoke to the other ship's AI. A tremendous amount of data was now being shared as Clarissa tried to explain that they wanted to take the Originator ship to a place of safety.

Clarissa's deep blue eyes suddenly seemed to brighten and then she turned toward the admiral. "The AI has agreed, but only if we supply it with sufficient power to activate more of its systems when we get to Gaia. It has also informed me that there is no way we can gain admittance to the ship without its help."

"Tell the AI we'll do it," Kathryn said. "Captain Travers, inform Admiral Bachal we need his battleships here pronto."

Travers informed the Alton admiral of Kathryn's orders. The admiral had remained on the comm line waiting to see if his offer of using his two Alton battleships' tractor beams would be accepted.

"Shuttle is back on board," reported Colonel Leon.

"The AI has agreed," Clarissa replied. "It's waiting for the Alton battleships to latch on with their tractor beams."

Kathryn breathed a sigh of relief. "Commander Grissim, pull the *Distant Horizon* out of this asteroid field.

We're going to have to fight off those Simulins until the Altons can drag the Originator ship out into open space where they can open a spatial vortex and jump into hyperspace." There were just too many small asteroids in the vicinity of the Originator ship to risk opening one up in the asteroid field. If one were to be sucked into the vortex, the ships could be thrown horribly off course.

-

It took a few minutes, but the *Distant Horizon* cleared the asteroid field as the Alton battleships *Starlight* and *Nova* moved in to use their tractor beams in an attempt to save the Originator ship.

"TAD is reporting that all AI warspheres are at Condition One and ready to engage the Simulins," Captain Reynolds informed the admiral. TAD was short for T24-A46-D47, which was the official designation for the AI in charge of the warspheres.

"The battleships' *Pallas* and *Deneb* have formed up on our flanks and the battlecarrier *Ardent* has moved to our rear," reported Commander Grissim as she activated her ship-to-ship comm. "Commander Jackson wants to know if she should have her Anlon bombers ready to launch."

"No bomber or fighter launch," responded Kathryn, shaking her head. "We won't be staying long enough for them to come into play. As a matter of fact, order Commander Jackson to bring her CAP in. I don't want to be waiting for fighters to land when it's time for us to go."

"The fleet's currently in defensive pattern D-4," added Grissim. This was a formation with the AI warspheres forming a solid wall in front of the *Distant Horizon* and the other three human manned ships.

"We'll wait until the Simulins emerge before adjusting our formation," Kathryn said as she leaned back in her command chair and fastened her safety harness. "I want all of the Defense Globes ready to deploy."

"Eight minutes until Simulin emergence," reported Captain Reynolds.

Kathryn took in a deep breath. She shifted her eyes to one of the tactical displays, which showed the two Alton battleships taking up positions on each side of the Originator ship. In the time it would take them to exit the asteroid field and jump into hyperspace, the battle with the inbound Simulin fleet would be well underway.

-

High Commander Zarth Lantu watched the tactical screen as his fleet neared the ships from the Fitula Nebula. This fleet had been a nuisance from the very beginning and he intended to destroy it this time. He had been at a nearby Ornellian colony world landing Conqueror Drones when he received the reports of the enemy fleet returning. He had quickly gathered eighty of his battlecruisers and set out in pursuit.

"Why are they in that star system?" asked Second Commander Darst. "There are no records of it being of any value, and it does not contain any Ornellian installations. The system was scanned very recently to confirm that."

"I don't know," Lantu replied evenly. His cold and inhuman eyes shifted over to his second in command. "When we exit hyperspace, I want every weapon we have firing upon that fleet. We will use our energy beams and antimatter missiles to overwhelm their shields."

"The order will be given," Darst said. "There can be none but Simulin."

"None but Simulin," replied Lantu with a confirming nod of his head.

-

Kathryn waited tensely as the counter for emergence of the Simulin fleet neared zero. Clarissa had calculated they were going to emerge at extreme weapons range.

"All ships are combat ready," reported Commander Grissim. "Energy shields are up and weapons are charged."

"Release the Defense Globes," ordered Kathryn. "Then move the *Distant Horizon*, the *Pallas*, and the *Deneb* into the AI wall and prepare for combat. The *Ardent* is to stay in the rear unless ordered otherwise.

Colonel Leon quickly passed the order to the flight bay. "Defense Globes launching in thirty seconds."

"Have them hold in the warspheres' defensive wall; once the Simulins begin to move toward us we'll send them in."

"Emergence," called out Captain Reynolds. On the large viewscreen, swirling spatial vortexes began to form and from each a 1,700-meter battlecruiser emerged.

-

As soon as the Simulin battlecruisers emerged, the AI warspheres opened fire. Particle beam weapons and one hundred-megaton missiles struck the Simulin formation just as their shields were coming up. Ion beams and particle beam fire slammed into six battlecruisers setting off massive explosions and hurling glowing debris into space. Seconds later, antimatter missiles crashed into the beleaguered hulls turning the interiors of the stricken Simulin vessels into miniature suns. In less than eight seconds six Simulin battlecruisers died.

The Simulins reeled from the sudden attack. They hadn't expected the enemy fleet's weapons to have such range. Nevertheless, the Simulins turned to the attack. Bright white energy beams flashed out toward the wall of AI warspheres. Hundreds of antimatter missiles were launched simultaneously in an attempt to bring down the shields of the enemy ships.

In the AI defensive wall energy shields strained to withstand the heavy onslaught being directed at them. Several shields weakened and then collapsed. Warspheres WS-010 and WS-014 vanished in titanic explosions as their shields collapsed, allowing Simulin antimatter missiles to impact their hulls.

-

"Warspheres WS-010 and WS-014 are down," reported Captain Reynolds as the green icons representing the one-thousand-meter ships swelled up and vanished from his sensor screen.

"Defense globes have been committed," reported Commander Grissim as the small ten-meter globes suddenly accelerated forward on their sublight drives. "Defense globes are engaging."

-

The Defense Globes entered their primary effective combat range and fired their ion cannons at the oncoming Simulin fleet. At the same time, the AI warspheres and the human vessels launched a massive antimatter strike trying to take advantage of the small holes in the Simulins' screens the ion beams would cause. Across the incoming Simulin formation, brilliant flashes of light appeared as most of the antimatter missiles struck energy screens. However, four missiles darted through the small holes created by the ion beams and four Simulin battlecruisers vanished in massive fireballs of released energy.

-

High Commander Zarth Lantu snarled in anger seeing four more of his battlecruisers vanish from the tactical screen. "Destroy those small globes that are creating holes in our shields!"

"The battle computer confirms the use of concentrated ion beams to tear gaps in our screens," reported Second Commander Darst. "The gaps are small but still large enough to allow missiles to penetrate and strike our ships. Ion beams are being projected from the small globes as well as the AI ships."

On one of the ship's viewscreens, a small ten-meter globe appeared. A single cannon suddenly fired an ion beam toward a Simulin battlecruiser.

"Use our defensive batteries to take those spheres out!"

"Order has been sent," replied Darst.

-

"They're firing upon the Defense Globes," reported Captain Reynolds as nearly a dozen of them suddenly vanished from his sensor screen.

"The *Starlight* and the *Nova* have just about cleared the asteroid field," added Commander Grissim as the large viewscreen suddenly shifted to show the three ships. The two Alton ships had somehow anchored themselves to the hull of the Originator ship and were using their subspace drives to move the vessel.

Kathryn felt the *Distant Horizon* shake violently and several red lights appeared on the damage control console. She looked over at Colonel Leon inquiringly.

"Only slight damage to the hull in sector seventeen," she reported. "All compartments are still airtight."

"Firing ion beam," said Major Weir. The *Distant Horizon* had the largest ion beam and it could easily create a hole in a Simulin screen.

"Firing antimatter missile," added Clarissa as she used her abilities to guide the sublight missile through the small hole the ion beam had created in a Simulin battlecruiser's energy screen."

"Target is down," confirmed Captain Reynolds.

"What is that?" Darst uttered in shock. Upon the ship's main viewscreen, a monstrous ship was emerging from the system's asteroid field. Two other ships were anchored to it using their sublight drives to move the ship away from the asteroids.

High Commander Lantu gazed at the apparition on the screen in disbelief. For the first time in his long career, he felt actual fear. "Run that ship against the database in the battle computer and see if it can identify it." Lantu had a strong feeling it would not be able to.

Darst did as ordered and after a moment turned back toward the High Commander. "There is no such ship in our records."

Lantu took a deep breath. He had a horrifying suspicion who that ship belonged to. "Run a scan of the hull material of the vessel and compare it to the material that comprises the Great Sphere."

Darst's face turned pale at the order but did as instructed. The results came back quickly and he turned toward High Commander Lantu. His voice quivered as he gave the answer. "They're the same."

"Then that's a ship of the builders of the Great Spheres," Lantu said, his eyes growing wide with concern. "We can't let them escape with that vessel."

"It's out of our weapons range," reported Darst.

"They're accelerating," added the sensor operator. "Detecting a massive energy spike."

"They're opening up a hyperspace vortex," warned Darst.

On the viewscreen, the three ships suddenly moved forward and entered a massive spinning vortex. Moments later, the vortex collapsed and the ships were gone.

Lantu knew if that monster ship was allowed to escape, it could mean the end of Simulin dominance in this galaxy. If the AIs and their allies from the Fitula Nebula succeeded in unlocking the science that ship contained, it could spell disaster.

"Track those ships!" he ordered. "We must not let them escape!"

"Long-range sensors are useless," the sensor operator reported. "They're being jammed."

Lantu's shoulders drooped as he realized what that meant. Unless he could end this battle quickly, the ancient ship would be out of his reach. "Order all ships to close with the enemy. We must eliminate them!"

In space, the battle intensified. Half of the Defense Globes had been eliminated and the others were under heavy attack. The Simulins were concentrating their powerful energy beams on just a few of the AI warspheres, attempting to bring down their shields so they could be destroyed by antimatter missiles.

Warsphere-016 was being subjected to a heavy onslaught of Simulin beams and its energy shield was under extreme stress. Suddenly a brief hole appeared in the screen and four Simulin energy beams slammed into the hull, blasting deep craters into the armor of the ship. Flaming debris was ejected from the wreckage as secondary explosions shook the warsphere. The energy screen flickered and then failed completely. Moments later a Simulin antimatter missile changed the one-thousand-meter ship into glowing plasma.

"Warsphere-016 is down," reported Captain Reynolds as the green icon vanished from his sensor screen.

"How many Defense Globes are left?" demanded Kathryn as the lights in the Command Center flickered.

"Twenty-eight," Clarissa answered.

Kathryn turned toward the AI. "Clarissa, I want those surviving Defense Globes to each target a Simulin battlecruiser. Use their ion beams to blast a hole in the Simulin energy screens and then ram."

"I assume you want to overload their reactors when they ram?" asked Clarissa as she took over command of the Defense Globes and sent them on their way. She sent the globes weaving in a complicated pattern to increase the likelihood of their survival.

"Yes," answered Kathryn. "I want to blow the hell out of those Simulins!"

"Globes are nearing the Simulin ships," reported Captain Reynolds as he watched the progress of the globes on his sensors. "Twenty-two globes inbound. Simulins are targeting them heavily with their defensive weapons."

"Fifteen globes inbound," Reynolds reported a few seconds later. "Impact with Simulin energy screens in eight seconds."

"Ion beams firing," Clarissa said, as she tried every trick she knew of to get as many of the deadly globes to their targets as possible.

"Eight globes inbound," reported Reynolds. "Detonation!"

On the main viewscreen, which had been switched to show the approaching Simulin formation eight brilliant balls of light suddenly grew and then slowly faded away.

"Seven targets destroyed," Captain Reynolds reported. "The eighth globe detonated against an energy shield."

-

In space, the two opposing fleets were now at pointblank range from each other. In the Simulin formation multiple energy beams from six AI warspheres struck two Simulin battlecruisers, tearing through their energy shields and opening up numerous compartments to space. Antimatter missiles arrived and the two Simulin ships were turned into small suns.

The Simulins in turn were targeting the AI ships as they deemed them the biggest danger due to the multiple particle beams they were able to fire and the ion beams. Another AI ship found itself under heavy attack as the entire Simulin fleet fired their energy weapons in mass upon the hapless vessel. The screen was instantly overwhelmed and the warsphere was blown apart in a violent explosion.

"Warsphere-004 is down," reported Captain Reynolds in an even voice.

"We need to leave," Commander Grissim said between clinched lips as the *Distant Horizon* vibrated from energy beams hitting the ship's shield.

Kathryn nodded. "Short jump to Ornellia."

"Ornellia?" asked Captain Grissim with a confused look.

"Yes," Kathryn responded. "The Simulins will be through with their attack upon the planet. "We'll jump there and then plan our next move."

"Lieutenant Strong, plot a jump to Ornellia," Grissim ordered. "I want to be able to leave this system in two minutes!"

"Plotting," Kelsey answered as she quickly brought up the hyperspace equations as well as Ornellia's spatial coordinates.

The battle continued with both sides taking damage and then suddenly the AI warspheres and the human ships turned away from the battle and accelerated away. Moments later, numerous spatial vortexes formed and the ships quickly entered them to vanish from the system.

"They're gone!" Darst reported, his face showing intense aggravation at the enemy fleeing the battle.

"Can we track them?" Demanded High Commander Lantu.

Darst studied a computer screen for a moment and then turned back toward the High Commander. "They're going off in the direction of Ornellia, but the battle computer says this is but a feint to draw us away from the course the other three ships took."

Lantu nodded his agreement of that assessment. "Plot the most likely course of the three ships they're trying to protect. We won't be fooled by this trick. Finding that ship of the builders of the Great Spheres is our highest priority. I want hyperspace messages sent out to all battle groups as to what we found here. Ships need to be sent out along the line of flight the three ships have taken. They must be heading back to the Fitula Nebula. We can't let them get there!"

The *Distant Horizon* exited hyperspace in the Ornellian System followed closely by the rest of her fleet. Fifteen AI warspheres, two Federation battleships, and one Federation battlecarrier appeared in the system as the spatial vortexes they had exited vanished.

"Report," ordered Kathryn as she breathed a sigh of relief. The long-range sensors were showing no Simulin ships in the Ornellian System and only a few at extreme range, nearly ten light-years distant.

"Picking up a lot of debris around Ornellia," Captain Reynolds replied as his hands moved across his screens touching various icons. "There are no ships in the system, either Ornellian or Simulin. The defensive grid around the planet has been destroyed as well as the shipyards and research stations."

"All communication frequencies are quiet," added Captain Travers.

"Are we going in to Ornellia?" asked Colonel Leon. Petra was hesitant to see the devastation she knew the Simulins had probably done to the planet.

"Yes," said Kathryn, taking in a deep breath. "We owe it to the Ornellians to see if anyone survived on their capital world."

"Picking up elevated radiation levels across the planet," Clarissa reported. "If there are survivors, they'll be scattered and probably in deep shelters."

Commander Grissim approached the admiral. "What about Admiral Bachal and the Originator ship? The Simulins are bound to be searching for them."

Kathryn nodded. "We set up three potential rendezvous points. Clarissa, contact TAD and inform the command AI to send its ten least damaged ships to the first rendezvous point. I'll feel better if that Originator ship has a more powerful escort. Also, set up an additional rendezvous point for us to meet them before they enter the nebula shielding Gaia. Let's meet three hundred light-years away from Gaia to be on the safe side. We might have a very large reception committee waiting for us when we get back home."

"You think the Simulins will gather their forces outside the nebula?" asked Grissim.

"Yes," Kathryn answered, her eyes focused on her second in command. "It's what I would do. Once we're inside the nebula, the Simulins can't reach us. They'll do everything they can to try to capture that Originator ship."

It took a few minutes for the AIs to separate their ships into two separate fleets. Once it was done, the ten selected warspheres accelerated and entered swirling white spatial vortexes and vanished from the Ornellian System. TAD sent Clarissa a final message promising to be at the rendezvous location with the Altons and the Originator ship.

"Take us to Ornellia," Kathryn ordered. It was time to see what the Simulins had done to the planet.

An hour later, a silent command crew stared aghast at the large viewscreen in the front of the Command Center at the devastation done to the Ornellian home world. Every city with a population in excess of ten thousand had been nuked. In addition, large numbers of Conqueror Drones were moving about on the surface. The planet's atmosphere was darker from the dust and ashes from the nuclear strikes. In some areas, nuclear winter had already set in.

It was hard for Kathryn to contain her anger knowing billions of Ornellians on this world and upon their colonies had been ruthlessly exterminated. "Are there any signs of survivors?"

"We're picking up some scattered fighting in some of the mountainous areas," confirmed Clarissa. She was using the ship's short-range sensors to carefully scan the surface of the planet.

Kathryn activated her ship-to-ship comm. She wanted to speak to the battlecarrier *Ardent*. "Commander Jackson, I want you to scramble all of your fighters and bombers. Have them armed for surface strikes against Conqueror Drones. We will be launching our fighters and bombers as well. Our first strikes will target the mountainous regions where there is a greater likelihood of survivors."

Major Weir walked over to stand close to the admiral. "We could use our defensive railgun batteries to take out some of the drones," he suggested. "I would need Clarissa's help as the target areas will be very small."

"Clarissa?" asked Kathryn, looking over toward the AI.

"I can do it," the AI replied. "You should warn our fighter and bomber pilots that some of these drones may have surface-to-air missiles. These are probably the Simulins' more modern drones and could pose a danger."

"I'll pass the warning on," Kathryn replied.

-

Down inside a small bunker complex on Ornellia, Dax Matol gazed in sadness at the viewscreens, which showed the battle going on above him. The small bunker complex he was in charge of sheltered 607 Ornellians, most of them young families. On the surface, his last sixty soldiers fought a losing battle against the horde of Conqueror Drones that had recently descended upon them.

"It won't be much longer now," his second in command spoke in a soft voice. "We're running low on ammunition."

On one of the viewscreens, four Conqueror Drones had pushed into the collapsing defenses. One of them grabbed an Ornellian soldier and promptly used its large pinchers to tear him in two. Dax grimaced at the gruesome scene and turned his eyes away. "I've set up the last of our heavy explosives throughout the complex. Once the drones penetrate into the first bunker, I'll set them off. Our young people will not face the drones!"

"I have contacts descending from space!" the Control Center's sensor operator suddenly reported. "I think they're human!"

-

Captain Lacy Sanders was in her Talon fighter leading her squadron of ten against the Conqueror Drones besieging the meager defenders below.

"This is Echo One flight leader, stay away from the Ornellian defensive line and try to take out the Conqueror Drones moving up to attack."

"Let's go fry some crabs," said Lieutenant Ronald Stehr in Echo Two.

"Crab legs for supper tonight!" proclaimed Cindy Maherst in Echo Three.

"Might be a little tough to chew," responded Clancy Borsht in Echo Six.

Captain Sanders allowed herself to smile. She had a well-trained squadron and it was time to put that training to the test. "All Echoes, engage." With those orders, Lacy pushed her flight control forward and the deadly fighter dove toward the ground and the waiting drones.

In the Control Center of the bunker complex, Dax watched spellbound as the human fighters suddenly dove toward the surface and began firing explosive rounds at the incoming Conqueror Drones. Small explosions carpeted the forest floor, blowing the advancing drones apart. Flames and dark smoke rose above the treetops, blotting out the sun.

"Quick," Dax said, wanting to take advantage of the human help. "Order our soldiers to pull back into the outer bunker. That will give the humans a clear field of fire!"

The order was quickly given and on the viewscreens, the surviving Ornellian soldiers turned and bolted toward the concealed entrance to the bunker.

Up above, a squadron of six Anlon bombers saw the Ornellians sudden withdrawal. Without hesitation, the flight leader ordered his bombers in to unload their heavier munitions. Moments later, the forest floor and the slopes around the hidden underground bunkers erupted in towering explosions, annihilating most of the remaining Conqueror Drones. As the bombers pulled away, the Talons moved in to ensure not a single Conqueror Drone escaped.

Across the entire planet, 180 Talon fighters and 120 Anlon bombers were busy annihilating every Conqueror Drone they could find. From the orbiting human warships railgun rounds rained down on any group of Conqueror Drones that could be detected by the ships' sensors.

For hours, the squadrons attacked the multitudes of Conqueror Drones on the surface. During that time contact was made with a number of deep underground bunkers on the planet still in hiding from the drones.

After speaking to the leaders of the complexes, Admiral Barnes sent shuttles down carrying supplies as well as weapons. She knew there was little else she could do. Areas around bunker complexes were cleared of drones to allow them to scavenge for other supplies and to prepare for a long period of time underground. Kathryn stressed the importance to the commanders of the bunkers of staying hidden lest the Conqueror Drones learn their location. She also informed them that once the fleet left the Simulins would probably return and land more drones.

"There doesn't seem to be a lot of Simulin ships on the long-range sensors," commented Commander Grissim. Anne had been expecting to see an inbound Simulin fleet at any moment.

"I suspect they're off chasing our other ships," Kathryn answered. "We need to begin winding up our ground operations. Another hour and I want us to be on our way."

"I estimate we've eliminated 64 percent of the Conqueror Drones on the surface of Ornellia," Clarissa announced. "Between our Talon fighters, Anlon bombers, and railgun rounds our attack has been overwhelmingly successful."

Kathryn leaned back in her command chair with a deep sigh of regret. She wished there was more she could do for the Ornellians. She knew the likelihood of their long-term survival wasn't great. The Conqueror Drones were very good at seeking out survivors and eliminating them. Perhaps someday she would return to Ornellia with a fleet to free the planet and see if anyone had survived this apocalypse. However, that was far in the future. Now she needed to leave the system and meet up with the Originator ship. That ship might hold the key to all of their futures.

Chapter Thirteen

Admiral Race Tolsen sat in his command chair feeling impatient. They were in orbit around a small airless moon in the Zatel System. Kelnor Mard and Reesa Jast had taken the exploration cutter down to the surface to explore some relatively intact ruins. The cutter had been down on the surface for nearly two hours, and the two scientists had not reported any of their findings. Race was growing concerned and was wondering if he should send more marines down to check on the situation. What if the Simulins had already been here and there were Conqueror Drones inside the complex?

Major Drake Nolan was in the Command Center speaking with Major Jonathan Daniels, the tactical officer. "Captain Abrams is reporting they lost communications with the exploration team nearly an hour ago."

"It may be some type of interference from the materials the Originators used to construct this place," suggested Daniels. "Our scans can't penetrate the surface. We're not sure what's down below or how deep beneath the surface the Originators built."

"I think I can answer that," Captain Davis responded from his sensor console. "While it's true our scans can't penetrate the material the Originators used in their buildings, we can penetrate where it's not. From the results of my last sensor scans, the Originator complex is quite extensive beneath the surface of the moon."

Race gazed at the viewscreen, which covered the front wall of the Command Center. It showed a desolate surface with numerous asteroid impact craters. The complex the two Altons scientists had entered was near a small range of mountains, which towered up above the cratered surface of the small moon.

"Major Nolan, inform Captain Abrams that if she hasn't heard from the exploration team in another thirty minutes, she's to lead a team to find them and report back. Also, have another squad of marines standing by in the Alpha flight bay ready to be deployed if needed."

"Yes, Admiral," Nolan replied. It wouldn't take long to have a shuttle prepped and a squad ready to go.

"Altons and their interest in science," muttered Madelyn Arnett with a frown on her face. "Sometimes they get so wrapped up in their explorations they forget to follow even simple communication protocols."

"That may be true, but the marines with them shouldn't have," Race responded evenly. He knew as well as everyone else how Altons loved to do research, and the draw of this underground complex and the mysteries it might contain may have proven too captivating for the two Alton scientists causing them to take some unnecessary risks.

"Sensors are still clear," Captain Davis commented. "No sign of any ships within sixteen light-years."

This was a relief to Race. So far, Simulin ships had been reassuringly absent. "Remind the captain to be careful. While we didn't detect any signs of any recent landings, that doesn't mean there aren't a few Conqueror Drones lurking in those underground passages."

"Message sent," replied Major Nolan. "I'm sure my marines are taking all the necessary precautions. The shuttle and the support squad will be ready in ten minutes."

One thing Nolan had done on this mission was to ensure all the marines who had gone down to the surface of the moon had armor piercing rounds as well as the more powerful explosive rounds. Both had been designed specifically to take out a Conqueror Drone. If it was necessary to send down another squad, they would be equipped in the same way.

-

Captain Lindsey Abrams frowned in frustration. It had been thirty minutes since she had received orders from Major Nolan to go out and search for the exploration team if they didn't make contact.

"Corporal Haggard, is your team ready to disembark?" asked Captain Abrams as she checked her Alton environmental suit.

"Yes, Captain," answered Haggard.

Lindsey looked at the corporal and the two privates behind him. "We need to go out and find out why the exploration team has missed their comm checks."

The two privates looked uneasily at one another.

"Do you think they're Conqueror Drones in that complex?" asked Private Sandra Carton as she checked to make sure she had armor piercing rounds in her assault rifle.

"I doubt it," Lindsey replied as she picked up her own rifle and slammed a clip of armor piercing rounds in place. "More than likely the material the complex is built from is interfering with communications. We'll go in, find the team, and then report back to the *WarHawk*."

Going to the airlock, Lindsey led her marines down the ramp and toward the entrance to the Originator complex. Behind her, the airlock hatch slid silently shut. She had left four other marines on board for security. In addition, the twenty members of the ship's crew were on watch. Even the cutter's laser turrets were activated in case they were needed. Lindsey hoped she was right and the exploration team wasn't in trouble.

-

Kelnor Mard led the exploration team deeper into the mysterious complex. He wasn't sure but he felt they had descended a good two thousand meters. In a sealed off room near the surface, Reesa had stumbled across a map which seemed to indicate there was an intact computer center at the bottom of the complex. It was one of the few rooms they had managed to open.

"How much farther?" asked Sergeant Brenda Wilde.

She wasn't happy about being out of contact with the exploration cutter and Captain Abrams. However, she couldn't leave the two Alton scientists and she was hesitant to send any of her squad of marines back to report in. She felt there was safety in numbers and had decided to keep everyone together.

"Not much more," Kelnor answered as he paused to catch his breath. There was obviously some type of power system in operation as the gravity had gradually increased the deeper into the complex they descended. Their instruments were even showing an atmosphere though it was too thin to breathe.

Sergeant Wilde looked around her in the lights from her suit. Each of the environmental suits had two bright lights, which they were using to light their way. Besides the two Alton scientists there were four research assistants, who were carrying much of the scientific gear, as well as five other marines. "Let's take five and then we'll move on. Kelnor, if we don't find anything in the next half hour, I'm going to insist we turn back."

"We're almost there," responded the Alton scientist, turning to face Sergeant Wilde. "Ten more minutes at the most."

"We've come so far," Reesa added. "We can't turn back now!"

Corporal Metz walked over to stand next to the sergeant, his assault rifle cradled in his arms. "They're probably already hunting for us," he commented.

"We left markers for them to follow," Wilde replied.

With a deep sigh, Brenda knew when she got back to the cutter she was going to get an ass chewing for being out of contact for so long. When they first discovered their comms didn't work inside the complex, she should have sent a marine back to the captain to ask for instructions.

After five minutes she indicated for Kelnor to lead the way again. They were going down a corridor and occasionally they would find wide steps that led farther down. From the size of the steps, Lindsey thought the Originators must have been very tall, taller than the Altons. Even the ceilings of the corridors were far above their heads.

As they continued to walk through the corridors, they came across numerous rooms, all of which were sealed from entry. Several times they stopped and tried to force the doors open, but they refused to budge.

At last, Kelnor came to a stop before what appeared to be a metal hatch. The metal of the hatch seemed to reflect a dim glow from their suit lights. Kelnor stopped and looked back at the sergeant. "This is it," he announced.

Brenda stepped forward and examined the hatch, not seeing any way to open it. "How do we get in?"

"Hopefully with this," Reesa said, reaching into the pocket of her suit and pulling out a small round globe slightly smaller than her fist. "I brought this from Albania. It's one of the few artifacts discovered when these worlds were first explored."

"What is it?" asked Brenda, looking questioningly at the small globe. It was copper colored and its surface was perfectly smooth.

"We think it's a key," Kelnor explained as he took the small globe and inserted it into a circular depression next to the hatch.

For a moment nothing happened and then the globe began to glow. A grinding noise came from the hatch and it slowly slid open. Through the open hatch bright lights began to come on, revealing what looked like a control room.

"It's intact!" exclaimed Reesa, her eyes filling with excitement. "In all of the exploration reports at Astral there's no mention of any of the exploration teams finding something like this."

Kelnor began to step inside when Sergeant Wilde stopped him. "What happens if the hatch shuts?"

"We'll leave one of our assistants out here and several of your marines. If the hatch shuts all they have to do is remove the key and insert it again."

Brenda nodded. They had come this far, they might as well see what was in the room. "Go on in, we'll follow."

Captain Lindsey Abrams was getting more aggravated the farther into the complex they descended. Sergeant Wilde should have known better than to go this far without attempting to reestablish communications.

"I think I can hear voices up ahead," Corporal Haggard said as they descended another flight of stairs.

Getting to the bottom Lindsey could see several marines about twenty meters farther down the corridor. It only took a few moments to reach them. She was surprised to see they were standing in front of a large hatch lit up by a light from within.

"Report!" she barked, striding up to the two marines.

"Captain," uttered Private Richard Trent, coming to attention. "We have found what appears to be the control room for this complex. Sergeant Wilde, the two Altons, and the others are inside."

"Corporal Haggard, I want you and Privates Mason and Carton to stay out here. I'm going inside to see just what the hell is going on!"

Lindsey stepped inside and came to a complete stop. The room she was in was full of equipment and what was more astonishing, it seemed to be working. "What's going on?" she demanded, seeing Sergeant Wilde standing next to the two Altons.

The sergeant turned around and saw Lindsey. "Captain, we've found the control room for this complex."

"I thought there were no functioning Originator artifacts," said Lindsey, stepping over closer to the two Altons. Her curiosity at what was around her was pushing her anger at Sergeant Wilde to the back of her mind for now. She would deal with the sergeant later.

"Not until now," Reesa said with a big smile. Even through her helmet, her look of excitement was obvious. "From what we can tell this control room has a self-repair system. This entire complex can be brought back to life if needed."

Lindsey shook her head in disbelief. "It's two million years old! How can anything that's been here that long still function?"

"Originator technology," Kelnor answered. "The Originators built things to last."

Lindsey looked around the large room seeing the Altons' assistants busy at several consoles. "What are they doing?"

"Downloading information," Kelnor explained. "We managed to access the complex's computer system."

"Do you understand what's being downloaded?"

Reesa shook her head in disappointment. "No, however, we have a translation program on the *WarHawk* we got from Astral. It's not complete, but we think given enough time we can decipher what we're downloading."

Lindsey paused, feeling confused. "If your people once came to this world, why didn't they mention this complex was intact?"

"That's a big question," admitted Kelnor as he examined some data flowing across a screen in front of him. He shook his head, as he didn't understand what he was seeing. "Perhaps they were afraid of what was here. From what we know of the exploration of this star cluster, all exploration expeditions were banned shortly after the report on this complex was filed."

"A mystery," said Lindsey, drawing in a deep breath. "How much longer until you're finished?"

"Twenty minutes," replied Kelnor. "Then we can return to the cutter and go back up to the *WarHawk* to download this data into the ship's computer and begin running it through the language program."

"Twenty minutes then, and no more," warned Lindsey. She turned to face Sergeant Wilde. "When we get back to the *WarHawk*, you and I are going to have a long conversation about exploration protocols."

"Yes, Captain," answered Sergeant Wilde, turning pale.

Lindsey stepped back so the Altons could finish up their work. At least there didn't appear to be any danger. However, there were reasons for protocols and failure to adhere to them could resort in serious repercussions. She just wanted Sergeant Wilde to understand that.

-

Admiral Race Tolsen was standing in one of the *WarHawk's* two large flight bays waiting for the exploration cutter to arrive. Next to him stood Major Nolan. This flight bay held two heavy shuttles, two small cargo shuttles, forty Talon fighters, and twenty Anlon bombers. The fighters and the bombers were anchored securely to the deck along the walls of the flight bay. At the far end were two large circular hatches behind which thirty Defense Globes resided. The other flight bay was set up very similarly. They had just been about to launch the shuttle with the squad of marines when the research team had emerged from the complex.

"Cutter is approaching," Commander Grissim reported over the mini-comm in Race's right ear.

"Captain Abrams seemed pretty excited about what they found in the Originator Complex," commented Nolan as he saw the large cutter enter the flight bay, passing through the atmospheric retention field.

Race nodded. He had spoken briefly with Kelnor Mard, and the Alton Originator expert had confirmed a significant discovery. Race was hopeful that perhaps they had found the secret as to where the Originators' Dyson Sphere was located, if the sphere actually existed. He was also a little concerned as half a dozen Simulin ships had been detected on the long-range sensors. Currently, the *WarHawk's* entire fleet was operating under stealth mode with the stealth energy shields up.

The exploration cutter set down in its docking berth and magnetic clamps rose up out of the deck to lock the ship securely in place. Moments later, the main airlock hatch opened and Captain Abrams as well as the two Alton scientists appeared. Seeing the admiral and the major, they descended the ramp and made their way over to the two officers.

"We found it!" exclaimed Reesa with an excited look in her eyes. Her thick white hair even looked a little disheveled.

"Found what?" asked Race, wanting to know what the Alton scientist was so excited about.

Reesa took a deep breath and then replied. "We found an intact computer core inside the complex. We managed to activate it and download most of its files."

"Two million years and it still worked?" said Major Nolan with disbelief in his eyes. "How is that possible?"

Kelnor looked at the major and said. "The Originators used building materials far in advance of anything we have. Also, keep in mind this complex is on an airless moon. Most of the complex was in a vacuum, which protected it from deteriorating. There is also a good possibility that even the sections we accessed where there was an atmosphere only had one because the complex detected our presence. Most likely the complex has an automatic self-repair system that has kept its essential systems operating over all of these years."

"So, what is in the files?" Race asked, his curiosity growing.

"We don't know," Reesa confessed with disappointment showing on her face.

"We need to run the files through an Originator language program we brought with us," Kelnor said, showing patience. He had learned over years of research that some things couldn't be rushed unlike Reesa, who was much younger and tended to rush into things.

"How long will that take?" asked Race. He didn't like staying in one system too long. Every hour they stayed here increased the likelihood of the Simulins stumbling across his fleet.

Kelnor let out a deep sigh. "A few more days. It will take that long for the language program to decrypt the files. The program only contains an estimated 9 percent of the Originator language."

This worried Race. He didn't want the Simulins to find this system, particularly with an intact Originator complex on the moon. He could destroy it with a Devastator Three or even with an antimatter missile though he hated destroying something that had survived for over two million years.

"I think it's best if we jump to another star system," he said after a moment. "If the Simulins find us here they may be just curious enough to do a search. We can't have them finding this complex."

"Excellent idea," said Kelnor, nodding his head in agreement. "I want to go to the Command Center and begin uploading the files into the ship's computer."

"Let's do it then," Race said, turning and motioning for the two Alton scientists to follow him.

Captain Lindsey Abrams stepped over closer to Major Nolan. "We had trouble maintaining communications once the research team went inside the complex," she informed him.

Nolan gazed at the captain for a long moment and then spoke. "Let's go to my office and we can discuss it, particularly since I imagine there'll be more of these research missions. I don't like the idea of not being able to communicate; too many things can go wrong in those types of situations."

"Yes, sir," Lindsey replied. "We need better protocols to handle these research missions. If we don't, then someone else is likely to be killed."

It was two days later and Admiral Race Tolsen was in his quarters sipping on a cup of coffee as he read the latest department reports. The *WarHawk* and the other ships of the fleet were performing within expectations and thus far had eluded detection by the Simulins. Engineering had fine-tuned the ship's power system until it was now running at optimum levels. Even the Altons, who had helped to design the ship's upgraded Fusion Five reactors, seemed impressed. Jalen Dothan was the ship's chief engineer as well as being an Alton and was highly qualified in reactor design. His assistant engineer was human and had been working overtime with several other technicians to increase the ship's power efficiency.

Race was interrupted from his thoughts by a knock on the hatch to his quarters. Putting the reports down, he got up and walked over to the hatch, opening it.

"Admiral," said Kelnor Mard respectfully. Reesa Jast stood just behind him with an excited look on her face. "Can we come in?"

"Certainly," responded Race, stepping to the side and gesturing for them to enter.

After the three of them sat down Race looked over at Kelnor. He suspected the reason the two Altons had come to see him was because they had news about their translation program.

Kelnor and Reesa were sitting on the sofa and Race was across from them. "How is the translation program doing?"

Reesa's face seemed to glow as she spoke. "It's done! We just finished going through some of the data. It's remarkable what was stored in that computer core."

"The Dyson Sphere?"

"It's real," confirmed Kelnor with a slight nod of his head. "However, sadly enough, that's not where the Originators went."

"Then where are they?" Race had assumed the Originators had evacuated all of their worlds to go and live inside the megastructure.

Kelnor sighed and leaned back closing his eyes briefly. "It seems the Originators were experimenting with a pathogen that would greatly enhance their life spans."

They were seeking immortality," explained Reesa, taking a deep breath.

"It did succeed in extending their lives, but it had some unintended side effects," Kelnor added. "Their birthrate rapidly began to decline and a strange illness appeared."

"Declining birthrates sounds like what happened to the Altons on Astral," commented Race, wanting to hear more.

"Yes, but this was much worse," Kelnor said with sorrow in his eyes. "The pathogen, over time, mutated until it became virulent. The first evidence something was wrong was the declining birthrate. Almost immediately after that, the Originators began to die. They could find no explanations for the deaths and examinations of the bodies failed to reveal any clues. It took them several years to learn the pathogen they had injected themselves with to give them longer life spans had changed their DNA on the molecular level. The change was very slight, but it was prone to sudden mutations, which normally led to death within two to three days."

Race looked intently at Kelnor, guessing where this was going. "Are you telling me they all died from this disease?"

"Yes," Kelnor admitted, his shoulders drooping. "It took years, but in the end they all perished. Before they did they destroyed all evidence of their advanced civilization to ensure no one else made the same mistake they did."

"What about the complex on the airless moon?"

"Their last redoubt," Reesa said. "A group of their scientists fled with their families to the moon in the hope of someday perfecting a cure. That day never happened."

"You once told me they had a population of three to four hundred billion," Race said, realizing the size of the calamity that had befallen the Originators. "How could they have made such a colossal mistake?"

"Arrogance," responded Kelnor. "The same type of arrogance which led my people to build the AIs so many years ago. They thought their science supreme and dared to challenge the natural order of things."

"We have our own life-extending drugs," Race said worriedly. "The same thing could happen to us."

"Ours are not like the Originators'," Reesa said. "The life-extending drugs used in the Federation and by my own people only slow down the aging process. They don't attempt to stop it."

Race reached over to the small table next to his chair and picked up his coffee cup. He took a long sip as he thought over what the two Altons had just told him. Setting the cup back down, he looked over at Kelnor. "Do you know where the Dyson Sphere is?"

Kelnor hesitated and then slowly nodded his head. "Yes; it's in this star cluster very close to Capal Four."

"Crap," muttered Race, shaking his head. "How close?"

"Four light-years," Reesa said softly.

That wasn't good as they suspected the majority of the Simulin ships in the star cluster were at Capal Four. "If we jump into the system where we suspect the Dyson Sphere is, the Simulins will probably detect us."

"That does pose a problem," admitted Kelnor, looking expectantly at Race. "What are we going to do?"

Race took a deep breath. He could only see one option. "We jump to Capal Four and destroy the Simulin ships."

Reesa turned pale at hearing this announcement. "Is there not any other way?"

Race shook his head. "Not unless we want to lead the Simulins to the Dyson Sphere."

Kelnor and Reesa looked at each other. Kelnor despised violence but understood that at times it was necessary. Reesa on the other hand was one of the Altons who had a disposition that didn't find violence so repulsive.

"We'll jump close to Capal Four and then send one of our ships in close to scan the system," Race explained. "Once we know what's waiting for us there we can make our battle plans."

"Then we're going to fight the Simulins," said Kelnor evenly.

"Yes," Race answered, his eyes focusing on the Alton. "We're going to fight the Simulins and either drive them out of this cluster or destroy them." Unfortunately, Race knew it wouldn't be that simple. War never was.

Chapter Fourteen

Admiral Race Tolsen stood in front of the large viewscreen in the battle dreadnought *WarHawk*. A yellow G-2 star beckoned in the center of the screen. Capal Four was twelve light-years away and for the moment held his attention.

"*Corvus* has jumped," confirmed Commander Madelyn Arnett as the dreadnought vanished from the tactical display.

"The ship should arrive at Capal Four in twenty-four minutes," reported Taalon Briez, the navigation officer.

Race nodded and walked back to his command chair and sat down. From their current position, they were only nine light-years away from where the Dyson Sphere supposedly resided. He had already focused the large viewscreen on that section of space. It had been disappointing as it revealed nothing, just darkness where a star should be. Even the long-range sensors failed to show anything at the coordinates.

"I've run some simulations on the movement of the nearby stars," Kelnor said as he stepped away from the ship's primary computer station. "They are moving in a pattern which confirms something of high mass at the indicated location."

Race tapped the fingers of his right hand against the armrest of his command chair as he considered Kelnor's words. "At least we know it's there."

Race was highly curious as to what they would find when it was finally safe to jump to the system. He could barely contain his excitement at the thought of exploring the Originator's Dyson Sphere, assuming they could find a way inside.

Colonel Brice Cowel breathed out a deep sigh. "How soon do we launch our attack?"

This brought Race's thoughts back to the task at hand; the Dyson Sphere would have to wait a little bit longer. The Simulins in the Capal Four System had to be dealt with first.

"As soon as the *Corvus* returns and we can find out what we're facing." Race knew for now they dared not approach the Dyson Sphere with the Simulins so close. If the Simulins were to discover the Dyson Sphere, it could spell disaster.

-

Commander Edison Smart was sitting in his command chair in the two-thousand-meter dreadnought *Corvus*. He was watching a counter on one of the tactical displays slowly counting down toward zero.

"What do we have on the long-range sensors?"

"Picking up Simulin warships," the sensor operator reported as he studied the data on one of his screens. "So far seventeen confirmed though there could be more in lower orbits around the planets in the system."

Commander Smart took a deep breath and considered his options. His mission was very simple; sneak into the Capal Four System and take scans of the Simulin ships. He was going to exit hyperspace on the fringe of the system next to the rocky asteroids and comets that orbited far out past the system's ten planets.

"The Simulins are bound to detect us coming in toward them," Colonel Jeffry Grayson, the executive officer, said uneasily. "They may be waiting for us."

"Perhaps," Commander Smart answered as he leaned back and folded his arms across his chest. "We're not staying long enough for them to respond. We're going to jump in, take some in depth sensor scans, and then jump back to the fleet."

Grayson heard the commander's words but questioned whether it would be that easy. Very seldom did anything go as planned.

A few minutes later, the *Corvus* dropped out of hyperspace and quickly activated her stealth energy shield. They had only been exposed to possible sensor scans for a scant few seconds, but the Simulins should have detected their inbound trajectory and were probably watching to see where they would appear.

Commander Smart turned toward the ship's sensor operator. "I want those sensor scans as quickly as possible; we don't dare stay long enough to allow the Simulins to respond to our hyperspace jump. There's a good possibility they detected an energy spike when we exited the spatial vortex. Keep an eye on those warships and let me know if they show any indication of preparing for a hyperspace jump."

"Scanning," the sensor operator replied as his hands flew over the control console in front of him. "It will take twelve minutes to get a complete scan of the system."

Edison nodded. "We'll stay at Condition One until further notice. Navigation, I want a jump plotted back to Admiral Tolsen. If the Simulins show up, we're leaving."

Several tense minutes passed as Commander Smart watched the nearby tactical display, which was constantly updating as new data came in from the sensors. So far, seven planets were showing as well as numerous moons and several minor asteroid fields. There were also fourteen Simulin ships appearing as red threat icons. As of yet there had been no reaction from the Simulin ships to the presence of the *Corvus*. Edison was starting to wonder if the Simulins had failed to detect the *Corvus's* approach.

"Final scans are coming in," reported the officer in front of the sensors.

On the tactical display, three more planets appeared, and one of them was surrounded by red threat icons. Edison took a moment to count them and then shook his head. There were eighteen Simulin ships around the planet. That meant a total of thirty-two enemy vessels were in the system.

Grayson was watching the nearer group of Simulin vessels when he saw several turn and begin accelerating toward the *Corvus*. "Commander, I think we've been spotted, or at least our hyperspace vortex was when we emerged."

"Do we have identifications on those ship types?" demanded Edison, looking intently at the sensor operator. He didn't want to go back to Admiral Tolsen without that vital piece of information.

"Yes, sir, there are ten battlecruisers and the rest are support cruisers. I'm also picking up energy spikes from several of the nearer Simulin vessels."

"Helm, get us out of here; take us into hyperspace immediately."

Moments later, the *Corvus* accelerated and entered a swirling blue-white vortex. Shortly afterward the vortex vanished, leaving no sign of ever being there or of the dreadnought.

White vortices formed and four Simulin escort cruisers burst forth. They scanned the area, but there was no sign of any vessel. On their long-range sensors, they could see a vessel in hyperspace leaving the area at a very high rate of speed. There was no point in pursuit as they wouldn't be able to catch it.

Commander Smart allowed himself to relax as it became clear the Simulins weren't going to follow them back to Admiral Tolsen. They had succeeded with their mission in finding out how many Simulin ships were in the Capal Four System. Now it was up to the admiral to find a way to destroy them.

—

Race was in his private office meeting with Commander Smart, Commander Arnett, and Kelnor Mard. They were discussing the sensor readings the *Corvus* had taken in the Capal Four System.

"The third and fifth planets both have Originator ruins on them," confirmed Kelnor as he studied a projection of the locations of the Simulin ships in the system. There was a small holographic table in the admiral's office and they were using it to display the ship locations.

Race walked slowly around the three-dimensional image, gazing thoughtfully at the Simulin ships. "Most of them seem to be around the third planet," he said after studying the hologram for a few moments.

"It was the Originator capital," explained Kelnor. "Or at least from the data Reesa brought back from Astral, we believe it was their capital. The ruins on that planet cover much of its surface, more so than any other world our people found in their early searches."

Commander Smart was also studying the holo display. "It may indeed be their capital, considering how close it is to where we think the Dyson Sphere is located."

"We have to destroy those ships!" uttered Race emphatically. "If we don't and they send word back to their galaxy of what we've discovered, we could face a massive invasion, particularly if they gain control of the sphere."

Kelnor had an impassive look upon his face. He disliked talking about war but knew in this situation there was no other choice. "This fleet was designed to be able to take out Simulin ships. I can assure you they have never faced vessels such as ours."

"Perhaps," Race responded, his eyes narrowing sharply. "Don't forget about the *Distant Horizon,* she was also very heavily armed. She's as strong as our own dreadnoughts and these Simulins may be aware of her capabilities."

"Our beam weapons are more powerful," Commander Arnett was quick to point out. "Our energy shields are also. We've made some advancements since Rear Admiral Barnes left on her mission."

Race walked back to his desk and sat down. "I don't want us taking anything for granted. Their largest concentration of ships is around the third planet. In all probability, they will detect our approach and be ready for battle. This could get ugly really quick. Don't forget their technology is at least on a par with our own."

"So what do we do?" asked Commander Smart, looking at the admiral. "Do we send word back to the Federation or the Altons that we need more ships?"

Folding his arms across his chest, Race shook his head. "I don't believe we can afford to wait. The Simulins are only four light-years away from the Dyson Sphere. We have to attack and attack now before they learn of it or accidently stumble across it."

After the meeting and once the others had left, Race stepped into his quarters and took a moment to rest. Here he was about to make one of the biggest decisions of his life and he had no way to notify his superiors of the actions he was preparing to take. Much like when he had destroyed the Simulin fleet at the galactic center, Race was taking a risk. If he failed, then in all likelihood the Simulins would discover the Dyson Sphere and bring war to the Federation and the galaxy. Race sat down and thought briefly about his family.

His sister, Massie, would never believe what he was about to do or even where he was. Just being within this star cluster inside Shari space was a tremendous risk. If the Shari found his fleet and discovered it was from the Federation, then war would be inevitable. It also brought up another question; why were there no Shari ships inside this cluster? They had detected Shari vessels outside the cluster but none since.

Race remained seated for several more minutes and then got up to fix himself a cup of coffee. Shortly he would be going to the Command Center and giving the order to set course for Capal Four and the Simulins. If they were successful in defeating the Simulins, then their next destination would be the Dyson Sphere. "Massie, you would never believe any of this," Race said aloud as he took a deep drink from his steaming cup. "I'm just glad you're back home where it's safe."

Finishing his cup of coffee, Race straightened his uniform and exited his quarters. It was time to find out just how powerful his fleet was.

Forty minutes later twenty-one blue-white spatial vortexes opened up in the Capal Four System spewing forth the massive vessels of war. The Simulins had detected the inbound fleet and hastily rearranged their ships into a defensive formation. There had been just enough warning to gather all of the ships in the system into one fleet. They were mystified as to what race this could be approaching so rapidly. However, they were confident their superior technology, particularly their weapons, would be able to deal with this impending threat.

The High Commander of the Simulin fleet gazed intently at his tactical screen as red threat icons began appearing. Twenty-one large icons were shown exiting hyperspace nearly in combat range of his fleet. On one of the Command Center's viewscreens a large cylindrically shaped ship appeared.

"What does the battle computer say of these vessels?" he asked, turning toward his second in command. They had detected a single hyperspace entry into the system hours earlier and even tracked the vessel as it approached the system and then left it at a high rate of speed.

"Alton," the Second Commander replied. "The ships most resemble those built by the Altons."

The High Commander was silent as he thought about what that might mean for the upcoming battle. The Altons were a very advanced race. Since coming to this galaxy, the Simulins had taken the time to learn what races might be the biggest threat to their goal of eventual conquest. They were not pleased to learn several very large galactic empires controlled most of this galaxy. It was also daunting to discover the Altons were an older race and highly advanced, perhaps as advanced as the Simulins themselves. It would take a huge commitment of Simulin forces to subdue and eliminate the organics of this galaxy. That was why it was crucial for them to find the Great Sphere. So far their searches of these old worlds had failed to shed any light on where the sphere might be.

"Why are they here?" asked the Second Commander.

The High Commander's eyes suddenly widened. "The Great Sphere; they must know of it! They have come here searching." He turned toward the Second Commander and spoke in a cold and harsh voice. "We must destroy this fleet; they cannot be allowed to find the Great Sphere. If they were to find the sphere our plans to conquer this galaxy could be met with failure."

"They shall be destroyed," responded the Second Commander. "There can be none but Simulin."

"None but Simulin," replied the High Commander.

Race was in the Command Center watching the tactical displays. He had formed his fleet into a disk formation facing the Simulins with the *WarHawk* at the center. The Simulins were in a defensive globe formation and slowly moving away from the planet to give them room to maneuver if needed.

"Weapons are ready to fire," reported Major Daniels from Tactical.

"All ships are at Condition One," added Commander Arnett. She was using her mini-comm set on ship-to-ship to communicate with the rest of the fleet.

"Four minutes to combat range," reported Captain Davis from Sensors.

Race took a deep, steadying breath. He always felt apprehensive when going into battle. "I want all weapons to fire as soon as we're within range. Also, launch all of our Defense Globes as well as those of the rest of the fleet." The *WarHawk* had sixty of the small ion beam globes and the other dreadnoughts had thirty each. If he could use the globes' ion beams to knock holes in the Simulins' energy shields, he might just be able to win this battle with minimal losses. It was a tactic the Simulins wouldn't be expecting.

The two fleets continued to close, Admiral Tolsen's fleet in its disk formation and the Simulins in a globe. The Simulins had their ten battlecruisers at the heart of their formation with the escort cruisers surrounding them.

As soon as the two fleets reached engagement range, the two fleets began exchanging weapons fire. From each ship in Tolsen's fleet small, ten-meter globes began launching. As soon as the globes left the flight bays, they activated their energy shields and accelerated toward the Simulin formation.

"Defense Globes are away," reported Major Daniels. "Their energy shields are activated and their ion beams are powering up."

The *WarHawk* shook slightly as several Simulin energy beams struck her powerful shield but failed to penetrate.

"Shield is holding at 92 percent," reported Colonel Cowel.

"Firing particle beam cannons and power beams." Major Daniels was directing the firing of the weapons from his tactical station. Eleven weapon techs sat in front of consoles that controlled the various weapons the *WarHawk* was equipped with. The battle dreadnought was the most powerful ship ever built by the Federation or the Altons.

Race turned his attention to the large viewscreen lit up from weapons fire. White energy beams, violet power beams, and the more deadly bright blue particle beams were evident as they flashed across space seeking targets.

On the screen, a Simulin eleven-hundred-meter escort cruiser had been bracketed by a number of power beams as well as particle beams. Its energy shield flared up into the ultraviolet and then collapsed, leaving its hull unprotected. Power beams drilled into the hull, blasting out huge chasms and particle beams tore deep into the ship, wreaking havoc with the interior systems. The ship suddenly shook violently and then exploded as its power systems were compromised.

"Simulin escort cruiser is down," reported Captain Davis evenly.

"The *Falcon* is under heavy attack," warned Commander Arnett. "Commander Braes is reporting his energy shield is down to 40 percent and the ship has sustained some minor damage." Commander Setol Braes was an Alton and a very shrewd tactician.

"Move the *Corvus* and the *Jaden* closer to her to help give her support," ordered Race.

The large viewscreen suddenly shifted to show the *Falcon*. The two-thousand-meter dreadnought was being attacked by a number of Simulin ships and her shield was glowing brightly from the massive onslaught of numerous energy beams. Even as Race watched one of the beams penetrated, blowing a massive hole in the side of the dreadnought. The ship seemed to shudder and her shield flickered. Two more energy beams penetrated, blasting large sections of armor off the ship to send them drifting off into space. The screen suddenly filled with light as a Simulin antimatter missile penetrated the weakened screen and detonated inside the damaged area. When the screen cleared, there was nothing left of the *Falcon* other than a mangled mass of molten metal and wisps of glowing gas.

"*Falcon* is down," reported Captain Davis in a shaken voice.

"Defense Globes are in firing range," reported Major Daniels.

Race shifted his gaze back to one of the tactical displays, which showed the six hundred and sixty small ten-meter globes rapidly closing with the compacted Simulin fleet formation. Even as he watched, they began to vanish as Simulin defensive fire started to destroy them.

"Fire the beams," Race ordered grimly. He was feeling pain at the loss of the several thousand Humans and Altons on the *Falcon*. "I want the ion beams followed up with a full spread of antimatter missiles from every ship in the fleet. I want this battle over with and I want it over with now!"

"Yes, sir," replied Major Daniels as he moved to comply with the order.

In space, the Simulins were attacking with their powerful energy beams and swarms of antimatter missiles. They had already managed to overload the energy shield of one of the approaching ships and now they were turning their fury toward another.

-

The High Commander in the Simulin flagship grimaced as his ship shook violently and the safety harness holding him in place bit tightly into his skin.

"Their shields are very powerful," reported the Second Commander. "Perhaps more powerful than our own. It's taking multiple energy beams and antimatter missiles to penetrate."

"What of those small globes that are approaching?"

The Second Commander paused as he checked with the ship's battle computer. His face paled as he turned back toward the High Commander. "The globes are armed with an ion beam that is capable of penetrating our shields. The battle computer says we must destroy them before they fire on us!"

"Too late!" called out the Simulin at the sensor console. "They're firing."

The High Commander looked at the ship's main viewscreen; hundreds of strange beams were being directed toward his ships. "Destroy the globes!" he ordered, his voice filled with anger. "Hit them with our antimatter missiles!"

-

The six hundred and twelve remaining Defense Globes fired simultaneously, targeting all the Simulin escort cruisers. The Alton built dreadnoughts and the battle dreadnought *WarHawk* followed up the ion beam strike with a massive barrage of one hundred-megaton sublight antimatter missiles. The ion beams struck the shields, tearing four-meter holes in the protective barriers. Many of the inbound missiles impacted where the screens were undamaged, but so many missiles had been fired that others flashed through the small holes, striking the vulnerable armored hulls of the eleven-hundred-meter ships.

Across the Simulin defensive formation, deadly antimatter energy was released, disintegrating armored hulls, interiors, and Simulins. The ion beam and antimatter strikes were so massive there was little the Simulins could do in defense. Escort cruiser after escort cruiser was torn or blasted apart. When the Defense Globes stopped firing, all the Simulin escort cruisers were battered wrecks or in most cases drifting and glowing debris.

-

The Simulin High Commander gazed at the viewscreens in his Command Center in shock. Never in his long life had he seen Simulin ships destroyed so easily. For the first time in his career, he knew fear. Fear of the unknown and what these ships might mean to the Simulin conquest of this galaxy. If there were many more where these came from, this galaxy might pose a threat to the Simulin Empire itself.

"All battlecruisers are to continue to fire; we can still destroy these organics." The High Commander knew it was his duty as a Simulin to inflict as much damage as possible on this fleet, even if it meant risking his last remaining vessels.

The Second Commander passed on the order, recognizing the fact these organics were a serious threat. "What if they find the Great Sphere?" he asked as he turned back toward the High Commander. "What will become of us if they learn the Old Ones' science?"

"Then our empire will die," answered the High Commander coldly. "We are Simulin and we will do our duty. Death to the organics for there can be none but Simulin."

"None but Simulin," answered the Second Commander though he was no longer quite so certain.

—

"All the Simulin escort cruisers are down," Captain Davis reported in a subdued voice as he gazed at the destruction caused by the Defense Globes and the antimatter strike. The Simulin defensive formation was full of drifting wreckage. "The Simulins are still targeting the Defense Globes."

"The *Yellen* is under heavy attack," reported Commander Arnett. "Her energy shield is down to 30 percent and she's taking substantial damage."

"Move the *Raven* and *Starling* in front of her to take some of the beams while her shield regenerates," ordered Race. On the ship's main viewscreen, numerous small explosions of white light marked his dying Defense Globes. "Prepare for a second ion beam strike targeting the remaining Simulin ships."

"Setting it up," responded Major Daniels as he swiftly passed on the orders to his tactical team.

The *WarHawk* suddenly shook violently and alarms began sounding. On the damage control board, several lights turned a glaring red.

"Energy beam strike to cargo hold twelve," Colonel Cowel reported. "Only a fraction of the energy penetrated the screen, but it was enough to cause some damage. The hold is open to space and I'm sealing off the outside corridor."

Race looked intently at the colonel. "Casualties?"

"Six," Cowel replied. "There may be others."

"Admiral, the *Yellen* has just been struck by an antimatter missile!" called out Commander Arnett, her face turning pale.

"Her energy screen?" asked Race as the main viewscreen shifted to show the stricken dreadnought.

"No," Cowel answered with a deep sigh. "The missile penetrated her screen and detonated against the hull. I have contact with Engineering; they're reporting heavy damage and their shield is down to 5 percent. They have no contact with the ship's Command Center."

"Major Daniels, launch that strike now!"

"Launching," Daniels answered as his team sent orders to the other ships of the fleet as well as the Defense Globes.

-

In space, the four hundred and twelve surviving Defense Globes fired their ion cannons at the ten Simulin battlecruisers. At the same time, the remaining dreadnoughts and the *WarHawk* launched full spreads of antimatter missiles aimed at the areas on the Simulin energy screens where the ion beams were impacting. Over five hundred one hundred-megaton missiles slammed into the energy screens of ten seventeen-hundred-meter Simulin battlecruisers. On one battlecruiser, a missile detonated on the bow, blowing apart all six of the huge energy weapon spires. On other battlecruisers, the interiors were turned into molten metal and glowing gas. The heart of the Simulin formation looked as if a small nova had gone off.

-

The Simulin High Commander gasped for air as his ship was pummeled by forces he had never expected to face. On the damage control console, most of the lights had turned red and alarms were sounding. The Command Center was filling full of smoke from shorted out control consoles. The air was becoming difficult to breathe.

The Second Commander turned around and announced in a grim voice. "We've lost Engineering, our subspace drive has been destroyed, and the hyperdrive is not responding. We've lost communications with most areas of the ship."

"The rest of the fleet?"

"Gone," answered the sensor operator.

The High Commander took a deep breath. His eyes were beginning to burn from the smoke. He wasn't afraid to die. What concerned him was the fact that he had no way to send a warning back to Simulin space.

"Energy shield is down," reported the Second Commander in a detached voice.

The High Commander nodded. He didn't reply. Death was part of a Simulin's duty to the empire. The High Commander closed his eyes and took a deep breath. There was nothing more he could do.

The *WarHawk* fired two antimatter missiles at the last surviving Simulin battlecruiser, turning it into a miniature sun.

Captain Davis turned toward the admiral. "Last Simulin battlecruiser is down."

"Admiral, the chief engineer for the *Yellen* is requesting assistance. He has emergency power restored; however, many areas of the ship are open to space. He fears they lost the biggest part of the crew."

Race gazed at the large viewscreen showing the heavily damaged dreadnought. The ship's hull was torn open in numerous areas from energy beam strikes. A good three hundred meters of the bow was nothing more than mangled metal where the antimatter missile had struck. Other areas of the hull looked burned with deep chasms where explosions had gone off. A fiery glow was coming from some parts of the ship indicating out of control fires still burning inside. It was obvious the ship couldn't be repaired with the resources they had at hand.

"Have the *Raven* and *Starling* begin evacuating the survivors. I want that ship searched from bow to stern to make sure we leave no one behind." Race knew a lot of people, both human and Alton had just died on that ship.

"It could have been worse," Commander Arnett said in a measured voice. "We were lucky. The Simulins didn't expect to face the ion beams the Defense Globes are equipped with."

Leaning back in his command chair, Race gazed about the Command Center. The tension and the anxiety in the room were rapidly dwindling as the battle was over. "Major Daniels, land the remaining Defense Globes. Send out a few Talons to check the debris to see if they can spot anything useful. If they do we can send out some of our smaller shuttles to bring the wreckage into one of our landing bays."

"How soon before we set out for the Dyson Sphere?" asked Kelnor, who had remained silent during the battle. He was feeling ill from the carnage they had caused as well as the loss of so many lives.

"Shortly," Race answered. "We'll finish the evacuation of the *Yellen* and then destroy her. Once we've swept the debris field, we'll leave."

Kelnor nodded. He was anxious to see the Dyson Sphere. Looking over at Reesa, he knew she was feeling the same. He could see her face was very pale; he wondered if this was the first time she had seen actual combat of this magnitude. He would speak with her later to help allay her fears.

Eight hours later, the *WarHawk* and her fleet of eighteen dreadnoughts made the hyperspace jump to the system that supposedly contained the Originators' Dyson Sphere. Blue-white swirling vortexes appeared and the fleet emerged into a system of darkness. There was no sign of a star, no planets, no moons, no asteroids, and no belt of comets or icy remnants.

Commander Arnett was gazing at the tactical display as it updated. "Wow, talk about depressing." She looked over at the admiral. "What if there's nothing here?"

"It's here," Captain Davis replied from his sensor console. "While we're not detecting the Dyson Sphere we're picking up an object of mass."

"It's strange being in a star system and there being no light," said Reesa as she gazed at the main viewscreen, which showed a sea of stars.

Kelnor reached forward and made some adjustments on his console. Instantly, the screen changed to show another area of space. The stars were still visible on the periphery of the screen, but a large circular object in the center was dimly apparent in the pale light from the stars. It was very dark in color.

"Is that it?" asked Race, standing up and striding over to stand in front of the massive viewscreen.

"Yes," Kelnor said simply. "We're probably the first people to see the Dyson Sphere in over two million years."

The Command Center was silent as everyone gazed at the massive artifact in front of them. It was hard to fathom that anyone could build such a structure around a star.

"How large is it?" asked Colonel Cowel. He felt a cold chill run down his back at what he was seeing on the screen.

"It's three AU in diameter," replied Captain Davis. "I've reset our sensors and we can now detect the object. It's made of some type of material that wasn't reflecting our original scans."

Race straightened his shoulders and looked around at his crew. "We've found what we came here for. I intend to take the fleet in closer, and we'll do a careful survey of the exterior of the sphere."

"There should be some way in," commented Reesa, her eyes alight with the excitement of discovery. "Can you imagine the amount of living space there must be inside?"

Race turned and looked over at Captain Denise Travers, who was sitting in front of Communications. "Send a hyperspace message back to the Federation informing them of what we've found. Give them the exact coordinates and add that we're beginning to survey the Dyson Sphere and will attempt to find a way in."

They had left a string of hyperspace communication buoys so they could contact Federation space. Supposedly, the Special Ops people had a fleet on standby to come in and assist with protecting the Dyson Sphere in case the Simulins or the Shari were to come across it. Race would feel a lot better with more warships to help protect this discovery. It would be a disaster if the Dyson Sphere fell under the influence of the Simulins or the Shari.

"Set a course for the Dyson Sphere at forty percent sublight," Race ordered.

By using the sublight drive at that power setting, it would take them a number of hours to reach the sphere. That would give them plenty of time to take readings on their way in. It would also help to ensure there were no surprises waiting for them. Race was intensely curious as to what they would find. He allowed himself to smile. His dreams of being an explorer had finally come true and here in front of him was the discovery of a lifetime.

—

High Lord Aktill of the Shari was back aboard his flagship after a meeting with the Shari High Command. His fleet had been heavily reinforced and he had been given direct orders from the Shari Grand Council of High Lords.

He was to proceed to the Rylus Cluster and search it to see if it was the source of the unknown ships that had been attacking the empire for the last year. The unknowns were very powerful, and numerous Shari vessels had been lost in the engagements. Most of the battles had been fought between small task groups. This would be the first time the Shari had committed a major fleet.

"I feel uneasy about our orders," commented Lower Lord Samarth, who was Aktill's second in command. "The Rylus Cluster has been forbidden to us for generations. It is said that no one who has gone into the cluster has ever returned."

"Rumors and superstition," replied Aktill dismissively. He had also heard those old stories.

For centuries, the Shari had avoided the cluster as entry into it had been prohibited by the AIs as well as the Grand Council of High Lords.

"Nevertheless, I greatly fear this is a mistake," Samarth stated with a deep sigh.

High Lord Aktill was silent for several long moments. He knew many in the fleet shared the same fears and concerns Samarth did. "We have a fleet of three hundred warships," he pointed out. "There is nothing in the Rylus Cluster we need to fear."

Lower Lord Samarth nodded his acceptance of Aktill's words. He just hoped the High Lord was correct and the rumors of the fate of those who had dared to venture into the Rylus Cluster were wrong.

Chapter Fifteen

Fleet Admiral Jeremy Strong stood on top of a large hill overlooking the new Fleet Academy. Across a small flat plain, numerous white buildings made a stark contrast in the desolate, windswept countryside. On the far side of the complex of buildings was the large spaceport, which served the facility. Jeremy had chosen this desolate location as it was away from the civilian areas and the lush green belt that circled the planet at the equator. They were nearly eighteen hundred kilometers to the north of the green zone, and the land was more arid, much warmer, and water was scarce.

"Feels like I'm back on the Moon again," said Kevin, who was standing next to him.

"Classes have already started in some subjects," Angela added from where she stood on Jeremy's other side with her arms folded across her chest.

"I understand Ariel plans on teaching several classes," commented Kevin with a chuckle. "I don't know if I would want to be in those classrooms."

Angela looked over at Kevin with a knowing smile. "You would have to do your own homework," she said teasingly. "Ariel would know instantly if it wasn't your work or if someone had helped."

"I'm sure Ariel will do just fine," Jeremy replied as he looked across to where a power beam installation was being installed.

When the defenses for the complex were finished in a few more weeks, it would be protected by a functioning energy shield and twenty power beam turrets. The Fleet Academy was equipped with four Fusion Five reactors for power generation so power was not an issue. There was some discussion of installing power beams around New Eden and Clements as well.

"I wish Kelsey and Katie were here for the dedication ceremony tonight," said Angela with a sigh. "I miss them."

"We all do," Jeremy said. It had been a difficult few months with Kelsey gone on the *Distant Horizon*. Kevin had been less of his usually humorous self since his wife had left to go on the mission.

"Jeremy, we may have a problem," Ariel's youthful voice spoke over his mini-comm in his right ear. "The battlecruiser *Gaia* just returned from checking on Simulin activity outside the nebula and her commander is reporting a massive Simulin fleet is assembling."

Jeremy looked at his two friends in alarm, seeing they too had heard the message.

A look of concern crossed Kevin's face as he looked over at Jeremy. "Do you think they've found a way into the nebula?"

"I doubt it," Jeremy replied. "Andram and the other Alton scientists think it will be years yet before that becomes a threat. No, this is something else."

"I have run some simulations based on the reports from the *Gaia*," Ariel added. "The Simulins are not forming up to attack the nebula or to keep us in; they're forming up to keep something out."

"The *Distant Horizon*," gasped Angela, her eyes growing wide with worry. "They're on their way back!"

Kevin looked confused. "But it's too early for them to be returning."

"Not if they've found something important," Jeremy responded as he thought over what Ariel had said.

"Damn! I bet Angela's right." Kevin gazed out across the Fleet Academy to the spaceport where their shuttle was. "I wonder what they've found this time."

"Whatever it is they've stirred up a hornet's nest," Ariel said over the comm. "From the scans the *Gaia* took, I would estimate at least two thousand Simulin ships are outside the nebula with more arriving every hour."

Kevin looked stunned at the number of ships. "Where did they get the ships? That's more than they had protecting the energy collecting stations around the blue giants."

"I believe they're bringing in ships from further out," Ariel answered. "The *Gaia* observed small fleets of anywhere from twenty to forty vessels arriving on a steady basis. They may be calling in everything they have in an attempt to stop the *Distant Horizon* from getting back to us."

Jeremy took a deep breath. The dedication ceremony was going to have to wait. "Ariel, contact the Command Staff and have them assemble on the Clan Protector. We'll be leaving the Fleet Academy shortly. Go over with them the data you have so far, and inform them we believe this is an attempt to stop Rear Admiral Barnes from returning with her fleet."

"What are you planning, Jeremy?" asked Kevin. He was greatly concerned for the safety of his wife as well as the others in Rear Admiral Barnes' fleet.

"We're going to go get them," Jeremy answered in a steadfast voice. "We'll assemble a fleet and when the *Distant Horizon* arrives, we'll go out and engage the Simulins." He was concerned about Rear Admiral Barnes fleet and if it was still intact. The fact that so many Simulin ships were assembling indicated the *Distant Horizon* had encountered the Simulins somewhere, and the odds were there had been a battle. He was also interested in finding out just what the exploration ship had discovered that had caused this massive reaction by the Simulins. It had to be something extremely significant.

"The odds won't be good," Ariel pointed out over the comm. "We'll be heavily outnumbered."

"I know," Jeremy replied evenly. "But whatever Rear Admiral Barnes has found, the Simulins want it back. I intend to see they don't get it."

An hour later, the shuttle carrying Jeremy, Kevin, and Angela docked with the Clan Protector. The large Carethian shipyard was nearly unrecognizable as a ship from all the changes made. Jeremy made his way to the conference room while his two friends caught a shuttle over to the *Avenger*.

Entering the conference room Jeremy saw that the other admirals were already there. They stood in unison as Jeremy came into the room.

"As you were," Jeremy said, as he walked to the head of the table and took his seat. As soon as Jeremy sat down Ariel appeared standing just behind him and to his left side.

"I've told them about the gathering Simulin fleet," Ariel said.

"Do you really think it's the *Distant Horizon* returning?" asked Admiral Jackson.

Jeremy looked over at Jackson and nodded. "It has to be, it's the only explanation for such a show of force."

"Is there any possibility of this being an attempt to pierce the nebula?" asked Admiral Sithe. "We could be facing an attack here at Gaia."

"I don't believe so," Jeremy responded. "The simulations Ariel has run almost all point to it being Rear Admiral Barnes' fleet. The Altons have also confirmed this isn't an attempt to penetrate the nebula; it's too soon."

He had taken this possibility very seriously and contacted several Alton scientists on his way up to the meeting from the shuttle. The Altons had been insistent it was too early for the Simulins to have come up with a method to travel through hyperspace that had been disrupted by the hyperspace disruption buoys.

"Rear Admiral Barnes is returning!" boomed Grayseth, his large brown eyes shining with intensity. "The Simulins are gathering to do battle. We must prepare to go on the hunt to help our brethren."

"To take on a force of this size will be dangerous," Admiral Cleeteus said, his brow wrinkled in a frown. "We will take some losses."

"We only need to hold them off long enough for the *Distant Horizon* and her fleet to enter one of the tunnels," Jeremy said. "I know it's a risk, but it's one I believe we have to take. Whatever they've discovered has really stirred up the Simulins."

Admiral Sithe shook his head in worry. "They will attempt to follow us down the tunnel. With the number of ships we'll need to take, they may be able to follow us back here. Our hyperjumps may take longer."

The other admirals looked at one another. This was something they hadn't thought about.

"I may have a solution for that," Jeremy said.

"So, how large a fleet are we taking?" asked Rear Admiral Susan Marks.

"I'm still working out the details," Jeremy admitted. "I need to have Ariel run some simulations and then we'll ready the fleet."

"What about the AIs?" asked Admiral Jackson. "The Command AI couldn't get here in time for the meeting. It's down on Borton inspecting the newest group of AIs that have been created. Kurene is also at the master Codex installation overseeing the imprinting of the AI programming."

"I'll be contacting the Command AI shortly," Jeremy responded. "I just want to stress the importance of the fact that if this is indeed Rear Admiral Barnes returning early, then they have made an important discovery, which they feel was important enough to cut short their mission. It's imperative we find out what that discovery is."

"We go on the hunt," growled Grayseth, standing up, towering over the conference table. "The evil ones of this galaxy must be destroyed!"

"We go on the hunt," agreed Jeremy solemnly, gazing at his large Carethian friend. "Everyone get your commands ready. Recall all crewmembers who are on leave. I want all fleets ready to resume full combat operations in twelve hours."

Jeremy looked around his group of admirals. They all had determined looks upon their faces. This was a good group, and he knew they would follow him to the ends of the galaxy if he so ordered.

Twelve hours later the sixteen-hundred-meter battleship *Avenger* made its third short hyperspace jump and exited back into normal space inside a clear area of the nebula. The location was two hundred thousand kilometers across and created by specially built Alton satellites, which used their tractor beam technology to keep this area clear. One more jump would put them out into open space where the Simulins would be able to detect them.

"The rest of the fleet is exiting hyperspace," Ariel reported as she used the ship's sensors to scan surrounding space. "The Command AI is requesting it be allowed to send one of its ships to the edge of the nebula to observe the Simulins and to report back when and if the *Distant Horizon* shows up. It will be one of the fifteen-hundred-meter ships that's equipped with a stealth energy shield."

"Permission granted," answered Jeremy. "Remind the Command AI to make sure the ship stays just inside the nebula to help reduce the chance of accidental detection."

"Message sent," responded Ariel. She looked back at Jeremy, her hands on her hips with and a serious look upon her face. "The Command AI has responded they will take every precaution to avoid detection."

Jeremy turned his attention to one of the four large tactical displays in the Command Center. He had brought two hundred of the large fifteen-hundred-meter AI ships, ten human battleships, ten battlecruisers, twenty strikecruisers, twenty Alton battleships, and twenty Alton battlecruisers. In addition, Grayseth was present with his flagship, the *Warrior's Pride*, and ten Carethian battlecruisers. That gave him a fleet of two hundred and ninety-one warships.

"What now?" asked Kevin from his sensor console. Due to the gas in the nebula, his sensors could detect nothing outside the cleared area.

"We wait," answered Jeremy. He knew it could be hours or possibly days before the *Distant Horizon* and her fleet showed up. However long it took, he was determined he would be ready to move out and engage the Simulins when the time came.

Commander Malen turned toward Jeremy. "All vessels have made transit."

Jeremy nodded. "Have all ships go to Condition Three until further notice." At Condition Three, the alert level was still high enough to respond quickly if the exploration dreadnaught was detected.

"This reminds me of when we were hiding in the gas giant the first time we were waiting on the *Distant Horizon*," commented Angela over their private comm channel.

"Only this time they have a powerful fleet to protect them," Kevin said. "I'm glad they had the AI warspheres with them."

"Feeling different about the AIs?" asked Jeremy. Kevin had always mistrusted the AIs ever since they arrived in the Triangulum Galaxy though over the last few years he had been gradually coming around to accepting them.

"They've upheld their end of the bargain," Kevin said grudgingly.

Jeremy leaned back in his command chair. Since becoming fleet admiral this was going to be the first really major fleet action he would fight. He had already instructed Ariel to run battle simulations for possible action against the Simulins. He'd also given Ariel control of the *Avenger* and four strikecruisers, which would be serving as the flagship's escorts. With Ariel in command, this would be a deadly combination against the Simulins. In addition, all the ships in the fleet were updated with better shields and more powerful power beams and particle beams.

"The Command AI is requesting permission to keep its ships at Condition Two," Angela reported.

Jeremy looked over at her and nodded. "Permission granted." The AIs didn't need rest and could stay at a high alert level indefinitely if needed.

Looking at the viewscreens in the front of the Command Center, Jeremy could see a number of ships being displayed. A large fifteen-hundred-meter AI sphere was on one screen, an Alton battleship was on another, and even Grayseth's flagship, the *Warrior's Pride*, was showing.

"They'll make it back safely," Ariel said over the private channel. Her lips on her hologram didn't even move, as it wasn't necessary when communicating this way. "Clarissa will keep them safe and the Simulins wouldn't be assembling such a large force outside the nebula if they had managed to intercept the ship and whatever it is they've discovered."

"I know," replied Jeremy softly. "This is a reminder for all of us just how dangerous this galaxy is and how powerful the Simulins still are." What concerned Jeremy the most, besides the *Distant Horizon*, was the fact he was going to have to fight a major fleet battle and some of the ships with him wouldn't be going back to Gaia.

—

The *Distant Horizon* and the ships with her dropped out of hyperspace three hundred light-years from the nebula which hid Gaia. The ships quickly formed up and began scanning the system. This was the system they were supposed to meet Admiral Bachal in.

"Nothing," reported Captain Reynolds after a few minutes as the ship's sensors reached the far side of the system.

"They may have their stealth energy shields activated," suggested Commander Grissim.

Kathryn relaxed slightly. That had to be the explanation. "Captain Travers, send a message to Admiral Bachal on the *Starlight* requesting they report their current position."

Captain Travers adjusted the comm frequency and sent the message. For several long seconds, he sat at his console waiting for a response and then it came. "They're forty-four million kilometers starward from us."

"I have them," Clarissa announced a few moments later. "I've spotted them with the ship's optics."

"Send the coordinates to Lieutenant Strong," ordered Kathryn. "We'll jump to them immediately and decide upon our next move." Kathryn felt relieved the fleet was here. On their trip through hyperspace to this star system, they had detected numerous Simulin ships moving in this direction. There was no doubt in Kathryn's mind the Simulins were gathering a blocking force to attempt to intercept her fleet short of the nebula.

A few moments later the ships jumped, emerging from hyperspace a few thousand kilometers from the *Starlight*. On the main viewscreen, the two Alton battleships appeared still linked to the massive Originator vessel. In addition, the ten escorting warspheres were also present.

"All ships accounted for," reported Commander Grissim.

"No obvious damage," added Colonel Leon. She turned away from her command console. "Permission to stand down from Condition One." Petra wanted to give the crew some rest before they continued on toward Gaia.

"Go to Condition Three," Kathryn replied. "Have the AI warspheres stay at Condition One."

"I have one group of Simulin ships on the long-range sensors," warned Captain Reynolds. "Seven light-years distant and heading toward the nebula."

Commander Grissim gazed at one of the tactical displays showing the seven Simulin vessels. "They must be calling in every ship they can to try to stop us."

"We may have to fight our way into the nebula," commented Colonel Leon.

Kathryn pursed her lips as she thought. She didn't see any way they could avoid a battle. "We'll stay here for eight hours with our stealth energy shields up. Once everyone has had time to eat and get some rest, we'll make our move."

"Admiral, I've checked and the two Alton battleships have managed to extend their stealth shields to cover the Originator vessel as well," Captain Reynolds informed her. "That's why we couldn't detect them."

Kathryn nodded. The material the ship was made of was undetectable anyway, but the added shield was further insurance against detection. Looking up at the main viewscreen, she saw the three ships. She was still in awe at the sheer immensity of the Originator vessel.

"I have contact with the AI on the Originator ship," Clarissa said. "He's asking if it's okay to siphon some energy from the two Alton ships so it can activate more of its systems."

"He?" asked Katie in surprise. It had never occurred to her the AI on the Originator ship would consider itself to be male. This could be an interesting development.

"Can he do so without causing problems to the *Starlight* or the *Nova*?"

"Yes," Clarissa replied. "He has stated very clearly he's not a danger and nothing harmful will happen."

"Andram?"

The Alton turned to look at the admiral. "Unknown; we know so little about the Originators other than they were very advanced."

"Do we dare risk allowing it to activate more of that ship's systems?" asked Colonel Leon. "For all we know it could be preparing to blow us all into space dust."

"I think it will be safe," Mikow added as she thought over the AI's request. She was sitting next to Katie at the main computer station. "I believe that by helping the AI it will encourage it to trust us. Right now that AI is alone and everything and everyone it knew is gone."

"You're saying it's lonely?" asked Kathryn in surprise.

"Possibly," Mikow answered.

"Very well, I'll contact Admiral Bachal and see if he has any objections. Clarissa, once we've agreed to do this, you need to monitor the energy transfer to ensure no harm comes to the two Alton battleships and the AI doesn't siphon off too much energy."

"Yes, Admiral," Clarissa responded. "The AI on the Originator ship will be thrilled to hear we'll furnish the energy. He's been very upset about how few systems on the ship are still functioning."

A few minutes later and the details were worked out. On the large viewscreen, a dim blue glow suddenly appeared around all three ships as the energy transfer began.

"How much energy does a ship of that size need?" asked Colonel Leon as she stared transfixed at the screen. Petra still wasn't sure this was a good idea.

"Once again, unknown," answered Andram. "We have no idea of the power that ship once generated or what systems are still functional."

Kathryn looked around at her command crew. "I want everyone to get some rest and let our backups handle the Command Center. Clarissa, contact me immediately if there are any problems." One thing about Clarissa, she didn't need any rest. Kathryn had come to depend on her more and more, and it was comforting to know she was always keeping watch.

Kathryn made her way to her quarters and after taking a long hot shower, lay down to try to get some sleep. As she closed her eyes, she wondered what her father was doing back on Ceres. Even though they hadn't been close since she entered the Fleet, Kathryn knew it had to have been heart wrenching for him to learn she wouldn't be coming back. But now that might change. With the secrets the Originator ship contained, perhaps there might be a way to return to the Human Federation of Worlds. Just maybe she would get to see her father again some day. As she drifted off to sleep, she thought about the outings her father had taken her on as a young girl. She really missed the closeness they once had shared and those happy, carefree times.

-

Jeremy gazed apprehensively at the latest report sent back by the AI ship, which had positioned itself near the periphery of the nebula. Thirty-two hundred Simulin ships were now situated in small attack formations along the outside of the nebula, waiting.

"That's a hell of a lot of Simulin ships," muttered Kevin over their private comm channel. "What chance are we going to have against them?"

"We only need to hold them off for a few minutes," Jeremy answered evenly. "Just long enough for Rear Admiral Barns to make the jump into one of the tunnels."

Ariel was listening and spoke. "There is a 92 percent probability the Simulins will attempt to follow Rear Admiral Barnes into the nebula. From the number of ships they have gathered, whatever it is the *Distant Horizon* has found has frightened the Simulins."

"I didn't think anything could get under the Simulins' skin," commented Jeremy. "Ariel, any idea on how soon the *Distant Horizon* and her fleet will be arriving?" Every hour that passed more Simulins ships were appearing. It almost looked as if they had called in every ship within hyperspace range of the nebula.

"Soon," Ariel responded. "From the latest reports from the AI sphere, the Simulins have been adjusting their fleet formations. I would say they expect Rear Admiral Barnes' fleet to arrive within the next twenty-four hours."

Jeremy turned toward Commander Malen. "We're jumping. I want to put us at the extreme edge of the tunnel just behind the AI ship. We have to be ready to jump to the *Distant Horizon's* location as soon as they arrive." Jeremy knew the survival of Rear Admiral Barns' fleet might depend on how quickly his fleet could jump to their emergence point.

"We'll be strung out in the tunnel," warned Commander Malen with a narrow frown. "It may make it difficult to emerge from hyperspace in a coherent formation."

"I know," Jeremy replied. "But it's a chance we're going to have to take."

-

The *Distant Horizon* and her fleet were on the last leg of the three hyperjumps they had to make to reach the safety of the nebula. As they approached, their long-range sensors began to pick up Simulins ships.

"How many?" asked Kathryn as the tactical display began to light up with red threat icons. They had suspected the Simulins would be waiting for them. Now they just needed to find a safe way to enter the nebula.

"Several thousand," Clarissa answered as she studied the data. "They're close enough to all the safe tunnels that they'll intercept us before we have a chance to enter."

"It will take Admiral Bachal a while to calculate his jump due to the mass of the Originator ship," Colonel Leon added. "We're going to have a fight on our hands."

"Clarissa, how many ships of the fleet can you control at once?"

The AI looked over at the admiral. "I can fight with the *Pallas* and the *Deneb*, but it would be better if I let the AI warspheres fight on their own."

Kathryn nodded her agreement. "As soon as we emerge, I want the *Ardent* to move over close to the Alton battleships to help protect the Originator ship." Somehow or another she had to get that ship to Gaia.

Commander Malen moved over closer to Kathryn. "Admiral," she said in a soft voice. "Against those numbers I don't know if we can survive long enough to make the hyperspace jump into the passageway."

"I know," Kathryn acknowledged. "But it's the only chance we have. If we can't make it into the nebula, the Simulins will destroy us."

High Commander Zarth Lantu gazed fixedly at the long-range sensor screen. Only moments before the sensor operator had reported an unknown fleet inbound toward the Fitula Nebula.

"It's them," stated Lantu. "Can we calculate their probable emergence point? It's essential we jump as soon as they emerge and before they can escape into the nebula." It was aggravating that the AIs and their organics had made the nebula impossible to travel through in hyperspace.

Second Commander Darst worked at a console for a moment and then turned toward the High Commander. "The battle computer has predicted their probable emergence point. We can have fourteen hundred ships there as soon as they emerge."

"Send the order," Lantu said. Since he had originally spread the word about the AIs and their organic allies finding the Old Ones' ship, he had been given command of its capture. "Remember, the Old Ones' ship is not to be harmed. We want it for study." He was confident he had enough warships to ensure the Old Ones' ship could not escape into the safety of the nebula.

Jeremy was awakened from his sleep by Ariel suddenly appearing next to his bed. This was something he had gotten used to over the years.

"I've located them," Ariel announced excitedly. "The *Distant Horizon*, two Federation battleships, one Federation battlecarrier, and fifteen AI warspheres are inbound toward the nebula."

"What about Admiral Bachal and his two Alton battleships?" Jeremy rolled out of bed and reached for his uniform.

"That's the strange part," Ariel confessed with a confused look on her face. "I'm picking up a large object that doesn't meet any ship profile in our database."

"How soon before they emerge?"

"Sixteen minutes. I've calculated their probable hyperspace emergence point."

"Get the fleet ready to jump; I want to arrive at that location twenty seconds after they drop out of hyperspace. Sound the Condition One alert and prepare the fleet for immediate combat operations."

It took Jeremy only a few more minutes to get ready and then he set off in a sprint toward the Command Center. They were about to learn just what it was Rear Admiral Barnes had found. He had a strong suspicion it had to do with the large object Ariel had detected on the long-range sensors.

-

Kathryn waited tensely as the *Distant Horizon* and the rest of the fleet prepared to exit hyperspace. They were traveling much slower than normal due to the two Alton battleships being attached to the Originator ship.

Gazing at the nearby tactical display, the area they were going to exit hyperspace at was still vacant of any Simulin ships though she knew that wouldn't last long once they emerged.

"Once we exit the vortex how long before Admiral Bachal will be ready to jump again?"

"Twelve minutes," replied Clarissa. "The stress of carrying the extra mass of the Originator vessel is putting a strain on the hyperdrive cores and it will require a minimum of twelve minutes of cool down before they can risk jumping into the nebula."

"Twelve minutes," said Commander Grissim with a deep frown on her face. "I don't know if we can survive for twelve minutes if the Simulins hit us hard."

"We have to," Kathryn answered. She knew the odds were not in their favor.

"Hyperspace exit in two minutes," called out Lieutenant Parker from his hyperdrive console.

"We're at Condition One and all weapons are ready," added Major Weir.

-

"I hate this," muttered Katie over the private channel she shared with Kelsey. "I didn't expect to arrive back home in the midst of a space battle."

"We'll make it," responded Kelsey, looking over at her long time friend. "Rear Admiral Barnes and Clarissa will see us through."

"I hope so," Katie replied. "I so want to see Kevin again. I'm beginning to believe he was right and we should have stayed at Gaia instead of insisting on going on this mission."

"We did the right thing," Kelsey said. "If we hadn't gone we would have regretted it."

"Hyperspace exit in one minute," called out Lieutenant Parker.

Katie let out a deep sigh. "I know you're right; I just hope we both get to see our husbands again."

-

Kathryn felt the gut wrenching feeling as the *Distant Horizon* dropped out of hyperspace just short of the gaseous nebula that hid Gaia. On the nearby tactical display, other green icons began to appear as the rest of the fleet emerged.

"All ships are present," reported Captain Reynolds as the data from the ship's sensors came in.

"Lieutenant Strong, calculate a jump into the nearest tunnel," Ordered Kathryn. "We're jumping as soon as Admiral Bachal reports their drives are ready."

Alarms suddenly began sounding and red threat icons began appearing all around them on the tactical displays.

Kathryn leaned forward and activated her ship-to-ship comm. "All vessels, our main priority is to protect the two Alton battleships and the Originator ship. Commence combat at your own initiative." She then turned toward Clarissa. "The *Distant Horizon* and the battleships are yours to command."

Almost instantly the *Distant Horizon*, *Pallas*, and *Deneb* moved closer together and then fired in unison at the nearest Simulin battlecruiser, which was uncomfortably close. Its screen lit up in a brilliant flash of light and then it was overwhelmed as the *Distant Horizon's* ion beam fired, blasting a hole six meters across in the shield. Two very carefully placed Devastator Three missiles flashed through the gap and the battlecruiser died a flaming death.

"Simulin battlecruiser is down," reported Captain Reynolds. "All other ships are engaged."

In space, more Simulin ships were jumping into the battle. Energy beams blasted away at the energy screens of the AI warspheres, trying to knock them down. The AIs were firing their ion beams and particle beam weapons as rapidly as possible with the AI ships working in pairs firing upon single Simulin targets.

On warsphere 0-019, the AI in command felt its vessel shudder violently and red warning lights began to flare up on the damage control console. The ship suddenly shook again like a giant hammer had struck it and the AI was thrown violently against the wall. Righting itself, the AI looked toward the AI at the damage control console. "Report."

Before the AI could respond, a Simulin energy beam cut through the Control Center, annihilating everything in its path.

"Warsphere 0-019 is down," reported Captain Reynolds, startled at how rapidly the Simulins had destroyed the vessel.

Kathryn looked at the main viewscreen showing the battle. The screen was full of light and even as she watched, another AI warsphere exploded as numerous Simulin vessels pounded it with their energy beams and sublight antimatter missiles.

"Warsphere 0-003 is down," reported Captain Reynolds as the *Distant Horizon* shook violently.

"Severe damage to the outer hull at section K-17 near Engineering," called out Colonel Leon, her voice taking on an alarmed note. "We have several fires out of control."

Commander Grissim stepped over to the damage control console and studied it for a moment. "Vent those areas to space," she ordered.

"There are still people in there," protested Petra, her face turning pale. "They'll die if we do that!"

"We'll all die if those fires reach Engineering or the starboard ammunition and missile storage bunkers."

Colonel Leon nodded and, reaching forward, did as ordered. A few moments later, she turned back toward the commander with a bleak look on her face. "Areas have been vented; the fires are out."

"Get rescue teams in there as soon as possible," Commander Grissim ordered. "There was survival gear inside and some of the crew may still be alive."

"I hope so," Colonel Leon replied as she began contacting damage control teams to respond to the effected area.

More alarms suddenly began sounding on the sensor console. Commander Grissim looked grimly at the nearby tactical console, expecting to see more red threat icons appearing. Instead, friendly green icons began flashing into existence; a lot of them!

"It's Fleet Admiral Strong," announced Clarissa in a pleased voice. "Ariel says they're here to rescue us!"

"How did they know we were coming?" asked Kathryn in shock as even more green icons continued to appear.

"Ariel says they detected the Simulin fleet gathering outside the nebula and guessed it was in response to something we had discovered."

Kathryn let out a deep sigh of relief and looked over at Kelsey. "You're husband's here and I'm damn glad he is!"

-

"We're going to live," spoke Katie happily over their private comm. "I was so afraid I wasn't going to see Kevin again."

"We're not out of this yet," Kelsey mentioned. "We still have to survive long enough for Admiral Bachal to be able to jump out of here."

Katie nodded, but she wasn't so frightened anymore, not with the *Avenger* so near. Jeremy would get them out of this situation

-

"What the hell is that?" uttered Kevin, staring in awe at the main viewscreen, which showed an unbelievably large vessel with two Alton battleships anchored to it.

"It's an Originator ship," explained Ariel as she came to stand next to Kevin. "That's what they discovered. It has an AI on board they've managed to establish contact with. They haven't been able to gain access to the vessel so they brought it back here to keep it out of the Simulins' hands.

"I knew it!" Kevin said, shaking his head and looking over at Jeremy. "Every time they go out they discover something incredible. First the Dyson Sphere and now this!"

"Rear Admiral Barnes is reporting they need another eight minutes before they can jump," Angela said. "The Originator ship is causing the hyperdrives on the Alton battleships to overheat. They've linked to it so they can use their hyperdrives to move the ship through hyperspace."

"More Simulin ships are jumping in," warned Commander Malen as more red threat icons began appearing on the tactical displays. "We're badly outnumbered, Jeremy."

Jeremy could see from looking at the tactical displays she was right; they were in danger of being overrun. "I want all ships to move into a defensive formation around the two Alton battleships and the Originator vessel. We have to buy them the time they need to jump. Ariel, you have control of the *Avenger's* weapons as well as the four strikecruisers. Don't get us killed."

"I won't," promised Ariel as the *Avenger* suddenly shifted direction and the four strikecruisers formed up on her flanks. "It's time to go kill some Simulins."

The excitement in Ariel's voice anytime she was given command of the ship made Jeremy nervous. However, she had been designed to be the AI of a warship and her desire for combat was deeply rooted in her basic programming.

High Commander Lantu gazed in aggravation at the tactical screen. More AI ships and their organic partners had jumped in.

"The battle computer is predicting a 96 percent chance of victory," Second Commander Darst said. "We have them badly outnumbered."

"Then this is our chance to take the Old Ones' vessel as well as deal a heavy blow to the AIs and their organics. Order all ships to attack!"

The battle grew more intense as thousands of energy weapons, power beams, particle beams and antimatter missiles were pummeling both fleets. In the Simulin formation, four escort cruisers exploded in bright flashes of light as their shields were overwhelmed by the ferocious attack. Two seventeen-hundred-meter battlecruisers were torn apart as Alton battleships used their powerful particle beam weapons against them. Other ships were incurring major damage as their shields were relentlessly battered down.

In the Federation fleet, two fifteen-hundred-meter AI spheres exploded as Simulin antimatter missiles penetrated the weakened screens, destroying the vessels. An Alton battleship died in a fiery blast as twenty Simulin vessels focused all of their energy beams on the powerful warship. A human battleship had its stern ravaged by Simulin energy beams before an antimatter missile turned the vessel into a blazing star.

Jeremy held onto his command chair as the *Avenger* shuddered violently. On the main viewscreen, the Simulin battlecruiser they were attacking suddenly blew apart as Ariel used the firepower of the *Avenger* and her four escorting strikecruisers to kill it.

"We're losing ships," uttered Kevin, finding it difficult to keep track of the destruction. "So are the Simulins."

"Six more minutes," Commander Malen reported as Ariel shifted to a new target.

Jeremy closed his eyes briefly and then looked around the Command Center. Everyone was working at peak efficiency and focused on their jobs. Their very survival might well depend on what happened in the next few minutes.

"Alton battlecruiser *Starmist* is down," reported Kevin. "Federation strikecruiser *Wolfhound* is down."

"We're losing ships too fast," Commander Malen said between clinched lips.

Jeremy looked at the viewscreen. There were burning and dying ships everywhere on both sides. "We can't withdraw," he said firmly. "We have to give the Altons time to get their hyperdrives working."

Kevin glanced over at Jeremy, seeing the determined look on his face. "We'll make it," he said. "We have to!"

-

Rear Admiral Barnes was watching the ongoing battle on both the giant viewscreen and the two tactical displays. She winced every time a green icon faded away.

"AI warsphere 0-012 is down," reported Captain Reynolds as the one-thousand-meter vessel disappeared from his screen.

"The *Pallas* is reporting heavy damage," reported Captain Reynolds.

"Commander Lewis says their energy shield is down to 18 percent and they have numerous compartments open to space."

"Have them pull back to the Originator vessel," ordered Kathryn.

A sudden light filled the large viewscreen and then faded away.

"What was that?"

"The *Pallas*," Clarissa said with a pained look on her face. It was very seldom she ever lost a ship she was in charge of. "Two Simulin antimatter missiles penetrated its energy screen."

"Lieutenant Strong, do you have that jump plotted?" Kathryn asked in a calm voice. She had to stay strong for her crew. She could see the frightened looks beginning to appear on some of their faces.

"Yes, Admiral," Kelsey responded.

"Admiral," Clarissa said with a puzzled look on her face. "The AI on the Originator ship wants to know if he should immobilize the ships attacking us."

"What?" exclaimed Kathryn, looking intently at Clarissa. "I thought it didn't have enough power to activate any of its weapons?"

"This isn't a weapon," Clarissa explained. "The AI says he just managed to repair the system and bring it online. It's purely defensive, but he says it will stop the attack against us."

"Do it!" ordered Kathryn as she watched several more fifteen-hundred-meter AI ships die on the large viewscreen.

Moments later the lights in the Command Center flickered and suddenly, on the viewscreen, the Simulin ships stopped firing. A blue glow surrounded them.

"Get me a report on what's happening out there," demanded Kathryn. "Clarissa, inform Ariel of what we've done."

Captain Reynolds studied his sensor screens for several long moments. "The Simulin ships have stopped firing and seem to be drifting without power."

"What did the AI on the Originator ship do?" asked Kathryn, allowing herself to take a deep breath.

"It siphoned off all the power from the Simulin vessels," Clarissa said after a moment. "He says if we want to destroy them, now is our opportunity."

Kathryn leaned back in her command chair stunned. She looked back over at Clarissa. "What does Fleet Admiral Strong want us to do?"

Clarissa paused for a moment as she communicated with Ariel. Then she glanced over at the admiral with a grim look upon her face. "Destroy them!"

Rear Admiral Barnes quickly contacted her surviving ships and passed on the order. An opportunity like this might never come again. If they could destroy this Simulin fleet, they could substantially reduce Simulin power in the Triangulum Galaxy.

Kelsey looked over at Katie with an *I told you so* look. "We're going back to Gaia," she said.

"Guess I'm cooking Kevin hamburgers for supper," Katie admonished with a pleased look.

-

Jeremy watched without remorse as his fleet methodically destroyed the assembled Simulin fleet. Their shields were down and from what they could tell from the sensors, the Simulin ships were without power.

"The Originator ship did this?" asked Commander Malen in awe. Just the power to do something of this magnitude was beyond imagining. An entire fleet immobilized in just moments!

"Yes," Ariel replied. "From what Clarissa has told me, the AI on the ship managed to get one of its defensive weapons operational."

"If this is a defensive weapon, I'd hate to see an offensive one," stated Commander Malen.

"Clarissa, what's the status of our fleet and Rear Admiral Barnes fleet?" asked Jeremy. He knew they had lost quite a few vessels.

"Total losses to both fleets are two Federation battleships, four Federation battlecruisers, four strikecruisers, four Alton battleships, six Alton battlecruisers, thirty-six of the fifteen-hundred-meter AI spheres, and eight of the one-thousand-meter AI warspheres.

"What about Grayseth?" he knew the big Bear liked to put his ships in the most dangerous fighting.

"Grayseth lost six of his battlecruisers."

Jeremy shook his head. The losses were bad but not as bad as they could have been. They would hold a memorial service once they returned to Gaia. "What about the Simulins?"

"Eighteen hundred and forty ships confirmed destroyed," Ariel reported. "The rest of their fleet is staying back. I would guess they're confused about what happened to the ships that were attacking us."

"Admiral Bachal reports they're ready to jump," Angela said. She had a smile on her face, knowing her friends had survived.

"Let's go home," Jeremy ordered. He looked at the viewscreen, which was focused on the gargantuan Originator ship. "We have an AI to ask some questions too. Perhaps now we can finally find a way to destroy the Dyson Sphere."

Chapter Sixteen

Jeremy, Kelsey, Kevin, Katie, and Angela were all seated on the stage of the large graduation hall in the new Fleet Academy. Jeremy had just finished giving his speech about how pleased he was to have the new academy open and following in the tradition of the older one on Earth's moon. Currently, Admiral Jackson was giving a closing speech about how the future graduates of the academy would be a shining symbol to the inhabitants of Gaia.

Also present on the stage were Clarissa and Ariel. Holographic imagers had been placed throughout key areas of the academy complex to give the two beautiful AIs access. Clarissa and Ariel were standing slightly behind Admiral Jackson with their hands clasped behind their backs and at perfect attention in their dark blue fleet dress uniforms. Both AIs looked amazing and were drawing their usual amount of attention. Clarissa had even toned down her voracious curves so as not to appear too distracting.

The graduation hall was crammed full of the first year students as well as the faculty. There were students from three different races present: Human, Carethian, and Alton. There were even a few AIs present, hovering at the back of the hall. Several science AIs had been chosen by Kurene and Mikow to teach classes at the academy.

"I feel like I'm back on the Moon," whispered Kelsey, looking around at all the people present. "This graduation hall looks so much like the one back home."

Jeremy smiled and nodded. "Yes, but back then I didn't know you were from Ceres and an admiral's daughter."

Jeremy was referring to the fact that during the time he had been at the academy, the citizens of Ceres had not as of yet revealed themselves to the people of Earth. Only a few higher ups knew of their existence, including Jeremy's father.

It was only later during the *New Horizon* incident that he had learned of the hidden Old Human Federation of Worlds base inside Ceres and of Kelsey's heritage.

As they listened, Admiral Jackson presented his closing remarks. Upon completion, Rear Admiral Susan Marks approached the podium and dismissed the students. Susan was going to be responsible for the academy and for the immediate future had been reassigned as the top administrator. She had been excited to be given the opportunity to train the future officers of the fleet.

As the students filed out, Jeremy and the others stood up and approached Susan and Admiral Jackson.

"I think you have a great group of first-year students," Jeremy said, smiling at Susan.

"I hope so," she said, sounding optimistic. "We have twelve hundred students in this first class."

Katie looked thoughtful and then asked. "How many do you think will make it to their fifth year?" She knew back on the Moon only about 30 percent made it through the classes and rigorous training.

"We're not sure," answered Susan with a slight frown. "Back in the Federation, you have the best students out of billions of people attending the Fleet Academy. Our population isn't quite that large. What we're talking about doing is as the students advance in their training we'll begin to group them into what specialties they need to go into. I'm guessing only about 8 to 10 percent will qualify as officers, the others will be trained to fill subordinate roles and perhaps after a few years of actual shipboard experience will be able to advance as suitable officer candidates."

Ariel and Clarissa walked over to the group. "I'm teaching advanced hyperspace navigation," Ariel said with a pleased smile. Her dark eyes flashing with excitement.

Clarissa shook her head. "I don't think I would have the patience to teach a class."

Jeremy was still amazed at times how human his two AI friends sounded. "Clarissa, how is our new AI friend doing?" Since arriving back at Gaia with the Originator ship, the entire planet was intensely curious about the monstrous vessel now in orbit.

Clarissa pursed her lips and then replied. "He's been quiet. I think he's having a hard time accepting that all the Originators are gone and so much time has passed. He spent most of it in stasis with his systems running on minimal power."

"Do we know what happened to the Originators?" asked Kelsey.

"He says it was a disease," Clarissa responded with sadness in her eyes. "The result of an experiment that went catastrophically wrong. His ship was the last one to leave the Originator worlds in the hope of finding a cure. They failed and the Originators on board all died, but not before they hid the ship in the asteroid field and disabled most of the ship's systems."

"Two million years," mumbled Kevin, finding it hard to comprehend the ship was that old. "What would have happened if the Ornellians had never found the ship?"

"The AI would have died," Clarissa replied. "Once its power was depleted its program would have faded away."

Ariel had a knowing, almost haunted look in her deep dark eyes. "It almost sounds like what happened to me after the original *Avenger* crashed on Earth's moon. My power was nearly exhausted when Jeremy and Katie's fathers came aboard the ship. They managed to restore enough power to enable me to activate a few of the ship's essential systems."

"I remember my father talking about that years later," Jeremy said. He could still hear his father's powerful voice telling the story of the discovery of the *Avenger* on the Moon and how it had reshaped human history.

"I'm glad we have a new Fleet Academy," Angela said. "To me it makes Gaia seem more like home."

"Has the AI revealed anything that might be of use to us about the Dyson Sphere?" asked Susan, raising her eyebrow.

"No," Jeremy answered with a frown. "He has so far refused to talk about it. It's almost as if the Dyson Sphere is a forbidden subject."

"He hasn't recovered all of his memories yet," explained Clarissa, jumping in to defend her new AI friend. "Some of his core memories are still jumbled and I've been helping to sort through them. I'm sure he will be more helpful when he has fully recovered all of his memories."

"He's letting you into his core programs?" asked Katie, thinking about the possibilities.

Clarissa shook her head. "No, not exactly. Only the surface regions. The deep and highly technical stuff he's blocking access to. We still have a lot to go through."

"I don't like the sound of that," commented Admiral Jackson. "Are we sure this AI is safe? I mean, look at what it did to the Simulins' fleet, and that was supposedly only a defensive weapon!"

"He's safe," Clarissa quickly said reassuringly. "He just needs time to sort everything out and get sufficient systems on the ship repaired."

"How's he repairing the systems?" asked Katie. In the Federation and even on Gaia they used spider robots for construction as well as basic repairs in the shipyards.

"Nano technology," Clarissa replied cautiously.

"Micro robots!" exclaimed Kevin, his face turning pale at the thought.

Clarissa nodded. "The ship has a small factory capable of creating the nanobots. The AI then programs them as to what needs to be repaired."

"Did you know about this?" asked Kelsey, looking accusingly at Jeremy. Nano technology, while not unknown in the Federation, had been banned due to the dangers that came along with it.

"Yes," Jeremy admitted. "However, we believe at some point the AI is going to need some raw materials for its nanobots. When that happens, we may have a bargaining chip to gain access to some of its technology."

Kevin shuddered, imagining millions of microscopic invaders swarming down on Gaia. "I hope you know what you're doing."

"We're taking precautions," Jeremy answered. "Andram has assembled a team of Alton scientists to monitor the situation. The Altons have experimented with nano technology in the past and are familiar with it. They've assured me that if the proper precautions are taken, we have nothing to worry about."

Admiral Jackson looked around the group before speaking once more. "Thanks to the Originator AI a lot of Simulin ships were destroyed in the battle outside the nebula. Is it possible the Dyson Sphere is now vulnerable to attack?"

Jeremy looked penetratingly at the older admiral. He had a sharp mind and was thinking along the same lines as Jeremy. "It's possible. From the size of the fleet they assembled they had to have pulled some of the vessels from the blue giant cluster as well as the Dyson Sphere." He paused and looked over at Ariel, who was now standing slightly behind him and Kelsey.

"We have a six-week window before the Simulins can bring in sufficient ships from some of their known worlds to replace those destroyed. If we're going to attempt to destroy the Dyson Sphere, it needs to be now. We may not get this opportunity again."

"There's only one problem," Susan said, cocking her eyebrow. "How do we get our ships inside the Dyson Sphere? It's obvious we can't destroy it from the outside."

Jeremy turned toward Clarissa. "Susan's right, we need a way inside. Clarissa, somehow you have got to get the AI on the Originator ship to tell us how to get inside the sphere."

Clarissa was silent for a long moment. "I'll try. So far, he has refused to speak of the Dyson Sphere. It's almost as if something terrible happened there."

Their talking was interrupted as Rear Admiral Barnes stepped up on the stage and walked over to the group. She and the other admirals had been touring the academy. "I was told the banquet is nearly ready to begin and your presence is required in the main banquet hall."

Kevin's face lit up and he smiled broadly. "Sounds great to me."

"They're not serving hamburgers and fries," Katie said threateningly.

"No," Kevin replied with a smug grin. "But they're serving steaks and right now a good medium rare one will work just as well."

Katie grimaced. "I don't see how you can eat something that's not properly cooked."

"If you cook it too much the steak loses its flavor," Kevin explained. "You should try it sometime."

"No thanks," Katie said, shaking her head. "Well done is fine by me."

"Let's go," Jeremy said, taking Kelsey's hand and starting toward the steps that led off the stage. "We don't want to keep them waiting. I remember how hungry I was while I was attending the Fleet Academy."

"Yes," Kevin said in agreement. "We could really put it away back in the day."

-

As the group left the stage, Clarissa and Aril were left alone. They would shift to the banquet hall using the holographic imagers shortly.

"Do you thing the Originator AI will reveal how we can enter the Dyson Sphere?" asked Ariel. She knew Jeremy really needed this information

"Maybe," Clarissa replied. "I think I've earned its trust, but I don't want to do anything to violate that."

"It's lonely," commented Ariel in understanding. "I think it's up to you and me to show it that it's not alone."

Clarissa nodded her head in agreement. So far there had been minimal contact between Ariel and the Originator AI. Clarissa hadn't wanted to overwhelm it. "After the banquet, I think it's time for you to become better acquainted with my new friend. I think you will like him; he's actually very pleasant to be around."

Moments later, the two AIs vanished as they switched to the banquet hall, leaving the massive room in silence.

In space above them, the Originator AI was still trying to learn just who these beings were that had rescued it from oblivion.

-

After the banquet was over, Jeremy took Kelsey up to the large hill, which overlooked the Fleet Academy. Below them, the pristine white buildings stood out against the reddish soil of Gaia.

Kelsey took a deep breath of the fresh air. There was an atmospheric retention field recently installed around the complex. It allowed for a higher humidity and even a few small ponds with fountains had been added. Trees and other plants had been put in place to add sufficient greenery to make the Fleet Academy almost look like a lost oasis.

"You're planning on attacking the Dyson Sphere, aren't you?" Kelsey said in a soft voice.

She knew her husband very well, and he wasn't one to shirk his duty. For the time being they were safe here inside the nebula, but there was no way to know if the Simulins had used the Dyson Sphere and its numerous hyperspace vortices to find another way to attack the Milky Way Galaxy.

Jeremy took a deep breath and looked over at Kelsey. "Yes, we have to. If we can destroy the Dyson Sphere then perhaps someday we can defeat the Simulins in this galaxy."

Kelsey stood silently, holding Jeremy's hand. She squeezed it gently and then said. "Someday, I want us to have children. It would be nice if they could be raised in a galaxy without war."

"It seems as if that's all we've ever known," Jeremy responded. "From our days in the Fleet Academy until now we've gone from one battle to the next."

"My father used to say I could do or become anything I wanted," Kelsey said as she gazed off toward the distant spaceport. The sun was setting behind them and the hill was beginning to project its shadow toward the academy buildings. "I think he always thought that I would follow in his footsteps and take over as fleet admiral at Ceres."

"Guess I screwed that up," Jeremy responded.

"My mother was pleased when we started going out together," Kelsey replied. "I don't think she wanted me following in my father's footsteps. I just wished she could have seen her grandchildren."

Jeremy reached out and put his arms around Kelsey, pulling her closer. "I think they both understood how important it was for us to take part in the war against the Hocklyns and the AIs."

"I know," Kelsey responded. "They told me so in the messages they left." All of their families had left recorded messages for the Special Five to listen to when they awakened from cryosleep.

Jeremy looked into Kelsey's deep blue eyes. "I promise you someday our fighting will be over and we can raise our family in peace. I want children the same as you."

Kelsey giggled and stepped out of Jeremy's arms. "Can you imagine what Clarissa and Ariel will do with our kids?"

Jeremy grimaced. "I try not to think about it."

Kelsey reached out and took Jeremy's hand once more. "Let's go back to the academy. We need to say goodbye to Rear Admiral Marks and then go back up to the *Avenger*." She was staying with Jeremy on the *Avenger* for now. She didn't think the *Distant Horizon* would be going anywhere soon and when it did, she wasn't certain she was going to be on it.

Early the next morning Jeremy was back in the Command Center of the *Avenger*. Ariel was at his side briefing him on her experiences from the previous evening.

"I have sixteen students signed up for my advanced hyperspace navigation class for the next semester," she said with pride in her voice. "I can't wait to start teaching."

"You will be a good teacher," Jeremy replied. He was going to have Katie monitor Ariel's classes to ensure the AI didn't get carried away with her enthusiasm.

"We've been detecting stronger power emissions from the Originator ship," Commander Kyla Malen said, stepping over closer to Jeremy.

Jeremy looked over at Ariel for an explanation.

"Clarissa says it has restored one of its secondary power generators," the dark haired AI explained. "I visited with it briefly last night, and the AI seems quite reasonable."

"That's one hell of a secondary power source," Kyla said, shaking her head in disbelief. "It's putting out more energy than a Fusion Five reactor."

"It needs the power for repairs," Ariel replied. "The Originator AI is keeping Clarissa briefed on all of its efforts to repair the ship."

Jeremy looked at one of the ship's main viewscreens, which was focused on the massive vessel. At five-thousand-meters in length and six-hundred-meters in diameter, it was a colossal spaceship. "We need a name for that AI as well as for its ship."

"I'll check," Ariel said as she closed her eyes briefly. She had a habit of doing this anytime she asked Clarissa a question.

Jeremy looked around the Command Center. Only about one-third of the normal command crew were present. Since they were in orbit around Gaia and not expecting to be leaving anytime soon, many had gone down to the planet on leave. There were still enough crew on board that the ship could respond to an emergency for a limited amount of time if it had to go into combat.

"The ship is called the *Dominator*, and the AI has a long complicated numerical identification," Ariel said after a moment of conversing with Clarissa. "He has told Clarissa he can be called Kazak."

Commander Malen eyes narrowed sharply upon hearing the ship's name. "*Dominator*," she said. "That sounds intimidating."

"Why was the ship named the *Dominator*?" asked Jeremy, agreeing with Commander Malen. He had assumed the Originators were a peaceful race similar to the Altons.

Ariel hesitated for a moment, as her eyes suddenly grew wide. "It's a warship," she said finally. "Kazak was hesitant to mention that as he didn't want to frighten us."

"Why did the Originators feel the need for a warship with all of their advanced technology?"

"Kazak says it can't answer that question as it has been classified by the Originators and only an Originator can access it."

Commander Malen shifted her gaze to the viewscreen and the Originator ship. "If that's a warship, can you imagine what type of weapons it must possess? Just one of that ship's defensive weapons disabled nearly half of the Simulin fleet!"

Jeremy nodded. He wondered if he had made a mistake in allowing the Originator ship to go into orbit around Gaia. "Ariel, is there any chance Kazak will see us as a threat?"

"Doubtful," Ariel answered promptly. "He's pleased we rescued him and his ship from the asteroid field. He has stressed a number of times that neither he nor his ship is a threat to us."

Jeremy sat down in his command chair and looked broodingly at the large vessel on the screen. Somehow, he needed to find a way into the Dyson Sphere. He was convinced if he could get a fleet of ships inside he could destroy it or at least damage it to the point where it would be useless to the Simulins.

High Commander Zarth Lantu opened his eyes to find himself in an infirmary. He tried to move his head and found it was restrained. His entire body felt as if it was on fire, and he found it difficult to breathe. There were several tubes inserted into his throat.

"Calm down, High Commander," ordered a medical technician standing nearby. "You were seriously injured and it has taken us time to heal your body to the point we could awaken you."

"My ship?"

"Destroyed along with over eighteen hundred other vessels," the med tech replied. "You and a few others were found alive once we began searching the wrecks for survivors."

"Why was I rescued?" asked Lantu. Normally destroyed ships were not searched for survivors as they were deemed to have failed in protecting the Simulin race.

"Information," said another voice as an older Simulin approached Lantu.

Lantu saw immediately, from the markings on the uniform, that this was a Supreme High Commander, one of only two in this galaxy.

"I have spoken with the others we took off the destroyed ships. We know the weapon that immobilized our ships came from the Old Ones' vessel. What do you know of this?"

"Only what our sensors recorded," answered Lantu, finding it difficult to speak. "The AIs and their organics found the ship in Ornellian space and managed to take it into hyperspace. We pursued it and sent word for other ships to join us at the Fitula Nebula. I believed if we could destroy the AI ships and the others we could gain control of the Old Ones' vessel."

"You failed!" the Supreme High Commander said in a harsh voice. "Now the vessel had been taken inside the nebula where, for the time being, it is out of our reach."

Lantu remained silent, as he knew the Supreme High Commander was speaking the truth. "What are my orders?"

"None," the Supreme High Commander said mercilessly. "You have failed the Simulin race."

Turning away from High Commander Lantu, he stepped over to a console and turned it off. Instantly the equipment keeping Lantu alive stopped functioning. With one long, convulsive breath, the High Commander died.

"There can be none but Simulin," the Supreme High Commander said as he turned to leave the room.

"None but Simulin," responded the med tech. Failure in the Simulin race wasn't tolerated.

Chapter Seventeen

Admiral Race Tolsen gazed at the large viewscreen in the front of the Command Center of the *WarHawk*. The entire screen was filled with a closeup view of the Originator Dyson Sphere. For several weeks, the fleet had slowly charted the megastructure seeking an entrance or a sign something was alive inside.

"Nothing," grumbled Colonel Cowel, shaking his head in frustration. "For two weeks we've circled that thing and we don't know anything more about it than we did when we first arrived."

"I wouldn't say that," responded Kelnor, turning around to face Cowel. "We know a lot more. We know the Dyson Sphere's exact size and we've made scans of its surface in an attempt to analyze the composition of the material it's made of. We know the sphere doesn't reflect back most sensor scans. There are no obvious entry points though we know they must exist. There has also been no reaction to our presence either positive or negative."

Brice continued to gaze at the Alton scientist. "As I said, we have learned nothing."

"There has to be a way in," Race said, staring with narrowed eyes at the Dyson Sphere. "Are we simply overlooking it?" He was just as anxious as everyone else to see what was inside the sphere.

Reesa looked over at Kelnor and then at the admiral. She took the small round globe out of her pocket and gazed at it speculatively. "This key opened up the Originator's Control Center in their hidden outpost. If we can find an entry port on the Dyson Sphere, it may provide a way for us to get in."

"We need to move closer to the sphere and take more detailed scans," stated Kelnor. "Reesa is correct; if we can find an entry port, the key she has may provide us a method of entry."

Race stood up and walked over to Reesa. He held out his hand and she gave him the small globe. It felt cool to the touch and was completely smooth. It was surprisingly heavier than he had expected. Handing it back to her, he spoke to Commander Arnett. "Put us in a closer orbit to the Dyson Sphere. We're looking for a hatch or anything that might indicate a possible entrance point into the sphere. There has to be one somewhere."

"Admiral," called out Captain Davis from his sensor console. "I've got Shari warships on the long-range sensors."

"Where, and how many?" Race returned to his command chair and set down. The long-range sensors had been quiet for the last two weeks. There had been no sign of Simulin or Shari vessels. Now that had changed.

"Fifteen," reported Captain Davis. "They're jumping into all the nearby star systems."

Commander Arnett's face took on a look of concern as she looked knowingly at Race. "They're running a search pattern, either looking for us or the Simulins."

"They'll find the remains of the Simulin ships we destroyed in the Capal Four System," warned Colonel Cowel. "The Simulins will suspect a Federation fleet was the cause."

"We're running with our stealth shields up," Race said. "They can't detect us." However, he agreed with the colonel. An analysis of the weapons used in the battle from the debris would indicate Human or Alton ships were involved.

"No, but they're bound to intensify their search once they find the battle scene," added Colonel Cowel. "The Shari will find out the Simulin ships encountered a powerful fleet, which will lead them to suspect our involvement and they'll be hunting for us."

Race knew the colonel was probably correct. "We'll worry about the Shari if they detect us or find this system. The Dyson Sphere hides this system's sun so the likelihood of them finding it is infinitesimal." At least Race hoped it was. "Commander Arnett, put us into orbit around the Dyson Sphere at two hundred thousand kilometers."

High Lord Aktill stared at his viewscreen and the large debris field they had found in the system. More mystifying were the ruins, which had been detected on two of the planets. He had sent several teams of Shari soldiers down to the surface of one of the worlds and a team reported encountering dangerous robotic creatures that had killed most of its members. Further sensor scans revealed a large number of these robots on the surface and High Lord Aktill had hastily recalled all of his soldiers.

"Reports from the surface indicate the ruins are of immense age," Lower Lord Samarth said. "This civilization died out eons before we even became thinking beings."

"We have found several worlds with ancient structures," Aktill said. "These dead worlds may be the source of all the rumors and superstition which surrounds this cluster. The AIs were also very old; perhaps they knew of this ancient race and that is why they banned us from exploring it."

"That may be so, but why are the unknown ships here in this cluster and who destroyed them?" asked Samarth. There was much about this he didn't understand. "We've found debris from another ship type, but so far we haven't been able to identify the race it comes from."

"What were they fighting over?" asked Aktill as he thought of the possibilities. None seemed to make any sense.

These worlds were all dead; there was no reason for any other race to be here.

Lower Lord Samarth turned away from the sensor console where he had been studying some data on the ship debris field. "Sensors indicate the unknown ships were destroyed by energy weapon and particle beam fire. There is also evidence of antimatter warheads being used."

"The humans!" swore High Lord Aktill, his eyes narrowing sharply. "They have dared to enter our space."

"If it was the humans, where have they gone? The debris field is recent."

High Lord Aktill stood still thinking about his next move. If the humans had come to the Rylus Cluster, they had violated Shari space. That was an act of war. "Call in the rest of our ships from the outlying areas of the cluster. We will do a thorough search using this system as the starting point. I suspect the unknowns and the humans are searching for something in this cluster, which has something to do with these ancient ruins. That is the only explanation for their presence."

"But what can they be seeking?" asked Samarth, looking confused. "There's nothing here."

"Look below us," Aktill said, pointing to one of the viewscreens showing the surface of the planet they were orbiting. "That's a very ancient civilization. We have no idea as to how advanced they were. What if somewhere in this cluster they left a cache of their technology, which would explain the unknown's presence as well as the humans."

"Perhaps," Samarth responded with a doubtful look upon his face. "I will send out the recall message to our other ships."

Aktill nodded as he folded his powerful arms across his chest. If the humans were here in Shari space, he would find them and destroy them. When he made his eventual report to the Shari Grand Council of High Lords, there was little doubt in his mind they would declare a state of war between the Shari Empire and the humans and their allies.

Several days passed and Race's fleet continued to orbit the Dyson Sphere but much more closely. They had located several areas on the surface that were possibly hatches. Some of them were twenty to thirty kilometers in diameter. There were also a few structures that might be some type of control centers.

"What do you think?" asked Commander Malen. She had one of the large hatches up on the main viewscreen so they could study it in detail.

Before Race could respond, an alarm began sounding on the sensor console. Captain Davis quickly shut it off.

"We may have a problem, Admiral," Davis said as a green icon on his sensor screen began blinking. "The stealth shield on the dreadnought *Jaden* is down."

"What? How?" Race couldn't believe their bad luck. As large as the dreadnought was, it would show up on the Shari long-range sensors. Race wasn't certain what their detection range was, but there were so many Shari vessels in the surrounding systems the *Jaden* was bound to set off an alarm.

"It was an accident," Commander Arnett said. She was speaking to the commander of the ship. "A crewman was doing routine maintenance on a power coupling when it shorted out. The crewman was killed and the short cause a power feedback, which momentarily compromised the stealth shield. They have it back up now, but it was down for nearly twenty seconds."

"Is that time enough for the Shari to detect the *Jaden*?"

"Yes, Admiral," Captain Davis answered. "I strongly suspect the Shari will shortly know we're here."

"Gather the fleet into defensive formation D-03," ordered Race, taking a deep breath. "Send out an emergency FTL message indicating our location may have been compromised."

The message would be transmitted along the line of FTL buoys they had placed between Federation space and their current location. It shouldn't be detectable to the Shari. With any luck a reinforcing Federation fleet would be here in a few days. At least Race hoped it would. As many Shari ships as they had been detecting, he doubted if his fleet could defeat such a large force even with their advanced weapons.

High Lord Aktill was inspecting the soldiers aboard his flagship when he received a message requesting his immediate presence in the Command Center. He dismissed the troops and quickly made his way through the ship's corridors until he was once more standing on his command dais. "Report!"

"We've detected a contact four point two light-years distant," Lower Lord Samarth informed him.

"Has it been identified?"

"No, High Lord," Samarth answered. "The contact only appeared briefly before it vanished."

"An anomaly or false contact?"

Samarth shook his head. "No, we've checked our systems. Several other ships reported the same contact."

"What type of star is at that location?"

"That's the problem," replied Samarth, looking confused. "There is no star at those coordinates."

Aktill took a moment to consider his options. That contact needed to be investigated. The human fleet he was searching for could be hiding in open space away from any star system with its power limited to avoid detection. "Send a battlecruiser and two support cruisers to investigate. I want to know if anything is there."

Aktill watched as his orders were swiftly carried out. If something was indeed at that location, he would summon his entire fleet and investigate it in force. If it was the suspected human fleet, he would destroy it. He was also mystified about one thing; if this was indeed the humans, why were they still here?

Race was sitting in his command chair watching the nearby tactical display showing the Shari ships in the Capal Four System. He frowned worriedly as three Shari ships suddenly vanished, indicating they had jumped into hyperspace. "Where are those ships going?" It had only been a few minutes since the *Jaden* had briefly lost its stealth shield.

Captain Davis studied his long-range sensors, which were capable of detecting a ship in hyperspace. "Straight for us."

"Is there any chance they won't detect our ships?"

"I don't think they'll be able to detect us as long as our stealth shields are up," Davis answered. "However, I don't think they'll miss the Dyson Sphere if they spend any time scanning this system. If anything, they'll detect the presence of an object of mass."

Race nodded his acceptance that the Shari were about to find the Dyson Sphere. "Communications, send out an additional FTL message that we expect the Shari to discover the Dyson Sphere within the next hour."

The minutes slowly passed and the tension in the Command Center steadily grew. Suddenly alarms sounded on the sensor console.

"Contacts!" called out Captain Davis as three red threat icons blossomed in the nearby tactical display.

"Go to Condition One," ordered Race as he leaned forward gazing at the contacts. "How close are they?"

"Sixty-four million kilometers," Davis replied. "Their sensors should be coming online shortly."

Race nodded and took a deep breath. He had orders not to allow the Shari to take control of the Dyson Sphere though he doubted if they would be able to find anyway to enter. Not without the key that Reesa had.

"Detecting sensor scans," Davis reported as several lights on his console lit up.

Commander Arnett was standing at her command console watching the red threat icons intently. "One battlecruiser and two escorts. We could take them out."

"No," replied Race, shaking his head. "They don't know we're here. It will take them awhile to figure out what they've found. Every minute we can delay combat is one minute closer our reinforcing fleet will be."

"We don't even know if they're on the way," pointed out Colonel Cowel. "Or if there's a fleet at the coordinates we've been sending our messages to."

Race didn't reply. This had been a concern to him as well. Was the Special Ops department powerful enough to assemble a fleet large enough to hold the Dyson Sphere against the Shari? The Altons would probably contribute a few ships, but most likely not many since so much of their population was opposed to war. The fleet would be composed primarily of ships from the Human Federation of Worlds and there was no way the Federation Council was going to allow a large fleet to enter Shari space without their permission. Race couldn't see how Special Ops could conceal the movement of so many ships in the first place. He was expecting, at the most, a large task group of thirty to fifty vessels. He had a sinking feeling from all the red threat icons of Shari ships they had detected in recent days that was not going to be enough.

The Shari ships stayed in the system for nearly two hours, even moving to within twenty million kilometers of the Dyson Sphere before accelerating away on their subspace drives and then entering hyperspace. It was obvious they had been afraid to jump in the massive gravity well created by the Dyson Sphere and the star it shielded.

"They're gone," Commander Arnett said as the red threat icons vanished from the tactical display.

"Yes," Race replied. "But they'll be back as soon as they can assemble their fleet. Take us back to Condition Three and let everyone get some rest. We've probably gained a few hours."

Race turned his attention back to the Dyson Sphere. They were about to fight a fleet battle over possession of the Originator megastructure. He just hoped it was worth it.

High Lord Aktill stared in disbelief at the results of the sensor scans taken by the battlecruiser *Crimson Glory*. The first sensor scans had shown very little, but once the sensors had been changed to a different frequency, a massive object had become visible.

"It encompasses the system's star," Lower Lord Samarth said in awe. "Who could build such a structure?"

"The inhabitants of these dead worlds," answered Aktill. A construction project of this magnitude was something far beyond anything the Shari were capable of. "Their science must be truly advanced."

"You sound as if they may still be alive."

"Possibly," Aktill replied. On one of the Command Center's main viewscreens, an image of the object was being projected. It was very dark and difficult so see with only the light of the stars to illuminate it. "They may have abandoned their worlds to live inside of this sphere. Our own scientists have speculated such a sphere could serve a race for tens of millions of years, if not longer."

"That's why the unknowns and the humans are here," Samarth said in realization. "They are seeking this sphere the people of these worlds built."

Aktill nodded his head. "Yes, they seek the science the sphere contains as well as contact with its builders if they still survive."

"What are we going to do?"

"The Rylus Cluster is inside Shari space," Aktill replied in a firm voice. "If the inhabitants of that sphere are dead then it is ours to possess."

"What if they're alive? With the science they obviously have at their disposal it might be wise to leave them alone."

"We'll deal with that possibility when it occurs," Aktill responded dismissively. "For now, we will gather our fleet and take possession of the system the sphere is in. We'll let the Grand Council decide what to do with it after that; it's not our decision to make."

"And if the humans are there also?"

"We destroy them!"

Two full days passed and Race was beginning to wonder when the Shari would attack. There was a possibility they had reported the discovery of the Dyson Sphere to their superiors and were waiting for orders or reinforcements. Either didn't bode well for Race's fleet.

"Admiral, the Shari fleet is beginning to enter hyperspace," reported Captain Davis.

So it begins, thought Race. "Take the fleet to Condition One and prepare for immediate combat."

Instantly alarms began sounding and red lights began flashing. The crew quickly went to their battlestations knowing they were about to fight a major engagement against the Shari.

Race looked over at Commander Arnett. "All ships are to drop their stealth shields and bring their defense shields online."

Madelyn nodded and quickly passed on the order over her ship-to-ship comm.

Race heard a subtle change in the normal background noise as the *WarHawk's* powerful defense shield was energized.

"All weapons ready to fire," reported Major Daniels from Tactical.

"Stand by to deploy defense drones," ordered Race. Their only chance against a Shari fleet as large as this one was to use the drones' ion beams to blow holes in their energy shields.

"What about our fighters and bombers?" asked Colonel Cowel.

"Those too, but not until the Shari arrive and we're about to engage in combat. Have all bombers armed with Shrike missiles to be used against Shari ships with weakened shields. The fighters will fly cover for them."

Colonel Cowel quickly passed on the orders to the other ships as well as to the *WarHawk's* two flight bays.

Race turned his attention to a nearby tactical display showing the inbound Shari fleet. He took a deep breath and fastened his safety harness in preparation for combat maneuvers. Once again, former Fleet Admiral Streth had placed Race and his command in harms way. Race was beginning to wonder if he got out of this one if it might not be time for him to retire from the fleet.

-

High Lord Aktill wasn't surprised when a number of red threat icons suddenly began materializing on the tactical screen. They were still over a light-year away from the target.

"Humans?" asked Lower Lord Samarth, staring at the red icons.

"Most likely," Aktill responded. "We must be prepared for combat once we emerge from hyperspace."

Aktill gazed at the tactical screen, pondering the significance of the human ships being at the sphere. How had they learned of it to begin with and how had they destroyed the unknowns' ships? From what he had been told, no Shari warship had ever managed to do so. It seemed to indicate the humans had some very powerful weapons, which might be very detrimental to Shari ships.

-

Race sucked in a deep breath as the Shari fleet began to exit hyperspace. Hundreds of red threat icons began appearing on the four tactical displays in the Command Center. "Ship types?"

"One hundred and fourteen battlecruisers and one hundred and eighty-six support cruisers," Captain Davis reported as the information appeared on one of his data screens. "Distance is twenty million kilometers."

"All ships are at Condition One," added Commander Arnett.

"Ready to deploy defense drones," reported Colonel Cowel.

"All weapons systems are online," informed Major Daniels.

Race looked around at his command crew. "Let's close the distance. Launch the drones at the six hundred thousand kilometer mark as well as the fighters and bombers. Switch to attack formation A-14."

-

The two fleets quickly moved toward one another. The Shari formed up into a disk formation facing the advancing Federation fleet, which was in a cone formation apex forward with the *WarHawk* leading the way. As the fleets passed the six hundred thousand kilometer mark, hundreds of defense drones began to launch as well as the fleet's fighters and bombers.

"Defense drones are away," reported Colonel Cowel as three hundred and seventy small amber icons suddenly appeared. "Fighters and bombers are launching now." Between the *WarHawk* and the eighteen dreadnoughts, they had 1,160 Talon fighters and 760 Anlon bombers. They were represented by smaller green icons.

"Fleets are continuing to close; combat range in forty seconds," called out Captain Davis.

Race studied one of the tactical displays for a long moment. "Have the fighters go in with the defense drones to help draw fire away from them. We need to use the drones before the Shari realize what they're capable of."

More alarms suddenly began sounding on the sensor console. "Admiral, I have multiple contacts on the long-range sensors," Davis added as he studied the new contacts on his screen.

"Simulin or Shari?"

"Federation and Alton!" called out Captain Davis in astonishment. "They'll be here in forty minutes."

"Major Daniels, initiate jamming on all subspace and hyperspace frequencies. I don't want the Shari to know we have reinforcements inbound." Race was feeling vastly relieved knowing reinforcements were so near. How they had managed to get here so soon he would find out later. For now he had a battle plan he needed to execute.

"Commander Arnett, keep us at extreme engagement range. I want to draw this battle out until our other ships can get here." If he could avoid a short-range engagement, he could limit the damage to his fleet. Once the Alton and Federation ships arrived, it would change the odds, and then he could commit his ships fully to the battle.

Madelyn nodded, quickly passed on the orders, and then she turned toward the admiral. "That fleet must have been close by; it's too much of a coincidence for them to arrive at nearly the same time as the Shari."

"We'll find out about that later," Race responded. "Right now we have a long range battle to fight. I'm authorizing one pass for the Defense Globes and the fighters, and then I want them pulled back to the fleet."

Race shifted his attention to the large viewscreen on the front wall of the Command Center showing one of the Shari vessels. A large cylindrically shaped spaceship was being displayed. It was dark and menacing with numerous energy weapon turrets and small hatches indicating possible missile tubes. The ship on the screen was a Shari battlecruiser and was eleven-hundred-meters in length.

-

As the defense drones and the fighters neared the Shari fleet, they began to be targeted by the Shari ships. The defense drones and their fighter escort went into a weaving pattern as they attempted to dodge the incoming defensive fire. Occasionally a Shari energy beam would spear one of the fighters and it would vanish in a brilliant fireball. The Defense Globes had a minimal energy shield and were more resistant to the Shari weapons fire. As the drones and the fighters drew nearer the Shari fleet, the defensive fire became more heated. More fighters and now an occasional defense drone died as energy weapons blew them apart.

-

High Lord Aktill watched the inbound bogeys with growing concern in his eyes. He had learned from past battles not to underestimate the humans. "Focus all of our firepower on those inbound targets."

"Yes, High Lord," Samarth responded.

"All long-range communications and sensors are being jammed," reported the sensor operator. "We can't detect anything beyond two million kilometers and our communications are restricted to short-range only."

"Why would they jam our sensors?" asked Samarth with growing concern. "What is it they don't want us to see?"

High Lord Aktill had a chilling feeling he wasn't going to like that answer. He needed to destroy this human fleet as soon as possible. Looking at one of the viewscreens, he gazed at a deadly monstrosity. A warship, obviously of human and Alton design, was being displayed. It was three-thousand-meters in length and four-hundred-meters in diameter. The bow of the vessel was a globe six-hundred-meters in diameter and the stern, where the engines were located, flared out to five-hundred-meters. It was the largest warship he had ever seen.

"The small globes are firing," reported Samarth. Then his face turned pale. "They're firing some type of beam weapon that's tearing holes in our energy shields!"

-

The inbound Defense Globes fired their ion beams, blasting small four-meter holes in the Shari shields. Almost immediately, the two particle beam turrets each globe was equipped with fired their dual beams through the holes, carving deep glowing rents into the hulls of numerous Shari vessels.

From the dreadnoughts and the *WarHawk*, sublight antimatter missiles slammed into the hulls of Shari ships through the small holes in the shields created by the ion beams. Throughout the Shari formation glowing suns appeared as ships died under the unrelenting attack.

The Shari were also firing back. Their weapons fire was now divided between the attacking Defense Globes, fighters, and the human fleet, which was at extreme weapons range. Even so, they fired their batteries of energy weapons while their missile tubes slid silently open. Hundreds of sublight missiles with thirty-megaton warheads flashed from the tubes and accelerated toward their targets.

Race grimaced as the *WarHawk* shook violently for over a minute. When it settled back down he looked inquiringly at Colonel Cowel.

"Nuclear missiles, big ones," he reported. "Over thirty of then impacted our energy screen. There was no damage to the ship. Energy screen is holding at 88 percent and is regenerating."

"Our other ships?"

Colonel Cowel listened for a moment to his long-range comm, which was set to the fleet frequency. "The *Trieste* and the *Raven* are reporting minor damage."

"It could have been worse," Commander Arnett commented. "We're at extreme weapons range and their energy weapons are nearly impotent at this distance. Our vessels were designed to fight Simulins so we have a distinct weapons and energy shield advantage."

"Our beam weapons are nearly useless also," Race reminded the commander. "Captain Davis, what are the results of our defense globe strike?"

"Sixteen Shari escort cruisers destroyed and seven of their battlecruisers. Many others have sustained damage. They're refocusing their attention to the fighters and the Defense Globes in an effort to remove that threat. They've even launched a few nuclear missiles, detonating them in our fighter and defense globe formations."

"Pull them back," Race ordered, not wanting to lose his pilots. "They've served their purpose. The Shari have stopped their advance."

-

High Lord Aktill gazed in anger at the viewscreen where the Shari battlecruiser *Tarnnith* was being displayed. The battlecruiser was missing a major portion its bow section. A good two-hundred-meters had been blown away and another one-hundred-meters was a mangled jumble of twisted metal. The ship still had life support functioning but had lost its energy shield.

"Have them pull back to the rear of our formation," ordered Aktill.

"Analysis of the weapons the small globes used against us indicates some type of high energy ion beam that is disrupting our energy shields," Samarth informed the High Lord. "The humans are pulling their small attack ships and the globes back toward their formation."

Aktill took a few moments to study the tactical situation. "We'll give our ships some time to repair what damage they can. When repairs are completed, we'll advance to pointblank range and hammer the humans with our energy weapons and missiles. If we concentrate our fire on just a few of their ships at a time, we should be able to bring their shields down and destroy them."

-

Precious minutes passed as Race waited tensely for the Shari to resume their attack. Their jamming was even preventing them from detecting the inbound Federation fleet though Race knew it had to be getting near.

"Shari are advancing," warned Commander Arnett as several warning alarms sounded on the sensor console.

"They want a short-range engagement," commented Colonel Cowel with concern in his eyes. "They must hope that at that range they can bring down our shields."

Race nodded his head and then flipped his mini-comm over to ship-to-ship. "We have a Federation fleet inbound toward our position. It should be here momentarily. However, the Shari are going to reach us first. All ships continuous fire; let's show the Shari we aren't to be messed with."

"Weapons firing!" called out Major Daniels as his tactical team went to work.

-

The Shari fleet had closed to optimal weapons range. Space was full of destructive energy beams, power beams, and particle beam fire. Beams of destructive energy flashed back and forth between the two fleets. An energy beam penetrated the shield of a Shari battlecruiser, blowing an energy beam turret to shreds and blasting out a huge gaping hole in the hull of the ship. Other energy beams penetrated the weakening shield, ripping open compartment after compartment. Inside the ship, frantic Shari raced trying to close emergency hatches and bring the spreading fires under control. Then a Devastator Three missile detonated and fifty megatons of energy turned the ship into molten metal.

In the human formation, dozens of Shari battlecruisers were firing every weapon they had at the dreadnought *Raven.* Its shield flared brighter and brighter as numerous thirty-megaton nuclear warheads impacted the energy shield. Finally, an energy beam penetrated, raking the hull leaving a deep gash in the side of the ship. Inside, alarms sounded and emergency bulkheads slammed shut. Two other energy beams penetrated the weakening shield, boring deep inside the two-thousand-meter vessel. Secondary explosions began shaking the ship, sending sections of the hull drifting off into space. With a bright flare the energy shield failed, leaving the vessel suddenly defenseless from the Shari missiles. Six thirty-megaton explosions suddenly tore the ship apart, leaving glowing wreckage and wisps of burning gas, which quickly faded, as there was no oxygen to keep it burning.

"Dreadnought *Raven* is down," reported Captain Davis in a shaken voice. "They battered its shield down with multiple energy beam strikes and nuclear missiles. Sensors indicate six explosions in the megaton range destroyed the ship."

Race grimaced at hearing of the ship's destruction. Over three thousand people, both Human and Alton, had just died. "Keep all weapons firing. Take those Shari ships out!"

"I have Federation ships exiting hyperspace at seven hundred thousand kilometers," reported Captain Davis excitedly.

"Admiral, I have a Rear Admiral Massie Tolsen on the comm," reported Captain Denise Travers from Communications. "She wants to know if you need any assistance."

Race reeled in shock at hearing those words. Massie? Here? A rear admiral? "Put her on my comm frequency."

"Hello, big brother," a familiar female voice said. "I see you've gotten yourself into another predicament."

"Massie, I don't know how you became a rear admiral but we need to eliminate this Shari fleet before they take word of the Dyson Sphere back to their empire."

"On our way," Massie answered. "And Race, I knew from the beginning you hadn't resigned; so do Mom and Dad."

"Ships still emerging from hyperspace," Captain Davis said. "I'm detecting at least one hundred and twenty Alton battleships inbound to intercept the Shari. There are

Federation battleships, battlecarriers, battlecruisers, and strikecruisers in the fleet as well."

"How many ships total?" asked Race, still finding it hard to believe his sister was actually here.

"Last count is five hundred and twelve."

Commander Arnett turned toward Race with a big smile on her face. "Talk about a relief fleet!"

"Shari are attempting to withdraw!" called out Captain Davis. "They're disengaging and turning away."

"We can't let them," Race said determinedly. "I want that Shari fleet destroyed! Send in the bombers, Defense Globes, and the fighters."

-

High Lord Aktill looked in shock at the main tactical screen. It was full of new red threat icons rapidly closing with his fleet. Even as he watched, he saw on one of the many Command Center viewscreens another of his battlecruisers explode as it was turned into a miniature sun.

"More Federation ships, including Alton battleships," said Lower Lord Samarth as he listened to panicked reports coming in from across the fleet. "Our ship commanders want to know what their orders are."

"We leave," Aktill said in a shrill voice. "The humans and their allies have invaded our empire. We must get word back to the Shari Grand Council that we are now at war and what we've found here!"

-

For many minutes, the battle continued in full fury. The Shari were now outnumbered and heavily outgunned. Ship after ship died in blazing pyres of antimatter destruction. Occasionally a Federation vessel would fall as a squadron of Shari vessels managed to blast a shield down in their frantic attempt to escape. A few Shari vessels did manage to fight themselves to safety and upon escaping the battle jumped into hyperspace.

-

"Some of the Shari ships have escaped," announced Commander Arnett as she watched them vanish on the tactical display near her.

"How many?" asked Race with a sickening feeling. Those ships would race back to their empire and report on the battle. He greatly feared he had just plunged the Federation into another galactic war.

"Forty-seven," Captain Davis answered. "Some of them are heavily damaged and probably won't make it back to their empire."

"However, some will," Race said with a deep sigh. He turned back to Commander Arnett. "Let's get search and rescue out there. We have some fighter and bomber pilots who need to be rescued. See what help our damaged ships need. Captain Travers, get my sister back on the comm. I need to meet with her and find out just what the hell is going on and how she became a rear admiral."

-

Race was sitting in his quarters when a marine opened the hatch and his younger sister walked in. She was dressed in the dark blue uniform of a rear admiral and had a big smile on her face. Race stood up and felt relief at seeing Massie.

"Hello," she said, walking over and giving Race a big hug. She stepped back and looked at him. "I saw the Dyson Sphere on my way over to the *WarHawk* in my shuttle. My God, Race; it's gigantic!"

Race looked down at his sister. He was slightly taller than she was. "Yes. Now the big question is, what are we going to do with it?"

"Explore it and learn more about the Originators," Massie said excitedly, her eyes lighting up. "My support fleet will be here shortly and there are ten Alton science ships coming."

"I don't understand," Race said with a frown spreading across his face. "How did you become a rear admiral and where did you get that fleet?"

"It was the Altons," Massie explained. "I was already in line for rear admiral and Ambassador Tureen got Fleet Admiral Nagumo to approve it. The Altons had already assembled their fleet and demanded the Federation Council supply suitable numbers of warships in case your secret mission discovered the Dyson Sphere's location. Ambassador Tureen went in front of the Federation Council as soon as your fleet left. There was quite a ruckus when Ambassador Tureen told them about the Originators and that there might be a Dyson Sphere in Shari space. Just the thought of the Shari gaining control of such an object frightened the council into agreeing with Ambassador Tureen's demands."

"Remind me never to play poker with him," Race said, shaking his head amazed at what the Alton ambassador had managed to accomplish. "I still don't understand where all the Federation ships came from."

"Every fleet near the Shari border was ordered to rendezvous with the Altons. I was given command of the Federation forces and told to respond to whatever threat the Shari might pose to the Dyson Sphere if you managed to locate it. Alton Admiral Lankell is the overall commander of the mission. He has experience from the war with the Hocklyns and the AIs and is a very good tactician."

"I still don't understand why you were given command of such a large force. Aren't there other admirals in the fleet with you?"

"Yes," admitted Massie, looking a little aggravated. "Some of them were hesitant to accept my command, but after a dressing down from Admiral Lankell, they changed their minds. Also, Ambassador Tureen was very insistent I command the Federation forces."

Race sat back down, indicating for his sister to take a seat also. "So, just how does Admiral Lankell intend to defend the Dyson Sphere? Enough Shari vessels escaped to send word to their Grand Council as to what we've discovered here."

"The Altons have a two-fold plan," Massie answered. "A large Alton fleet is going to Shari space with an ambassador to speak to the Shari Grand Council of High Lords. They want to have this star cluster declared neutral territory with the Altons promising nothing learned here will ever be used against the Shari Empire."

"What if they refuse?" Race couldn't see the Shari accepting this request.

Massie let out a deep sigh. "In the supply fleet there are twenty Alton Indomitable Class battlestations as well as a number of fleet repair vessels. We're going to build a base close to the Dyson Sphere powerful enough to repel any foreseeable Shari attack."

Race nodded. The next few months were going to be highly interesting. He was surprised the Altons were taking such a lead role in this with their population being comprised of so many pacifists. Then again, how often did one get to explore a Dyson Sphere built by a race that had been extinct for over two million years?

Massie stood up and gazed at her big brother. "I want you to take me on a tour of the *WarHawk*. You do know you have command of the most powerful ship ever built."

Race stood up and smiled. "Yes, she's quite a vessel." As they left his quarters, Race felt immense relief knowing his sister and his parents knew he hadn't been forced to resign from the fleet. With Massie here his life would be quite interesting; things were never dull when she was around. With the ships that had just arrived and the supply fleet inbound, they were going to get to explore the Dyson Sphere. Race wondered what they would find when they got inside. He had always wanted to be an explorer and now that wish was going to be granted.

"How's Mom and Dad?" he asked as they began walking off down the corridor with two marines escorts. "I want to hear all about home." As they ambled down the corridor, Race listened as his sister spoke of their parents.

In space, the Dyson Sphere waited. For two million years, no living being had walked its surface. That was about to change.

Chapter Eighteen

Jeremy stared at the viewscreen in the *Avenger* as the sixteen-hundred-meter battleship once more emerged from hyperspace. They were deep within the blue giant cluster and nearing the dark matter nebula, which hid the Dyson Sphere. It had taken some coaxing, but the Originator AI had finally furnished Clarissa with a code to allow them access to the interior of the sphere. It had even told them where the best entry point would be. They had been stealthily moving through the cluster once again using the T-Tauri stars for their hyperspace exits so as not to be detected by the Simulins. It helped that the dense hydrogen clouds in the nebula played havoc with long-range sensors, making detection even harder.

"All ships have exited hyperspace," Ariel reported as she checked the ship's sensors. "No signs of Simulin ships."

Jeremy nodded. They had only detected a few since they had entered the nebula and those had been at extreme range.

"Distance to the first target?"

"Eighteen light-years," Ariel answered promptly.

Jeremy activated his ship-to-ship comm. "All ships, twenty minutes until we jump to tunnel target one." That should allow all the drive cores to properly cool.

Looking at the tactical displays, they were full of green icons. If they failed to destroy the Dyson Sphere, it would cripple his fleet strength for years to come. He had brought ten Federation battleships, twenty battlecruisers, sixty strikecruisers, seventy Alton battleships, fifty Alton battlecruisers, three hundred AI fifteen-hundred meter spheres, and all one hundred and twenty of the one-thousand-meter AI warspheres. A total of six hundred thirty ships would be going into battle in an attempt to destroy the

Dyson Sphere. If they failed, none of them would be returning home. He had left Admiral Jackson at Gaia with a substantial force as well as Grayseth and his Carethian ships. Grayseth had objected stringently about being left behind, but Jeremy had patiently explained to his large Bear friend that if the fleet failed to return Grayseth would be looked to for leadership of the colony. That placated the Bear and he had reluctantly agreed to stay at Gaia.

"All systems functioning at optimum levels," Commander Malen reported as she stepped away from her command console. "Ship is at Condition Two."

"Are we doing the right thing?" Kevin asked over the private comm channel that connected him and Angela with Jeremy and Ariel. He had voiced his concern earlier to Jeremy about taking so many of their warships and dedicating them to this battle.

Jeremy took a deep breath. This was something he had debated with himself for many long hours as well. It has been tempting to stay inside the nebula where they were safe from the Simulins. The Altons were using another one of their technologies to thicken the gaseous clouds that surrounded Gaia, making them too dense to travel through in hyperspace. They were also doing this in other areas of the gaseous nebula to make finding a safe passage through almost impossible. They needed several years yet to accomplish their plan and once it was finished, the nebula would finally be safe from Simulin attack. Even when the Simulins finally figured out how to travel through the higher bands of hyperspace currently being scrambled by the hyperspace interference buoys, the thicker areas of the gas cloud would protect Gaia.

"When the relief fleets arrived they brought specific orders from Fleet Admiral Nagumo and Fleet Admiral Streth we were to do everything in our power to take the battle to the Simulins. That was over two years ago."

Kevin looked at his sensor screens and then back toward Jeremy. "I have a lot of respect for both fleet admirals, but they aren't here."

"By attacking the Simulins we're protecting the home galaxy from attack," Angela said. "Brace and I have talked about this. We can't just hide in the nebula forever. I know it's a risk, but it's one I believe we have to take."

Ariel looked at Jeremy and then spoke. "If we're successful destroying the Dyson Sphere we prevent the Simulins from calling in major reinforcements from other galaxies they may control. It will also allow us to build up our AI fleet to take on the Simulins for possession of this galaxy."

Kevin leaned back in his chair and gazed at his console. "We have the Originator ship; we could learn a lot from it."

"It may even allow us to go home someday," Jeremy added.

Angela looked over at Jeremy and then to Kevin. "We are home," she said in a soft voice. "Gaia is ours and our children's future."

Kevin nodded his agreement. He had long since given up any hope of returning to the home galaxy. Gaia was a good world and it was where he and Katie would someday raise their children.

The twenty minutes quickly passed and the massed fleet jumped back into hyperspace. Their first target was one of the seven hundred and forty kilometer energy collection spheres just outside of the tunnel entrance to the Dyson Sphere. The plan was to jump in, engage whatever ships were present and then destroy the sphere. Once that was done a blockading force would be left behind to secure the entrance to the black matter tunnel while the rest of the fleet entered and attacked the Dyson Sphere.

-

The *Avenger* exited the swirling blue-white spatial vortex just twenty thousand kilometers from the Simulin energy collection sphere. Around her, hundreds of other vortexes opened as the rest of the Federation fleet exited hyperspace.

"Contacts!" called out Kevin as his sensors began picking up Simulin vessels. "Seven battlecruisers and ten escort cruisers."

"All ships, formation A-03," Jeremy ordered over the ship-to-ship comm. Formation A-03 was an attack formation resembling a half sphere with the flat side facing the Simulins. Damaged ships could fall back and be replaced by the ships in the rear of the formation.

-

In space, the Federation fleet quickly formed up and began advancing toward the Simulin warships and the massive collector station. On the station alarms sounded as the Simulin crew was summoned to battlestations. Hundreds of energy cannons were activated and missile hatches slid open. The station's powerful energy shield snapped into existence as the station prepared for combat. Never in the long history of the Simulins had someone dared to attack one of the stations. A frantic message was sent down the black matter tunnel sending word of the impending attack and requesting fleet reinforcements.

The Simulin fleet formed up around the station to help give it added protection. The station was essential to help provide the energy needed to operate the intergalactic vortexes. It could have a crippling affect on operations if it were damaged or destroyed.

As the Federation fleet entered optimal engagement range, the collector station opened fire and space became full of hundreds of powerful energy beams, each seeking to destroy one of the incoming attacking ships.

-

Jeremy winced as the *Avenger* shook from several powerful Simulin energy beams smashing into the ship's energy shield. "Maximum acceleration and close to pointblank range," he ordered. Jeremy planned to overwhelm the Simulin defenses. This was a battle he needed to win quickly so they could enter the tunnel and make their way to the Dyson Sphere before Simulin reinforcements arrived.

"Weapons firing," reported Lieutenant Preston.

"AI sphere 227 is down," reported Kevin as the fifteen-hundred-meter sphere vanished from his sensors.

Looking at the viewscreens, Jeremy could see countless explosions lighting up space. This battle was just a precursor to what was waiting for them inside the black matter nebula.

-

The Simulin warships were under heavy attack. Not just one or two but dozens of particle beams were striking their shields. The beams were causing the shields to flare up brightly and then they began to penetrate. Particle beam fire slammed into the stern of a Simulin battlecruiser, blasting a hole completely through the vessel. A well placed Devastator Three missile exploded in the damaged area, blowing the ship apart. The other Simulin ships were rapidly suffering the same fate as their defenses were overwhelmed. In less than thirty seconds, all seventeen Simulin warships had been ruthlessly eliminated.

However, the Simulin energy collector station was another matter. It had a powerful energy shield and was heavily armed. Its energy weapons reached out and overloaded the shield on an Alton battlecruiser. The cruiser was cut to pieces as dozens of energy beams tore it apart. From the missile hatches of the station, two hundred sublight antimatter missiles flashed out and struck one small section of the advancing Federation fleet formation. Four strikecruisers died as they were instantly turned into miniature suns.

-

Jeremy grimaced as the destruction of the four strikecruisers was reported. "Rear Admiral Barnes, it's your turn," he said over the comm, which connected him to the *Distant Horizon*. They had a plan to destroy the station and now was the time to implement it.

-

From the center of the formation, the *Distant Horizon* fired its powerful ion cannon from its bow. The beam flashed out and impacted the energy screen of the Simulin station. For long seconds, the beam tore at the shield as the full power of the exploration dreadnought's Fusion Five reactors fed it energy. Then a twelve-meter hole suddenly formed in the station's screen and four one hundred-megaton antimatter missiles flashed through. Each missile detonated simultaneously within one kilometer of each other, shaking the station to its core. Molten metal flared up and huge pieces of the station's hull were torn loose.

The station's screen flickered briefly, but that was long enough to allow more antimatter missiles to penetrate as well particle beams. More titanic explosions rattled its surface as the beams cut deep trenches into the armored hull. The damage was now so severe that internal explosions began to rock the station. The Simulin energy collection station had a tremendous amount of energy stored from the surrounding blue giant stars and now the energy containment systems became compromised. The energy was suddenly released, tearing through the station. In a blinding explosion, the station blew apart, sending flaming debris in all directions.

-

"Target is down," Kevin reported as the large red icon swelled up and slowly began to dwindle. "I can't even measure how much energy was released in that explosion."

Jeremy breathed a long sigh of relief. The first part of the attack had been a success. He spoke once more over the ship-to-ship comm. "Admiral Sithe, prepare your blocking fleet. All ships that received substantial damage will be staying with you. All other ships prepare for hyperspace jump to the Dyson Sphere."

On one of the tactical displays, Admiral Sithe and his task group moved away from the attack formation. The admiral from New Providence had twenty ships under his command. His personal battleship, the *Star Defender*, two battlecruisers, two Alton battleships, four Alton battlecruisers, eight fifteen-hundred-meter AI spheres, and three AI warspheres. Their job was to keep the dark matter entrance to the Dyson Sphere clear of any incoming enemy ships until the fleet returned from its mission.

"What did we lose?" asked Jeremy. He was aware of some of the losses.

"Four strikecruisers, one battlecruiser, two Alton battlecruisers and one fifteen-hundred-meter AI sphere. We have one strikecruiser, one Alton battlecruiser, and two fifteen-hundred-meter AI spheres that have suffered medium to heavy damage."

"Have them remain here," ordered Jeremy. "The rest of the fleet will proceed down the tunnel and attack the Dyson Sphere."

Jeremy's orders were quickly carried out, and in a matter of just a few minutes, he had the fleet ready to make the jump down the narrow corridor. The corridor was 1.6 light-years long and only twelve million kilometers in diameter. Any miscalculation in a ship's jump could see its hyperdrive become too unstable if it came too near the side of the tunnel and could easily result in the destruction of the vessel.

"Fleet is ready to jump," Ariel reported.

Jeremy took a deep breath. He still had time to turn back, but he knew what duty required of him. He spoke the words in a steady voice. "Initiate jump."

The *Avenger* dropped out of hyperspace into a sea of perpetual darkness. Jeremy gazed at the viewscreens which were void of stars or any other illumination. He had known what to expect from studying the data the *Distant Horizon* had recorded when the exploration dreadnought had dared to enter this darkness alone. Even so, it still sent a cold shiver down his back.

"Contacts!" called out Kevin as his sensors began picking up inbound Simulin ships. "I have twenty battlecruisers and thirty-two escort cruisers inbound at three hundred thousand kilometers."

Commander Malen shifted her gaze from the nearby tactical display to Jeremy. "There are probably other Simulin ships we haven't picked up yet."

Jeremy looked at the viewscreens, which still showed nothing but darkness. "How far are we from where Kazak said we need to go to enter the Dyson Sphere?"

"One point two billion kilometers," Ariel answered promptly. "I've already calculated the jump coordinates. We'll be jumping inside the gravity well of the Dyson Sphere, but our hyperdrives should be able to handle the stress."

"Transmit the coordinates to all ships," ordered Jeremy, shifting his gaze to Commander Malen. "How long until the Simulin ships reach combat range?"

"Eight minutes at their current speed," Malen answered. "I think they're waiting for reinforcements as their intercept speed has slowed substantially."

"We'll jump in five," Jeremy said with a determined look on his face. He had no intention of fighting a battle at this location.

Inside the Dyson Sphere, Simulin Supreme High Commander Nathalee stared in growing anger at the ship's viewscreens. He had just received a report informing him of the attack on the energy collector. "The AIs and their organic allies have destroyed the H-03 collector station and a large fleet has just exited hyperspace outside the Great Sphere."

"They dare attack us here!" cried High Commander Tarnell. "None of their weapons can harm the sphere. It's impervious to all known energies."

Supreme High Commander Nathalee was a shrewd leader and knew at times all was not as it may seem. "The AIs and their allies have a ship of the Old Ones. They may have discovered something, which could be of danger to the sphere or us. We must be wary in case they find a way to enter. If they can be kept outside we have nothing to fear."

High Commander Tarnell nodded. He was confident this attack by the AIs and their organics would be thwarted. Even if they managed to get inside, there were over eleven hundred Simulin warships, which could be used to destroy them. "Should we send a summons to the galaxies nearest us to send reinforcements?" There were three such galaxies where additional ships could be rushed to aid in the battle if needed.

"No," Supreme High Commander Nathalee replied coldly. They were Simulin and the most powerful race in the known universe. To request aid would indicate to his superiors he was not capable of command. However, it would be prudent to take precautions just in case the AIs and their organic allies had learned something of significance from the Originator ship. "Have ships standing by in case they need to be sent to summon more Simulin warships."

Nathalee turned to the ship's battle computer and began questioning it about the reason for this attack. After a few minutes he was satisfied the Great Sphere was in no danger. The battle computer had stated the AIs and their organics would most likely engage the defense fleets outside the Great Sphere and then leave the way they had come once they realized they could not do any harm to the sphere itself or gain entry.

The *Avenger* was one thousand kilometers above the Dyson Sphere. Even at this distance, the pull from the mass of the sphere upon the ship was substantial.

"Is this the correct location?" Jeremy asked as he gazed at the dark object on the viewscreens. The screens suddenly changed and a dim view of the Dyson Sphere appeared. Below them was a smooth metallic surface with what looked like a small structure over to one side.

"The small structure is the control center for this access hatch," Ariel explained. She was standing in her customary spot just to Jeremy's left and slightly behind him. "That structure is five kilometers in height."

Jeremy gazed at the screen trying to see the edges of the hatch. This close to the Dyson Sphere was overwhelming. It was beyond belief that any civilization could build a megastructure like this.

"Have Clarissa transmit the code," ordered Jeremy after a moment. Now they would find out if the access code Kazak had provided them would work. If they couldn't gain entry to the interior of the sphere, then their mission would be a failure.

"Simulin ships are jumping in," warned Kevin as alarms began sounding on his console again. "Admiral Bachal is moving into a defensive position with the Starlight and the Alton battlecruisers to intercept.

Jeremy nodded. Admiral Bachal's job was to keep this area of space free of Simulin warships until Jeremy returned with the rest of the fleet.

"Clarissa's transmitting now," Ariel said in her youthful and vibrant voice.

On the viewscreen, nothing happened. Several long seconds passed and Jeremy was beginning to fear the access code had failed when suddenly the hatch seemed to peel back into the hull of the Dyson Sphere, leaving a great circular opening.

"How large is that?" asked Commander Malen, focusing her eyes intently on the main viewscreen.

"Thirty kilometers," Ariel responded. "Scans indicate the entrance tunnel below us is fifteen-hundred-kilometers in length."

Jeremy took a deep breath and spoke over the ship-to-ship comm one more time. "All ships, we're about to enter the Dyson Sphere. Undoubtedly, there will be Simulin ships waiting for us on the other side. Good luck and good hunting."

"Message from Admiral Bachal," Angela reported. "He says he will be waiting for us to return."

Jeremy nodded. "Ensign Striker, take us in."

-

Supreme High Commander Nathalee could not believe what his sensors were telling him. The AIs and their organics had managed to open a hitherto unknown corridor, which led into the interior of the Great Sphere. Already their ships were emerging. While it was true they couldn't cause great harm to the sphere, they could possibly damage some of the energy collectors, particularly those near the central sun, which could hamper the operation of the intergalactic vortices.

"Send our ships through to the other galaxies," ordered Nathalee. He realized now he should have done this earlier. In his arrogance, he had underestimated his foe. It would not happen again. "All ships will form up on the *Silent Victory* and we will move to engage the enemy."

"It will be over an hour before reinforcements can arrive," pointed out High Commander Tarnell.

Nathalee knew this could not be helped. "It is our duty to defend the Great Sphere. There can be none but Simulin."

"None but Simulin," High Commander Tarnell responded.

-

Jeremy stared at the now well-lit viewscreens. They showed a massive world. It was beyond anything he could have imagined. As they accelerated away from the surface of the Dyson Sphere, they saw that it was divided up into giant squares. Each square was a world unto itself.

"There's enough living area here to hold over two million planets the size of Earth," Ariel informed Jeremy. "Atmosphere is Earth normal and so is the gravity."

"Just how big a surface area are we talking about?" Jeremy asked. On the viewscreens, he could see hundreds of the large squares of the Dyson Sphere. Some were complete water worlds, others seemed to be jungles, some rolling plains, and even a few held mountains covered in deep snow.

"8,980,000,000,000,000 square kilometers," Ariel answered.

"Any signs of cities or inhabitants?" Jeremy shook his head. The number Ariel had spilled out was nearly incomprehensible.

"No," Ariel replied. "There is some evidence of there once being cities in some areas, but there are no structures still intact."

"There are metal roofs over some areas," pointed out Kevin, gazing at the viewscreens. "Is it possible the cities we're looking for are there?"

"Possibly," Ariel acknowledged. "Kazak would know."

"Unfortunately, he's not here and we can't ask him," Commander Malen said. She looked at the viewscreens, gazing at the giant world spread out beneath them. "Some areas seem to be in darkness; how is that possible?"

Jeremy turned toward Ariel, expecting an answer. He knew she was probably communicating with Clarissa on the *Distant Horizon*. Andram and Shilum were on the exploration dreadnought and might be able to offer an explanation.

"There are a number of energy collector rings close to the Dyson Sphere's sun," Ariel explained. "They're set to rotate around the star in such a way as to give all areas of the Dyson Sphere eight hours of darkness each day."

"How long are the days on the Dyson Sphere?" asked Kevin, cocking his eyebrow.

"Thirty-one," answered Ariel. "The days here are much longer than on Earth or Gaia."

Warning alarms began sounding on Kevin's sensor console. "Simulin ships exiting hyperspace in close proximity."

Jeremy turned anxiously toward Kevin. "How close and how many?"

"They're still emerging," answered Kevin, as red threat icons began to appear in the tactical displays. "So far over seven hundred at a range of eighty thousand kilometers."

"How far to the nearest intergalactic vortex?"

"Two million kilometers," Kevin answered promptly.

Jeremy nodded and then spoke over his ship-to-ship comm. "All ships, initiate operation *furnace fire*."

Far above the Dyson Sphere, the Federation ships accelerated away from the approaching Simulins vessels. Their destination was one of the seven intergalactic vortices the Simulins kept open at all times.

"What are they doing?" asked High Commander Tarnell in confusion. "They can't be planning on going through the vortex. It leads to one of our galaxies, and we have a large fleet on the other side."

Supreme High Commander Nathalee was uncertain as well. "What does the battle computer say?"

Tarnell stepped over to the computer and then a few moments later turned back toward the Supreme High Commander with a look of concern on his face. "They're going to try to destroy it and release the stored energy that powers the vortex."

"We must stop them!" cried out the Supreme High Commander, his eyes growing wide in shock. He could not allow the AIs and their organics to damage the Great Sphere.

"Too late," replied Tarnell, pointing to one of the ship's viewscreens focused on the vortex area.

On the screen, hundreds of powerful antimatter explosions began going off around the swirling intergalactic vortex. Huge bursts of blinding light surrounded the vortex area as the surface was repeatedly pounded by the deadly missiles.

"Engage those ships!" grated out Nathalee in a grim and cold voice. "We must not allow them to damage or destroy that vortex or we will lose contact with the galaxy it's connected to." Nathalee knew his career was probably over. The Simulin Grand Council would not tolerate his failure in allowing the Great Sphere to be attacked. His entire bloodline would face deletion if the AIs and their organic allies managed to damage the sphere.

-

The Simulin ships let fire with every weapon they possessed. The seventeen-hundred-meter battlecruisers activated their energy cannons and the deadly beams flared out to strike the ships of the enemy. Missile hatches slid silently open and sublight antimatter missiles flashed out to strike defense shields. In fury, the Simulins attacked as they tried to defend the Great Sphere from the AIs and their organic allies.

Energy beams from a pair of Simulin battlecruisers slammed into the energy shield of an Alton battleship. The shield held steady and then half a dozen antimatter missiles detonated, causing the shield to weaken in one small spot. A Simulin energy beam penetrated and struck the ship's armored hull, cutting deep inside the ship. Emergency hatches activated and interior energy shields snapped into place, cutting off the damaged areas. Then the energy shield regenerated, stopping the Simulin beam.

Full squadrons of Simulin battlecruisers and escort cruisers were targeting individual Federation ships. Ten Simulin battlecruisers were concentrating their fire on a fifteen-hundred-meter AI sphere. Its screen radiated higher and higher until a massive influx of Simulin antimatter missiles caused it to fail. Across the hull of the huge warship, explosions rattled its surface as Simulin energy beams slammed home. Large, gaping chasms were opened up in the hull and then a dozen antimatter missiles arrived, changing the vessel into molten metal and glowing plasma.

-

"AI ship 437 is down," reported Kevin as the ship vanished from his sensors. "Other ships are receiving substantial damage."

Jeremy looked worriedly at one of the main viewscreens where an Alton battleship was besieged by several squadrons of Simulin ships. The top section of the vessel suddenly exploded and debris started drifting away from the ship. Then an antimatter missile slammed into the stern of the battleship and the vessel vanished in a fiery explosion.

The viewscreens on the front wall of the Command Center were steadily shifting, showing other ships joined in heavy combat. Even as Jeremy watched, a Federation battleship was blown apart as numerous Simulin energy beams penetrated its energy screen followed by several antimatter missiles.

"Battleship *Nomad* is down," reported Kevin in a grave voice.

"We have numerous ships reporting heavy damage," Commander Malen added with growing worry on her face. "We can't take this pounding much longer."

Jeremy took a deep breath. "Are we causing any damage to the Dyson Sphere?"

"Very little," Ariel answered with deep concern showing in her dark eyes. "Our sensors are indicating energy shields have been activated around the vortex area."

"What if we fired directly into the vortex? Is there any chance we could destabilize it?"

"No," Ariel responded. "I'm now detecting a powerful energy shield directly above the vortex."

The *Avenger* shook violently and alarms began sounding on the damage control console. Red lights began appearing, indicating the hull had been compromised.

Jeremy looked around the Command Center. The crew were at their consoles showing no fear of what was occurring around them.

"We can't destroy it," Kevin said in a grim voice. "Jeremy, we're losing ships. Two AI warspheres have just been destroyed. The damage to the fleet is mounting."

"Ariel, is there any target we can hit which might damage the Dyson Sphere?"

Ariel shook her head. "I'm talking to Clarissa and she's making inquiries of Andram and Shilum. They feel now that the interior is protected by energy shields to prevent just the type of damage we're trying to cause." Ariel paused as if listening to someone. "The Command AI is volunteering to use some of its ships to ram the Dyson Sphere with their antimatter warheads set to detonate on contact."

"Will that work?" Jeremy hated the idea of sacrificing ships in such a manner, but they had to find a way to damage or destroy the sphere.

"I'm running calculations now," Ariel replied. A few moments passed and then she spoke. "No, the energy shields are too powerful. Even if we rammed the sphere in some of the worldlets, I don't believe we would be able to cause significant damage. Our only hope is to destroy the area around one of the vortexes releasing the energy being used to keep them activated."

Commander Malen looked over at Jeremy. "What do we do?"

"Keep fighting until we figure out how to destroy the Dyson Sphere," Jeremy answered determinedly. "We're never going to get this opportunity again."

In space, the AI warspheres were in the midst of the battle with the Simulins. They were the most powerful ships in the fleet and moving directly into the center of the advancing Simulin formation. Particle beams were flashing out, followed by multitudes of one hundred-megaton antimatter missiles. The heart of the Simulin formation was a furnace of burning and dying ships.

A heavily damaged warsphere rammed a Simulin battlecruiser sending both to their deaths in a fiery funeral pyre. Two warspheres combined and blasted down the energy shield of a Simulin battlecruiser and then raked its hull with particle beams, causing devastating damage until an antimatter missile detonated blowing the ship apart.

Three AI warspheres were surrounded by sixty Simulin battlecruisers and had their shields repeatedly pummeled by Simulin energy beams and antimatter missiles until the shields weakened and failed. In three horrendous explosions, the warspheres were destroyed.

-

Supreme High Commander Nathalee gripped the armrests on his command chair as the *Silent Victory* received a jarring strike from several antimatter missiles. "Report!" he demanded in a harsh voice.

"We're losing ships," High Commander Tarnell answered as he consulted the battle computer. "Chance of Simulin victory is at 12 percent, chance of AI victory is at 14 percent. The battle computer is reporting a 74 percent probability of the battle resulting in a stalemate with most of the ships from both sides being eliminated."

"What of the Great Sphere?"

Tarnell consulted several other Simulins who were working the ship's science consoles as well as sensors. "The Great Sphere has activated hitherto unknown energy shields to protect itself. The AIs and their organic allies are not causing significant damage."

Nathalee nodded. The activation of these energy shields was an interesting facet of data. It indicated the Great Sphere had a guiding intelligence defending itself from attack. This was information the Simulin Grand Council would find useful. If a way could be found to communicate with this intelligence, then perhaps it would be possible to access other areas of the Great Spheres.

"Continue the attack," ordered Nathalee without hesitation. "These AIs and their organics are enemies of the Simulin race and must be eliminated. There can be none but Simulin."

"None but Simulin," replied Tarnell.

-

Rear Admiral Kathryn Barnes grimaced as she saw a Federation strikecruiser vanish in a fiery explosion from a Simulin antimatter missile.

"The fleet is sustaining heavy damage," Clarissa reported. "Fleet Admiral Strong is hesitant to withdraw as we many not be able to return again. In all likelihood, the Simulins will increase the size of their defense fleets at the tunnel entrances to ensure this."

Kathryn could sense the growing desperation she knew must be sweeping across the fleet. Only the AIs would be void of this horrible feeling. "Andram, is there anything we can do?"

The Alton scientist hesitated for a moment and then turned toward Kathryn with a grave look on his wizened face. "I may have found a way to destroy the Dyson Sphere."

"What?" exclaimed Colonel Leon, her eyes growing wide in astonishment. "How?"

Andram turned back around and adjusted the ship's large viewscreen. Instantly, the central sun appeared surrounded by half a dozen dark ribbons of power collection stations. "We destroy the system's sun."

Kathryn leaned back in her command chair in shock at hearing those words. "Is that even possible?"

"Yes," Andram answered. "Shilum and I have been doing some calculations. If we take the *Distant Horizon* to the outer edge of the corona of the star and launch all of our antimatter missiles into the photosphere, it should cause a sufficient reaction to cause the star to go nova. It will take some precision because all of the missiles need to detonate within milliseconds of one another to cause the photosphere to become unstable enough."

"We've lost another battlecruiser, and two more strikecruisers," Captain Reynolds said in a grim voice. "We've also lost eighteen warspheres in the last seven minutes."

"Clarissa, if we do this, can the *Distant Horizon* escape the nova?"

Clarissa was quiet for a long moment and then answered. "No, Admiral. The nova will be nearly instantaneous and we most likely won't be able to activate our hyperdrive in time to escape. The sheer mass of the sun and being so deep inside its gravity well may cause the drive to fail catastrophically when we jump into the outer regions of the corona."

"Can we send some of the AI ships to do this?" asked Commander Grissim.

"No," replied Andram, shaking his head. "Only the *Distant Horizon* possesses an energy shield powerful enough to allow us to get as close to the corona of the star as we're going to need to be. We're actually going to be within the outer edges."

Kathryn closed her eyes briefly. She had always known there was a possibility she could die in her service to the fleet. Now it seemed as if that time had arrived. There were six large shuttles and four small cargo shuttles in the ship's flight bay. "Commander Malen, give the order to evacuate all nonessential personnel." She looked over at Katie and

Kelsey. "That includes the two of you as well as Andram, Shilum, and Mikow." She wasn't going to be responsible for the deaths of two of the Special Five, and Jeremy would need the three Altons and their knowledge.

"Admiral," protested Andram, you may need me to coordinate the missile strike."

"Clarissa, can you launch the missiles to do the job?"

"Yes, Admiral," Clarissa said softly. "I can do it. There's no reason for Andram or any of the others to stay."

"What's the nearest ship that can take on our shuttles?"

"The AI command ship is nearby," Commander Grissim answered in a steady voice. "It has ten warspheres and twenty of the fifteen-hundred-meter spheres as escorts."

Kathryn nodded. That would be a safe place for her people. "Clarissa, contact the Command AI and inform it of what we're getting ready to do." She looked around at Andram and the others who were still standing in the Command Center, hesitant to leave. "Go now," she ordered. "Or I'll have you escorted to the shuttle by marines."

"Goodbye, Admiral," Kelsey said, her eyes filled with shock over what they were about to do. She had never imagined anything like this.

"It's been an honor," Katie added as she walked over to Kelsey's side. She looked over at Clarissa and a tear formed in her eye. "Clarissa, I'm so sorry."

"Its fine, Katie," said Clarissa, turning toward Katie with a weak smile. "You have always been my best friend. Don't forget me."

"I won't," sobbed Katie as she turned and left the Command Center followed by the others.

The Command Center was quiet for a long moment and then Kathryn began giving orders. "Clarissa, expedite getting them off the ship and anyone else we can get to those shuttles in the next few minutes. I want to make our hyperspace jump to the star as soon as possible. Contact Ariel and tell her what we're preparing to do."

"I already have," Clarissa replied as she squared up her shoulders.

—

"They're going to do what?" exploded Jeremy, his eyes taking on a look of disbelief.

"Andram and Shilum have figured out how to cause the central sun to go nova. They're already evacuating all nonessential personnel to the Command AI's ship. Clarissa says we have twenty minutes to get out of the Dyson Sphere before the nova reaches us."

Kevin looked over at Jeremy and then spoke with his voice almost in a whisper. "They're sacrificing the *Distant Horizon* to destroy the Dyson Sphere."

"It's the only way," Ariel replied in a somber voice. "I've run the calculations with Clarissa, and the plan will work."

"How soon before the shuttles reach the Command AI's ship?"

"They're already docking," answered Ariel. "The Command AI has sent twenty of the remaining warspheres to cover the *Distant Horizon* until they're ready to make their hyperjump."

Jeremy looked at one of the viewscreens, which showed the exploration dreadnought. He couldn't believe he was agreeing to this. Over the ship-to-ship comm, he contacted all of his remaining ships. "We're leaving. I want a short hyperjump to the exit tunnel and then full subspace speed until we're out. Once we've cleared the Dyson Sphere, we'll jump to the dark matter tunnel entrance and then jump out. Timing is of the essence."

—

Aboard the *Distant Horizon*, Kathryn watched as the rest of the fleet disengaged from the Simulins and opened up spatial vortexes to jump the short distance to the escape tunnel. Once she was satisfied all the ships were gone except her escort, she turned to Commander Grissim. "Make the jump to the corona. Clarissa, as soon as we jump, the remaining AI warspheres are to join Fleet Admiral Strong."

Moments later a swirling blue-white vortex formed in front of the *Distant Horizon* and Lieutenant Styles quickly flew the exploration dreadnought into it.

Kathryn was nearly thrown from her command chair as the ship exited its vortex in the outer edge of the star's corona. Alarm bells were ringing and multiple red lights were appearing on the damage control console.

"Hyperdrive is down," confirmed Clarissa in a calm voice.

"Chief Engineer Jalat is working on it," Commander Grissim reported. "He doesn't know if it's repairable."

Kathryn nodded. They had known this might be a one-way trip.

"Admiral, the energy shield is rapidly weakening," reported Colonel Leon from her command console. "I estimate three or four minutes is the longest it will remain up."

Taking a deep breath, Kathryn looked around her command crew. Most were watching her, their eyes showing little fear. "I've been proud to be your commander," she said. "I couldn't have asked for a better crew. Take solace in the thought that what we're about to do will protect our home galaxy as well as Gaia." She turned toward Clarissa. "Launch the missiles and Clarissa, I want you to know that I consider you a friend."

"Thank you, Admiral," Clarissa responded as she activated the complicated launching process she had set up. The *Distant Horizon* had thirty-six missile tubes and she had nearly two hundred missiles to launch. She had adjusted the missiles' subspace drives to allow for multiple launches and for all them to arrive on target simultaneously. It would be a rapid launch and she could have all the missiles launched in twelve seconds. "Missiles launching."

Rear Admiral Kathryn Barnes, the daughter of Governor Barnes of Ceres, closed her eyes waiting for death. She just wished she could have seen her father one last time.

-

The two hundred missiles arrived at their target within milliseconds of one another. Already the intense heat was causing the missiles to melt. In a massive explosion all the missiles detonated, each releasing one hundred-megatons of antimatter energy. The star seemed to recoil in on itself and then it exploded. Raw energy raced outwards toward the surrounding energy collection rings and the Dyson Sphere. The energy collection rings were destroyed in seconds and still the ravaging energy continued outward.

-

Supreme High Commander Nathalee leaned back in his command chair in shock. The AIs and their organic allies had done the impossible. They had found a way to destroy the Great Sphere.

"Nine minutes until the nova reaches us," reported High Commander Tarnell. "The battle computer estimates a 98 percent chance the Great Sphere will be destroyed."

Nathalee did not respond. He had failed in his duty to the Simulin Empire and now one of its most important assets was about to be lost. He would pay for that failure with his life and the lives of every Simulin in his fleet.

-

The nova swept outward and approached the Dyson Sphere. The Simulin ships that had survived the fleet battle were snuffed away like insects. All across the Dyson Sphere emergency energy shields came into being. However, even those powerful shields hadn't been designed to withstand the all-consuming force of a nova. The shields resisted briefly. Then they failed and the full power of the nova smashed into the Dyson Sphere. For a moment, nothing happened, and then the entire sphere blew apart in a cataclysmic explosion. Its dense hull material became fuel for the raging energy of the nova and then the nearly impossible happened. The exotic material of the Dyson Sphere caused the nova to greatly expand in renewed force and fury. In a heartbeat, the star turned into a supernova and that energy now raced toward the edge of the dark matter nebula.

-

Jeremy watched the *Avenger's* sensors, which were recording what was happening down the tunnel of the dark matter nebula.

"The star has turned into a supernova," Ariel reported in an even voice. "The Dyson Sphere has been destroyed."

"What will its effects be on the dark matter?" asked Commander Malen.

"Unknown," Ariel answered. "It will have to be studied. Nothing like this has ever happened before."

Jeremy was silent for a long moment. He had lost numerous ships during the battle inside the Dyson Sphere. Worst of all he had lost the *Distant Horizon* and those aboard her. The evacuated crew from the exploration dreadnought were already docking with the *Avenger* and would soon all be safely aboard. Jeremy turned toward Ariel and saw the lonely look upon her face. "I'm sorry about Clarissa, we'll all miss her."

"I know," answered Ariel in a soft voice. "Jeremy, if you don't mind I would prefer not to be in the Command Center for awhile."

Jeremy nodded in understanding. They were all going to have to deal with these losses. "Commander Malen, as soon as the survivors from the *Distant Horizon* are all on board set a course for home."

"Yes, Admiral," Kyla responded.

Jeremy looked back at the viewscreens showing the dark matter nebula. What they had accomplished today would change this galaxy. No longer were the Simulins undefeatable. They were now cut off from major reinforcements from their other galaxies and had lost a large portion of their warships. While this battle had been won, there were still many more waiting in the future. Jeremy was also determined no one would ever forget the great sacrifice made inside the Dyson Sphere. Today new heroes had come to light. Heroes whose sacrifice would always be remembered.

Epilogue

Jeremy stood atop the large hill, which overlooked the Fleet Academy. At the top of the hill was a new dark gray granite obelisk. On each side of the obelisk were two walls, also constructed out of granite. On the obelisk and the walls were the names of everyone who had died in combat since they had come to the Triangulum Galaxy.

A set of wide steps had been cut into the hill and led all the way down to the academy below. A large parade ground faced the hill and the monuments at its top. Upon the parade ground, thousands of fleet officers, academy cadets, and other military personnel stood at attention to honor those who had fallen in the line of duty.

All the surviving admirals, the Special Five, and Ariel stood before the obelisk in silence. At the top of the obelisk was an engraved picture of Clarissa in her dress blue uniform without insignia, a slight smile on her face. Below her name and picture were that of Rear Admiral Kathryn Barnes and the officers of the *Distant Horizon*.

"She would have liked this," spoke Ariel in a soft voice.

"I miss her," said Katie with tears flowing down her cheeks. "She died once before and this time I can't bring her back."

"Governor Barnes would have been proud of his daughter," Admiral Jackson said in a solemn voice. "She gave her life for the future of so many others."

"I remember when she first came aboard the *Distant Horizon*," Kelsey said, looking at the others, remembering that day so long ago. "We all wondered what type of admiral she would be; now we know. We couldn't have asked for a better commanding officer for the ship."

"As with the Fleet Academy on Earth's moon, all cadets will be required to climb these stairs to honor those who have fallen," Rear Admiral Susan Marks said in a grave and resolute voice.

"Rear Admiral Barnes died an honorable death for her clan," Grayseth added in a much softer voice than normal for the large Bear. "Her clan is now all the people of Gaia: Human, Alton, Carethian, and the AIs. Her sacrifice has ensured our home will be safe and our children can be raised without fear."

Jeremy looked up toward space to where he knew the Originator ship was. Kazak had been quiet since learning of Clarissa's death. He had spoken a few times with Ariel and had promised to speak more in the future. There was no doubt that someday the Originator AI would give them access to the ship. Until then, there were other things that needed to be done. Already Jeremy had ordered the AI shipyards above Borton to be expanded. He had met with Daelthon and ordered him to begin constructing more battlecruisers like the *Gaia*. There were also plans to add another construction bay to the Clan Protector.

Only the day before he had met with Admiral Jackson and several others to discuss sending a fleet to the Ornellian Empire to drive off whatever Simulin vessels might remain and to see how many survivors there were on those worlds. No longer were they going to hide in the protective environs of the nebula. They would be taking the battle to the Simulins for control of the Triangulum Galaxy. They would also be seeking out more allies.

They had achieved a great victory destroying the Dyson Sphere. While Jeremy hated that they had to destroy the megastructure, he knew it was for the best. It helped to drastically weaken the Simulins and ensure Gaia would remain free from attack. People could now live a more normal life and plan for their future.

A few days earlier, Angela had confided in Jeremy that she and Brace were going to try to have a child. Katie and Kevin had hinted at the same thing. The future was changing and they would have to change with it. Gaia was their home now, and it was going to be a wonderful world. Looking out over the sea of people who had turned out for the memorial ceremony, Jeremy was confident a great future was ahead of them and someday the Triangulum Galaxy would be one of peace. He just had to make sure that future happened, and as fleet admiral, there was no doubt in his mind that he would.

If you enjoyed *The Lost Fleet: Oblivion's Light* and would like to see the series continue, please post a review with some stars. Good reviews encourage an author to write and also help sell books. Reviews can be just a few short sentences, describing what you liked about the book. If you have suggestions, please contact me at my website, link below. Thank you for reading *Oblivion's Light* and being so supportive.

For updates on current writing projects and future publications, go to my author website. Sign up for future notifications when my new books come out on Amazon.

Website: http://raymondlweil.com/

Other Books by Raymond L. Weil
Available on Amazon

Moon Wreck (The Slaver Wars Book 1)
The Slaver Wars: Alien Contact (The Slaver Wars Book 2)
Moon Wreck: Fleet Academy (The Slaver Wars Book 3)
The Slaver Wars: First Strike (The Slaver Wars Book 4)
The Slaver Wars: Retaliation (The Slaver Wars Book 5)
The Slaver Wars: Galactic Conflict (The Slaver Wars Book 6)
The Slaver Wars: Endgame (The Slaver Wars Book 7)

-

Dragon Dreams
Dragon Dreams: Dragon Wars
Dragon Dreams: Gilmreth the Awakening
Dragon Dreams: Snowden the White Dragon

-

Star One: Tycho City: Survival
Star One: Neutron Star
Star One: Dark Star

-

Galactic Empire Wars: Destruction (Book 1)
Galactic Empire Wars: Emergence (Book 2)
Galactic Empire Wars: Rebellion (Book 3)
Galactic Empire Wars: The Alliance (Book 4)

-

The Lost Fleet: Galactic Search (Book 1)
The Lost Fleet: Into the Darkness (Book 2)
The Lost Fleet: Oblivion's Light (Book 3)

-

The Star Cross (Book 1)

Galactic Empire Wars: Insurrection (Book 5) March 2016
The Lost Fleet: Genesis (Book 4) 2016
The Star Cross (Book 2) 2016

ABOUT THE AUTHOR

I live in Clinton Oklahoma with my wife of 43 years and our cat. I attended college at SWOSU in Weatherford Oklahoma, majoring in Math with minors in Creative Writing and History.

My hobbies include watching soccer, reading, camping, and of course writing. I coached youth soccer for twelve years before moving on and becoming a high school soccer coach for thirteen more. I also enjoy playing with my five grandchildren. I have a very vivid imagination, which sometimes worries my friends. They never know what I'm going to say or what I'm going to do.

I am an avid reader and have a science fiction / fantasy collection of over two thousand paperbacks. I want future generations to know the experience of reading a good book as I have over the last forty-five years.

14871760R00185

Printed in Great Britain
by Amazon.co.uk, Ltd.,
Marston Gate.